THE TRIGGER MAN

A TRIGGER MAN THRILLER

AIDEN BAILEY

INKUBATOR
BOOKS

Published by Inkubator Books
www.inkubatorbooks.com

ISBN (eBook): 978-1-83756-251-0
ISBN (Paperback): 978-1-83756-252-7
ISBN (Hardback): 978-1-83756-253-4

for Alyssa, with love, and the many adventures life will bring you

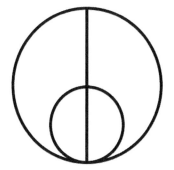

PROLOGUE
SAHEL, MALI

Rookie CIA officer Katie Siegel lay sprawled on her back, pain racking every inch of her broken body. Except her legs. She couldn't feel any pain from the waist down.

She couldn't feel anything.

A noise like a high-pitched squeal screamed in her ears, but it seemed to be coming from inside her head.

What had happened?

Glancing left and right wasn't possible, because the motion caused her already searing frontal lobe to throb with unbearable agony. Her peripheral vision told her only that she lay in a semi-desert, that the heat of the sun burned, and the air was orange with dust and smelled of motor oil.

Only minutes ago, she and two CIA paramilitary officers had been powering their four-wheel drive through the isolated fringes of the southern Sahara, swapping jokes and bad-mouthing their boss, for sending them into this hellhole on a pointless mission in the first place.

The next minute, there had been a flash, bright like the

always-searing Saharan sun. Then smoke and metal propelling everywhere, and her body catapulting out of her seat, circling forward until the scrubby, gravelly earth raced up at her...

When she had regained consciousness, Katie knew she was dying.

The pain didn't hurt so much now. Instead, she felt coldness, and she knew this was because she was bleeding out. There weren't enough fluids in her body to regulate her core temperature anymore.

Finally able to turn her head, she glanced left, towards the remains of their shattered and ripped-apart four-wheel drive. Beyond, the flat Sahel spread in all directions towards every compass point. It was a landscape of dusty reds and oranges, widely spaced acacia trees, craggy riverbeds that hadn't seen water in decades, occasional sand dunes, and patches of dried grasses. It wasn't a place she ever imagined herself dying in.

1

SAHEL, MALI

Less than two kilometres away, the horizon spewed a black cloud of death.

Somebody, or some bodies, had just died.

And they had not died well.

Mark Pierce slammed down on his speeding Toyota Hilux's brakes. He swore under his breath as he skidded to a brutal stop. Nothing felt right. Everything stank of a set-up.

With his AK-47 assault rifle raised and ready, the CIA paramilitary operator stepped out into the heat, the sand, and the oppressiveness of a baking and hostile landscape. The blue turban wrapped around his head flapped in the unrelenting oven-like breeze. His boots pounded dust in the semi-desert of the Sahel.

He stared down the iron sights of his weapon.

But the scene of destruction was too far away to ascertain details.

Cursing still, Pierce returned to his battered four-wheel drive and drove again.

But the drive was complicated by an old riverbed with

edges too steep to drive into. Pierce had to divert two further kilometres perpendicular to his direction of travel just to find a crossing. Twenty minutes later, diverting over rough terrain, Pierce spotted the dust trail of what he thought was another vehicle disappearing over the far horizon.

When he reached the smouldering wreckage, he expected trouble.

He soon found it, but not in the form he expected.

The three CIA operatives he'd been sent to rescue, their deaths were now ignoble. Corpses little more than ragged strips of meat. For the two men, their body parts resembled game kill after hyenas had finished picking at their carcasses — though hyenas had not killed them. The woman was intact, but with many broken bones, and a shard of metal that had sliced open half her abdomen was a wound she would never have survived. He replayed the incident in his mind. The CIA's four-wheel drive had hit a landmine. The vehicle had catapulted into the sky. Flipped at least once before the chassis tore into three discernible pieces, then crashed back onto the earth. The war-torn West African nation of Mali did that with strangers, defeated them with random acts of brutality. Their path to death wasn't unusual.

Pierce sighed. He considered if he should pity these Central Intelligence Agency men. Their deaths, at least, had been quick. An ending without pain. There were far more horrific and agonising fates they might have faced as field operatives for the Directorate of Operations, and now never would.

Pierce was almost jealous.

Soon the wind dropped, and visibility improved. Pierce slung his AK-47 and undid the blue turban covering his face and head. He dressed as a Tuareg, one of the many local nomadic people of this region, because of the practicality of their garb and because of its effective disguise. Along with his turban, he wore a medium-length cotton shirt over his cargo pants, T-shirt and tactical armour-plated vest. Tuareg men by tradition never showed their faces. A perfect cover to mask his Americanness. Anyone who saw him from a distance wouldn't presume he was a foreign devil.

He grabbed his satellite phone and dialled CIA Headquarters in Langley, Virginia.

"Code in, please?" A friendly but firm response from the other side of the planet. Female. American. Accent West Coast. She sounded young, perhaps late twenties or early thirties. College graduate because of her clear enunciation.

He both missed and detested the familiarity.

"Three, one, Delta, one, Echo, nine, Bravo."

Pierce heard her breathing over the otherwise silent line.

"ID confirmed," she said after a few seconds. "Go ahead, Trigger Man."

"Weather is clear... I repeat, weather is clear." The report was a fake. This was a code confirming he wasn't under duress.

"Good to hear, Trigger Man. Patching you through now."

"Thanks."

The line fell silent. His hearing turned to the winds whistling across the flat plains. His clothes beat against him as if fighting each other. The sun rippling in the boiling skies resembled an all-seeing eye focused only on him. He blinked away sand particles that got in his eyes.

He scanned for movement. Bad actors roamed northern Mali, spoiling for a fight. Enemies ready to murder him for his water, his guns and his four-wheel drive. Crazy jihadists prowled these lands like computer-coded zombies in post-apocalyptic first-person shooter games. Fanatics who'd murder him for no reason. Al-Qaeda and Islamic State wannabes looking to prove their fanaticism with an easy kill.

Mali was the new ground zero in the War on Terror.

Mali was now the most dangerous country on the planet.

For eleven months, Mali had been Pierce's theatre of operation.

"Mark Pierce?"

A man's voice. Pierce pictured mid-fifties, Caucasian and Ivy League educated. Accent? Pierce wasn't sure, but he sounded New England. Maybe Boston.

"Yes, sir." Pierce spoke with respect even though he didn't yet know if this CIA case officer deserved his deference. They had never met, never talked before today. "I take it you're Idris Walsh? The new Head of Special Ops, North Africa Desk? The man who authorised this crazy, fucked-up mission I find myself knee-deep in?"

Walsh chuckled without humour or joy. "I'm told you're the closest operative to my team. Did you find them?"

"Yes, sir." Pierce considered offering further intel, but he hadn't warmed to the man's gruff tone. He'd leave it to Walsh to ask direct questions while he got a read on the man.

"Are they... dead?"

"Yes, sir," Pierce answered without emotion. "Two men. One woman. All dead."

Walsh groaned. "What the hell happened?"

"Landmine. You can guess the rest."

"And the money?"

"Money?" Pierce recalled there had been no mention of missing funds during his mission brief.

"Eleven million dollars, Pierce. Is it there?"

Pierce frowned. If eleven million dollars blew to pieces

along with the team and their vehicle, there would have been signs. Burned bills littering the earth or falling like snowflakes out of the sky. Legal tender spread far and wide across the Sahel. It seemed likely that, if there had been money here, it had disappeared with the vehicle he had glimpsed disappearing over the horizon.

"No, sir. No money."

"And the hostages?"

"Hostages?" Again, this was news to Pierce. He considered how much his CIA superiors had *not* told him.

He decided he didn't respect Walsh. No CIA operations officer with a shred of integrity sent men into the field without sharing all intel in their possession. Pierce had not been told who had requested his latest assignment deep within insurgence-controlled West Africa, but he would continue to assume it was Walsh, judging from his line of questioning. Pierce's blood boiled, knowing he was alone with no understanding of what was transpiring. In the spy game, good intel was often the difference between a successful mission and ending up dead. The three CIA operatives' cause of death was becoming clearer.

Walsh cleared his throat. "Yes, hostages? Five, snatched off the streets of Timbuktu yesterday. They dead too?"

Ignoring the woman because she was intact, Pierce recounted the other body parts. Four arms. Four legs. Both male. Enough to build two corpses. "That's a negative, sir."

"Fuck!"

Pierce scanned the clearing horizon now that the dust storm was settling. He took his time to complete a full-circle reconnaissance but saw only a few hundred metres in any direction. The Sahel — as they called these sub-Saharan lands — was a flat, desolate landscape with no discernible geographical features, and acts as the dividing zone between the lifeless Saharan dunes of the north and the lusher southern savannas. He sensed something wasn't right. Or was he sensing Walsh's bullshit? Regardless, there was nothing out here. His situation appeared secure for the moment. "When were you intending on reading me in, Walsh?"

Not "sir". No respect anymore. It was Pierce operating way outside the wire, in the heart of insurgent-controlled territory with no realistic backup. From his cushy corner office in Langley, it should be Walsh looking after Pierce.

"I don't like the tone, Pierce."

"I don't like missions where you withhold information critical for my survival."

Walsh growled again. He almost blustered further insults when he instead took a deep breath and slowed his breathing. "Okay. You've made your point, Trigger Man. I've lost three good operators. I'm fucking angry about that right now."

"They're dead. Nothing we can do. But I'm *not* dead. If you want my help, brief me."

"Okay! Okay!"

"What was the purpose of the eleven million dollars?" Pierce did a quick calculation in his head. An average U.S. note weighed about a gram. If he assumed the $11,000,000 comprised $100 notes only, that was still 110,000 bills, weighing in at 110 kilograms. More than the weight even of a heavy man, requiring at a minimum four bags to transport. If the notes were smaller denominations, the weight would be even greater.

Walsh sighed. "That was for a hostage exchange. An al-Qaeda-affiliated group holding a bad actor with intel that could shift the political and military landscape here in West Africa. We planned a Timbuktu exchange. Then a third party snatched the hostage before we could."

"A bad actor? A local or a Westerner?"

"Westerner, and that's all you need to know right now."

Pierce gritted his teeth. Then, distracted, he noticed that a new dust cloud grew on the horizon. He raised his AK-47, looked down the iron sights. The haze might be the abating sandstorm, but Pierce thought it unlikely.

"Pierce?"

Ignoring Walsh for the moment, he watched the rising dust for a good long count to ten. The cloud was growing in size, and it was moving towards him.

It was common to spot thin, ebony-skinned men on motorcycles ploughing dust trails from one isolated village to the next. Sometimes he spied women with tiny children carrying fuel on their heads, kilometres from the nearest settlement. Horsemen or camel riders were often Tuareg nomads who may or may not be in league or at war with al-Qaeda or Islamic State, or a dozen other ideological-based groups with a fondness for murder. Recently, he'd started spotting Wagner mercenaries from Russia inserting themselves into these desolate battlegrounds. So many factions warring in Mali it was nearly impossible to keep track of who was who. He'd treat any people he encountered in the Sahel as hostile. No exceptions. If they got too close, he'd shoot first to scare them away. The second shot would be to kill.

The alternative was to end as dismembered meat like his CIA peers.

"Sir, no offence, but I'm in the middle of insurgent-controlled territory. I've just identified an unknown number of potential hostiles approaching my position. Is a drone watching? Do you know who they are, and what might connect them with your botched operation?"

Walsh blustered. "No drones available, Pierce. That's why I sent *you*."

It was Pierce's turn to growl. He could die here because of Walsh's incompetence. "Perhaps you could get a drone here ASAP, *sir*? Predator or Reaper preferably. Hellfire missile ready?"

"No can do, I'm afraid. Committed to other operations."

Pierce identified several technicals in the dust cloud. "Technical" was military terminology for Utes, four-by-fours and pickup trucks fitted with tripod-mounted machine guns, rocket launchers and flamethrowers. At least five of the rusted, battered vehicles ploughed through the gravelly desert towards him. Whoever these people were, they wouldn't be friendly.

"Sir, we're done talking. I'll extract myself from this situation — if I can. If I make it back to Gao, I'm returning to my original mission. You're on your own—"

"That's a negative, Trigger Man." Walsh raised his voice. "Extract yourself, then call back. I've reassigned you to my team—"

Pierce ended the call. He wasn't in the mood for pleasantries or signoffs. The technicals numbered seven and were less than a kilometre from him. He could clamber into his battered Hilux and try to outrun them, but he didn't like his chances.

Instead, he scanned the dusty road ahead, searched until his eyes spotted the glint of metal he hoped would be there.

His tactic was risky, but when he looked up again and saw how close his enemy was, he no longer had a choice.

2

His odds of survival weren't good. Pierce steadied his AK-47 and sighted the approaching convoy of armed technicals. Sweat beaded on his skin. He had to keep his cool to survive the impending minutes.

The men in the trucks wore dark or khaki desert clothes covering their bodies and faces. A few vehicles displayed black flags with the Shahada Islamic creed scribed in white Arabic letters. Words that translated to *There is no god but God. Muhammad is the messenger of God.*

Pierce sighed. Only fanatics flew these flags.

As the seven technicals decelerated, Pierce steadied himself. He checked for shaking in his hands, but for the moment he was in control. He slowed his breathing and heart rate.

The first brutal strike never came.

Not yet. The insurgents didn't comprehend what lay at their feet...

Men and guns weighed down each vehicle. The convoy was comprised of four Toyota Land Cruisers, two Ford

Rangers and one Mitsubishi Triton. He could see that the crew were a mixture of fairer Arabs and dark-skinned Africans, with the Arabs carrying the largest weapons and acting as drivers. AK-47s were their most common small arms. Mounted armaments included five DShK Soviet Union-era heavy machine guns while two technicals featured SPG-9 Kopye 73mm recoilless guns. The Kopyes no doubt fired high explosive anti-tank or HEAT rounds. A single direct hit would reduce Pierce to smaller meat fragments than the two dead CIA men.

The Triton stopped the closest. The insurgent behind the tripod-mounted Kopye soon recovered from the rough drive and now pointed the deadly recoilless gun at Pierce's heart.

Pierce kept his AK-47 raised and ready. It was an ineffective weapon against the sheer firepower aimed in his general direction, but Pierce knew a secret these fanatics did not. With their reckless driving, it was only by luck they hadn't already killed themselves.

"*As-salamu alaykum,*" called the insurgent behind the wheel of the Triton. *Peace be upon you* being the universal greeting of both fanatic and moderate Islamists.

"*Wa 'alaykum as-salam,*" Pierce responded in the traditional manner. *And peace be upon you too.* It was positive they were conversing. He might still negotiate himself from this predicament, but he doubted it.

The driver stepped onto the gravelly desert and approached. He drew a 9mm Beretta M9 semi-automatic pistol from his cracked leather belt and waved the muzzle in the air. His other hand unravelled his khaki turban, revealing a thick beard. The whites of his eyes encircled his irises and looked ready to pop out of their sockets. "Brother? Do you pledge allegiance to Allah, the one true God?"

Pierce took another slow, deep breath and responded in Arabic. "I humbly serve the one true God. May Allah give me strength to continue to serve him."

The words brought a smile to the insurgent's face. "No reason to point your Kalashnikov at me, brother. If you are true to the faith, you need not fear us."

Pierce kept his AK-47 raised. He wasn't religious in any sense and supported no ideology that proclaimed itself as the single source of truth or righteousness, but he'd pretend if it appeased these fanatics and kept him alive. Either way, he wasn't ready to surrender his assault rifle.

"Why are you not at home with your wife and children?" asked the wide-eyed insurgent.

Pierce sensed the man was itching for a kill, searching for signs Pierce was not as devout as he claimed.

"Did you pray to Allah this morning?" the insurgent asked.

Pierce sighed. The conversation was pointless, as expected, and he wasn't in the mood for any religious dogma. His eyes motioned to the crumpled chassis of the CIA four-by-four and the dismembered bodies, surprised that the fanatics hadn't yet taken an interest in the earlier violent confrontation. His glance produced the desired effect. The leader turned, noticing the wreck.

"You did this?" he demanded.

Pierce nodded. "Foreign American devils. They deserved it."

"Perhaps you are one of us after all. Who taught you how to fight?"

Pierce said nothing.

"My problem, brother, is that we came to meet these men. They had an important prisoner in their custody. We came to claim him, but now... You seem to have ruined our plans..."

Pierce's expression remained impassive despite his concerns. The story contradicted Idris Walsh's earlier claims. Someone was lying. "You're Ansar Dine?"

The leader grinned, impressed by Pierce's guess.

"I'll take that as a yes." Pierce knew Ansar Dine were a sect of jihadist killers aligned with AQIM, or al-Qaeda in the Islamic Maghreb. A terrorist organisation with no regard for the life or liberty of others who didn't follow their ideology. "Who is your master?"

"I am in charge." The wide-eyed man chuckled as he scratched his beard.

"No!" Pierce lined his gun up on the fanatic's chest. "Who is your regional commander?"

"Brother, don't make me laugh."

"Everybody has a boss."

The insurgent smirked. "Hilarious. Why should I tell you?"

"Because he owes me, a reward for killing these infidels."

The insurgent considered Pierce's demand. "I think you should forget compensation, my friend. I serve the will of the Saifullah. You know of him? Yes? No? If you do, you'll soon wish you did not."

Pierce nodded. Saifullah, the Sword of Allah. The name gave him chills. Pierce kept his face impassive and said, "I know of this man."

The Sword of Allah's real name was Kashif Shalgham, a powerful and psychopathic regional commander of Ansar Dine and former officer of the Libyan Army. In his early days he'd tortured political dissidents for Muammar Gaddafi. His favourite drug was sodium thiopental, used as a truth serum but also to incapacitate his victims while transporting them from one torture site to the next.

When Gaddafi's regime collapsed, Shalgham fled the country. He turned up in Syria years later, training Islamic State fanatics to fight as real soldiers. Now with Islamic State all but decimated in the Middle East, Shalgham had reappeared in the Sahara, leading an army of Ansar Dine killers pledged to terror and barbarity. A high-profile terrorist no one had succeeded in assassinating, although many Western powers had tried for over a decade.

Ansar Dine's headquarters were the Adrar des Ifoghas, a vast and arid mountainous region on the border between Mali and Algeria. Three hundred kilometres north of Pierce's current location and deep within the Sahara Desert, it was not an easy region to reach or explore, and even more difficult to leave again. Shalgham's wandering bands of insurgents murdered trespassers who strayed too close.

Shalgham himself had fought long and bloody battles across Mali and Algeria. His aim was to enforce Sharia law across West Africa. There were reports he had reignited the practice of crucifixion. He'd bound countless men, women and children to X-shaped crosses erected in the hottest regions of the desert, disembowelling them and leaving them to die in the heat and the sand. Pierce wished only to encounter this sick excuse for a human being through the sights of a sniper rifle.

"You should forget the Sword," the insurgent responded. "It will displease him that you interfered in his operations. You know what he does to men who betray him?"

Pierce stilled his breath. He'd heard enough.

"You should be grateful that we will kill you first. No one inflicts more pain than Saifullah himself—"

The fanatic didn't get the chance to finish. No longer interested in this pointless conversation, and now that the man had voiced a clear threat, Pierce switched targets and fired a full burst into the reflective metal he had spotted earlier: a landmine, two metres from the leader and untouched since the convoy's arrival. The CIA team had died because of these hidden explosives. Why assume there was only one mine buried in this location?

Pierce hadn't.

The sky grew thick with noise, flames and black smoke. The landmine detonated with an explosive force greater than Pierce had expected. Perhaps three or four mines clustered together had triggered simultaneously.

Three technicals and their occupants catapulted into the air. The leader suffered the quickest death as his arms, legs and organs scattered across the desert. The HEAT rounds in the SPG-9 Kopye-mounted Triton fuelled the first detonation, shredding the vehicle into tiny fragments. Two of the Land Cruisers caught in the explosion rolled and flipped, crushing the men and the machine gun in their trays.

Pierce staggered on his feet as the blast wave hit him. He struggled to breathe for a few seconds as the explosions sucked oxygen from the atmosphere. But he was prepared for the pressure wave. None of this slowed him. Pierce ejected the AK-47's first banana-shaped magazine, locked in a second and pulled back on the charging handle. In under three seconds he fired controlled bursts towards the four intact technicals, pinning them. When the magazine emptied, he sprinted for his Hilux while reloading a third magazine, and then he clambered into the cabin.

Once behind the wheel, he engaged the ignition and drove fast, south the way he had come.

Soon he was pushing eighty kilometres per hour on the dusty gravel road.

He glanced in the cracked rear-view mirror and cursed.

Another dust cloud materialised from the smouldering wrecks.

The four remaining technicals, three with machine guns and one with a recoilless Kopye, were chasing him.

3

Pierce floored the accelerator, churning a cloud of sand behind him. Bullets pounded through the air. Dust exploded in tiny puffs on the road each time a projectile hit the earth. Soon he too was driving in the dust, limiting his visibility.

He glanced again in the rear-view mirror. Four technicals pursued. A black Land Cruiser was gaining, with the white Land Cruiser dropping behind. Closing in was the tan-coloured Ranger, with the second white Ranger further behind. The gunner on the tan Ranger must have been choking on the grains of sand pelting his face, but this didn't slow him in taking hold of the Kopye trigger grip and lining up Pierce in his sights. The missile fired, igniting as soon as it left the barrel and rocketing towards Pierce's Hilux.

Pierce pulled hard on the wheel. The vehicle spun in a sharp circle, tilting for a few seconds, balancing on two wheels. The rocket shot past his window, close enough to feel its hot fiery tail. Somewhere out of visual range, he heard and then felt the explosion's heat as his tyres dropped back onto the sand.

The manoeuvre had closed the gap between him and his pursuers. Worse, he had turned in a half-circle and now faced them head-on.

Without thought, he accelerated. Pushed the odometer to eighty and aimed for the tan-coloured of the two Ford Rangers racing towards him.

The insurgents, surprised by Pierce's brazen tactic, fired their weapons and came hard at him.

Bullets erupted around Pierce and tore into his Hilux's chassis. The windshield and side windows shattered. He turned his head as fragments of glass pounded him and the interior of the cabin. The turban protected his flesh from the most serious cuts, but his hands on the wheel suffered, soon covered in a dozen shallow lacerations.

Ignoring the pain, Pierce continued to drive at the convoy.

Two men on the tan Ranger rushed to load a new rocket into the Kopye.

Pierce kept a steady path, aimed again for the tan Ranger, which had levelled with the Black Land Cruiser.

When less than fifty metres separated Pierce and the two lead technicals, the insurgent at the wheel of the tan Ranger succumbed to his fear. He pulled to his right, hoping to avoid a head-on collision. But he didn't see the black Land Cruiser to his right and crashed into its side. The Land Cruiser wobbled, then flipped. That was all Pierce saw before a gap opened in the convoy, and he rushed past as the remaining white Land Cruiser and white Ranger whipped past him, heading in the opposite direction.

As the distance between them grew, Pierce glanced back.

The upside-down black Land Cruiser skidded on its roof across the gravelly sand. It soon disappeared inside an angry fireball that erupted from its centre mass. Pierce knew its fuel tanks must have ruptured.

One technical incapacitated. Three to go.

The three remaining technicals were turning, ready to rejoin the hunt.

Pierce turned his gaze again to the road ahead and realised he was barrelling towards a patch of dunes. He spotted flat gravelly terrain to his left and headed there instead. Sand was difficult to drive through and not suitable for speed. And, without a windshield, he couldn't afford for more coarse silica grains to blast into the cabin and blur his vision.

The three behind him kept with their chase. Tripod-mounted weapons fired again, their bullets missing him as another HEAT rocket blasted a nearby rocky pinnacle into a thousand pieces. Despite his luck so far, Pierce knew his odds weren't great even with his enemy's numbers already halved. If he were to escape alive, he must use every tactic available to him.

He twisted and turned, accelerated and braked in erratic movements, lessening opportunities for his enemies to find him in their crosshairs. But these manoeuvres cost him speed, and soon his enemies were gaining again.

Pierce grabbed his AK-47 and rested it on the lip of the already shattered passenger-side window.

When the technicals were less than thirty metres behind, Pierce braked hard.

The white Ranger leading the convoy howled past on his right.

Pierce, ready with his assault rifle, peppered the gunner with a dozen bullets, killing him.

But he missed the driver.

Dropping the AK, Pierce spun the wheel and pressed his foot on the accelerator. Just as he was gaining traction and moving ahead of the three pursuing technicals, he felt a thump on the chassis.

His speed dropped away. His engine lost power.

He looked again into the intact rear-view mirror.

Insurgents in the white Ranger had thrown a grappling hook with a chain, and its barbs had embedded into Pierce's tray. Now Pierce was towing their vehicle through the rugged terrain.

The tan Ranger, with its high-explosive anti-tank rockets, accelerated up on Pierce's left.

Pierce saw his opportunity. He abandoned the tug of war and turned in a circle to his left before the tan Ranger could pass him.

The driver saw too late the tensing chain, now parallel to the horizon, slice through the air towards him. With both Pierce and the white Ranger now hooked onto him and moving at speed, the chain became taut between them and sheared the tan Ranger's cabin, caught in the middle, decapitating the driver and passengers.

The chain then snapped, whipped through the haze like a striking snake to shatter the skull of the insurgent arming the tripod-mounted weapon on the white Ranger. His body cleaved in half. Blood and gore projected into the sky as the vehicle ground to a halt.

Free again, Pierce pushed up the gears of his Hilux and turned in a wide circle, once more facing back the way he had come.

The odds had shifted. He was no longer the prey in this confrontation, but the hunter.

The last white Land Cruiser, which had lagged behind his fellow insurgents for reasons Pierce could not understand, now raced back into the battle and came head-on towards Pierce. These insurgents would keep fighting even with their reduced numbers. They had mastered their fear. They believed paradise awaited when they died. Fanaticism made them unpredictable, reckless and willing to die as martyrs.

Pierce turned the wheel, aiming for his last foe as they raced at each other. He released the steering wheel, then covered his face with his bloody hands the second before he crashed head-on into the white Land Cruiser, flipping it on its side.

The impact was sudden and jarring. Pierce's seat belt caught, saving him from flying through the gap where the windshield had been, but the strap compressed his rib cage, hitting him like a sledgehammer to the chest.

When his vehicle came to a stop, Pierce clambered out, AK-47 at the ready. His body ached with bruises and cuts, but he ignored them.

He checked his bleeding hands. They weren't shaking.

They never did until the violence ended.

He dashed on foot over to the toppled white Land Cruiser and fired a burst of his AK into the cabin, killing all the upside-down insurgents who were still moving inside the decimated vehicle.

Satisfied he had neutralised this threat, Pierce turned to the insurgents pinned into the white Ford Ranger fifty metres behind him. They were attempting to untangle the grapple chain from the sheared Ranger, which in the chaos had wrapped around the axle of its front left tyre.

Pierce ejected the spent magazine of his AK-47 and locked in another. He pulled back on the charging handle, then lined up his last foes in the weapon's iron sights. When the insurgents noticed Pierce advancing, they were too late to react. Several short bursts made quick work of them.

4

With blood dripping from his cut hands, Pierce checked for survivors. Most of the Ansar Dine insurgents were dead or fatally wounded, thrown from their vehicles and bleeding in the rugged desert with jagged wounds and broken bones, or peppered with multiple bullet wounds from Pierce's earlier shots. He put each barely living man out of his misery when he found them, with single shots to the head using his favoured 9mm Glock 19 semi-automatic pistol.

He let one insurgent live. A man with a shattered knee. He looked to be in his forties, dressed in black cloth and a matching turban. Dust covered his thick beard and eyebrows. An Arab, Pierce guessed he was probably Libyan or Algerian. He smelled as if he hadn't washed in years.

After patting his body down to check for weapons, Pierce grabbed the man by his shirt and dragged him ten metres across the gravelly desert. Pierce wanted him terrified for his life, fearful that Pierce would do anything to get the information he wanted from him at any cost. The insurgent's knee bounced on the undulating surface, and he screamed from the pain.

Pierce dropped him and pointed the Glock at the man's intact knee. "This is how it works," he said in Arabic. "I will kill you. Nothing will change that. Your only choice is a quick, humane execution. Or..." He let the words hang in the sand-choked air. "I won't explain what will happen if you don't cooperate."

The man cursed in Arabic and spat at Pierce.

Pierce squeezed the Glock's trigger. The gunshot was loud even after the brutal noises of the recent battle. The insurgent's other kneecap shattered, and he wailed in further agony.

"Perhaps I do need to explain."

The insurgent panted. Sweat covered his face. The dry desert heat pushing forty degrees Celsius would only add to his discomfort. Pierce watched the man's expression soften as he came to terms with his fate. His legs were useless. He couldn't walk out of here. Pierce wouldn't leave him any water, or any weapon with which to end his misery. He was at Pierce's mercy.

"Why were Ansar Dine here?"

The insurgent growled.

Pierce fired a second bullet across his head.

The crippled man recoiled from shock, then cried, "Please, have mercy on me!"

"Answer my question."

"We're looking for a prisoner. A hostage. The Saifullah wants to do business with him. A Frenchman."

Pierce grimaced. "What is his name?"

The man covered his head with his forearms as if they

might protect him from bullets or a beating. "Please, I don't know the Frenchman's name."

Pierce pointed to the wreckage of the CIA's four-by-four. "What about them? What was their involvement here?"

The bleeding-out insurgent shook his head. "I don't know who they are. I promise."

Pierce sensed the man was telling the truth; he knew nothing about the CIA team. "You know little, don't you?"

"Please. Kill me quickly. May Allah have mercy on my soul."

Pierce licked his lips. Idris Walsh's and Ansar Dine's versions of events differed. Walsh's version of events involved an $11,000,000 exchange with hostages for a Western bad actor who held important information regarding the political and military landscape of West Africa. Meanwhile, this insurgent believed the Western bad actor was one of the hostages, a Frenchman who wished to do business with Ansar Dine's leader, Saifullah. Too many contradictions worried Pierce, and neither side seemed to know who the third party was, who now presumably had the hostages. He needed to understand the many pieces of this puzzle before he called in. "If Ansar Dine don't have the hostages and neither do the Americans, who does?"

The insurgent shrugged. "I don't know." His face was slick with sweat. His pulped knees seeped thick red blood into the ground beneath him. He wouldn't last much longer regardless of Pierce's actions. This was the Sahel. Injuries were a death sentence in these hostile conditions. "We planned to meet the Frenchman in Timbuktu. Another group snatched him first, from right under our noses. We tracked them into the desert, hoping to catch the upstarts. Please, I know nothing else."

This time, Pierce didn't believe him. "What about the eleven million U.S. dollars? You haven't mentioned that."

"There was money?"

The surprise on the man's face told Pierce everything. Perhaps the man was telling the truth, and Ansar Dine knew nothing of the ransom money.

Pierce raised his pistol and pressed it against the insurgent's forehead. "One last question."

The insurgent nodded, then closed his eyes, accepting his fate. "Very well. If I answer, you promise to kill me quickly?"

Pierce nodded. "I do, but I shouldn't. I know what Ansar Dine represents. You've no doubt murdered many innocent people. Beaten and tortured those who don't follow your twisted version of Islam. Recruited children as soldiers and raped women. Are you going to tell me I'm wrong?"

The man shook his head. "I have done those things. I regret them now."

"Lots of monsters regret past actions when faced with the certainty of their own death. Repenting in the face of oblivion isn't noble. It's an act of self-preservation. It doesn't make your life worth any more than the trash it was a minute ago."

"Is that your question?"

"No." Pierce laughed and shook his head. "Where will I find Saifullah?"

"He hides in the Adrar des Ifoghas."

"I already know that. It's vast." Pierce knew the Adrar des Ifoghas covered an area roughly the size of Michigan. "I could explore it for years and never find him. You need to be more specific."

The insurgent nodded. "I've never been there myself. I'm

told his hideout is near an oasis, close to the Hand of the Prophet."

Pierce pulled a shard of glass from his index finger that was bothering him and threw it away. "Hand of the Prophet?"

The insurgent gasped. In the last minute his face had paled, and his eyes had lost focus. He was losing blood fast. "A rocky outcrop, five pillars of natural rock. They resemble a hand."

"Near an oasis?"

The dying man nodded.

"Where exactly?"

"That is all I know, I promise—"

Pierce didn't realise he had squeezed the trigger, put a single bullet through the insurgent's cranium. He had killed his enemy without thought.

He studied his hands. Now they were shaking.

It would take minutes, maybe half an hour, before he got his tremors under control.

Yet he had acquired the information he needed.

And a new objective.

5

SAHARA, MALI

Darkness, sobs, unbearable heat and the stench of urine characterised the long, stifling drive. It took a day and a night of frantic off-road travel before Awa Sissoko accepted that an unknown group had kidnapped her. Her life was in peril. She didn't understand why.

Cord bound her hands. A hessian bag tied over her head itched on her skin. Insects trapped inside crawled on her face and hair no matter how many times she shook them away.

Her fear felt unbearable.

Between the long periods of tears, sobs and near catatonia, Awa sensed other captives confined in the truck.

This was not surprising. During lucid moments, her mind replayed her kidnapping. It started with her walking home with her required pills, safe in her pockets, secured from the hospital's dispensary. Two men with assault rifles appeared from nowhere. They snatched her and the group of white foreigners she was passing. One kidnapper was dark-skinned and the other an Azawagh Arab. They spoke a mixture of Arabic and Bambara. Her language. Her own people held her hostage.

Awa sobbed for hours. She recalled horror stories of African girls stolen from schools in Nigeria. Sex slaves to pleasure the perverse Boko Haram terrorists in the northeast of that nearby African nation. She didn't believe Boko Haram had captured her, but one of the similar fanatical groups that had overrun much of Mali since the military coup in the capital, Bamako, over ten years ago now. Awa was no schoolgirl. She was twenty-five. That didn't lessen the likelihood that she now faced a future of abuse and sexual servitude.

The white people were financial hostages. Their wealthy families back in Europe or America would be coerced into raising suitable ransoms for their loved ones' return. But Awa was nothing more than a theatre nurse at Timbuktu General Hospital. She was lucky to have a job and a vocation — considering her medical affliction — but her salary was a pittance compared to even the lowest-paid foreigners. She had no money. No family to pay for her release either, other than an ageing mother who relied on Awa for food and the roof over their heads. There could only be a single purpose for her capture...

The kidnappers drove through the day before providing Awa and the prisoners with water.

A few hours later the truck stopped again. She listened as the kidnappers discussed a wrecked jeep they discovered with dead people inside. They argued about what they should do. She heard every word as they then discovered a treasure that made them ecstatic. They argued, then returned to the vehicle and drove again.

Judging by the angle of the heat on her skin, Awa predicted they were driving northeast. That scared her more. North and east were the fringes of the Sahel and the baking wastelands of the Sahara. No one ventured into the deep desert where nothing grew and no life existed, except for occasional Tuareg camel caravans and fanatics returning to their desolate hideouts. Midday desert temperatures could bake a human to death.

As evening approached, and the heat lessened, they stopped again.

The back door flung open. Calloused hands dragged her and the other captives from their mobile prison. The white prisoners whimpered, whispered their fears in French. She was the last out. A man ripped the hessian bag from her head.

Despite the late hour, her eyes immediately adjusted to the light.

The landscape was sand dunes and clumps of dead vegetation. A red sun dipped on the far horizon. The air was dry and crisp. There were no animal noises. The only sounds in the deep desert were the winds.

A captor appeared. The young man who'd snatched her in Timbuktu. He wore the same bright yellow T-shirt, loose pants and battered AK-47 strapped to his back. He shuffled to a well, dragged a bucket from its depth, then tipped the container onto his open mouth, quenching his thirst. Water splashed across his thin face and chest.

"What about me?" asked a second terrorist. Another dark-skinned young man, whom Awa didn't remember being at the Timbuktu attack. She saw him up close. His physical deformities caused her to draw in a sharp breath.

He had no hands.

His wrists ended in ragged stumps. Old wounds.

This second terrorist wore a dirty blue polo shirt and loose pants. He carried no weapons. Similar facial features suggested the two men were relatives. The handless man likely relied on his "brother" to survive in the world, performing daily domestic tasks most people took for granted.

The first terrorist passed the bucket to his brother. He took it in his stumps and drank, spilling water across his face and wasting more precious liquid.

Watching them, Awa remembered her own thirst.

She again examined her surroundings. She saw nothing but the truck, the well, the sand dunes and their congregation. They were deep inside the Sahara. There was no strength in her to fight her predicament. There was nowhere to flee.

The Western prisoners huddled as a group. Their number included a handsome white man in his late twenties or early thirties prostrate on the earth. Tension showed in his face as his hands gripped a seeping wound in his left shoulder. Two women in the later stages of life, wearing loose-fitting pants and shirts, trembled together and hugged. The last hostage was a stodgy male wearing khaki trousers and a dirty white shirt. A gold cross pendant hung around his neck.

A third terrorist leaped from the truck, startling Awa with his sudden presence. His skin was fairer. He, too, was young and had slung an AK-47 across his back. He kept a semi-automatic pistol tucked into the front of his pants and wore a turban and the loose-fitting clothes of the Azawagh Arabs from the northern regions of the Malian Sahara. His beard was long and fashioned in the style of pious Muslim men. The dark-skinned Malian men didn't dress as Islamic fanatics, but this Arab did.

"You need to water the cattle," the Arab commanded in Arabic. "They're still worth something, even with the Americans' money in our possession."

"What about her?" The brother with the AK-47 pointed to Awa. Either he had no concern that she might understand he was discussing her fate, or he presumed she didn't speak their dialect of Arabic — which she did.

The Arab shrugged. "She has her uses. It would be a waste to kill her so soon."

Despite the lethargic heat, Awa shuddered.

"Water!" demanded the Frenchman in his native tongue from where he lay in the sand. "We need water!"

Awa didn't wait for permission. She snatched up the empty bucket and dropped it into the well. When she sensed its weight fill with the life-giving liquid, she dragged it up again. A difficult task with her bound hands. She used her feet to secure the rope each time she shimmied her hands further along its length.

The Arab argued with the Malians, proclaiming at how Awa had acted without approval.

The armed Malian responded with derision. She performed woman's work. Why should the Arab complain?

Despite its weight and her bound wrists, Awa soon pulled the bucket up out of the well. She beckoned the white people to join her. Together, with cupped hands, they spooned the brackish, muddy liquid into their mouths. Water had never tasted so good.

The wounded Frenchman hadn't moved because of his injury. When the others had drunk their fill, she took the bucket to him. He couldn't move without jolts of pain surging through his shoulder, so she helped him drink.

"Thank you."

"What is your injury?" she asked in her limited French.

He glanced at his shoulder, pulled back his shirt from the bloody gash. The circular wound was red and raw. These terrorists must have shot him during the kidnapping.

"I need to check it."

He nodded.

Awa examined the entry and exit wounds. The bullet had gone clean through the muscle. No shattered bones or ruptured arteries.

"Can you help?" the Frenchman asked her.

She saw fear in his eyes. He knew, as she knew, they must treat the wound soon, or it would become infected. Without medicines or antibiotics, his injury was a death sentence.

"Can you?"

"I can try."

6

The memory of gunfire during the kidnapping was strong in Awa's mind. She'd felt her attackers had fired weapons as a scare tactic. Examining the Frenchman's bullet wound, she no longer believed this.

"Let me look." She crouched by his shoulder. "I'm a nurse. I know what I'm doing."

The Frenchman nodded. She noticed his face was handsome and rugged. His physique was slim and muscular. Long, wavy brown hair hung over deep blue eyes. Awa fantasised about getting to know him better — if they got out of this predicament alive. Local men were not interested in Awa because of her neurological affliction. Long ago she'd accepted she'd never have a relationship with an African man. She touched her pocket, checking for her pills, their remaining presence the single positive outcome of this mess.

"Are you ready?" Her hands gently explored the wound, causing him to flinch.

Distracted by movement, the Frenchman looked up and past Awa.

She followed his gaze. Behind her, two terrorists watched with dispassionate interest.

"I'm a nurse," Awa growled in Bambara. "This man will die if I don't treat him. Do you have antibiotics?" When they returned blank stares, she inquired, "Bandages? Clean water? I need to wash the wound."

Still no response.

She raised her voice. "He is no good to you dead; otherwise why kidnap him? I can save his life."

"You're a doctor?" asked the handless terrorist from the back.

Twice she'd explained she was a nurse, but they hadn't picked up on that. "I'm a medical professional," she said, not directly answering his question. If they believed she was a medical doctor, they might decide there were better uses for her than as a sex slave. "Do you or don't you want this man saved?"

The stares from the Malian gave her hope that her skills were worth preserving. In contradiction, the Arab's glare expressed both loathing and lust. Her skin prickled.

It was the Arab who answered. "The infidel hasn't bled out. He'll survive."

"He won't survive. I need to clean the wound to stop an infection. It is a miracle it's not already too late. Do you have alcohol?"

"It is forbidden to drink alcohol—"

"Not to drink!" Awa growled. "To disinfect the wound."

"She's right," said the handless man. He held out his stumps, acknowledging he could better appreciate the injury based on personal experience. Awa didn't doubt him. Only surgery in a sterile hospital could have saved him from his terrible maiming.

"What would you know?" The Arab was furious. "You are useless. I don't understand why we brought you here."

The handless man shrank into himself, afraid of the Arab.

The second Malian came to his rescue. "Because Oumar is my brother, that's why. You get us both, or none of us, Farid."

The Azawagh Arab from Mali's Sahel region slapped the Malian hard across the face. "Jali! Stop using our names," he said in Arabic. "Every piece of personal information you give the prisoners is a piece of information the infidels can use against us."

Jali cringed. "*You* used my name, just then?"

"Yes, to teach you a lesson. You don't have my experience—"

"In the al-Qaeda training camps?"

"Yes. Of course."

"They made you tough, did they?"

Farid's face reddened. "You don't understand our ordeals. The tests of faith, the endurance exercises, the scoring... and the cost of failure. But understand this, you wouldn't be alive now if it weren't for the special skills I mastered."

Awa remained motionless while the angry men argued. She kept her face impassive, suggesting she couldn't follow what they were saying. Farid acted as their leader, the most aggressive and least empathetic of the three. It was Farid whom she was most wary about.

The Frenchman responded with a harsh whisper, surprising them all with his command of the Arabic tongue. "The young lady is correct. I won't survive if my wounds are untreated. There is a trauma kit in my pack. Use that."

The kidnappers looked at the Frenchman with fury and curiosity.

"I am your most valuable prisoner. No? You want me to die?"

"I'll get the trauma kit," volunteered the handless man.

Farid snorted. "Don't be stupid, Oumar. How can you find anything?" He glared at Oumar's stubby wrists.

"My brother knows what he's doing," Jali said. He nodded to Oumar that he should go.

When Oumar disappeared, Awa held out her bound wrists and demanded in Bambara, "Cut them, please?"

Farid shook his head. "No!"

"You believe I will run? I'd die out here. I need unencumbered limbs if I am to treat this man."

Farid looked her up and down. She sensed his desire for her body. It took every effort not to shrink in his presence.

Jali pushed past, pulled a knife and cut the bindings. "You may have more military training than me, Farid. But you don't understand people as I do."

"Watch your tone, Jali, or—"

"Or what? You'll kill me and my brother? You don't have the will to complete the mission alone. Where we're headed, you need us as much as we need you. Despite your 'so-called' al-Qaeda qualifications."

"You imbecile! I'm ready to give my life for this cause. I don't think you are."

"*You cannot guide those you would like to, but God guides those he wills. He has best knowledge of the guided.*" Jali gave a sly smile. He had recited a passage from the Qur'an.

"I can judge you any way I want, Jali."

Awa watched as the two men argued. She didn't care who

was the most pious. She cared only for clarity on where they were taking them. She also feared the answer.

Oumar returned. He balanced the trauma kit between his wrist stumps. "This what you're after?"

Awa nodded. "Thank you." She took the kit and searched through its contents, finding haemostatic dressings, chest injury seals and airway control devices.

A kit issued to soldiers.

She put the thought from her mind.

Awa soon found what she needed: saline washes, bandage wraps, tweezers, wound cleaning wipes and antibiotic ointments.

"Do you have a name?" she asked the Frenchman.

"Lucas," he said, grimacing against the pain, or in anticipation of the added pain he'd suffer as she cleaned the injury.

"You've been shot before?" she asked, holding his stare. Her instincts told her he had been.

He expressed surprise. "What makes you ask?"

"I think you appreciate what is about to happen."

Lucas gritted his teeth and nodded.

"I need to pick out debris and dirt inside the entry and exit points. I need to clean it. You understand what this requires?"

"Of course."

She glared at the terrorists and asked in Bambara, "You understand as well? This man will scream. I will have to hurt him to heal him. You understand?"

Farid shrugged. "Do what you must. I care not."

"It will save his life?" asked Oumar, glancing again at his stumpy limbs.

"If we do nothing, out here, infection will kill him."

Lucas gripped her arm with his good hand until it hurt. His violent response shocked Awa until she saw the pain and fear in his eyes. "*Mademoiselle*, I don't want to wait any longer. I know what you must do. So just do it."

Awa grimaced. She couldn't decide if Lucas was angry or stoic.

He slipped off his belt and bit into it. He nodded that he was ready.

In the fading light, Awa began her work.

She had never heard a man scream and fight against the agony as much as Lucas did for the next three hours.

7

GAO, MALI

Bullets lodged in the chassis of Pierce's Hilux had torn the engine block apart, which now leaked transmission, brake, steering and coolant fluids. Sand inside the engine's many moving parts produced grinding and clunking noises.

With no windshield, dust had blasted Pierce's body on the journey back to Gao. His only protection was a pair of goggles. He'd stopped every fifteen minutes to top up oils and fluids and clean the engine with an air compressor. It was a losing battle.

He reached the first United Nations manned checkpoint at sunset. Kenyan soldiers in their blue helmets demanded identification. He offered code words identifying him as being with the UN forces. They let him pass and never questioned the state of his vehicle, his bandaged hands or the AK-47 resting on the passenger seat. Gao, like most of northern Mali, was an "open carry" zone. Locals secured whatever weapons they could, including assault rifles, as a protection against the insurgents and criminals who roamed the Wild West landscape. The AK-47 was not suspicious, while a modern M4 assault carbine would create unwanted attention.

Three hundred metres later, the engine groaned, spluttered and died. The steering wheel locked up, and steam gushed from the radiator.

Pierce grabbed his Glock 19 and slung his AK-47 and field kit over his back. Everything else he abandoned. Then he walked.

Built on the banks of the Niger River on the southern edge of the Sahara, Gao was a flat, uninspiring metropolis of eighty thousand inhabitants. Buildings were low and sand coloured. Sandy streets were wide and baked in the hot sun. Acacia trees grew in clumps on the broken footpaths, seemingly too healthy to belong in this town. Bullet holes peppered mud-brick fences and houses, reminders of the 2012 insurgent rebel occupation and later liberation by Malian and French forces. Burned-out and rusted husks of cars and tanks blocked occasional roads. Black paint obscured faces on faded billboards and shopfront advertising because artistic human representations were offensive to radical Islamists. The same fanatics had even painted over the cartoon camel heads.

Dark-skinned citizens in bright clothing walked the streets in their hundreds. Men and women laughed and chatted together again. Mopeds or motorcycles powered through the crowds. Sheep congregated in bleating herds or wandered alone. Trash collected by the wind gathered in corners.

A French EC665 Tiger attack helicopter swept low across the city with its air-to-surface missiles armed and aimed at people walking the streets. The military helicopter's spinning rotor blades and powerful engines drowned out all other noises as it passed over on a routine patrol, creating a short-lived storm of dust.

Gao was a city balancing on the edge of collapse, but Pierce felt at home. On the surface Gao was bland, but peel back the cracks and the metropolis had character. People laughed and stopped to pass the time of day unlike in the war-ravaged Yemeni cities he had operated in during past missions. Gao had suffered during occupation, but the insurgents had never broken the spirit of its citizens. It held a vibrancy unmatched by most other cultures that Pierce had experienced in many other corners of the Earth.

No one bothered Pierce as he walked. With his Tuareg disguise and his face hidden behind the blue turban, he looked as if he belonged. The concealing garb was a reason he favoured the AK-47 over the more modern U.S. assault rifles at his disposal. The Russian-designed weapons were everywhere in Mali.

He should have hiked to MINUSMA, the local United Nations super-base built to tackle the Malian military and humanitarian crisis in this region. Established by the French in 2013, MINUSMA was shorthand for *Mission multidimensionnelle intégrée des Nations Unies pour la stabilisation au Mali.* It had served as Pierce's home for the last year, one he shared with six thousand other foreign soldiers, peacekeepers, UN aid workers and administrators. But with the United Nations Security Council's recent questioning into the value of MINUSMA and its many failed operations and high death rate, and the Malian government wanting it gone, Pierce suspected it would not be around for much longer.

The base was several kilometres from his current position and a long walk in this heat. Its fortified walls presented the most secure facility within a thousand kilometres, but Pierce was dead tired. He needed a moment to think in a nearby semi-secure location. Too many aspects of his conversation with Walsh and the Ansar Dine terrorists bothered him. Until he learned more, MINUSMA might not be an ideal venue for recuperation.

He checked his hands.

Although only he would have noticed, they were shaking.

For the sake of his health and mental well-being, he needed rest — and food. If he couldn't get his shaking under control, it could affect his performance if he found himself in another violent confrontation.

He knew of a nearby bar frequented by both Malian men and foreign soldiers, the Regatta de Blanc. He headed there.

Thirsty and with his stomach rumbling, he stepped inside and sized up the patrons. A dozen male civilians drank in a few groups. Three German soldiers sat at the bar, knocking back Castels straight from the bottle. Salif Keita afro-pop played through a tinny speaker. Old fire damage blackened an interior wall. Another scar from the Islamist occupation period.

Pierce sat at the rear with an uninterrupted view of all the bar's patrons and exits. He rested his Glock on his lap, out of sight beneath the table but within easy reach should he need to shoot his way out of any unexpected confrontations. The AK he kept slung over his shoulder. When the waiter came, he ordered a Castel beer and a meal of lamb stew and couscous.

The food arrived by the time Pierce finished his first beer. He ordered a second Castel, then devoured his bowl, passing the food and drink under his turban as was Tuareg custom.

He hadn't eaten today, and the food was tasty and properly cooked. The alcohol calmed his thoughts.

The Germans watched him sporadically. They slung Heckler & Koch G36 rifles and wore the latest European body armour. Kitted soldiers and mercenaries were common in Gao. Pierce kept his movements slow and controlled so they wouldn't consider him a threat.

Five minutes passed without incident. By then Pierce had eaten most of his meal. Already he was feeling more energised.

He checked his hands. The shaking had disappeared.

Across at the bar a satellite phone rang.

One of the Germans answered it. After a terse conversation, the three soldiers paid their bills and disappeared.

In an instant, Pierce's senses switched to high alert.

He threw a heap of West African CFA francs on the table, more than enough to cover the meal and the drinks.

But before he could stand, three new mercenaries armed with FAMAS assault rifles moved into and took command of the bar. They ordered patrons to remain where they were as they covered all corners with their deadly bullpup-style weapons. FAMAS rifles fired 5.56x45mm NATO rounds at the rate of a thousand bullets per minute. They would make quick work of anyone who resisted them.

Pierce sensed their military training, but the men's aggressive and blustering nature suggested they weren't ex-special forces; they drew too much attention to their actions. Each man was muscular and large bodied. Dressed in desert camouflage and body armour, they displayed no insignia designating country allegiance.

Pierce returned to his seat and again rested his Glock on his lap. He gave no outward sign the men interested him, yet he observed them. As a paramilitary officer with the CIA Special Activities Center's Special Operations Group, known in the trade as SAC/SOG, in Pierce's experience there were no coincidences. Like attracted like. The moment these men had showed, he'd known they had come for him.

The tallest mercenary, a man with close-cropped black hair, a Roman hooked nose, angular chin and an ugly scar running from his left eye to his jaw, marched straight for Pierce. He raised his FAMAS rifle and pointed the muzzle at Pierce's head. "Hands on the table, Pierce!" he commanded in English with a strong French accent. "No sudden movements."

Pierce complied.

"Lose the disguise."

Pierce grinned behind his turban. "I need hands to do that."

"Then do so fucking slowly."

With careful movements, Pierce unwrapped the turban.

The mercenary smirked at Pierce's unmasked face. "Good. Now I have confirmation, hand over your weapons."

Pierce paused. "No!"

"Fuck you!" The armed man cocked an eyebrow. The scar twisted, parodying a second mouth. "Reassess your position, Pierce."

"No," Pierce said again. "This is Mali. Not the Cote d'Azur. Gao's an unsafe city to walk about unarmed."

"I'm not asking."

"I'm not complying. Besides, why should you fear me? There are three of you. Plus one out front and two round the back. Not a shoot-out I'd survive."

"How the fuck did you know that?"

Pierce grinned. His assessment was a guess based on

years of experience in similar missions. "I don't care how many you are. I'll keep my weapons while you talk. You came to talk, right? You'd have killed me already if that was your plan."

The mercenary grinned. "They said you were slippery."

"Tell me I'm wrong. Should I reassess and shoot my way out?"

"You'd be dead in seconds if you did."

"And so would you—"

"He's okay, Denault." A woman's voice from the back of the bar speaking English, also in a French accent. Eloquent. Refined. Cultured. Pierce didn't know France well enough to guess which region she was from, but he guessed it was somewhere nice.

Both men turned.

A slim muscular woman approached. She was as tall as Pierce. Her pale skin was as white as alabaster, and her platinum-coloured hair was tied in a bun. She was a classic beauty, with large eyes, full lips and well-defined bone structure. He guessed her age to be early thirties, the same as him. Yet there was an aspect to her that was otherworldly, not human. Hers was not a face he would forget.

Pierce couldn't draw his eyes away. She was equal parts runway model and assassin, dressed in the same desert-coloured uniform and body armour as the soldiers but that hugged her curves as if cut in the fashion houses of Milan. She passed Denault without acknowledging him and sat opposite Pierce. He realised what bothered him about her. One of her irises was green and the other grey. When he looked closer, he saw her eyes weren't different colours. Her left eye featured a dilated pupil, the mark of a condition known as anisocoria.

She ignored his stares as she drew her holstered PAMAS G1 9mm semi-automatic pistol and planted it on the table. Pierce recognised the gun as the French Army version of the Beretta M9.

"You're carrying a Glock 19. No doubt it's just out of sight on your lap." She motioned with her eyes that hiding it was not appropriate.

Pierce put his weapon on the table next to the PAMAS. The woman had access to impeccable intelligence. She knew Pierce's preference in firearms and what equipment he carried on his person. "I take it you are DGSE?"

"Good guess, Mark."

The General Directorate for External Security was France's foreign intelligence organisation — the equivalent to the United States' Central Intelligence Agency. As with the CIA, they specialised in paramilitary operations, intelligence gathering and security-risk neutralisation. DGSE was not an organisation that Pierce could dismiss now they had showed an interest in him.

"You have a name?" He didn't recognise her. With her striking features and unusual eyes, he would not have forgotten her if they had crossed paths before.

"You can call me Juliet Paquet."

"Juliet Paquet," he repeated. The name suited her. "Is that your real name?"

"Is Mark Pierce your real name?"

Pierce grinned. "Juliet Paquet it is, then." He reached for his Castel and drank the last of the cool amber fluid. "Since you've gone to so much trouble to meet, what do you think I can do for the DGSE?"

Juliet smiled like a cat that had just killed a pigeon. "Rather a lot, actually."

8

Juliet Paquet smiled away a little of the tension held in her facial muscles while the rest of her body remained rigid. From Pierce's perspective, she had no reason for concern. Three armed DGSE paramilitary officers guarded her, and three more waited outside. He was a single man without a ready weapon. If it came to a firefight, Pierce wasn't walking out of here alive. He'd be dead before he could fire a single shot.

"What is this about?" he asked.

"I'm here to dissuade you from your current mission."

"Which mission?" Pierce laughed. "You need to be more specific."

Juliet grinned, but there was no humour in her returned gesture. "This will go faster if we bypass the gameplay. You're in Mali with a kill order. Your target is the arms dealer Victor Vautrin."

"I can't confirm or deny that."

"No need. I know. I'm here to tell you your mission is

over. Joint orders, French and American. You're to hand over all intelligence you've so far gathered."

Pierce locked eyes with the unusual woman, held her non-symmetrical stare to gain a measure of her. To his surprise, she didn't glance away or blink. She was as skilled as he was in intimidation and sizing up opponents. Pierce presumed she knew as much about him and his career with the CIA as it was possible to know, because the mission she had described was exactly as his superiors had briefed him. That didn't offer many opportunities for bluffing.

"Why is the DGSE and not the CIA telling me my mission is over?"

"Because we're all in this together. The West versus the fanatics."

Pierce didn't believe her. "So that's the deal? I give you everything I have on Vautrin, promise to stop hunting him, and you'll let me walk out of here?"

Juliet nodded. "A sufficient summation of the situation. Yes, Mark, that is the deal."

Pierce leaned forward, ignoring Denault's warning stares that he was too close to his employer. "You appreciate Vautrin supplies weapons to AQIM, Ansar Dine, al-Qaeda and Islamic State?"

She shrugged. "So what?"

"Juliet, Vautrin supports the world's worst terrorists. That makes him a terrorist. That is why I'm hunting him."

"And why you will try to kill him when you find him. Yes, I know all this."

"Not try. I *will* kill him."

"You underestimate him."

Pierce shook his head. "I know Vautrin plays both sides. He

supplies the DGSE and French Legionnaires with weapons. I appreciate Vautrin can get arms into Mali like no one else because he knows all the supply routes and exactly who to pay off. But that doesn't change his betrayal or my mission. He'll receive the justice he deserves for his enemy action."

Juliet leaned back in her chair and gave Pierce a look suggestive that he disgusted her. "We're already in dialogue with Langley. Vautrin is worth more to us alive and serving the interests of French, U.S. and Allied intelligence agencies. Plus, you already understand why Vautrin went a little crazy."

Pierce nodded. "Because four years ago a U.S. air strike killed his only son and daughter. In Afghanistan if I remember correctly—"

"Murdered while securing weapon supplies for American troops — working for their father, I should point out."

"He blames America for their deaths. But I don't care about motives, Juliet. He turned against us. He made that choice."

She breathed deeply. "Mark, just play ball, please. This is way above your paygrade. You are compromising both our national security interests. The Americans and the French, and the British if they are important to you, need Vautrin back on the books."

"He made a deal, did he?"

She nodded. "He's promised to cease sales to insurgents and provide us with a mother lode of intel on West African terror cell networks. You don't get breaks like that every day. In return, things go back to how they were."

Pierce shook his head. "Are there no principles we abide by anymore?"

"Don't be naïve, Pierce. There never were, and there never will be."

He drummed his fingers on the table. "This is a great story, Juliet, but I've received no supporting information on what you've told me."

Juliet laughed with derision. "Mark, of course you haven't. You're a loner. I've seen your profile. You never check in with your case officers, even those you respect like Mackenzie Summerfield, unless it suits you. You don't enjoy hanging out with your own people when given the choice. Look at you now. You're eating in a dangerous bar in the heart of Gao after dark. This dive is a haunt for insurgents. You'd rather be here than back at MINUSMA base, where you should be when not in the field. Where I wouldn't be able to reach you without some high-ranking officer noticing, and we wouldn't be having this conversation."

Pierce stared at her, said nothing.

"I don't understand you, Mark. I realise much of your past is a highly classified secret, but I'm guessing something traumatic happened during that redacted period. You were hurt so bad, you trust no one. Believe me, I know what that feels like, but in this game, you have to count on your own people. Without trust in someone, you lose sight of what the game is all about."

Pierce took a moment to frame his answer. "You think your amateur psychological assessment of my inner workings will change my mind?"

Juliet lifted her hand in a signal. Denault and the other two mercenaries stepped forward and aimed their FAMAS assault rifles at Pierce. "I give the word, and Denault kills you. Denault and his men aren't DGSE; they are mercenaries and don't care about justice, alliances and nationalism, just about getting paid by following my instructions. In this situation, it is easier for me if you're a corpse, rather than trying to negotiate with you."

"Then why are you negotiating?"

"I need the intelligence you have on Vautrin. If you are dead, it will be more difficult to acquire. Plus, I don't want the headache of explaining to the CIA my connection with the death of one of their SAC/SOG operators."

Pierce calculated what steps he needed to take next. There was no way he was giving Juliet Paquet the intelligence she demanded, nor would he cease his mission to hunt Vautrin. At least not until he had unambiguous orders from the senior heads of the CIA, and even then, he might not stop. But he wanted to walk out of here alive and unharmed. Pierce had to convince Juliet that she had persuaded him. He formulated a plan of action, built upon tools he had established in-country during the preceding eleven months.

"Okay. I guess you *are* persuasive, Juliet."

She sighed. Relief spread across her mismatched eyes as she relaxed a little more. "Good. I'm glad we're getting somewhere."

"I'm taking a risk, handing over intelligence to a foreign agency. Even an allied one. For that, I'll need compensation."

She frowned. "What do you mean?"

"I want two hundred and fifty thousand U.S. dollars."

"You're joking."

Pierce shook his head. "I'm committing treason giving you this information. I need contingency money if I need to go into hiding, should my deceit come to light. So I propose this; there is a military-grade laptop in my field kit. Contains everything I have on Vautrin. It's locked down with state-of-the-art CIA encryption tools. If you try to hack it, specialist-installed software wipes the hard drive. I mean destroys everything."

"What are you suggesting?"

"I give you the laptop. You give me a phone number. We both go our separate ways. When I feel I'm a safe distance from Denault and your men, I call with the passcodes. You can log in and confirm the data. Once you're satisfied that I kept my side of the bargain, you transfer the money into a numbered account I provide."

"That's a lot of trust."

"I agree, on both sides." Pierce didn't wait for an answer. He carefully grabbed his Glock and holstered it while the barrels of three assault rifles tracked his every move.

Keeping his cool, he opened his field pack and removed his laptop. The Getac X500 was a booby-trapped device, designed to foil insurgents. Should it fall into the hands of terrorists, it was easy enough to hack. It then sent a transmission identifying its current GPS location while providing fake intel on CIA safe houses and black detention centres in the country. Those locations were kill sites, watched over day and night by U.S. Rangers ready to terminate or capture anyone who showed up. Terrorists fell for it all the time.

But the laptop had other uses, too.

He pushed the Getac across the table to Juliet Paquet. "The number, please?"

She recited a satellite phone number. "I guess you special forces types need not commit the number to paper?"

"No," Pierce said with a grin. He tapped his head. "It's locked away in here now."

He stood, picked up his Glock, then slung his AK-47.

Denault and his men closed in. Pierce sensed they itched

to squeeze their triggers and remove him from the world. They didn't hide their disgust for him. They wanted a reason to kill him.

Pierce stared down at the exotic beauty that was Juliet Paquet. The whiteness of her hair and skin was unsettling, and her eyes were mesmerising, almost as if she were unreal. "Either you shoot me, Juliet, or I'm walking out now."

She nodded. "We're done here," she said in French to her men.

The men lowered their weapons and opened their ranks, creating a path out of the bar.

He walked out without looking back.

Pierce marched into the poorly lit streets of Gao. He passed another mercenary standing in the shadows outside the bar. They watched him disappear.

In the last eleven months he had studied the city's layout. He took a surveillance detection route through narrower, lesser-travelled streets. He doubled back several times, stopped at random intervals and altered his walking speed until he detected not one but two men tailing him, but now they dressed like him as Tuareg nomads in long flowing blue robes and turbans. What gave them away were their FAMAS rifles. Too rare a weapon for Tuareg. They slung them as openly as Pierce slung his AK-47.

Pierce turned the corner of a sand-coloured building. Once out of sight, he dug his fingers into the wall's bullet holes and within three seconds pulled himself up onto the roof, where he lay flat and still, waiting for Denault's men.

Within seconds they turned the corner and halted. They whispered in French, querying each other where Pierce had gone.

Pierce dropped to the sandy road and clobbered the first mercenary on the back of the head, rendering him unconscious and dropping him.

The second mercenary turned, but not fast enough. Pierce closed the distance and punched him hard in the throat, compressing his airways.

As the man struggled to breathe, Pierce punched him again in the cranium, dropping him as quickly as his partner.

When Pierce was certain they were both incapacitated, he dragged them behind a wall out of sight. He didn't wish them further harm from muggers or insurgents. They were, after all, fighting on the same side. Certain they were breathing without difficulty despite his throat punch, he dismantled their weapons and scattered the parts. He took one man's radio and earpiece, fitting it into his ear canal, and started walking.

Within minutes Denault was checking in. "Fabre? Pelletier? Report?"

Pierce responded into the mic, "I don't enjoy being followed, Denault!"

"Fuck! Pierce? If you've killed them—"

"They're not dead. Their unconscious bodies are hidden three blocks east of the bar." It was actually four blocks. Pierce's aim was to distract Denault's men, to send them searching in the wrong place for the two downed mercenaries.

"They'd better be."

"I'll forgive this mistake, Denault. The deal is unchanged despite your pointless threats. Tell Paquet I'll call soon."

He pulled the earpiece out and threw it and the radio into the night.

After changing directions multiple times, Pierce found the empty shell of a ruined building and moved inside. Barely standing, the building was another casualty of the mortar and rocket attacks that still plagued Gao. Convinced the building was empty, he found a dark corner out of sight, unlocked his satellite phone and opened his tracking software.

Then he called Juliet.

"Where are Fabre and Pelletier?" Juliet growled.

"Near where I said."

"Near?"

"They'll be fine. Live with your mistake. You were a fool to have me followed."

For a moment Juliet said nothing. Pierce could hear her breathing. "We had a deal, Pierce."

"We still have a deal. Just don't try to play me again. Is the money ready?"

"Yes."

"Okay, these are the passcodes." He recited two strings of numbers and letters. Codes that would initiate a unique set of events. "The second code you need to key in one minute after the first; otherwise the data gets wiped."

"Very well. Hold a minute."

Pierce waited. Within seconds a light flashed on his tracking software. Juliet's location was about half a kilometre from his current position, inside a residential building on Avenue de l'Aeroport. Not inside any of the French military bases or forts, and nowhere near the UN super-camp, where it would be difficult to reach her. She was likely hiding out in a DGSE safe house. Like him, she preferred to operate outside of professional protocols. This would make his next task easier.

As Pierce packed his gear, Juliet spoke. "I'm in, but the system is running a diagnostic test. For God's sake, Pierce. How long will that take?"

"No idea." Pierce did know. This was a deliberate delay. He had ten minutes to reach Juliet's location. "Call me when it's done. I don't want anyone tracing me on an open line." He hung up, then dismantled his phone's battery and SIM card to ensure no one could track him.

Jogging, he reached the safe house in eight minutes. A minute of surveillance identified two of the mercenaries, wearing light-intensifier goggles, watching the streets from the roof.

Pierce took a flashbang grenade from his pack and lobbed it at the safe house, then looked away. The light would blind the mercenaries for at least five seconds, the noise would deafen, and the concussion wave would produce temporary balance disorientation. With light intensifiers, the disorientation would last much longer.

Just after the grenade detonated, Pierce sprinted to the front door, emptied a clip around the hinges until the wood shattered, then kicked it in and lobbed another flashbang into the house.

When the second grenade exploded, Pierce reloaded his AK-47 with his eyes shut, then stormed the building. Two mercenaries stumbled on unsteady legs just inside the entrance, trying to clear their vision. Pierce clubbed each with the stock of his assault rifle, rendering them unconscious. Then he fired into the roof, peppering the wooden ceiling with tiny holes, causing the men up there to reconsider coming after him.

Pierce moved quickly. All the rooms were empty except for one: the operations centre with laptops and monitors arranged across various fold-out tables. Juliet Paquet and Denault were the only occupants, and Denault was already firing his pistol into the door as Pierce glanced in. He ducked just in time. When the firing stopped, Pierce remained still, listening. He soon heard the unmistakable sound of a magazine being reloaded into the grip of a semi-automatic pistol.

Pinpointing the sounds, Pierce knew exactly where Denault was standing.

Crouching low, Pierce fired his Glock through the wooden wall.

Denault screamed and dropped to the ground.

Pierce stormed the room. Denault, lying on his side in the centre of the room, had grabbed his calf where Pierce had put a bullet through the muscle. Juliet stood in shock against the back wall, away from the surveillance tech.

Pierce pointed the Glock at Denault's head. "Drop the weapon."

The mercenary relinquished his pistol.

Pierce kicked the weapon away, then dragged Denault into a sitting position and pressed the muzzle of the Glock against his forehead. Juliet did not try to find a weapon of her own. She stood motionless with her hands by her sides, rubbing her fingers together. Her unusual, mesmerising eyes locked onto Pierce's stare.

"Call off your men!" Pierce pressed the weapon hard into Denault's dark hair. "You know what I'll do otherwise."

Juliet spoke into the radio. "All units stand down. I repeat, stand down."

"Raise your hands where I can see them."

She complied.

Pierce dragged Denault towards the desks, where there was a well-thumbed print-out of Paquet's personnel DGSE file, open to a page detailing her involvement with past UN missions. It seemed odd that Paquet was examining her own file, but he didn't have time to think further on the anomaly at this moment. Surveillance camera feeds on the monitors allowed Pierce to see all rooms inside the house, the roof and outside onto the streets. The two mercenaries above were the only active combatants. Despite Paquet's orders, he could see they were preparing to re-enter the safe house, weapons ready.

"Order them to dismantle their weapons, throw the parts away and then sit on their asses with their hands on their heads. Otherwise..."

Paquet looked like she was considering her options. Realising she didn't have any, she instructed the mercenaries to do as Pierce demanded. She warned her men that Pierce would execute her and Denault for non-capitulation. The men considered their options, then complied.

"Fuck, Pierce!" Denault spat his words and panted hard from the pain of the bullet wound. "No one gets the better of me! No one! If you don't kill me now, I'll come for you, and I'll fucking kill you!"

"Sure you will." Pierce swung the grip of his pistol hard against Denault's skull, stunning him but not quite knocking him out. He pointed the weapon at Juliet, grabbed her hard by the arm to immobilise her.

"We had a deal," she blustered.

"You think I'd betray my country?" Pierce asked, surprised that his bluff had duped her. "I haven't killed you or your men out of professional courtesy, but don't expect my generosity to last."

Juliet's striking green-grey eyes shrank and grew dark. "You don't know what you're getting into."

With one hand on the pistol still pointed at Juliet, and an eye on the monitor to ensure the mercenaries on the roof weren't moving, Pierce pulled an aerosol can from his pack. He sprayed the fine mist over Juliet's face and hands, then did the same to Denault.

She looked horrified. "What's that?"

"Infrared markers," Pierce explained with a grin. "They light you up with a signature our Predator and Reaper drones home in on. Identifies you as an insurgent."

Shock and surprise grew in Juliet Paquet's face.

"Can't wash it off. Takes a few weeks to wear off. Until then, I wouldn't leave this safe house if I were you."

"Don't think this is over, Pierce."

"It is over unless you interfere with one of my operations again." He fired bullets into the monitors, shattering the screens into hundreds of glass shards and metal fragments. Then he sprinted outside and disappeared into the night.

Pierce didn't like how much in the dark he was. He needed answers.

It was time to call Mackenzie Summerfield.

10

AGADEZ, NIGER

A storm gathered in the west. Moonlight lit up a mile-long wall of clouds rumbling across the horizon like a tsunami. Lightning flashed within its dark interior, and crackling thunder followed soon after. In the Sahara, storms never brought rain. When it hit the airfield, only dust and sand would fall from the skies.

With a blank stare, Mackenzie Summerfield glanced at her "near coffee" held loosely in her left hand. It tasted like layers of sediment. She guzzled the remaining black brew before the storm closed in and filled her cup with more sand, then stepped inside the air-conditioned Quonset hut.

The interior was fold-out desks and chairs, military-grade laptops and uplinked servers, connecting the forward operating intelligence centre to the CIA's vast, global information networks. A dozen CIA and Air Force intelligence officers tapped keyboards at their assigned workspaces. None looked up as she entered, for their work assignments were separate to hers. Summerfield was as uninteresting as the storm outside. Winds would rattle the building, and comms might go down for short periods, but that was all the damage it could do — other than ruin her coffee.

The facility was Niger's Air Base 201 — AB 201 as everyone called it — near the Saharan town of Agadez. Officially AB 201 was for the Niger people. In reality, it was a military airport to launch MQ-9 Reaper and Predator drones armed with air-to-surface missiles to take out Islamic fundamentalists operating across West Africa. The paved runway, when completed, would be long enough to land any aircraft in the U.S. Air Force fleet, including C-17 supply and transport planes. It would be from AB 201 that America's War on Terror would advance its latest offensive against the new ground zero. West Africa.

With this latest sandstorm, construction activities would again halt on the one-hundred-million-dollar-price-tagged air base. Sandstorms were regular occurrences, so this surprised no one. Building costs would rise, and the delivery programmes would stretch out. Only the pen-pushers in Washington would fail to understand the realities of infrastructure development in West African countries.

Summerfield sighed. She reflected on her morose mood, trying to understand her lack of motivation. Every day the dry heat wore her down, but her physical lethargy was not the cause of her depression. When she was honest with herself, Langley's latest request bothered her. Headquarters demanded a detailed report on her current operation, with specific references to Mark Pierce and his "unconventional" methods.

No one had asked her that before.

She didn't even know how to answer that question.

It was ironic that Langley had asked because the same people had assigned her to "the Trigger Man" three and a half years ago. No one wanted to or could work with this mysterious operative — except her.

No one would work with her, either.

But when provided the latitude to operate independently, Mark Pierce demonstrated a track record of neutralising high-level insurgents and delivering quality actionable intelligence. Few SAC/SOG Ground Branch operatives could claim the same. Summerfield had understood Mark's skills and encouraged him, not held him on a tight leash like his previous case officers. Mark responded in kind and kept her in the loop. As a team, they had delivered whatever was asked of them, proving the CIA wrong.

What had changed?

She pondered this question from her fold-out desk while staring at the situation report feeds on her battered laptop. Mark had been "dark" for twenty-four hours, which meant she was unable to do much but assess the latest intel reports that came across her desk. Villagers in Sierra Leone known to harbour Ebola carriers were being systematically murdered. Someone had tipped police off to the murder of a Parisian woman discovered half dissolved in a bathtub of acid. Interpol had arrested a Turkish counterfeiter in Istanbul for printing fake money for the Islamic State. It didn't seem to matter what the CIA achieved in its efforts to make the world a safer place, people still committed the most heinous crimes.

Summerfield leaned into her chair and tapped her pen against her teeth. Most analysts were quiet, unobtrusive introverts who sat motionless while they worked. She was the opposite, agitated and unsettled if she wasn't in motion, even if that was just squeezing a stress ball or stretching a rubber band between her fingers, much to the annoyance of her peers. If her seat swivelled, she'd be doing that too. Movement helped her think.

"Got a moment?"

Summerfield looked up and around. A late middle-aged, rugged yet refined man with a square jaw and full head of hair stood behind her. He wore civilian clothes, their tan colours resembling neutral desert textures. Blue eyes and neat grey hair distinguished him. He was handsome in a George Clooney kind of way.

The man reached out his hand, palm facing down. "Idris Walsh, H/ONA. Head of Operations, North Africa."

Summerfield shook his hand. His grip was firm. "Pleased to meet you."

"You're Mackenzie Summerfield?" He looked her up and down.

She nodded. Summerfield knew Walsh by reputation only, there were rumours of corruption, but he was smart enough that no evidence ever compromised him. Many considered him one of the best case officers ever to work in the Directorate of Operations. "I thought you were in Langley, sir?"

He grinned. "That's what I wanted people to think. You run the so-called Trigger Man, don't you?"

Summerfield hesitated. "What is your clearance to ask?"

He laughed. "I'm your new boss. Or I'm your boss's boss. Haven't decided the reporting structure yet. Either way, you're on my team now."

"That doesn't give you clearance."

His lip quivered for a moment before he answered without humour, "You think I'm testing you, Summerfield?"

"No! I'm just serious about national security."

"Anaconda Trident Seattle."

Summerfield shrank a little inside. That was the correct code. With the Trigger Man, Walsh operated on the same clearance level she did, perhaps higher. There was nothing he could ask that she wasn't obliged to divulge.

"We all good?" he asked in a manner suggesting it wasn't a question. "Tell me, why is Mark Pierce called the Trigger Man?"

Mackenzie shrugged. "It's not what most people assume."

"So... he's not some super-sniper who's taken out hundreds of Afghani and Iraqi insurgents, then?"

Summerfield shook her head. "I don't recall who assigned the code. His handler before me said it was because if you want to 'trigger' a volatile situation, shake things up, he was the man to do it."

Walsh looked amused. "And does he?"

"Shake things up?"

"That's what I asked."

She nodded.

"Sounds as if you've got your hands full. Let's talk and walk. Follow me."

He set off at a brisk pace. She followed him through the corridors linking the Quonset huts to a briefing room. The sandstorm hit as they entered, shaking the walls and supports. The whistling wind sounded like wailing ghosts from a horror movie.

"Take a seat." He pointed to a chair next to the small desk. Walsh wiped sweat from his forehead and sat opposite her. He raised his voice to be heard over the rattling structures and howling winds. "How long have you run Mark Pierce?"

"Over three years."

"So, you ran him during his operations in Yemen?"

"Yes. You should understand I'm not his first handler."

"You said. But you've run him pretty much since he joined the CIA?"

"Well, I don't know about that."

He raised an eyebrow. "Explain?"

"Sir, Pierce's records before three and a half years ago are sealed. No one knows his earlier history, but that doesn't mean he wasn't working for the CIA back then."

He grinned like he had caught her in a lie. "You think he was? Or know he was?"

"Speculating." The whistling winds and rattling building brought an ominous tone to their conversation, which now felt like an interrogation. She slowed her breathing so her emotions wouldn't get the better of her. "Pierce joined us already trained in covert operations and tradecraft. He must be ex-special forces. He speaks all five MASER languages, plus some others—"

"MASER?"

"New acronym describing the five most important languages for intelligence operatives: Mandarin, Arabic, Spanish—"

"—English and Russian," Walsh finished for her. "Not French?"

Summerfield laughed. "French isn't as important as it used to be. Plus, I don't think the acronym works if you include it."

"Trigger Man speaks French?" Walsh's unwavering stare seemed to bore right into her.

She nodded. "Passable. Can hold a very basic conversation. Couldn't write a report. Why all these questions?"

Walsh was motionless for a moment. Then he smiled

and showed teeth. "I heard three different case officers ran Trigger Man before you. None of them lasted a month."

"He's..." Summerfield searched for the right words. She risked presenting Mark as a rogue operative, always a nomad operating with his own agendas, and this wasn't far from the truth. "He follows unconventional routes to solutions that don't always seem obvious at first assessment."

"He's a loose cannon? A danger to himself and others?"

"No! He's intelligent. Don't underestimate him. He strikes me as a man who's operated alone for a long time without support. He's so used to running his own missions, he no longer knows how to follow the rules. Like something made him that way, and now we expect him to change his stripes into spots and become a team player—"

"He's not reporting in or returning to base when instructed. Like now, with him running loose in Gao."

"He's in Gao? I—"

Walsh interrupted, "You're in a relationship?"

"With Mark?"

He nodded. "First-name basis, I see."

"If you mean have I slept with him? No, I haven't. And I don't intend to, not that it's your business."

"This is the CIA, Summerfield. You'll appreciate how closely we watch each other?"

His comment caused her skin to crawl. "I've guessed your next question. Are we friends? I wouldn't even know how to answer that."

"Mykonos. Three years ago. You, he and another CIA paramilitary officer, Michael Abraham. Only two of you came home. Abraham somehow ended up garrotted to death."

Summerfield couldn't help but shudder as memories

returned, of long hours trapped in the dark house. How her attacker had tormented her again and again. She had survived only because of Mark's quick and brutal actions. Greece had changed everything, bringing them both closer together and tearing them apart. She shut the Mykonos mission from her mind before the memories became too awful to bear. Since then, she'd been reluctant to operate in the field again.

Once upon a time, Summerfield's role within the CIA was linked only to the Directorate of Analysis as a senior intelligence analyst, and a pure research role based in Langley had suited her fine. Then she'd met Pierce via teleconferencing during an operation in South Sudan, where she provided critical intel to him that no one else could, which saved his life during a tricky deception he'd miraculously pulled off that had caused their targets to fail in a terrorist attack. Two weeks later, the Chief of the Special Operations Group had seconded her and made her the Trigger Man's handler, because Pierce insisted he couldn't work with anyone else. The new role had terrified her at first, but somehow, they had gotten along, and they managed to work well together. And from that point onwards, the Trigger Man's missions became successful more often than not.

The new role, however, meant she was travelling constantly and into countries most tourists avoided, and most people had never heard of. Exotic travel had been exciting at first, like her student days backpacking in Africa, but that all changed with Mykonos. Secure Bases like AB 201 were the limits of what she could endure, and she didn't want to make this assignment more difficult than it was because of her own deteriorating mental state.

"That's right," she said, jutting out her chin. "It's all on file. I'm presuming you've read the after-action report?"

Walsh grinned. "I have. Like all AAs, it's what's *not* written that intrigues me."

Summerfield looked away, afraid that he would query her further. The Greek mission was not an aspect of her life she wanted to relive. Ever. The ordeal brought nightmares, even years later. "You still haven't answered my question."

"What question is that, Summerfield?"

"What is this about? Why are you interested in Mark — I mean Pierce?"

"That's two questions."

"I'm fine with you answering both," she said, maintaining eye contact. "Sir."

"What is this about? Mark Pierce works for me now. So do you."

"You've reassigned us?"

"Kind of. And I need someone who knows the ins and outs of the Trigger Man's mind, hence why you're still on the team. Plus, your geopolitical knowledge of Africa is exceptional. The big difference now is that I run him, not you."

Summerfield let the information sink in. This was a demotion. Before Mykonos, she had been an intelligence analyst who'd made the rare transition into the role of case officer. After Mykonos, she'd failed to cope with proper fieldwork, and apart from directing the Trigger Man, her role had returned to her previous analyst position rather than a field officer. She tightened her fists at the unfairness and arbitrary nature of further reduced responsibilities. "You'll manage Pierce directly?"

"That's what I said. You'll remain at AB 201, provide me with intel as I require it."

"I'm a case officer, not an intelligence analyst."

"You came first in your class from UCLA in African Politics and completed a master's degree on the geopolitics of North African insurgency. Applied for and were recruited by the CIA as an analyst — not a case officer. You speak Arabic, French and a half-dozen sub-Saharan languages, and you've presented detailed and well-received threat assessment reports from at least thirty countries across the continent. I also know you travelled to eighteen African countries during college semester breaks, so you know the region first-hand. Tell me I'm wrong, but you're wasted running field operatives."

Summerfield was furious. She might make an official complaint, but that would get her nowhere. She had no recourse but to accept her new duties.

She thought of Mark and already felt she was abandoning him. She didn't believe he would work well with Walsh. This new Head of Operations, North Africa was in for a surprise if he believed he could control a Ground Branch operative as unpredictable as the Trigger Man.

She nodded, realising it was better to cooperate than fight with Walsh... for now. "Okay, I'll brief Pierce, tell him the change of plan. It will be better coming from me."

Walsh laughed. "No need, Summerfield. Trigger Man and I have already talked. He knows I'm the new sheriff in town." He stood and shook Summerfield's hand again, smooth like a congressman asking for her vote in the next mid-term elections. "Welcome to the team."

11

GAO, MALI

Pierce walked into the MINUSMA super-base at twenty-three hundred hours, but not before UN security forces confirmed his coded identification, only then allowing him through the barricaded checkpoint.

Even at this late hour, military personnel and UN aid workers went about their business inside the base. With so many allied soldiers on patrol, Pierce relaxed for the first time in weeks. Relaxation lessened his tension, and he soon felt his exhaustion hit.

Despite his need to sleep, Pierce entered the male showers in the military accommodation block, stripped off his Tuareg disguise, then washed away weeks of grime and dust. Cleansed, he changed into fresh desert-coloured civilian clothes before heading outside to make a call.

"Mark Pierce?" a man called from the darkness between two temporary buildings he was approaching from.

Pierce turned. The soldier stepped into the main thoroughfare Pierce used, and stood under a base light; he was wearing desert camouflage and a blue UN peacekeeping beret. Pierce recognised the French Foreign Legion major. "Gabriel Travers!" The men shook hands, then hugged in a manly embrace. "Good to see you, my friend."

"You too." The major rubbed his copper beard with thick fingers. Tense muscles bulged beneath his uniform, and his sunken eyes carried a far-off stare. Travers looked as exhausted as Pierce felt. "How are you traveling, Mark?"

Travers slung a FAMAS assault rifle over his right shoulder despite being deep inside secure UN territory. Pierce was no different with his AK. It was never possible to feel protected in a war zone like Mali, even inside a protected military base. Personal security was second nature to men like Travers and Pierce.

"I'm fine," Pierce answered. "I'm still alive."

"And in one piece, I see."

"You didn't expect that?"

"I never know what to expect with you, Mark. Didn't know you were still in Mali."

"Nothing changed there." Pierce shrugged. "Too much to do."

Travers nodded. "I know what you mean."

The War on Terror was a shared effort between many allied nations. In Mali, there was an extra level of cooperation between the French and the Americans, the two biggest Western forces operating in the country. The risks were too great not to. Travers and Pierce had worked on several missions together in the last year. Assignments had taken them into the northern Sahel and Sahara regions. Their objectives were to "win the hearts and minds" of Tuareg tribes opposed to the fanatic insurgents, or neutralising AQIM and Ansar Dine strongholds. As a team, Pierce and

Travers had had their successes, but they'd had their failures too.

Off-duty, they had become drinking buddies, consuming non-alcoholic drinks in the so-called wet mess. They had experienced shared horrors in the battlefield and had saved each other's lives frequently. Theirs was a friendship difficult to break.

"What about you, Gabriel, you working tonight?"

Travers nodded. "Driving out at first light. Protective duty for a UN convoy supplying an interim aid mission in Tessalit."

Pierce sensed the man's worry. "That's the far north, near Algeria. Insurgent badlands. Why is the UN still out there?"

Travers laughed. "Short answer, refugees. So many displaced people either trying to make it to Europe crossing the Sahara, or heading south to refugee camps in the more stable neighbours of Burkina Faso and Niger. But our operations in Tessalit are in trouble, and they can't easily defend themselves. We're taking in supplies, then bringing the UN workers out before any more of them get killed. Leaving short-term aid for the local people but encouraging them to come here to Gao, where we can send them on to further refugee camps down south. We no longer have the will or resources to defend Tessalit."

"Good luck. Pity you're working. Want to grab a drink before you go?"

He shook his head. "I'd like to, but I need to ensure every vehicle in my convoy is operational. Last thing I need is a breakdown."

Pierce almost shared his earlier experiences with his Hilux, but his was a classified mission. He couldn't reveal any details no matter how innocuous. "Good luck, Gabriel. The convoy couldn't be in better hands."

Travers nodded. "Thank you, Mark. Before I forget, something odd happened a few days ago. A French journalist came looking for you."

"For me?"

"Yes. Knew you by name. Wanted a story from you, regarding arms smuggling in West Africa?"

Pierce's senses were on high alert. "Female?" His thoughts went to Juliet Paquet.

"No. Male. Told him I didn't know you."

Pierce grinned. "Good man. Was he tall? Short black hair and a Roman nose? Scar running from his left eye to his chin?" Despite the risks of sharing minor details of his recent actions, Pierce gave a vague description of Denault.

"No. This guy was handsome. Young, late twenties. Wiry frame, but fit."

Pierce nodded. That description matched no one he had encountered in Mali. "Don't suppose you got a name?"

Travers shook his head. "Sorry, my friend. I didn't ask, and he didn't offer one. That's odd now that I think about it. Journalists always give their name."

"No matter. Thanks for the heads-up."

"When I get back, we'll catch that drink... If you are still around. I don't know near enough stories about you."

"Sounds good."

They shook hands. "Keep yourself safe, Mark."

"You too."

Travers looked ready to say more. Then changed his mind, grinned and marched into the night.

Pierce waited a moment, reflecting on the news regarding the journalist. There was no doubt the mysterious man was a

DGSE operative working for Juliet Paquet. Someone inside the French government was intentionally compromising Pierce's mission.

Realising he had put off his call to Mackenzie Summerfield long enough, he dialled her number. He suspected when they spoke, the news he'd learned earlier would become official, that he worked for Idris Walsh now, and Mackenzie would get a transfer somewhere else. He felt sad. As his case officer, she had made his work bearable, and he hadn't warmed to Walsh in the slightest.

When the call connected, he coded in, "Three, one, Delta, one, Echo, nine, Bravo."

"Eight, five, Juliet, Zula, zero, zero, Alpha. Mark, nice of you to call." Mackenzie stifled her sarcasm with a yawn.

"Did I wake you?"

"It's the middle of the night. Everybody needs to sleep sometime, you included."

"How have you been?"

"Better."

"Is it true? I now report to Idris Walsh?"

"Yes." She kept her voice level and unemotional even though he sensed her tension. "Both of us, actually. But the same team."

It could have been worse. Together they'd continue to have each other's backs.

"Mark, there is…"

Pierce sensed her hesitation. She had important news to share, and while this was a secure line, the CIA and the NSA could listen in if they chose to. "When are we meeting?" he asked before she could voice her question.

"An Air Force CH-47 Chinook is transiting to AB 201 in the morning. Walsh wants you on it."

Pierce gritted his teeth. He was being called in to meet the new boss, a few hours' flight east by helicopter. Walsh was not in Langley after all. "Roger that. You're in Agadez?"

"Never left."

"Good, we'll catch up tomorrow."

"Mark...?" She hesitated again. Something was troubling her.

"We'll speak tomorrow, Mackenzie. I'm inside MINUSMA now, so nothing will happen tonight. We'll get to talk. Everything will be fine."

"Are you sure—?"

He ended the call before she could say more. He didn't believe everything would be fine, not with three dead CIA operatives, five hostages, eleven million dollars missing, an arms dealer on the loose equipping the insurgents, and the possibility that the Sword of Allah was planning an operation against the West here in Mali.

But Pierce couldn't concern himself with any of that now, for he was dead tired.

He claimed a hot bunk in the accommodation block and was asleep within seconds.

12

SAHARA, MALI

Startled, Awa Sissoko woke. Her throat felt constricted. She couldn't breathe.

The nightmare came back to her.

Ropes, bound around her neck, tightened whenever she rolled from one side of her body to the other.

It was sunrise. The same ropes bound the other captives. Two sets of nooses around their necks tied to opposite posts hammered into the sand, with the prisoner in the middle. To move towards one post tightened the rope tied to the other. Awa angled her fingers through the nooses to loosen the grip, but with bound hands this was difficult. She'd tried to untie the knots during the night, but they were too thick. No rope bound their feet, but to stand constricted the bindings further.

On her knees, resisting the urge to cough, she examined their camp. It wasn't much, with three bedrolls for the kidnappers and the dying embers of a campfire. The kidnappers kneeled on rugs at the crest of a dune, praying to Mecca. She watched the rising Saharan sun and knew she could not pray. She instead asked for God's mercy from her bound position.

Awa looked to the four captives. One woman sobbed, and the second lay unmoving in the sand. The older man stared expressionless towards the horizon. Lucas must have been the only prisoner to have slept during the night, for he looked refreshed despite his wound. Stirring from his slumber, he sat, wincing in pain when he moved his injured shoulder. He caught her staring and smiled. His confidence gave her hope. She didn't know why. Their situation was hopeless.

"What happened to your friend?" Lucas asked the older woman.

She didn't acknowledge him except to turn her sunken, bloodshot eyes and stare through him. Salt had dried on her cheeks where tears had run during the night.

"She isn't moving," Lucas said.

The woman sobbed.

"Is she a close friend? A sister?"

She sobbed louder.

Awa watched the prostrate woman for several minutes. She never moved. There was no rise and fall of her chest.

"How are you?" Lucas asked.

At first Awa didn't realise he was talking to her. She felt her own tears run along her cheeks. "My name is Awa. Awa Sissoko. I wanted to tell you, before they kill us."

He grinned. "They won't kill us. Awa is too pretty a name for you to die this day."

"They won't kill *you*. Me, I am worth nothing."

The older man snorted, as if what they said both amused and disgusted him. He refused to look at Lucas or her. He stared instead towards the rising sun, red as it danced on the hazy horizon. Its rays already heating the atmosphere after a long night in near freezing conditions.

"You're a priest?" Lucas asked.

The man said nothing.

"No need to answer. I've seen the gold cross around your neck. I listened to your mumbles during the night. Prayers, to a Christian god."

"The only God." He spat his words and bared his teeth. "I'm more convinced than ever of that now, watching these heathens—"

"I'm a Muslim," Awa retorted, not wishing to hear further disparaging words regarding her religion.

"Then you are as bad as them." The priest nodded towards the kidnappers bowed in prayer.

"No way are we the same!"

"Are you a missionary?" asked Lucas.

"What if I am?"

"In Mali it's illegal to convert Muslims to Christianity. You are here under false pretences."

The two men locked eyes. Awa sensed mutual hatred. Why did they want to fight each other when they had a greater enemy in their midst?

"My faith is strong," said the priest. "My soul is eternal. I don't fear death."

"No one really fears death, old man. They fear the pain that precedes it. When the Muslims discover you are a priest, I can assure you, your passing will not be quick."

"You will tell them?"

For a moment, Awa thought Lucas was considering his answer.

"It matters not what you say." The priest nodded to the

two women. "They lay with each other. Their fate will be worse than ours."

"We're not lesbians." The conscious woman half-sobbed, half howled her answer. "We're sisters. You disgust me suggesting so, even if you are God's representative."

"I am a man of the cloth. It pleases me to learn that you are not sinners. But I suspect our kidnappers may not see it that way."

"You'll be the one to tell them, won't you?" retorted Lucas.

The priest looked away, closed his eyes and mumbled another Christian prayer.

Awa felt sick in her stomach. She couldn't understand these Westerners, scheming to sell each other out, hoping to save their own skins. All thinking they were better than everyone else. Even Lucas. She'd believed he was a nice man, an understanding soul with depth. She didn't see that anymore.

"Lucas, why do you taunt him? The priest is not the enemy. They are." She nodded to the terrorists returning from the dune.

Lucas lost his smile. "The priest schemed through the night. He will bargain for his own life by betraying the rest of us. He fabricated a story that the sisters were lovers. He talked to himself during the night when he thought we were asleep—"

"How dare you!" countered the priest.

"Tell me I'm wrong!"

"*STOP IT!*" Awa yelled. "Listen to you. You're like children. If we are to survive this, we must work together."

The conscious woman stopped sobbing. She turned towards the kidnappers.

Awa followed her gaze. Jali and Oumar attended the fire. It was Farid who approached. A snarl distorted his angry face. "What is with the wailing?" he demanded in French.

"My sister, Jacqui," sobbed the woman. "Cut her free. She is unwell."

The Arab approached the motionless woman. He sniffed the air and prodded with his foot. When the prostrate woman remained unresponsive, he kicked her hard.

Jacqui's sister let out a squeal, but the inert body gave no response.

"She's dead," Farid snarled. "The infidel strangled herself during the night."

"*You* strangled her!" bellowed the sister. Her accusation became a sob, then a wail; then she howled like a beast possessed.

"Be quiet!" demanded Farid.

Her howls continued. The noise was inhuman.

"Be quiet! *BE QUIET!*"

He pulled at her noose, and her sobs halted. Soon she gurgled. Gurgles became coughs, then choking noises.

"Let her go!" Awa demanded, speaking Arabic, thereby betraying that she understood the enemy's language. "You've tormented her enough!"

Farid loosened his grip on the noose. The sister collapsed, breathed guttural gasps. Her bloodshot eyes wouldn't blink.

Farid approached Awa. He took her chin in his hands, forced her head to turn and stare up at him. "You need to be careful, pretty one. Where we're taking you, there will be no favours. Pray I keep you for myself and don't pass you on to my brothers. They might not treat you with the respect I will."

He held Awa's stare. Despite her fear, she refused to lower her gaze, waiting for him to break contact. He did so by shoving her head away with force. "You are mine, pretty one."

Then Farid returned to his companions, berating them in Arabic for not cleaning away a mess.

Awa slumped. She stared upwards. Lucas and the priest looked at her with pity. The sister wailed, oblivious to everything in the world but her dead sister.

And, Awa realised with a sense of unfathomable dread, their torment had only just begun.

13

Oumar Kone watched from a distance as Farid tormented the prisoners. The Westerners were no threat, yet the man gained pleasure in hurting the bound captives.

Oumar didn't understand Farid al Rewani's constant anger, or why his brother, Jali Kone, always carried a far-off stare. The men were young, handsome and strong. They had much to live for, yet they would throw their lives away in a jihad that didn't represent God's words as transcribed in the holy Qur'an.

They should consider themselves lucky they were whole. Not like Oumar. One missing hand, he might eventually have accepted that. Two missing hands left him an invalid for the rest of his life, constantly dependent on others for his survival.

Even mundane tasks required concentrated efforts and ingenuity to complete. The morning required him to empty his bowels beyond the rise of the nearest dune. For Farid and Jali, this task took minutes at most and required no thought.

Oumar had to pull down his pants, clean himself and dress again using his stubs. Loose pants with a drawstring were the only solution. He used teeth to tighten knots, but he could never get them snug, so they required continuous adjusting. A greater embarrassment was when he soiled himself and would require Jali's help. The humiliation was unbearable. His brother would give him a hard time during the cleaning and chastise him later for not being more careful. But he always cleaned him. Theirs was a bond of brotherhood.

As he walked to the camp, Oumar sobbed for his miserable existence. He had never lain with a woman or even kissed one. He never would. What woman would want him? He couldn't provide, couldn't be a complete man for her. He only had his brother, and Jali might not be around forever. Especially if he killed himself in this fundamentalist crusade that had duped his morality. But for now, Jali had prepared mint tea. He seemed sad when he saw Oumar, like his soul had left his body, leaving him as a grey husk. "You've performed your ablutions? Would you like me to clean your stumps?"

Embarrassed, Oumar nodded.

With his left hand, Jali took a cup of soapy water and washed both of Oumar's stumps. Muslims ate with their right hand, cleaned their privates with their left. Jali always assumed Oumar must use both stumps to clean himself because he used both to feed himself. Jali was not wrong.

With the washing complete, Jali offered Oumar tea. Oumar balanced the cup between his stumps. The mint was refreshing and sweet.

"Did you count the money?" Oumar asked after a few sips.

"I have." Jali looked away. "I threw away the cases we found it in, should they have a tracking device. The cases also seemed to be armour plated."

"What does that mean?"

"I don't know. The money belonged to serious people?"

"How much?"

He shrugged. "I needed five bags. I reckon it's just over eight million."

"Eight million?" Oumar was in shock. He found it difficult to imagine what so much money could buy. "Five bags contain eight million?"

"Maybe more. Maybe nine or ten."

"Ten million? U.S. dollars?"

Jali nodded. "Maybe even eleven or twelve. It's almost all in $100 notes."

Oumar wiped away the tears building in his eyes. "With that kind of money, just some of it, I could travel to Morocco, find our lost sister and live with her and her husband. Get prosthetic hands. I could feed and look after myself. Return to university and finish the engineering degree I started—"

"No!" Jali growled. He stood and looked towards the dunes, refusing to acknowledge his brother.

"I never wanted to be a soldier. I know you do, Jali, but this is not my dream—"

"No!" He was angry now. "You lost your hands, and our parents are dead, because of Western devils. They took our family fortunes. They must pay. Jihad is how we will bring them to justice."

"Then you fight. Let me leave. I accepted before because I had no hope until that money came into our possession—"

"No, Oumar. How many times must I say it? You need me. Who else will clean you when you soil yourself? Who else will cook for you? Dress you? Wash your clothes? No one! Because I am all you have now."

"But there is our sister?"

"She's gone. We'll never find her. But, Oumar, I need to fight, to prove I am a man. I need vengeance against the infidels—"

"You never talked like this before. It was only when Farid came into our lives—"

"Stop it! Do not speak of this again. We've committed ourselves to the Saifullah, the Sword of Allah. We've committed ourselves to jihad. Giving our lives serves a greater purpose, so if we die, so be it. Heaven will welcome us with virgins in our beds every night. Your hands shall return, and you will be a real man again."

The words stunned Oumar. This seeing him as something less than human, these were not sentiments Jali had voiced even a month ago. This was Farid's doing.

"How long were we living on the streets, my brother? Three, four years since the doctors released you from the hospital. That was not a life. This is."

Oumar's body tensed. His skin was numb. He had never felt this lost and alone since the day he had woken in the foreigners' hospital, recovering from the complex surgery, when the doctors explained they could not save the hands he didn't know he had already lost. At least their sister was long outside of the country before this tragedy struck them; she was in Morocco, married and living a better life.

"Oumar, this is our life."

There were many arguments Oumar might present, but he felt weak. He needed his brother. That was the horrible truth of his predicament. He didn't have the will to undertake the perilous journey across the Sahara to Tangiers alone. He was too afraid to try on his own. Until Jali believed in the same dream he did, this was their fate. Warriors, off to fight in the jihad, and die.

At least it would be a short life.

Farid returned from tormenting the prisoners.

Jali forced a grin and asked their companion, "What's wrong with the unmoving prisoner?"

"She's dead."

"Dead?" Oumar felt shocked that they could kill a prisoner so easily. "How?"

"She was weak. An old, infidel woman. This should not surprise you."

Oumar trembled, hoped that neither man noticed. "What now?"

"We leave," Farid said. "The Saifullah entrusted us with this important assignment. We must keep our promise and bring the surviving prisoners to his holiness, as he commanded."

"And offer him the money we stole from the Americans?" Jali asked.

"Yes. It was a most fortunate discovery."

Oumar almost sobbed. His brother had never spoken like this before either.

14

GAO, MALI

When Major Gabriel Travers witnessed the rising sun, it confirmed his mission was behind schedule.

Six white VAB armoured vanguard vehicles, built like bricks, sat upon four huge tyres, and two armoured PVP small protected vehicles with UN markings were ready to roll. Maintenance checks were complete. Fuel tanks were full, and the forty Foreign Legion soldiers with their UN blue berets had eaten, rested and kitted for the mission ahead. Their delay now came down to several missing crates of bottled water. One bureaucratic error halted everything. Travers was furious.

He stormed into the Legionnaire inventory supply tent. The corporal behind the desk stumbled to his feet and saluted. His face expressed his nervousness. He should be. Inventory supply was his responsibility. "Sir?"

"Where is my water, Corporal? Men and women need to drink."

"Sir, I've triple-checked. Records say the crates should be here—"

"And yet, they are not."

"Perhaps I can help?"

Travers turned. A striking woman had entered the supply tent without him noticing. Her hair was almost white and so was her skin. Her eyes were different colours. Tall and slim, she was beautiful yet projected an aloof demeanour. Her desert camouflage uniform carried no country insignia or rank, adding to her mystery.

"Who are you?"

"My name is Juliet Paquet."

"You a spy?"

"I prefer intelligence officer. DGSE, although this is not information to share with your troops."

Travers clenched his teeth. "It'd better be good, whatever it is you want."

"I'm traveling with you to Tessalit. So are my men. Seven, not including me."

"Under whose authority?"

She smiled, but there was no warmth in her gesture. "You know how this works, Major. I need not explain, but if you need confirmation, please call the DGSE and ask. Be aware, they might construe the call as interfering with an operation critical to national security."

A veiled threat. Travers had dealt with intelligence agencies and their field operatives before, including the General Directorate for External Security. They were a nasty bunch, smug with their secrets that no one else could know. Their pompous belief was that the whole French national security apparatus served them. They had forgotten that intelligence was there to support military action, not the other way around.

Before he could respond, she smiled again and motioned outside. "On the bright side, Major, I've found what you were looking for."

Travers stepped out into the dusty base. The sun was a red globe on the horizon, rippling in the baking skies. His men busied themselves loading plastic bottles onto the various trucks. The missing water.

"Where was it?" he asked, sensing she had walked up behind him, again without him hearing her.

"You're welcome, by the way."

Travers was in no mood to thank her. Her ploy might have been deliberate, a transparent psychological game so Travers would feel indebted to her when she had in fact delayed their departure. He turned and stared her down. "We leave when we have secured the water. Based on the likelihood of improvised explosive devices laid out on the route, and the number of insurgents operating there, it could take days to reach Tessalit. When we arrive, we're staying only long enough to drop off supplies and get the UN workers out. You can remain in Tessalit or return with us. I don't care. I care only about my mission."

She grinned. Her eyes were unsettling, like they weren't real. He could not look away.

"You are a passionate man, Major Travers. An attractive quality."

She touched his jaw and beard. Her skin was soft and caused a sensation akin to an electric bolt running the length of his body. He mused on what it would be like to kiss her, run his hands across her smooth skin. He imagined making love to her. She would be wild, uninhibited...

He shook his head and stepped back. She was a spy. Even if they were on the same side, he could not trust her. "We leave when I say we leave. I'm not waiting if you delay."

"I wouldn't either."

"You and your men can travel in Vanguards Two and Three." He pointed to two armoured vehicles where his Legionnaires were stowing the water bottles. "Everyone mucks in. You and your men work as instructed, but otherwise stay out of my way."

"No problem."

"Good."

Travers stormed off. He climbed into the command VAB and sat for a moment. As his mind calmed, he realised he was angrier with himself than with Juliet Paquet. Catering to the operational needs of spies was an unfortunate part of the business of soldiering. The sudden inclusion of the DGSE in his UN-sanctioned operation should not have surprised him. He was angry because for a moment he had considered betraying his wife and children. He'd considered making a pass at this woman.

Travers had felt lonely for a long time now and, when he was honest with himself, afraid. Every day carried the risk of death. Insurgents fired mortars into their camps, shot soldiers on patrol and hid improvised explosive devices on the roads. Without warning, death or maiming could befall any of them. There were moments when Travers sought release from his fear, and distraction in the embrace of a beautiful woman promised that...

But at what cost?

He removed his helmet and took out the photograph tucked in there. His wife, Esme, and his two young sons, Louis and Curtis, smiled back at him. The three hugged on their tattered lounge in their Paris apartment. His wife was beautiful; joy and pride in her children shone from her eyes. He remembered how special his family was, and why he fought terrorists. It was to protect his family and his people from the worst of humanity.

He touched his fingers to his lips, then to the photo and mouthed that he loved them. How long had it been since he had last held them in his arms? Three months? Four?

The driver's door flung open. A corporal climbed in and saluted. "Sir?"

Travers returned the salute. "Corporal, is the water loaded?"

"Yes, sir."

"Good, then let's roll."

"Yes, sir."

Travers checked in with the other drivers by radio. All Legionnaires confirmed they were ready. Travers gave the order. The corporal started the engine. They drove out, a convoy of eight armed United Nations vehicles headed into insurgent-controlled territory.

The easy part was behind them. The difficult part lay ahead. Travers silently vowed he would complete his mission without losing a single man or woman to the dangers prevalent in the north. He'd checked and double-checked every detail as best he could. Only bad luck could hurt them now.

Or the DGSE. Paquet and her men might still complicate matters.

15

MALI-NIGER BORDER

Pierce wouldn't have thought it possible, but Mali looked more desolate from the sky than from the ground. He watched the Sahara race beneath the Chinook helicopter as they flew east. The military aircraft's shadow flickered in the ripples of the dunes, grew small, then large again, depending on whether they were over crests or troughs.

Later the landscape shifted from dunes to flat gravelly expanses and occasional rocky outcrops. A lack of vegetation and the stretch of blue skies and rippling heat were the only consistency.

The pilot advised via headset that they needed to fly low for a time, to avoid collision with an allied fighter mission currently underway and unrelated to their activities. The area below was considered low risk. Pierce accepted this without question, knowing their course correction was nothing unusual.

Within minutes, they passed over a village with mud

huts, thorn trees, goats and camels, and an oasis with date palms.

Pierce heard and felt bullets impacting on the metal hull before he registered what they were.

The Chinook turned. The gunner retaliated with his .50-calibre machine gun. A volley of high-velocity rounds devastated the village. The noise was deafening. Flames arced from the barrel. The shells bounced hot and bright on the metal floor of the helicopter.

When the shooting ceased, the pilot completed another pass.

No one fired back this time.

Pierce looked out, not wanting to know the cost of their engagement, but he couldn't stop himself. Sometimes seeing was better than not knowing, and sometimes not. It could go either way.

Paths ran red with blood. Dozens of camels and scores of goats lay butchered in the sand. Some beasts, not quite dead, kicked in their agony.

Pierce searched for the shooters. He identified two teenage boys, their corpses ravaged with meaty wounds and their limbs spread unnaturally where they had fallen. An old rifle lay next to the larger boy. They had been herders, protecting their livestock and their livelihood.

The Air Force gunner cursed. His face turned red; tears gushed from his eyes. He had killed children, and his mind couldn't accept it.

The U.S. objective in Mali was to save lives, bring stability and prevent fundamentalist Islamists from creating a new caliphate like they had in Syria, Iraq and Libya. Nobody wanted Mali to become a new landscape from which to spearhead terrorist strikes against America and

Europe. But, today, retaliation with extreme force had failed, and might turn more victims towards the path of the insurgent.

"They could have been Ansar Dine or AQIM!" Pierce yelled over the helicopter's engines, not sure that the gunner could hear him despite their linked headsets. "You reacted appropriately, Airman."

"The hell I did, sir!" The soldier wiped tears from his eyes. "They were just boys."

"You didn't know. If they were insurgents, and you didn't shoot, it would be us down there now, bleeding to death."

Pierce's words had little effect. The shooting had scarred the gunner, and Pierce couldn't blame him. He hoped the man would accept his actions soon; otherwise his recriminating mind would devour his soul, destroying him.

For the next hour Pierce tried not to think upon the massacre, yet that was all he could do. The situation paralleled Victor Vautrin's internal conflict, his children massacred because U.S. forces had bombed the wrong target. Vautrin had allowed the injustice of a single incident to consume him. It had corrupted him with rage and turned him against his own people. Bad choices that made him a hunted man.

For Pierce, the war in Mali was also personal, but with a different emotional dimension. He knew his actions could improve this part of Africa. It was about protecting the Malian people, destroying the threat of terrorism so Malians could build their own economies and the prospect of freedom from tyranny. Vautrin was his opposite; he had chosen a path of retribution. He had sided with the terrorists and the doctrine of despair. If Pierce brought justice to Vautrin, with a gun or the international courts, then some good might come to this desperate West African landscape. But that involved finding Vautrin first.

Hours later they crossed into Niger, and the Chinook touched down at AB 201. Pierce identified radar stations, satellite dishes and Quonset huts. The near-completed airstrip was a line of black tarmac in the otherwise sandy environment. Until the airfield was complete, the U.S. Air Force could provide only limited drone support in this part of the world.

The heat was unbearable and the air dusty. Earth-moving equipment and ground compaction rollers moved across the base. Soldiers dug out the sand dumped over every flat surface during yesterday's sandstorm.

Pierce was the first out of the helicopter, his AK-47 across one shoulder and his travel pack slung over the other.

A man approached and shook Pierce's hand. He was late fifties, with a full head of grey hair and a firm jaw. Similar to Pierce, he was dressed in civilian clothes that blended with the desert. He grinned when his eyes locked onto Pierce's stare. "I'm Idris Walsh, but you already know that." His firm handshake lingered.

"Mark Pierce."

"I know. Welcome to Niger." He gestured to a distant group of Quonset buildings. "Home away from home, buddy. This is CIA central in the world's largest sandpit, and the other kids don't play nice."

The building interior was cool and artificially lit. Dozens of analysts, case officers and cyberwarfare specialists at makeshift desks watched Arab and African mugshots as they flashed up on their screens. Other terminals displayed real-time drone footage of villages or highways. Consumed by their work, the women and men talked into headpieces or tapped at keyboards, and otherwise ignored Pierce and Walsh.

"We'll go somewhere discreet. We need to talk."

Walsh led Pierce into a briefing room and closed the door behind them. Mackenzie Summerfield sat at the table, tapping away at her military-grade laptop. She had fashioned her dark hair into a pixie cut, accenting her long slim neck. She wore jeans and a cotton shirt. Pierce had seen her in a summer dress once and remembered that her arms and legs were slim and muscular, like those of a dancer.

She noticed Pierce, and her brown eyes lit up. "Mark!"

"Mackenzie, you're looking good."

"So are you."

He raised an eyebrow. "You looked surprised that I do?"

"I know how you've been living these last months, Mark."

Walsh stepped between them. "You two can catch up later. We need to talk." He gestured that Pierce should take a seat at the table. After pouring them all cups of water and black coffee, he sat with them. Out of habit, Pierce waited until Walsh drank before he did.

Pierce asked, "What were three CIA operatives with eleven million dollars doing in the Sahel?"

Walsh turned to Mackenzie. She raised an eyebrow at this revelation, as Pierce knew she would.

"Which parts doesn't she know?" Pierce asked.

"The eleven-million bit. Obviously, the fewer people who know, the better."

"If you want us to work as a team, *sir*, you need to keep Summerfield up to date with the same intelligence as me."

"Who said you were still a team?"

Pierce assessed the mood of the room, and it was tense. "I did."

Walsh stared, willing Pierce to break eye contact. Neither man backed down.

Walsh spoke first. "Fine, have it your way. I hear no one else can handle you, anyway."

"I handle just fine. It was the case officers before Summerfield who were fragile."

"Yes, well, let's dispense with the bravado bullshit. I'll allow you two to continue as a team, but you both report directly to me."

Mackenzie asked, "Under whose authority?"

Walsh grinned, as if her bold statement came as no surprise. "The Deputy Director of Operations made me Head of Operations, North Africa. That gives me the authority to select my direct reports. Unless that is unclear, we will move on?" He looked to Pierce, then Mackenzie, willing them to challenge his statement. "Let's return to business."

Pierce leaned forward. The next words out of Walsh's mouth would reveal his long-term objectives and how Pierce and Mackenzie fit into his schemes. "What business is that?"

"You already know the mission, Pierce. Find Victor Vautrin, and kill him."

That was not the response Pierce was expecting.

16

AGADEZ, NIGER

Idris Walsh leaned on the table and made a cage with his outstretched fingers. "You look surprised, Pierce?"

Pierce's face was a mask. He remembered a story told to him when he first landed in Mali, on why Tuareg men veiled their faces. Normally it was women who covered themselves in Islamic cultures, but not amongst the Tuareg. Men wore veils to hide their emotions. No wonder he felt an affinity to these lords of the Sahara, the only tribe of West Africa never subjugated by European colonialism in the previous centuries. The Tuareg men knew how to keep secrets and mask their intentions. He wondered if Idris Walsh was the same.

"Let's clear a few misunderstandings," Pierce said.

"Such as?"

"What were three CIA operatives doing in the Sahel with eleven million dollars in the first place?"

Walsh leaned back and chuckled, more relaxed than he should be. "We'll come to that."

Mackenzie gave Pierce a quizzical stare. He ignored her.

They would speak later, and he didn't wish to give Walsh any measure of the depth of their working relationship or the trust between them. What he had to say to Mackenzie was not for Walsh's ears, not until his new boss proved his trustworthiness, and that might take a while.

Pierce turned to Walsh. "Very well. But there is much more you are going to tell us."

Walsh laughed. "My mission has always been Victor Vautrin's downfall. If that's inside a CIA black prison, or ending his life with the Mozambique Drill, so be it. Pierce, just so we are clear, it was me who authorised your Vautrin mission in the first place."

Pierce raised an eyebrow. The CIA spymaster had his attention, hinting that he had been operating in the background for months now, directing Pierce's operations in the country. Walsh was slippery and could make any story sound like it was the truth. He had to be careful here.

"The problem is the French, Pierce. They want to forgive Vautrin. Get him back in play. Vautrin is well connected to the French president and moves a lot of arms around the globe to countries where the French government doesn't want anyone to know of their involvement. They're also convinced they can't get arms into Mali without him."

"Vautrin certainly has the right contacts and resources," Mackenzie added. Pierce sensed that she also didn't like the direction this conversation had taken. "Connections include Russian oligarchs, American businessmen and Saudi royals. He owns at least three Antonov cargo planes registered in Nigeria, and his personal funds total over forty million U.S. dollars."

"That we know of," Walsh added. "God, I could do with that kind of money."

Pierce said nothing. He wanted to hear Walsh's take on recent events. He still didn't understand Walsh's motivations in this scenario, or if they aligned with U.S. foreign policy. Something didn't sit right with him about the stories being told.

Walsh leaned forward, as if about to bring them both into his confidence. "The CIA can't show their hand, can't reveal that we're after Vautrin. That would rattle many allies, particularly the French. Pierce, Summerfield, this is a false-flag operation. Through our established cover networks in Gao, we pretended to be Ansar Dine, representing Kashif Shalgham, aka Saifullah the Sword of Allah, who was offering eleven million dollars for the capture of Victor Vautrin. Luck had it, Ansar Dine fell for it, and seemed to have better intelligence than we did, stating that they knew where Vautrin would be, and assigned two hot-headed, low-ranking insurgents wanting to prove themselves to complete the task of kidnapping him. Again, pretending to be Ansar Dine, we set up a meet with the money — that would be those three CIA operatives who drove over those unfortunate mines, Marcus Rowlands, Jake Wong and Katie Seigel — to make the exchange in the Sahel. We never intended to hand over the money, just take Vautrin by force, until the hot-headed duo had the bright spark idea of kidnapping a few more Westerners for good measure, unnecessarily complicating everything. Then we really did need the money. Can't have Western innocents dying and bringing unwanted media attention to this whole mess."

Pierce felt his eyes squint. "You did all this without informing me? Even though you've had me chasing Vautrin for months?"

Walsh shook his head like a schoolteacher disappointed

with his student's test results. "You weren't getting anywhere, Pierce. Plus, if you became compromised, I didn't want you tipping off anyone to this dupe."

"I'm not compromised."

"That you know about. I know your intentions are loyal, if you were wondering."

Another unprompted and barbed comment that seemed unnecessary in the current discussion. Did Walsh mean Paquet? Was she the leak he hinted at? Did Walsh even know about her? Too much he still didn't understand. "Let me get this straight. The plan was to kill the duped insurgents and take Vautrin into custody? Shalgham would never be the wiser, the insurgents would be out of the picture, and the French would blame Shalgham for Vautrin's disappearance?"

"Exactly."

"But your CIA team hit a landmine before securing Vautrin." Pierce remembered the distant vehicle he had spotted leaving the crime scene. He wondered if, in that moment, he had seen the insurgents making their escape with the funds they had "stumbled" upon. "I see now that your low-ranking, hot-headed insurgents and their hostages are on the fast track to Shalgham's real hideout in the Adrar des Ifoghas? About to hand over hostages and eleven million dollars he didn't ask for?"

"That's about it. Yes." The man displayed no emotion or care about the fact he was playing with the lives of innocents with his duplicitous scheming.

"Sir, I've been hunting Vautrin for many months, with no luck."

"I know. Perhaps you're just not any good at that kind of work."

Another barb, another attempt to get a rise out of Pierce. His eyes remained locked on Walsh. The comment about Ansar Dine knowing exactly where Victor Vautrin could be found seemed at odds with everything Pierce knew to be true. Perhaps Ansar Dine thought they had identified Vautrin, but had confused him with someone else, a third party perhaps, innocent and unconnected to the arms dealer. "I doubted Vautrin's ever been in Mali. It seems now the last lead I followed was one you created, taking me instead to three dead CIA operatives. How can you even confirm Vautrin was among the kidnapped victims?"

"I can't." Walsh flipped open his laptop, plugged a cable into the display screen on the far wall, and called up several dossiers. The first open file displayed an image of an old man with a priest's collar, looking as happy as someone who has just been told he has cancer and only weeks to live. "We've identified three kidnapped subjects from information provided by the French Ministry of Foreign Affairs and our contacts with the local police and military. This is Remy Leblanc, age fifty-nine. A Catholic priest from Lyon. He's in Mali on a tourist visa. You can guess what he's up to."

Images of two older women appeared next. Unlike the priest, the women smiled for the cameras. "These are Jacqui and Isoline Bisset. Sisters from Nice. Early sixties. They're in Timbuktu as volunteer aid workers. Working for an NGO."

There were many humanitarian, educational and health-care non-government organisations operating across Mali and in neighbouring West African countries. It didn't surprise Pierce when Mackenzie asked, "Which NGO?"

"A French one. I've looked into them. Nothing of interest, so let's move on." Walsh took in a breath. "The two other victims... Well, we haven't confirmed their identities. We're looking into it. Word is one is a young Malian woman. The other is a Westerner. He might be Vautrin."

"*Might?*" Mackenzie asked with a frown.

Pierce said nothing; he felt his supposition that Ansar Dine had gotten the wrong man held credibility.

"Yes, Summerfield," Walsh growled. "This is the goddamn CIA. We've always operated in the shadows, the realms of half-truths and inaccurate intelligence. You complain as much as my sister does, even though I bailed her out when she defaulted, *again*, on her home loan. You two should be grateful I've provided you with this much intel."

The biggest question in Pierce's mind, however, concerned the money. Eleven million was a lot of cash on offer to low-ranking insurgents in one of the poorest countries on the planet. A sum that would attract mercenaries, bounty hunters, and a host of other unwanted attention from every corrupt operator in the region. Even if everything else was legitimate, Walsh's actions with the money made no sense.

The spymaster said, "Your mission remains the same, Pierce. You get yourself into Algeria, find Vautrin and the money, and bring back both. If you can't do that, you make sure Vautrin never sees another sunrise."

"If it even is Vautrin—"

Walsh bared his teeth. "Let's assume it is. If nothing else, we're rescuing hostages. We all need good news stories. Hostage rescue makes us look fantastic. Especially when the victims are Westerners."

Mackenzie rolled her eyes so only Pierce could see.

"How do you expect me to pull this off?" Pierce asked.

Walsh loaded another dossier to the screen, of a dark-skinned man wearing a blue turban; he had weathered, leather-like skin and grey eyes. "You already know who this is."

"I do." Pierce recognised the man as Bachir Aghali, head of a powerful and well-armed Tuareg tribe that operated in the fringes of the Adrar des Ifoghas. Major Gabriel Travers and Pierce had engaged with Aghali in the recent past, training his men in soldiering and enlisting the tribe's aid in identifying Islamic State, Ansar Dine and AQIM strongholds across the mountainous region. Aghali was an ally, opposed to the Islamic fanaticism that was eroding the control he once held across his lands. It was his people dying at the hands of extremists. A common enemy assured his loyalty.

"You've guessed the plan, Pierce?"

He nodded. "Appeal to Aghali's good nature and ask for directions?"

Walsh grinned. "He should direct you to Shalgham's hideout. From there... Well, you can work out the rest."

"What do you need?" Mackenzie asked, pre-empting the conversation they would require regarding logistics, infil and ex-fil routes, and equipment for the mission.

Pierce smiled for her benefit alone. "The usual. An AK-47 and plenty of magazines. I've got my Tuareg disguise and Glock. I'll need rations, the usual medical and field kits, flashbangs and fragmentation grenades, a satellite phone, maps and plenty of water. I'll also need a skin kit and fifty thousand U.S. dollars."

Mackenzie asked, "A skin kit? For your wrist?"

Pierce nodded. "You never know."

"I'm sure I can get one in your skin colour."

He smiled and nodded a thanks.

Walsh shook his head. "I can't authorise fifty thousand dollars, not after you lost eleven million."

"I didn't lose it."

"Doesn't matter. It's all the same operation as far as the bean counters are concerned."

"I can't go to Bachir Aghali empty-handed."

"Ten thousand, then. Don't ask for more."

"Do you parachute in?" Mackenzie asked, deflecting their argument.

Pierce shook his head. "No, I need a powerful motorbike for mobility. That mountain range is huge. We're close enough for me to drive there in less than forty-eight hours. If I find our missing hostages, only then will I need an airlift for an ex-fil, presuming they are still alive."

"That's not a problem. I'll liaise with AB 201's Combat Application Group." Walsh referred to the 1st Special Forces Operational Detachment-Delta, once commonly referred to as Delta Force, an elite special mission unit of the United States Army, whose purpose was to complete missions like this one. "Or the regular army, if you don't need special forces support. Delta is prepping a hostage rescue mission as well, should you be unable to release them, but they need intel on the kidnappers' location first."

"I'll let you know. Oh, and I'll need a sniper rifle. Top of the range."

"I can get you an M40A5?" Mackenzie said.

Pierce grinned. "That will do nicely."

"And don't forget the eleven million dollars." Walsh leaned forward, ensuring Pierce's full attention. "I need you to return it. That single objective, Pierce, is critical."

17

ADRAR DES IFOGHAS, MALI

After almost a day driving through vast flat tracks of sand, rock and gravel, the peaks of Adrar des Ifoghas loomed from the horizon.

The landscape this deep inside the Sahara fascinated Oumar. The remote granite mountains were blocks weathered smooth by the winds that blew among wide, shallow valleys. For a time, a pack of hyenas watched them from the ridge of a rocky range, darker fragments of sharp rock contrasting against the beige sand and clumps of brown grass. Later, Oumar identified ancient rock art he had read about in *National Geographic* magazines, depicting big cats fighting and ancient hunters pursuing giraffes and antelopes. Less than six thousand years ago, the Sahara had been green and fertile. Difficult to believe looking at the landscape before him.

At one point, Oumar spotted a Tuareg salt caravan. He counted their numbers to pass the time. Eighteen men with rifles and sixty-eight camels each loaded with salt blocks transported south for sale at markets along the Niger River. Oumar alerted Jali and Farid to the caravan. But the Tuareg weren't approaching, so the men agreed to let them be and continued on their own journey.

He chose the truck roof as his viewing platform to get away from a sulking Jali and a constantly complaining Farid, both in the cabin below. Oumar said he would act as a lookout, but his motivation was solitude. His companions' choices disgusted him, and he feared for all their fates once they reached Saifullah's camp. This might be his last chance for peace, which the expansive mountainous landscape offered.

Oumar spotted a viper sliding across the track ahead. Jali swerved, driving over it, then stopped. The two men climbed out with AK-47s slung across their shoulders. Jali lifted the dead snake, its head crushed by a tyre. "Tonight's meal," he said without passion.

Farid scanned the northern horizon. "Not far now." He pointed to five peaks perhaps ten kilometres distant. From this angle, they resembled stubby fingers on a fat limb. "The Hand of the Prophet." Farid spoke with reverence. "It is a difficult drive. We won't reach it today."

"Will we camp here tonight?" Oumar asked.

Farid spat into the dust. "Don't be a fool. There is a guelta around that outcrop. We camp there."

Oumar nodded. Gueltas were Saharan water pools fed by underground drainage channels. Many were seasonal, but a few lasted all year round. Gueltas were the only reason people survived out here.

They drove for another hour, taking many false routes until they found the waterhole. Farid and Jali led the bound prisoners to the water, where they drank with cupped hands. Farid, Jali and Oumar did the same, using water canteens instead of hands.

Once hydrated, the prisoners collapsed, exhausted, in the sand. Oumar couldn't blame them. Farid insisted they be given only morsels to eat and again tied nooses around their necks so their sleep would be uncomfortable. Exhaustion, he explained, kept them pliable and too weak to escape. If a low-ranking Ansar Dine soldier like Farid could be this cruel, Oumar dared not to imagine what horrors Saifullah and his men would stoop to.

He would know tomorrow.

Oumar considered his options many times during their journey. He had no desire to become a jihadist. If he were to disappear, tonight was his last chance. But, alone, he wouldn't last a day in the desert. He needed his brother. Convincing Jali to flee with him was his only option.

"I'll make a fire." Without waiting for an answer, Jali marched towards a distant copse of thorn trees. Perhaps he too needed a moment of peace away from Farid.

The Arab took the stakes and the ropes from the truck and went about the business of constructing the constraining contraptions. The priest and the old woman begged for compassion. The black woman and the wounded Frenchman were more accepting of their fate.

Oumar watched while his stomach twisted in knots and his stumps sweated. He wanted to share words of humanity, anything to lessen the barbarity Farid inflicted on these poor people, but what could he do?

Farid first looped the priest, then the older lady with the nooses. As Farid dragged forward the younger Frenchman, wincing because of his wounded shoulder, the man said, "You're taking us to Saifullah, the Sword of Allah?"

"You'll meet him in the morning," Farid snarled. "Expect no mercy."

"Neither should you."

The statement caused Farid to pause. "I have nothing to fear. I am one of God's soldiers. When my end comes, I will know only paradise."

"Whatever you say."

Farid smacked the Frenchman over the head, then tied the nooses around his neck.

Oumar looked for his brother, but the copse was further than Oumar had estimated, and Jali was still walking towards it, five hundred metres distant or more now. Oumar turned and watched Farid. The Arab had the young Malian woman in his grip. Awa was her name, and he recognised again that she was pretty. Farid wasn't leading her to the stakes and the nooses. He was dragging her from the camp as she resisted, pulling against his grip.

"What are you doing?" Oumar asked.

"Nothing that concerns you."

Awa struggled, then screamed.

Farid shook her, covered her mouth with his hand. "Be quiet, woman, or I'll slit your throat."

"What are you doing?" Oumar asked again, although he already knew the answer.

Farid revealed a knife in his hand, thrust it in Oumar's direction. "Shut your mouth, fool, or I will open your throat and bleed you out like a lamb." He pressed the knife against Awa's throat. Her eyes grew wide with fear, and she ceased struggling.

"You're a virgin?" Realisation dawned on Oumar. "You don't wish to martyr yourself as a virgin."

"Shut your mouth!"

"You know rape doesn't count. It makes you less a man than you already are."

Farid threatened again with the knife. "I'll cut your throat, Oumar." His eyes darted towards where Jali had disappeared. Oumar sensed Farid didn't wish Jali to know of the unspeakable act he was about to commit, as if ashamed of his weak morals.

Oumar shrugged. "I don't care. Kill me. I have nothing to live for where you are taking us."

Every muscle in Farid's body tensed. "You saw nothing. Stay here. Watch over the prisoners. Take instructions from your brother when he returns. You understand me?"

"Why?"

Farid laughed. "You must have heard stories of Saifullah? His cruelty knows no limits. If I tell him you are a non-believer, he will trust my judgement, and your death will be long and agonising. So keep your mouth shut and say nothing."

His jaw muscles tensing, Oumar looked to Awa, an arm twisted behind her back and the knife pressed up against her throat. Her body shook, and sweat poured off her. Her eyes motioned for Oumar to act decisively and protect her. He was her only hope now. He held up his stumps, acknowledging how he was useless here. Oumar couldn't even save himself, let alone someone else.

Awa's eyes lost their hope, and Oumar sensed that a part of her had died inside. He felt responsible.

Farid grinned, recognising he was again in control. "Stay here, Oumar, and say nothing. Understood?"

Oumar nodded.

Farid turned and marched with Awa towards an outcrop, which would hide them while he assaulted her.

Oumar waited, sweating and shaking, until Farid and Awa were out of sight. Then he lifted the largest rock he could carry between his stumpy arms and followed them.

18

AGADEZ, NIGER

An hour after their briefing, Mackenzie Summerfield found Mark in an Air Force hangar, dressed again as a Tuareg. He looked like he'd been born for a life in the desert.

He was checking over a Honda Africa Twin 742 cc motorcycle that, for reasons no one at AB 201 could explain, had turned up from nowhere several months back and was being repaired by Air Force mechanics in their spare time. One mechanic claimed it was a Paris to Dakar Rally bike, an event that had run in West Africa until 2008. The failing security situation in neighbouring Mauritania had required the event organisers to move to South America.

The rusted motorcycle looked old and battered, yet Mark seemed convinced it would serve his purposes. The mechanics hovering around Mark didn't appear happy that the CIA had requisitioned their pet project for a matter of national interest. Perhaps they lingered to get their last look before it disappeared forever.

What surprised Summerfield more was Mark's insistence on working in the hundred-plus-degree-Fahrenheit heat. She was sweating without exerting herself. She didn't understand how he could keep going in the murderous temperatures.

Mackenzie pressed her hands against her hips. "I don't understand you. Wait a few hours until nightfall. Work when the temperature drops. If you get exhausted and lost out there because you can't think straight, the Sahara is a huge place to disappear in, forever."

Mark looked up and grinned. He led her outside, where the air felt hotter. The winds picked up, blowing more sand across the base, rising only a foot above the surface, resembling a low-lying beige mist. She felt the particles bash against the hem of her uniform.

"We can safely talk here."

"Why did you agree with Walsh so quickly?" She felt uncertain if she was mad at him or with the layers of deceit they were both facing. "Your mission. It's suicide."

Mark glanced around, ensuring no one could overhear them. "Did you feel Walsh wasn't telling us everything?"

Summerfield nodded. "I thought that was obvious." She had considered that she might have imagined too much, but not when Mark voiced similar concerns.

"Eleven million is too much to offer low-level insurgents."

"You think it's a payoff to someone else?"

Mark nodded. "It's also an odd amount."

"How so?"

"Ten percent of ten million plus ten million makes eleven. It's like someone asked for ten million and Walsh wants his cut. Ten percent."

"Walsh?"

He nodded.

"Over the years, I've heard occasional rumours whispered in the halls of Langley that he's corrupt, but that is all they are, rumours. That nothing sticks to him. Until today, I thought they were nothing more than office gossip from low-ranking CIA desk analysts who felt hard done by because their skills weren't properly recognised. But now... You think he's dirty?"

"I don't know... *yet*. But who is paying who? That is the real question."

"Mark, we have multiple players. Our elusive arms dealer Victor Vautrin. Kashif Shalgham, the so-called Sword, and his Ansar Dine thugs. And the kidnappers. Even though Walsh says the kidnappers are with Ansar Dine, we don't actually know that to be certain."

"True. But there are also two other groups we need to consider."

"Who? You mean Walsh?"

Pierce dusted sand off his white robes. "Yes. Although our spymaster's motivations remain unclear. The missing eleven million may or may not be for a legitimate CIA operation we don't have clearance to know about—"

"Something else you should know about Walsh... Mark, you remember Greece?"

He nodded, recalling their disastrous mission together during their early days as a team. "I told you, Mackenzie, only you and I will ever know the truth about what really happened. It wasn't your fault. Never your fault, and I'll take the blame if this comes out... which it won't."

She shuddered, remembering the prolonged period locked in a room with the madman outside threatening her again and again. "That's not the problem."

"What, then?"

"The CIA paramilitary officer... Michael Abraham. The man who... died..."

"What about him?"

She knew Mark felt no remorse for the dead operative, and she didn't blame him. She carried no remorse for the dead man either, but it seemed his past actions had returned from his grave to haunt them. "Mark, he was one of Walsh's boys, like the two CIA paramilitary operatives killed by the landmine, Wong and Rowlands. They all knew each other. Went through the Farm together, instructed by Walsh." She referred to the CIA's rigorous training facilities for new recruits, run out of the U.S. military base Camp Peary in Williamsburg, Virginia. "Did you know that?"

She watched Mark as he absorbed this information, no doubt putting pieces of the puzzle together in ways she could not.

When he didn't respond, she said, "Mark, it could be revenge. Walsh coming after us for killing four of his team. Men he was close to."

"I didn't kill the three operatives in the Sahel. Plus, why wait almost three years to avenge Abraham? Not that Walsh would have any reason to suspect it was anything but terrorists who killed him."

Mackenzie shrugged. She felt the sweat evaporating off her bare neck, and the sand in her clothes itching every inch of her skin. How could Mark be comfortable in this hostile environment? "This is a coincidence. The CIA trained you and me to never ignore a coincidence."

"True." He nodded. "This makes Walsh more of an unknown quantity than he already is."

"You said two groups? Who is the second?"

Mark described his encounter with Juliet Paquet, Denault and the DGSE paramilitary team in the restaurant in Gao, their insistence Pierce drop his hunt for Vautrin, and how Pierce had later attacked Paquet and her team and turned the tables on them.

"Are you crazy? And why the hell didn't you tell Walsh about all this?"

He shrugged. "I'm like you, Mackenzie, I don't completely trust Walsh. Besides, it might be the DGSE and Walsh who are working together. She also might feed intel to Vautrin, working for him with an agenda we don't yet understand."

Summerfield contemplated Paquet's unusual physical description. Recent information she had encountered leaped into the forefront of her mind, so she described the recent reports that had crossed her desk. He nodded but didn't seem concerned.

Frustrated at Pierce's relaxed attitude, Summerfield knew she'd have to go back over her reports and see if she could recall the connection she couldn't yet articulate, before she brought it up again. "I'm more convinced than ever that you're walking into a trap, Mark. We both are."

Mark smiled. "We have five groups. They can't all be working together."

"Some of them must be. Or one of them is pulling all the strings, behind the scenes."

"Maybe, but we don't know who aligns with whom. I can't find out unless I follow this mission to its conclusion."

"Mark, you'll be in the field soon. We can't talk openly again. We need a code to communicate over long distances. Remember, the CIA, DGSE and the NSA could tap into our satellite phone conversations if they choose."

Pierce grinned. "How about this, Mackenzie? We compare the Sahara to deserts in the various U.S. states. Saifullah and Ansar Dine can be Utah, the kidnappers New Mexico, Walsh California, Paquet and the DGSE are Texas, and Vautrin can be Arizona."

"And Bachir Aghali, your Tuareg friend, he can be Nevada."

"Exactly. If we get evidence that two groups are working together, we compare them as being like the Sahara. If two groups are working in opposition, we say their deserts aren't like the Sahara at all."

Mackenzie nodded. A simple plan and not easily decoded. Eavesdroppers might never recognise that they were talking in a secret language. "It's better than nothing."

"Keep your head about you, Mackenzie. You're smart, intuitive and empathic. You've kept me alive more often than you give yourself credit for. We've been in worse situations in the past and came out on top each time, thanks to you."

He was building her up. She appreciated the sentiment. The CIA was not renowned for offering credit where it was due, except for operatives killed in the line of duty. Then they talked endlessly on about what a great operative they had been, for the dead are never in the position to disappoint later. "I'm not so sure. My intuition tells me this is the worst situation we've faced. Worse than Yemen."

"Then we'll be careful."

She shook her head and crossed her arms. He was too reckless. "What is your plan, Mark, exactly?"

Mark stared off into the flat, shimmering desert to the north. More than a thousand miles of baking dunes, rock and mountains separated them from the Mediterranean Sea. A lot of nothing to get lost in. A lot of places to die.

"The money, Mackenzie. If the eleven million is real, it's critical to whatever is going on here. It is the catalyst to shake things up. If I secure the money, it stops the purchase of something important and will throw our enemies' plans into disarray."

"And if the money isn't real?"

"Then it's Walsh who is lying, and we learn something."

"Sir?"

Both Pierce and Summerfield turned. Two Air Force mechanics wheeled the Honda Africa Twin towards them. "Sir," one of them said again as he saluted, "it's ready. Fully serviced and fuelled. We have extra gas tanks strapped to the sides. Should give you enough range for your needs."

"Thank you, Airman." Pierce gave a salute. "I appreciate you giving up your bike."

The man scratched his grease-stained face. "Would have loved to race it in those dunes, but I guess it was never really mine."

"Doesn't change my appreciation."

The Air Force man nodded; then he and his companion returned to the hangar.

Pierce grabbed his pack and slung it over his shoulders. He secured the AK-47 across his back and climbed onto the bike.

"You leaving already?" Summerfield asked. It was 13:00 hours, one in the afternoon. Mark wouldn't get far before nightfall, and it would be better leaving fresh in the morning. Pierce always underestimated the value of a good night's sleep.

"I can reach the International Organization for Migration transit centre in Assamakka tonight, then cross into Algeria at first light tomorrow morning."

She shook her head and pressed her hands into her hips. "Mark?"

"Everything will be fine," he said with a wink, wrapping the blue Tuareg turban around his face so only his eyes showed.

Not wanting to do it, she touched him on the shoulder. She couldn't remember the last time she had physically touched another human. "Mark… I'll… miss you if you don't come back. Look after yourself, okay?"

His eyes twinkled like those of a college boy about to perform a dangerous party stunt. "I always do." The eyes he then hid behind mirrored sunglasses.

Mark Pierce gunned the engine, turned in a sharp circle throwing up dust, and then powered north, disappearing through the guarded gates of AB 201 and the haze of the rippling heat.

19

Long ago, Mackenzie Summerfield had noted that remote military bases in war zones compelled their personnel to work constantly. Not that their workload was excessive. It was fear that kept them busy.

A mortar could be fired into the base at any moment. A local worker might pull a concealed weapon and fire indiscriminately. Insurgents could unleash a chemical weapon attack. Summerfield had known too many soldiers and intelligence officers who had died unaware that death loomed nearby. Many had no time for surprise, and the three CIA operatives Walsh had sent into the Sahara were a case in point. In AB 201 there was a real possibility that, at any second, she could cease to exist.

The fear was abstract, but its effects were real. Like most people here, she couldn't sleep more than a few hours at a time. When not on duty, there was nothing to do, and moments of introspection brought anxiety into conscious thought. There were only so many hours a day you could eat, wash or exercise. Some people coped by watching reruns of old movies. Others devoured dog-eared paperbacks that were passed around the base like currency. Many played cards and lost their wages. The only outlet that took Summerfield's mind off the risks was work, so this afternoon she focused on the problems Mark Pierce had highlighted.

There was an aspect to Mark's story that bothered her. Specifically, it was the intelligence officer from France's General Directorate for External Security, Juliet Paquet.

Summerfield pulled the CIA file on the enigmatic woman. Paquet's known mission history since her recruitment was all laid out, as was her life before joining the service.

The French national had a double major in politics and journalism from the Lumière University Lyon and a master's degree, which she completed two years later. During semester breaks she vacationed in former French African colonies and Middle Eastern nations.

After graduating, an NGO journalism programme accepted her for work in the eastern highlands of the inappropriately named Democratic Republic of Congo. During her time in the city of Goma, she'd interviewed warlords from the terrorist organisation M23, clandestinely recorded mercenaries bragging about secret wars fought for diamond mining companies, and exposed a syndicate of wildlife poachers and their smuggling networks across Africa and Asia. With these successes it was no surprise that the DGSE recruited Paquet into their ranks. She could uncover any secret.

Paquet's first DGSE missions were in Algeria, recruiting the wives of al-Qaeda and Muslim Brotherhood fanatics, who provided excellent intelligence supporting French special forces operations in the country. Later the DGSE recruited her into their Action Division, and she ran operational missions in Iran, Kazakhstan, Egypt and Jordan. She was in Syria during the civil war and had barely escaped from an invading force of Islamic State fanatics in Aleppo. All this before she had turned thirty.

It was a little satisfying for Summerfield that, even with her perfect career and perfect looks, Paquet had never been in a serious relationship and had no dependencies. Either she was all about her career or, like Summerfield, men had scarred her and had become too traumatic to deal with.

Paquet's file included a complete set of fingerprints, digital identifiers for facial recognition software and her DNA profile.

Photographs of Juliet Paquet were many and informative. She was as Mark had described her: tall, lean and muscular, with porcelain skin, white hair and the striking looks of a glamorous Hollywood actress. The one aspect missing from photos was the anisocoria. The same condition that characterised rock star David Bowie where one pupil was permanently more dilated than the other. There was nothing in Paquet's files that suggested she had this feature.

While other analysts tapped away at their own keyboards, Summerfield pulled up yesterday's intelligence reports. She hunted for the file on the murdered Parisian woman half dissolved in a bathtub of acid. The police had filed new reports since yesterday's findings. Being fluent in French, Summerfield skimmed those reports. The dead woman was tall, slim and muscular with pale white skin and blond hair. The Parisian Criminal Investigation Division would usually have included fingerprints in their report, but the acid had dissolved away her skin. They had instead taken quality blood samples and determined the victim's

DNA. The CID hadn't matched it to any DNA records on their criminal databases, and Summerfield knew now that they never would. As she had looked at the Parisian woman's case file and Juliet Paquet's dossier, she realised something that seemingly no one else had. The dead woman's DNA markers did have an exact match. Juliet Paquet.

But if Juliet Paquet was dead, who was the woman Mark Pierce had met with yesterday?

She called Mark on his satellite phone. He didn't answer, so she left a message. "Hi. Thought about what you said regarding the Sahara desert. I was thinking, the Texas desert isn't real. Fake in fact. I'm thinking the Texas desert is really an Arizonian, New Mexican or Utah desert. But definitely not Texan."

Summerfield disconnected. She had left a jumbled message, but it would have to do. She hoped he made sense of her warning.

It was time for a break and coffee.

When she turned and stood, she gasped.

Walsh had been standing behind her. She could not guess how long he had watched her.

"Busy, Summerfield?"

"Joining the dots, or trying to."

"Your shift ended hours ago."

She nodded. "Didn't know there was a rule against working in my own time."

"There isn't." He looked everywhere in the operating intelligence centre except at her. "Something I should know?"

She licked her lips. She wouldn't volunteer any information unless he asked. But she had to assume he had seen everything she had pulled up on the Juliet Paquet file. "No. I was cross-referencing recent daily reports, in case anything corresponded to what Mark had told us."

"And was there?" he asked, still not looking at her.

"No."

"What was your hunch, then, that didn't pan out?"

Summerfield swallowed. "A Turkish counterfeiter arrested in Istanbul. I thought I might have seen a connection there to Vautrin."

"And was there?"

She shook her head.

"I was in Turkey recently, but it was nowhere near as exciting as here." Walsh leaned over her workstation, catching her stare now and holding it. "I didn't tell you, Summerfield..."

"Tell me what, sir?"

"I've seen Pierce's redacted files, the ones before he 'officially' joined the CIA's Directorate of Operations." He made quotation marks with his fingers. "Pierce isn't even close to his real name."

She sensed Walsh wanted her to ask him how he got access to the files, so he could tell her she wasn't cleared to know, but she wouldn't give him the satisfaction. "I hope you found them helpful, sir."

For a moment, his skin brightened like he was holding his breath. Then just as suddenly, his mask of calm and control snapped back in place. "Don't fuck this up, Summerfield. Mark Pierce is a goddamn hero. The service he's given to our country, the sacrifices he's made, you need to give him the respect he deserves."

That was not the response she expected.

"If you have anything to report, Summerfield, you come to me first. Understood?"

She nodded.

He returned the nod, then disappeared.

Summerfield didn't know how, or why, but she was certain Walsh had lied about reading Pierce's redacted files. So why did Walsh want her to believe that he had?

20

ADRAR DES IFOGHAS, MALI

The rock was heavy and awkward in Oumar's limbs, but he knew weight was his best weapon.

It wasn't difficult to follow Farid unnoticed. Awa's screams carried through the otherwise still air. He found them on the ground, hidden behind a large granite outcrop. Farid's back was to Oumar as he crouched over Awa, tearing at her clothes. She fought him, but his grip on her wrist was tight, and he twisted her in uncomfortable angles. She was no match for his strength and couldn't hope to win.

Then, while they were both distracted by this awful struggle, Oumar lifted the rock as high as he could and dropped it on Farid's head.

The noise was like a coconut cracking. The Azawagh Arab dropped suddenly, screaming as he did. Blood erupted from a deep gash along his skull.

Awa crawled out from under the man, her eyes wide with shock and wet with tears. Bruises were prominent on her lips and around her eyes where Farid had beaten her.

Farid rolled in the sand, screaming. The crown of his skull had collapsed inward, creating a bowl-like indentation, yet he lived.

Oumar lifted the bloody rock again, held it aloft, then dropped it again.

It landed flat on Farid's skull, crushing and splintering the bone, silencing him forever.

Farid's legs twitched for a few moments, nerves firing in confusion at the lack of signals from the brain, then stopped altogether.

Then Awa was on her feet, pulling her clothes back around her. Amid the horror, Oumar found himself noticing her loose cotton pants and bright, flamboyant Malian shirt of purple, blue and pink patterns, and a purple turban around her hair. The clothes, despite the ingrained dust and sand, looked good on her.

Her body shook, and she wrapped her arms around herself. "Thank... you."

Oumar shook too. He had never killed a man, and with a of moment of reprieve to acknowledge the gory mess, he was soon vomiting.

Awa waited until he could retch no more. "Oumar, you saved me. Thank you." She hesitated. "What should we do now?"

Oumar wiped the bile from his mouth with the sleeve of his shirt. He had been brave, attacking Farid, but the consequences now overwhelmed him. "I don't... know..."

"You saved my life." She couldn't stop shaking. "Why?"

"I... I couldn't..."

"We should run. Find help, then come back for the others."

He shook his head.

"We must! Come with me, please. I don't want to be alone out here."

"No, Awa," he said, wrapping his useless limbs around him. His eyes motioned back to the camp. "It's only my brother back there. He would never abandon me. I..."

"Why don't you want to run? Isn't he the reason you are in this mess?"

Oumar felt his back stiffen. "No, he isn't. I would have died many times if it were not for Jali." He held out his stumps as if that were all the explanation she required. "I need him. I owe him."

She reached out and gently touched the ragged skin at the ends of each limb. "What happened to you?"

Oumar shuddered, remembering the long night of terror, then waking in a hospital to discover he had lost both hands. He realised he hadn't told the story in a long time. No one asked anymore. Nobody ever wished to be in a position where they had to express their pity. "It's... complicated."

Her eyes flashed and caught his stare. "I'm sure it is, but I want to hear your story."

He held her gaze. She was pretty, taller than him and slim like the stylised stick figure totem statues he'd seen in Timbuktu's curio shops. He wanted to kiss her, but that would make him no better than Farid.

"Oumar, you can tell me. I'm a nurse; nothing shocks me."

"It... was a street battle in Timbuktu. Insurgents stormed our family home during a shoot-out with Malian Army and French commandos. They used my parents, my brother and me as shields. My older sister thankfully wasn't there, as she was already married and with her husband in Morocco. The French fired a mortar round into the house, killing my parents. Part of the roof came down, crushing my hands and knocking me unconscious. But I didn't know the extent of my injuries until I'd recovered from surgery."

"That's horrible."

"When we returned to our house, men had moved in. They threatened us with guns. We had no ability to fight, and the police ignored our pleas for justice. Jali and I have lived on the streets ever since…"

"What about your sister? Did you reach out to her?"

"Jali and I didn't know how. We didn't memorise her phone number or email, and all our devices were lost in the attack. I know she is in Tangiers, Morocco, but that is all. She is lost to us. I… just don't know what to do…"

Before he could say anything else, she stepped forward and hugged him.

At first, he was stiff in her embrace. He hadn't expected this. Then he wrapped his arms around her and sobbed as he savoured the touch of a woman. A sensation he never thought it would be possible to experience.

"We need to run, Oumar," she murmured. "This is not a safe place for us. Come with me, please."

Oumar remembered the ten or more million U.S. dollars back at the camp in the five bags. To consider the possibility of running and achieving any semblance of a normal life, he'd need funds. But he needed his brother more. "No! I can talk Jali round. With Farid gone, I can make him see sense. You should come with me instead."

Awa stepped back, shook her head. "No! I'm not going back. I can't risk being tormented, tortured… murdered."

"I must save the other prisoners. I must tell my brother what I've done."

She looked ready to burst into tears. He felt sorry for her, empathising with her fear.

"Wait here, Awa, if you must. I'll talk to Jali. Then, when I make him see reason, I'll come back for you."

She nodded, crawled into a shadowy crevice in the rock. He wondered how long she would wait before her nerves got the better of her and she fled further into this desolate landscape. If she did, she would die of thirst and heat exhaustion. He had to convince Jali to abandon his jihad for all their sakes.

Oumar turned, ran to the truck and the prisoners. The priest, the young man and the old woman remained tied with their nooses. Jali had returned and had dragged a dead tree branch to the camp.

"Where are Farid and Awa?" Jali asked, dropping the branch in the dust.

Oumar glanced down at his stumps and the blood splatter on his clothes.

Jali's eyes and mouth grew large in his face. "What have you done?"

Before Oumar could answer, they heard high-pitched voices and hooves pounding the earth. They both turned towards the noise. A dozen men on camels dressed in black and khaki with headscarves and brandishing AK-47s appeared from behind the sheer cliffs of a nearby rocky mountain range. Galloping towards them, they emitted what sounded like war cries.

Within a minute they had Jali and Oumar surrounded, racing circles around them as their camels grunted with thick saliva sloshing from their frothing mouths.

Jali dropped his AK-47 and raised his hands in surrender. Oumar did the same with his stumps.

A craggy man more than two metres tall climbed off his camel. Like the others, he dressed in black and slung an AK-47 across his back. His eyes were the deepest blue, resembling precious stones. A scabbard tied to his belt held a scimitar. He withdrew the weapon and pointed its tip at Jali's throat. The curved steel blade reflected the harsh Saharan sunlight into Oumar's blinking eyes. "You have trespassed into the Sword's territory," he said in Arabic with a deep, booming voice. "Why should I not kill you where you stand?"

21

Oumar could not speak; fear had paralyzed him. Jali, also, spoke not a word, but his silence seemed to be an act of defiance rather than a distress response. Yet when Jali caught the cold stare of the blue-eyed giant threatening with his medieval scimitar, he dropped to his knees as an act of submission. Oumar copied his brother.

"I should behead you." The brute spoke softly. There were no emotional inflections in his voice, and his movements were precise and fluid. A butcher in control of every aspect of his being. "Give me a reason not to."

"We brought gifts," Jali answered as he swallowed. "Three Western prisoners and funds for Saifullah."

The blue-eyed giant raised an eyebrow, but that was his only movement. The blade remained inches from Jali's neck.

Jali cleared his throat. "We are volunteers for the Ansar Dine cause. We offer our lives to achieve Islamic jihad."

A hint of a smirk appeared on the giant's face. "Who sent you?"

"Your people in Gao sent us. Pious representatives of Saifullah."

His smirk grew. "Really?"

Jali nodded. "Farid al Rewani is his messenger. He trained in your al-Qaeda camps as a loyal soldier. Your commander, Saifullah, instructed Farid that we capture these infidels and bring them to Ansar Dine."

The grin broke into a wide smile. "Is that so?"

Jali gazed downward. He seemed uncertain now. "I do not question my orders. I just follow them."

"This intrigues me, for I gave no such order."

Oumar looked up, and so did Jali. "You are Saifullah?" Jali asked with a shudder.

Sunlight glinted in the giant's icy stare. His nod was slight. "You have caused me a world of trouble. You took something that belonged to me." He turned to his men. "Beat them until I order you to stop."

Men were upon Jali and Oumar in an instant, punching and kicking with all their strength. The pain was sudden and sharp, and they spared no corner of Oumar's body. Soon he was prone on the sand, his limbs unable to protect him from beatings to his head, back, legs and feet. He heard his ribs crack. He felt welts and bruises materialise across his skin.

"Stop!" commanded Saifullah after a time.

The Ansar Dine fighters stepped back.

It hurt to move, and it hurt to lie motionless. Oumar's mouth dripped blood, and his arms were purple. No bones other than his ribs seemed broken, for which he was thankful.

"On your knees."

The insurgents dragged Oumar and his brother up onto

their haunches. The agony racking Oumar's body felt worse now than during his beating.

"I... don't understand?" Jali spoke through bleeding gums and a missing tooth. His left eye was so badly beaten it had swollen and closed over.

Barely moving, Saifullah said, "Bring the three Westerners."

Several Ansar Dine fighters raced to the French prisoners. Knives cut the binding nooses from the stakes, leaving the looped ropes around their necks. Bound wrists were left untouched. When the three Westerners dropped to their knees before Saifullah, only then did he look down upon them. His eyes fell to Lucas, and he smiled with satisfaction. "You live, I see." He spoke French with the same proficiency as he spoke Arabic.

Wincing with the pain of his bullet wound, Lucas held out his arms, demanding release from his bonds. Oumar noticed then that Lucas was sweating profusely and his body tremored. He must have a fever. An infection from his untreated shoulder injury?

Saifullah nodded. An insurgent cut Lucas's bindings, freeing him. The Frenchman dusted himself off, stood on wobbly legs, then checked his wound. The entry and exit holes looked hot and red. "This one," Lucas said, pointing at Jali with a shaky finger, "shot me."

"You seem to have survived," answered Saifullah.

"Thanks only to the nurse." Lucas gazed left and right, searching for Awa. "She's gone, and so is Farid. They can't be far." He looked expectantly back at Saifullah, as if they were equals deserving of each other's respect, and pointed. "They disappeared towards that outcrop not that long ago."

The blue-eyed killer nodded ever so slightly. A gesture

that propelled several of his men into action, who raced on their camels towards the outcrop.

Lucas inadvertently caught Oumar's stare. The Frenchman's expression suggested he knew Oumar had followed Farid and Awa to where they had disappeared, but he said nothing about this. Oumar didn't understand why, but he was grateful for Lucas's silence.

They waited many minutes. When the insurgents returned, they dragged Farid's near headless corpse through the sandy gravel, tied to a rope behind their camels. A trail of blood spread across the path behind them.

"Is this Farid?" asked Saifullah.

Lucas nodded. "What's left of him." Oumar expected Lucas to turn to him, but he kept his gaze on the bloodied corpse.

"And the woman?"

One insurgent shook his head. "She's long gone. There seemed to have been a struggle, Iman. She must have killed this one, then fled."

Saifullah turned in a circle as he examined the rugged landscape with careful eyes. "She can't have gotten far. Find her."

A half-dozen men took off on their camels. Shrieks bellowed from their throats. One fired his AK into the air, and the bullet blasts echoed off the mountain walls.

Saifullah turned to Lucas. "We are two days behind schedule, thanks to your ineptitude. You let these men capture you."

Lucas shrugged as if this were an inconsequential outcome. He shivered as if he were cold despite the burning heat. "We can reschedule plans, and not all the pieces are in place yet. Besides, I thought you told me once that Saifullah possesses infinite patience?"

The giant snorted.

"By the way, thank you, Shalgham." Lucas gave a short bow, then coughed from the pain that came from twisting his shoulder. "For coming to save me."

"I came only because I need you, as you need me." He turned to the priest and the older woman kneeling in the sand. "It's a shame. I could have turned a profit with these prisoners if other matters weren't so pressing." He lifted the woman's head, forcing her to look at him. Tears soaked her eyes, and her body shook with fear. "How much do you think you are worth?"

She couldn't speak. Her mouth fell open, and Oumar thought she was about to scream, but no sounds came forth.

"They're loose ends," said Lucas. "We can't have them reporting to anyone about our working relationship."

Kashif Shalgham thought on this a moment, then nodded. "You are right." He made eye contact with another of his men. That man returned the gesture, and soon several were hammering long stakes into the earth, then tying them together in pairs to form Xs.

When the priest realised what was about to happen, he screamed, then begged for his life.

Four crosses. Four prisoners.

Oumar and Jali fought back, but the insurgents were too many and easily restrained them. The old woman and the priest, however, did not resist as the insurgents bound their hands and feet to the stakes, at both the base and at the far ends of the stake, forcing them to also take a X-like stance with their legs and arms spread wide.

The priest muttered a prayer to the Christian god, asking for forgiveness for his life's many sins.

The giant loomed over him. "You think your god will save you?"

"You can butcher me, but my soul is eternal."

"This is not your land. These are not your people." In a flash of movement almost too fast to see, Shalgham swung the scimitar. A wide gash appeared in the priest's belly. Intestines and organs spilled out. Blood squirted from the priest's mouth, and he convulsed. The priest should have died in that instant, and that would have been merciful. Instead, he lingered, jerking against the pain.

Saifullah marched to the woman. She sobbed. He wiped his hand on her face, brushing her sweat-drenched hair from her eyes, and smiled. "None of this is your fault, is it?"

She sobbed and shook her head.

"You were in the wrong place at the wrong time. Nothing more?"

"No," she whispered. For an instant there was hope in her eyes, but it was a false hope.

"Then I'll make your death quick."

He swung the scimitar fast with barely a flick of his wrist, slicing her neck open. Blood squirted as jets of hot crimson liquid. Her head lolled and almost tore free from her neck, for the cut was deep. At least her ending was sudden.

Oumar dared to hope for the same mercy. The carnage before him was too much for his mind to comprehend.

Saifullah approached Jali.

Oumar's brother caught the giant's stare with his one good eye and didn't look away despite his fear. He would be defiant to the end. "We are not your enemy," he yelled as spit gathered around his mouth. "We are your soldiers, and we came here to fight for *you!*"

Saifullah grinned as he plunged the scimitar into Jali's gut.

Oumar looked away.

He heard screams and gurgles. An insurgent, enjoying Oumar's torment, grabbed his jaw and turned him so he had to watch, and slapped him hard every time he tried to close his eyes.

Saifullah twisted the blade again and again until a bloody hole opened wide and Jali's intestines spilled forth. But, unlike the priest, Jali's wounds were brutal and many, and he expired within seconds. The blank stare of pain captured in his final moments caused Oumar to look away and stifle a cry of horror.

Finally, the brutal man approached Oumar.

Blood dripped from the crimson blade.

The insurgent released his grip upon him.

Oumar's now sweaty arms slipped from his bindings, unintentionally, and he landed on his knees. With no hands or wrists, nothing held him to his cross. He looked up to see Saifullah's surprise. Oumar showed his ruined stumps.

Saifullah seemed to see Oumar's deformities for the first time and laughed. "I thought you were trying to escape."

Oumar shook his head and sobbed. "Please just kill me. I have nothing to live for."

"How did you lose your hands?"

"The infidels bombed my family home. I lost my hands when the roof collapsed."

The brute kept laughing. "Not because you are a thief?"

Oumar shook his head. He waited for the scimitar to

finish him, but the blow never came. He looked up again at Saifullah.

"You amuse me. You are like a performing monkey. I'll keep you alive, for now. I want to discover how you fend for yourself." He nodded to one of his men, who cut the bindings from Oumar's feet.

Oumar sobbed and curled into a ball. There was nothing left to live for, yet he lived. He only hoped Awa got away. She alone might escape this nightmare because of his one moment of bravery. It would be the single honourable deed he achieved in his short, pathetic life.

"If you don't keep up," Saifullah continued, towering over him, "we'll leave you behind."

Oumar couldn't move. Jali was dead, and he was now a prisoner, lost in the merciless heart of the Sahara, where the sun was an ever-present eye that burned into husks those who lingered too long. Every muscle ached, and his ribs agonised where the men had beaten him. He decided he wouldn't go anyway; instead he would just lie in the sun and let the heat bake him to death.

Then a shadow passed over his eyes.

Oumar looked up.

Lucas stared down at him. The man shivered and hugged his arms around his chest.

"Who are you, really?" Oumar asked.

Lucas rubbed perspiration from his brow with a shaky hand. "I guess it won't hurt you to know. You won't last long enough to tell anyone. I'm Lucas Vautrin."

22

SAHARA, MALI

Major Gabriel Travers scanned the dunes with his binoculars. His convoy was two hundred kilometres north of Gao now. Well inside insurgent-dominated territory. The dangers here were real. Backup was non-existent.

The sun beat down from the perfect blue sky — hot enough to fry eggs on the hoods of their VAB armoured personnel carriers. He sweated no matter how much water he consumed, and that reminded him. He had not drunk for some time and should do so now to remain hydrated. He was not good at keeping his fluids up even with the sun constantly reminding him how hot it was.

Travers had hoped for aerial support during the mission, but until AB 201 was operational, American and French drones provided air cover only ten percent of the time. Now was not an over-watch moment, so he relied on old-fashioned surveillance techniques. Constant observation through a pair of binoculars ensured they identified unwanted threats before they could strike. He would scan until his mechanics repaired VAB number three's broken axle.

The biggest threat was not a direct attack, for the Legionnaires were superior soldiers and commanded far greater firepower than any local insurgent could. Improvised explosive devices, mines buried in the road and suicide bombers were the real threats. They hadn't encountered any on this mission yet, but one could never be careful enough. That was why he watched, looking for any signs of danger.

"What is the problem?" Juliet Paquet asked. She had appeared from nowhere again, sneaking up behind him to stand by his side. Paquet had probably materialised from the other side of the nearest VAB parked just behind them, but still he didn't know how she did it.

He dropped his binoculars. "Axle broken on that VAB." He watched her drink from a plastic water bottle. Travers returned his gaze to the horizon and would not give her the satisfaction that her attractive face and shapely body might cause him to be weak-willed around her. "Mechanics are swapping it out. We'll be on our way soon enough."

"I'm not worried. You seem to know what you're doing."

He lowered his binoculars again and caught her stare. "If you're worried about Tessalit, I'll get you there. I've been with the Foreign Legion for twelve years. Never lost a soldier under my command or a civilian under my care."

She smiled as she finished her water. "I'm neither."

"I know. No 'spooks' have died on my watch either, if it worries you," he said, using the English slang for a spy.

Her only response was another perfect smile.

Travers didn't like Paquet. He held no affinity for any intelligence officers of the DGSE, but other spies he'd met during his work, such as Mark Pierce, didn't get under his skin like this woman did. She was arrogant, self-assured and superior. Her unusual appearance was both striking and otherworldly, and she worked her traits hard to get his men to help her with inconsequential tasks. But a pretty face could never make up for an ugly personality. He wouldn't let her trick him that way.

She was an enigma to Travers, yet there was an aspect to her that was familiar... And that bothered him the most.

He should put her out of his mind. She had no influence over his mission, and he didn't care why she needed to be in Tessalit, so why was he angry every time he was around her? Was it more than his single moment of weakness when he felt attracted to her?

Behind him, the major heard the sound of retching.

He turned to his mechanics busy working on the axle. One soldier had spewed up his lunch and what looked to be blood.

"What's wrong, Private?" Travers asked.

Sweat drenched the soldier. "I'm okay, sir. Suspect that something I ate has disagreed with me."

"I don't feel too good either," said another corporal on guard duty who was standing nearby. Then, suddenly, he too was throwing up, expelling bile and blood.

The major surveyed all the soldiers in his line of sight. A few had fallen and lay unmoving in the sand. Others were bent over, vomiting up their guts. He tensed, overcome with both fury and fear at what he witnessed. His instincts warned that they were under attack, and that he had let his men down by not seeing this assault coming earlier, but who was attacking them? A rational part of his mind argued this was only a bad case of food poisoning that had torn through their unit. But the instinctual, animalistic side of his brain was ready for fight or flight. Something was terribly wrong here.

Then Travers felt the sweat on his forehead under his combat helmet. He felt hot and clammy. His stomach was cramping.

"What the hell—"

Two of Paquet's mercenaries appeared from behind him, perversely calm and controlled.

He almost didn't believe it when they casually shot two of his vomiting men in the backs of their heads. Bone and brain matter exploded as gory mists. Paquet's men clearly weren't sick, and this sudden realisation terrified him.

He spied the DGSE intelligence officer approach from behind her mercenaries. She moved with ease and grace, and the smug smile fixed to her face sickened him.

Then the mercenaries moved to the next incapacitated target, and Travers tried to run to stop them, but his stomach turned, and cramps forced him to bend over. He watched helpless as the mercenaries executed a man with another bullet in the base of his skull. Thanks to the cramps in their guts and the bloody bile exploding from their orifices, no one could resist.

Not even him.

With an effort, Travers drew his PAMAS G1 9mm semi-automatic pistol and fired at the mercenaries. He hit one in the chest plate, knocking him backwards. The second man returned fire and hit Travers in his own body armour, forcing him on his ass.

Gunfire erupted around him. Short, controlled bursts from multiple directions made quick work of his Legionnaires, who were too sick to respond, too busy vomiting up their stomach linings to realise they were under attack.

Soon Travers was vomiting with them, blood and bile racing out of his mouth and nostrils, burning his throat as it came up. He wondered if it was something in the water; he hadn't quenched his thirst in some time despite the heat. The blood seemed too much, particularly for him. He shouldn't have that much fluid inside him.

He heard another gunshot. In the same instant his hand exploded as his pistol flung from his grip and his palm mangled into a meaty mess of blood, bone and sinew. Crying out in pain, he gripped his wrist and turned to find the deadly end of a pistol resting against his temple, with Juliet Paquet's finger on the trigger.

"Looks like your track record is at an end, Major."

"You poisoned us?" The sweats, the cramps and the aches in his muscles, he had put those down to stress and the heat. "The water bottles...?"

"Very good. Obviously not the one I was drinking from."

A tall mercenary stepped up behind her. He had close-cropped black hair, a bandage on his forehead and a red scar disfiguring the left side of his face. He wore the same desert camouflage uniform as the rest of Paquet's men and carried a FAMAS assault rifle with smoke wafting from the barrel. Travers wondered why he hadn't noticed this man before, for he was large and muscular even when compared to other special forces soldiers. Perhaps he had stayed out of Travers's way because of the stiffness in his left leg and the bruising on his face, which would have drawn questions. It had been the right strategy, for Travers now realised that this was the man Mark Pierce had asked about back in MINUSMA.

"We have accounted for everyone," said the man with the scar as he pointed at Travers, "except him."

Travers looked across the Saharan sands. Every soldier

under his command was dead, butchered while constrained by their ailments. He was the last Legionnaire left alive. The spook was right. His track record was in tatters.

He looked up at the unusual woman and wondered who she was.

Then he remembered why she was familiar.

Her facial structure was the same as the male journalist who had asked for Pierce in MINUSMA. He realised that they must be related.

"Why?" he managed.

"Don't take it personally. You no longer serve a purpose, that's all."

She pressed the weapon hard against his temple.

Travers closed his eyes and thought of his wife and children. He had failed them, and he would never come home to them.

He didn't have to wait long.

23

J uliet Paquet wasn't her true name. The DGSE intelligence officer was a cover that had served a purpose for a time. With Major Travers now a bleeding corpse at her feet, that purpose was at an end.

"That was easier than I hoped." Denault stomped his boots in the red-soaked sand behind her, cleaning them. Muscles rippled under his desert uniform and body armour. A shaved gorilla in clothes. "Ms. *Vautrin*."

She grinned.

Hanna Vautrin.

Daughter of the deceased Victor Vautrin and sister of Lucas Vautrin. Heir to the global Vautrin arms-dealing empire.

With sweat glistening off his tanned skin, Denault spat at Travers's body. A former Legionnaire himself, Denault would have been a handsome man if it were not for the ugly scar that disfigured one side of his face. "All the Legionnaires are dead. The convoy is ours. And, as I promised, we damaged no vehicles."

"Good."

He growled. "Yet Pierce wasn't amongst them."

"You'll get your revenge soon enough." She nodded to Denault's bandaged leg and bruised head. Denault had been smarting since Mark Pierce had gotten the better of him in the safe house. His hatred towards Pierce had become an obsession, and Hanna couldn't have that. She required his focus on their mission, for there was much to achieve before they could accomplish their ultimate aim. "He's out here somewhere, and I know we'll find him. You can have your fun with him then, but you are not to go after him. Not until our primary mission is complete."

"I should have killed him in Gao."

Hanna shook her head. "I needed to know if the CIA learned about me and my brother. If they had figured out the truth about who really died in that air strike in Afghanistan..."

"Your father?"

"Of course my father. The U.S. don't know he is dead. Which means the DGSE don't know either. We didn't get the intelligence I wanted from Pierce on what exactly they do know, but he confirmed what we hoped. The world believes my brother and I are dead. That makes everything easier for us when this is all over."

Hanna stared off across the horizon as she remembered her father's passing. Back when her hair was its natural jet-black. Back when she still thought the attention of boys, the gleam of Mediterranean yachts, luxury villas and hot sex was important. Back when her father constantly belittled her, hit her, and called her horrible names.

Memories that even today caused her to shudder.

It had been in Afghanistan's Helmand Province, a couple of years before America's final withdrawal from that war-ravaged nation. Victor had dragged her and her half-brother, Lucas, into the harsh, near-lifeless wastelands of deserts, goats, poppy fields, IEDs and snow-capped mountains, to train them on how to run a global arms empire. Nations like Afghanistan were where the money was and where the demand for weapons was high. Where Taliban warlords itching to exchange opium for assault rifles, rocket launchers, mines, grenades, and air-to-surface missiles were as common as chicken eggs. Victor figured if Hanna and Lucas demonstrated the wit to negotiate with hardened Taliban fighters, then they could sell weapons anywhere in the world, and he would finally be proud of them.

And then a missile had struck, suddenly and from nowhere. It had to have been from a drone, one operated by the United States Air Force. The camp had been obliterated in seconds. Even now, Hanna still woke from vivid nightmares of the event, of men on fire as air fuel burned away their skin as they begged from eyes without lids and mouths without lips. The night had lit up like a raging fire burning out of control in an oil refinery.

Lucas and Hanna had been far enough from the blast to survive, but not far enough not to sustain injury. Victor's latest contract intelligence officer, a former American CIA operator who went by the name Brad Tegmark, it was he who had secured them onto helicopters, flown them to a hospital in Quetta, Pakistan, and saw to their recovery and protection. He hadn't been anywhere near the attack when it happened, so he didn't suffer physically as Hanna and Lucas had in the weeks that followed.

Eventually Hanna's broken bones and bruises healed, and she started paying attention to the news.

The world was reporting that Hanna and Lucas had died, and that Victor had survived the missile strike.

She wondered: why?

Hanna sought out Tegmark, for he had stayed by their side since the missile strike. He'd protected them with bribes to keep the Pakistani government from becoming too interested in them, and he seemed able to materialise from nowhere a security detail sourced from local mercenaries, whenever they felt to be under physical threat. Reports from U.S. officials claimed the strike had been a "mistake", so-called "friendly fire". She didn't think so, and asked Tegmark why the lie had been allowed to propagate.

He'd explained it simply while he drank whiskey as he sat at the end of her hospital bed while a saline drip hydrated her veins, prominent on her skinny arms. She remembered dust particles in the air, seen in the streams of light radiating through the hospital windows, the interior heat like someone had left an oven door open somewhere, and the smell of something off, but otherwise indescribable. She never understood why her memories of that moment were so vivid. Perhaps it was because of what Tegmark had told her.

If Victor's customers thought he was dead, they would move on and find other arms dealers to trade with, and their profits and revenue streams would quickly dry up until the empire collapsed. The United States had wanted Victor's arms empire destroyed, because he sold weapons to too many of Uncle Sam's enemies, and murdering Victor was the quickest means of achieving this. Tegmark could not allow this to happen, not while he had a stake in the business, and he explained to Hanna and Lucas, as the new shareholders, they shouldn't want this to happen either.

Later, Hanna came to understand that the only reason Tegmark had saved her and her brother was not out of loyalty or compassion, but because, apart from their father, they were the only individuals left alive with knowledge of the account numbers and passwords to access the vast Vautrin cash fortune.

When her half-brother healed his bullet wound sustained during the missile strike, and when she had recovered from her lesser injuries, after years of barely speaking to each other, they recognised they needed to work together if they were to make their inheritance work for them. The siblings then seemed to see each other in a different light, and soon Hanna's and Lucas's petty differences of lifestyle choices and flippant commodity purchases were forgotten. As partners they took their first steps in asserting control over the family business.

They moved quickly to feed the rumour networks with further stories that it was Lucas and she who had died, and not their father during the assault. They also worked to protect themselves further in case Victor's killers had worked out the truth and were coming after them to finish off the job. They achieved this by hacking into their father's email account and obtaining state-of-the-art software that could mimic his voice on telephone conversations. Later they discovered that pretending to be their father during online negotiations with terrorists, paramilitary groups, third world police forces and militaries opened far more doors than they could under their real identities. When they met with buyers in person, they pretended to be nothing more than representatives of their phantom parent.

While he had lived, Victor had been distant towards Hanna and her older half-brother. Victor was emotionally cruel and physically abusive when they didn't live up to his expectations. He only talked to them on his terms, and the only topic of discussion was how they should improve themselves. But Hanna had loved her father and valued his lessons on buying and selling weapons. Victor's intention had always been to bequeath his children the multi-million-dollar business, but only when they proved themselves worthy. That day had never come while he lived.

The procession of boyfriends and the extravagant lifestyle of her past life were a rebellion against her father, but with Victor gone, her insurrection lost its purpose.

In time, Hanna and Lucas became more emboldened with their control over the business. While it was never stated explicitly, everyone in her inner circle knew she and Lucas were Victor's children. Their underlings also maintained the lie because everyone understood the power Victor Vautrin's name carried in protecting all their interests.

They removed Brad Tegmark from the picture after discovering he was skimming their profits by a significant margin, and it still stung that he'd gotten away before she could make an example of him. Meanwhile, negotiating with power-hungry and psychotic African warlords, Mexican drug lords and Western spies made her feel powerful. There was a thrill in exchanging weapons of death and destruction for cash, diamonds, opium and cocaine that romantic flings of the past had never satisfied. The power of profit was superior to any sex she had previously enjoyed with the young handsome boys she had once considered essential in her life.

In time, Hanna recognised how she could be merciless

towards her underlings. How she enjoyed her cruelty, and they didn't, but accepted her behaviour because she paid them. Her "niceness" she reserved only for clients, and even then, clients demanded a level of "hardness" in their interactions; otherwise they would not take her seriously.

Overnight, Hanna had become her father.

To understand her new power, she convinced a Somali warlord to let her execute one of his prisoners. Hanna had taken a 9mm Browning semi-automatic pistol and pressed it into the forehead of a young Kenyan man gagged and bound on his knees in the dust. She squeezed the trigger and, amid the recoil and deafening noise, watched as the man's cranium disintegrated into a cloud of crimson mist and slivers of skull and brain tissue. Before committing the act, she had thought she might have felt terrified. Instead, she realised just how far power could extend. There was no greater aphrodisiac than to control the power of life and death over another human being.

Her only regret in her own life so far was never learning the identity of her mother. Her father had taken that secret with him to the grave. All Hanna had ever gleaned from Victor was that her mother was a ridiculously expensive prostitute who had tried to blackmail him when she had fallen pregnant. Hanna never knew her mother's name or her fate. Her father referred to her only as "the slut" or "the bitch". Hanna wondered sometimes if a critical aspect of her upbringing was lacking because of a mother's absence, but what that deficiency might be, she could never articulate.

Victor had been an asshole, but she appreciated the driven and focused woman he had created in her. Mali would be how she would honour him, but also how she would show him that she was better than him. Her scheme was so much more brazen than anything he could have ever imagined, and she would finally prove to herself that he had been wrong about her all along. She was worthy of the empire that had been unwittingly thrust upon her.

"Your father is dead," Denault said, drawing her back to the present. "He cares for nothing anymore. You need not hide behind his memory any longer."

Hanna turned, wiping sweat from her forehead. She hadn't intended to daydream. She never let her guard down around anyone, and certainly not in front of psychopaths like Denault. "It is necessary! The French president has pardoned Lucas and me to allow us more freedom to trade arms and support his interests in West Africa. But he also believes we are in hiding, fearful that Victor's enemies will come for us if our true status is revealed. Ironically, he wants us back in business, as a legitimate face for the Vautrin empire, because the French still need to move arms around the world, particularly here where France controls many economic interests. But if the French president discovers it was us, and not my long-dead daddy, who's been supplying AQIM and Ansar Dine with weapons used against French troops, that will change, and he'll drag you down with me. Thanks to our conversation with Pierce, it seems we are in the clear."

Her anger was getting the better of her. She breathed and forced a smile until she once again masked her emotions. "No one knows the truth. Not the CIA. Not the DGSE and not MI6," she said, referring to Britain's secret intelligence service. "A contact would have chirped by now if they did." She considered the forgers and hackers she'd had to utilise, the money she'd had to spend, and the pressure she'd had to apply to corrupt employees of the DGSE to ensure her cover identity as Juliet Paquet was thorough. The fake legend had held, so it was money and pressure well spent.

She'd expended similar sums for information on what the CIA had gathered on the current status of the Vautrin family and their global arms trading business. A corrupt CIA contractor was willing enough to provide the information, in exchange for a large sum of money. Another Brad Tegmark; the country seemed to be full of his kind. Once the transaction was complete, to make sure he never talked, Hanna arranged for him to die from a cocaine overdose, an "unfortunate accident" that was never considered suspicious, ensuring any links back to Hanna were now closed off. She took back the money too, which he had naively asked for in cash.

The contractor's information proved invaluable. The CIA believed Victor had lived while Hanna and Lucas had died in Afghanistan, exactly as she had hoped. But what troubled Hanna was new information concerning a CIA operator, Mark Pierce, tasked with tracking down and assassinating her father in West Africa. The scant information she had been able to obtain on Pierce suggested he was a highly competent operative, with a track record of successful missions in Yemen and now West Africa. His file also criticised Pierce as secretive, unwilling to share gathered intelligence with his superiors, including Mackenzie Summerfield, his handler, on a regular basis. This suggested Pierce might already know of her bluff, but hadn't told anyone else yet. She'd hatched a plan to meet Pierce disguised as Juliet Paquet and gather what information she could from him. That meeting hadn't gone at all as she had planned, but it had confirmed that Pierce hunted Victor, not Lucas and herself, which she was grateful to know.

"So we proceed as planned?" Denault asked. "It all seems unnecessarily complicated."

Hanna's laugh was harsh. "We're already committed, my brave former Legionnaire." Her hand stroked the stubble on his chin, the side without the scar, knowing that he enjoyed her touch and that flirting was the quickest way to stop him thinking with his brain. "You know what is at stake here. If we pull this off, the war in West Africa escalates, and you and I become richer than Saudi Aramco."

The mercenary sneered. The red scar twisted like it was its own mouth with its own cruel grin. "I must admit, despite the daily challenges you have put me through, I like your plan."

"How long before the next surveillance satellite passes over?"

He glanced at his Luminox F-117 Nighthawk wristwatch. Denault did always like his expensive toys. "Four hours, twelve minutes. A British Skynet 5 satellite. As we planned, our construction contacts at AB 201 will have 'problems' with the runway today, so no drones will be in the skies, ma'am."

She smirked. Everything was proceeding as scheduled. "We have that long to make it look like insurgents killed the Legionnaires and destroyed these VABs."

"Not a problem at all, ma'am. My men are already on it."

24

In under thirty minutes, Hanna Vautrin, Sergeant Jean Denault and six of their mercenaries had two VABs prepped for sacrifice, one of which had the broken axle. They stripped Legionnaires of their uniforms and weapons, then crammed their bodies inside the two vehicles. Nine armed and uniformed Legionnaires they left where they had fallen outside so the scene resembled an insurgent attack. They buried the vomit, shit and piss with sand, and cleaned faces and uniforms as best they could. Eventually someone might work out that the Legionnaires had been poisoned, but the bullet wounds peppering the corpses hopefully would deter anyone from looking too closely for a more complicated means of killing them. And she only needed the ruse to last long enough for her plan to reach its end point, less than a week from now.

Denault propped an LRAC F1 anti-tank rocket launcher on his shoulder and engaged the firing mechanism. His giddy expression mimicked a schoolboy playing with matches. The 89mm shaped-charge rocket sped across the dunes as the fins folded out, providing stability. Denault's aim was true, and his missile entered the VAB's open door. In an instant, the armoured personnel carrier disintegrated in a fireball of fuel, flesh and metal.

Hanna stepped backwards as the concussion wave rushed past her, although its destructive energy dissipated into a strong breeze at this distance.

Denault lowered the launcher and smirked. "Not much left. It will take the CIA days to determine the wreckage contains only a single VAB."

"That's long enough," Hanna answered.

Another mercenary aided Denault as they loaded a second warhead. Denault turned towards the second VAB, two hundred metres in the opposite direction, and fired again. As before, the rocket raced through the open door, and the second VAB disintegrated.

This time Hanna smiled with him. The former French Foreign Legionnaire was a natural marksman.

"Makes the job fucking worthwhile, ma'am!"

"Blowing things up?"

"Of course. You don't become a soldier because you like to repair things."

She studied him, as it occurred that he had never explained the scar on his face. "How did you get that?"

He stiffened. His mouth curled into a hideous snarl.

"I thought you said no one had ever bested you?"

Denault's snarl turned into a grin. "The Cambodian fuck who gave me this, he might have bested me. But I found him again, gutted him from his groin to his throat. I bested him... permanently, so my record stands — or will stand again when Pierce is dead." He gritted his teeth. "Spraying us with deodorant and lying that it was an infrared tracker for their drone... Pierce will pay for that too."

Hanna shrugged, unimpressed with Denault's obsessions and not believing his story either. "Well, it's time to move."

The mercenaries split between the four remaining VABs and the two armoured PVP vehicles. Hanna joined Denault, who drove the first of the PVPs. They headed east towards the Adrar des Ifoghas. When the ground became rocky and their tracks were no longer visible, Denault commanded the convoy to stop.

Hanna dialled a memorised number on her satellite phone.

"This is Scorpion Nine-Three," answered a Russian-accented voice in English.

"Scorpion Nine-Three, this is Cobra Eight-Four."

"Copy that, Cobra Eight-Four."

"Proceed with Stage One. Repeat, proceed with Stage One." Hanna provided the caller with GPS coordinates, first for the VAB wreckage, then with secondary coordinates for her location. "ETA?" she asked, requesting their estimated time of arrival.

"Fourteen minutes, Cobra Eight-Four."

Denault turned the PVP in a wide circle and parked facing the direction they had come. They waited a quarter of an hour in silence before they spotted the twin turboprop Antonov An-32 transport aircraft appear in the hazy blue, flying low over the horizon. The cargo plane came straight at them, cruising somewhere between fifty and a hundred metres above the sand, a dangerous altitude but necessary. The winds the aircraft produced scattered the sand beneath its path, obliterating the tyre tracks of the convoy, churning up a temporary sandstorm.

Hanna gritted her teeth, suppressed a grin and called the pilots again. "Well done, Scorpion Nine-Three. Now drop your cargo."

"Roger that, Cobra Eight-Four."

The Ukrainian cargo plane had once belonged to her father; he used it to transport weapons across Europe, Africa and Asia. It belonged to her now and served the same purpose. The original owners were the Libyan Air Force, which was ironic, considering whom she and her half-brother were in league with.

Hanna watched the aircraft gain altitude and turn in a wide circle. When it prepared for its next pass over their position, it was well over a kilometre high. She watched three crates drop from the rear cargo ramp. Parachutes released, and the precious cargo floated to the earth, creating small dust clouds when the crates landed on a flat and rocky track of desert. Honeycomb crunch layers under the cargo absorbed much of the impact.

The Antonov kept climbing, on its return journey to Lagos, where Hanna rented a hangar at Murtala Muhammed International Airport, and it soon disappeared from view.

The crates contained Composition C-4 explosives and packages of ball bearings, bolts and nails. Once she felt that the crates were stable, the mercenaries loaded the cargo into the UN vehicles, their work completed in nineteen minutes. The men then dismantled the crates and collected the parachutes. Hanna had chosen C-4 for its shock-absorbing ability during the parachute operation and because it was an explosive commonly used by terrorists, making it difficult to trace.

When nothing remained to suggest they were ever here, they drove further into the rugged granite mountains towards the highest peaks of the Adrar des Ifoghas.

"Any spy satellites that might have seen all this?" Hanna asked.

Denault checked his top-of-the-range Iridium 9575 Extreme satellite phone for messages, then shook his head. "My Russian hacker says no. He should know, he's been tracking satellites as a hobby for decades."

"I hope he is reliable."

"Oh, he is. He'd be dead by now if he wasn't." Denault turned to Hanna and caught her stare. "You sure you want to see this through, ma'am? There are easier strategies for making money."

"We stick with the plan."

"You could make us a lot of enemies. We could still back out."

She ran her hand along the back of his head, a gesture of affection. "Oh Jean, you worry too much. Everyone will think this is my father's doing. He'll 'die' officially this time, take the blame while we escalate the war in Mali and get stupidly rich with the new contracts I've secured."

"With the French government backing us?"

"Elements of the French government, Denault, who have pardoned us already. And I'll get my revenge on the Americans, tying them up in another costly war that none of their citizens want to pay for in a country most of their people have never heard of."

She grinned again. As the Americans were fond of saying, "Everything was going to plan."

They drove for several hours to the next rendezvous, a large rocky overhang on the edge of the mountain range that satellites or drones couldn't see beneath, and there they prepared a camp. Then the mercenaries set about wiring the UN vehicles with the C-4, ready for the next stage of their operation.

25

TRANS-SAHARA HIGHWAY, NIGER

Pierce made good time traversing the Trans-Sahara Highway. The 4,500-kilometre paved road stretched from Lagos on the Indian Ocean to Algiers on the Mediterranean Sea. His route was the middle section between the Niger towns of Agadez and Assamakka, where the roads were at their worst. Unpaved tracks here received only laughable maintenance, and it was a zone where car wrecks were more prominent than the scant road signs or other commuters.

He passed through Arlit at dusk, a dusty industrial town at the halfway point of his journey. On the edge of the Air Mountains to the east, and vast landscapes of flat desert to the west, Arlit was sand-coloured buildings, sandy streets and dust everywhere, lit in orange hues. Pierce considered stopping for the night, but the near full moon provided excellent visibility. Delays would lessen his chance of finding the kidnapped victims alive, so he pushed on.

On the outskirts of Arlit was an International Organization for Migration transit centre, a quasi-refugee camp for processing displaced persons escaping the violence brought on by wars in Mali, Nigeria, the Central African Republic and other neighbouring nations struggling with internal conflicts. He spotted a few campfires contained behind the barbed-wire security fence that surrounded the IOM transit centre. Wood was a scarce commodity this deep into the Sahara. Refugees faced a daily dilemma; forgoing portions of their food rations for wood bought on the black markets that sprang up in these camps. Rice and flour weren't nourishing when raw.

Many of the interned were victims of immigration scams and ruthless people smugglers. West Africans hoping to escape the violence and hardship in their homelands handed over their life savings to buy passage across the Trans-Sahara route, only to find their initial payments were never enough. The lucky ones made it to Europe, but many ended up in camps like this. Those less fortunate were abandoned in the desert without food or water, or forced to make perilous border crossings on foot, covering distances of thirty kilometres or more to transition from one people-smuggler convoy to the next. Many were left to die when transit routes became too risky for the smugglers to use, leaving families shattered and children as orphans. Often smugglers abused, exploited and trafficked women and children, many of whom would never be seen or heard from ever again.

Pierce hated refugee camps. Not because of the help they offered, but because camps reminded Pierce of just how fucked up some corners of the world were, of how a few power-hungry warlords and terrorists could create so much unnecessary suffering for hundreds of thousands of people.

The irony that his mission to save a few Europeans held

precedence over the disaster unfolding before him was not lost on Pierce. He would rescue the kidnapped Westerners if he could, but a more important personal objective was the eradication of those responsible so they couldn't create more of the misery that congregated in the camp before him.

He passed Arlit and kept driving.

Once he was beyond the IOM transit centre, the highway deteriorated further, little more than a sandy track slowing his progress. This deep into the Sahara, the landscape transformed into dunes stretching from horizon to horizon. The occasional near-lifeless tree or vegetation clump and rocky outcrops were all that broke up the monotony.

Pierce figured he would reach the town of Assamakka by about 22:00 hours. The town was near the Algerian border, where he would refuel and refresh his water supplies if he could before continuing overland three hundred kilometres west towards the Adrar des Ifoghas. He hoped to reach his destination by midday tomorrow. This route was preferable to driving through Mali, as the risks of encountering landmines and improvised explosive devices buried in roads were less likely in Algeria.

He considered again his choice to drive overland rather than entering the area by air. Helicopter inserts couldn't help him; he had witnessed first-hand how desert tribes reacted to rotary aircraft prowling over their lands. Tribes packed their camps and moved on in case whoever those helos brought were coming for them. He'd learned of a network of spotters and runners operating throughout the Adrar des Ifoghas who spread the word whenever they discovered intruders. His choice to drive in disguised had been the right one. Aerial insertion would have alerted Shalgham to Pierce's presence, and his enemy would disappear.

A high-altitude low-opening jump might have also been possible, but there was always the risk of a HALO jump being spotted during the day. At night the risks of hitting a mountain peak or landing on a treacherous outcrop before Pierce deployed his chute were too great.

On a more fundamental level, Shalgham, Ansar Dine and the kidnapped victims' locations were unknown. Aerial insertion might have dropped him hundreds of kilometres from where he needed to be. Riding into the mountains dressed as a Tuareg on a reliable motorcycle seemed the only sensible option because he needed mobility here.

But there was more to his decision than managing calculated risks. Pierce needed to be in control, or more accurately, he wouldn't allow Idris Walsh to control him. There was an aspect to Walsh that Pierce couldn't trust and couldn't yet articulate. His instincts insisted that he kept his new superior at a distance until he had a better understanding of Walsh's motives.

At around 23:00 hours he stopped to quench his thirst. Two encrypted messages from Mackenzie Summerfield waited on his satellite phone.

The first garbled voice message suggested that Juliet Paquet was not a DGSE intelligence officer as she claimed, but an imposter working for other interested parties. This revelation brought more questions than it answered, but it was information Pierce could use. He now appreciated that the woman had played him as much as he had played her the previous night. This made her a far more dangerous opponent than he had given her credit for. Who was she really, and how was she connected to Vautrin, Shalgham and the missing money? The answers to those questions might be fundamental to understanding the risks he would face in the coming days.

The second message was an official report with satellite images and GPS coordinates provided by the U.S. National Reconnaissance Office, the department that operated the United States' network of spy and surveillance satellites. A brief but condolent message informed Pierce that Gabriel Travers's UN convoy had come under attack. Based upon analysis by the NRO's satellite imagery department and the CIA, unknown assailants had killed all participants during the ensuing firefight. Their summary reports suggested insurgents had taken down the Legionnaires while their vehicles had congregated into two groups during a period of routine vehicle repairs. Bullet-riddled bodies lay spread across the battlefield. Imagery confirmed Major Travers was among the dead.

In the morning the CIA would send in a crime scene investigation team to learn more.

Pierce tightened his fists and clenched his teeth. Over two dozen women and men and a respected ally were dead, killed in the line of duty. The Legionnaires were soldiers; they knew the risks of their chosen profession, but this knowledge didn't dull the loss.

Pierce would mourn and unleash his anger later. Not now, not while he was on a mission. The living depended upon him even if the dead never again could. The mission took precedence over his feelings.

As Pierce started up his Honda Africa Twin, he wondered if the kidnappers, Vautrin or the mysterious Juliet Paquet had a connection to the convoy attack. What no one had mentioned in any of the reports were insurgent bodies. The Legionnaires must have taken out some insurgents, so was it another group that had attacked them, such as a professional mercenary outfit? Like the soldiers under Paquet's command, who knew how to fight without losing casualties or who were cunning enough to remove their dead and wounded when the battle was over? There were no tyre tracks or footprints leading to or from the battle, which was also confusing.

He could have called Mackenzie to discuss his concerns, but he didn't see the point. Conversations would serve as little more than an outlet for his suppressed anger, and no one at AB 201 deserved his fury, least of all his only friend in the CIA. Anything he shared with Mackenzie, he had to presume Walsh would also hear, and until Pierce ruled out the possibility that Paquet and Walsh were working together, because anything was possible at this stage, he would keep his theories to himself. Mackenzie was smart; she would come to the same conclusion he had.

He sent a message to Mackenzie, thanking her for the updates, told her where he was and which direction he had taken, and then he kept driving.

He reached Assamakka at 00:00 hours. The moon was high in the heavens, and the Milky Way was brilliant in its arch from one horizon to the next. The town wasn't much, with a gas station that was little more than a pump and a lean-to shack. He woke the proprietor, paid the exorbitant price for the fuel and stocked up on bottled water. Pierce thought about asking the tall, emaciated man if there was a house where he could secure a bed for the night, then changed his mind. Assamakka was a transit route for people smugglers, and they might become too interested in him if he stayed, especially with his expensive bike. He pushed on and drove west.

With the Trans-Sahara Highway far behind him, Pierce lost all signs of civilisation and powered into Algeria unannounced. Hundreds of kilometres of starlit sand dunes lay before him.

It would be a long night before the sun rose again.

26

ADRAR DES IFOGHAS, MALI

Oumar woke suddenly. The horizon shone with an orange and purple hue, denoting that the sun would soon appear. Men and camels jostled around him as they packed up their camp and prepared to leave.

The young invalid sat, shedding layers of sand that had settled on his sleeping form during the night. He coughed; his throat was dry. Yesterday's bruises and cuts ached across his body. A gentle exploration of his chest revealed that his hurting ribs were merely cracked and not broken. He called to the Ansar Dine fighters, asking for water. They ignored him or laughed. Despite his miraculous good fortune yesterday, unless he secured a benefactor, he faced a slow and agonising death from dehydration.

It took a moment to perceive Lucas Vautrin watching him from where he sat in the sand, looking gaunter and more haggard than he had yesterday. He sweated and shivered as a fever gripped his body. Despite the heat, he wrapped a blanket around him, and his breathing was like a hyena's panting. When Oumar caught the Frenchman's stare, the wounded man took a swig from his water bottle with his good arm. He stared at Oumar for a moment before beckoning him over with a nod.

Oumar approached.

Lucas held out the water bottle. When Oumar grabbed it between his stumpy limbs, Lucas maintained his shaky grip. "Don't drink it all."

Oumar nodded, took the bottle and quenched his thirst. He left half for Lucas. Thirsty, he wanted to consume it all, but he controlled his impulses.

"How did Shalgham find us?" Oumar asked.

"He has spies all over this region. It wasn't hard." Lucas's bullet wound, still open and weeping, was also red and inflamed. When he caught Oumar staring at it, the Frenchman also glanced at his wound. He set about reapplying the dirty bandages one-handed. "It's your brother's fault. It was he who shot me."

Oumar looked away. The mention of Jali brought pained memories of his brutal death and how he had almost shared the same fate. Would it have been a blessing to die together? He'd be in heaven now, his hands restored and perhaps paired with a nice young woman who wished to be his wife.

Lucas's body shook as he tied a final knot in his dressing to secure it, and used his teeth to pull it tight. "I might forgive you. You and Awa were the only ones who tried to help me."

"Is it improving?"

"It's infected. I have a fever. There are no more clean bandages." He laughed and looked away, then drank more water. "It's fucking ironic, really. If I don't get medical attention soon, I'll die. And you were the one who let Awa escape."

Nodding, Oumar kept silent. His feelings towards Lucas were difficult to understand. Part of him loathed the man. Another part felt sorry for him. "Farid would have raped her."

Lucas shrugged. "I appreciate you killing the turd. But letting Awa escape..."

"I didn't... She just..."

"Disappeared?"

Desperate to change the subject, Oumar asked, "Who are you? Really?"

Lucas laughed again. "I told you, Lucas Vautrin."

"Is that name supposed to mean anything to me?"

His shoulders slumped. "No, I suppose not."

"Why are you here?"

The Frenchman smirked, enjoying Oumar's ignorance. "My family has a business relationship with the Sword of Allah. I'm seeing a joint project through to its completion." Then his eyes lost their shine, and his lips pursed. "As to this fucking kidnapping business of yours, I don't know what you hoped to achieve, but you've caused me a world of unnecessary pain and delay. You fucked things up rather well."

"What kind of project?"

Lucas snarled. "You're a nosy turd, aren't you?"

Oumar looked to his feet. He realised he detested Lucas and his own misplaced sympathy. The Frenchman had stood and watched without comment during the crucifixion and subsequent slaughter of Jali and the hostages. Lucas cared for no one but himself. He cared for Awa only because her medical training might save him, and he tolerated Oumar because he needed help during his ailment.

Oumar thought upon his survival. What point was there in antagonising the man with returned taunts or by questioning the morality of his past actions? He needed Lucas as an ally just as he had once needed his brother. Better to act as a loyal servant and hope for a miracle to save him.

His mind visualised Awa. He'd liked the nurse. She was pretty and kind. During the night, memories of her hug had comforted him. He should have fled with her when he'd had the chance. It seemed Ansar Dine had not found her, but that just left her to die alone of thirst. Her fate and his were the same, but dying together seemed preferable to a long torturous death as a prisoner of Ansar Dine.

"I'll make a deal." Lucas's announcement drew Oumar's morose thoughts back to their conversation. "You aid me. Be a crutch and help me walk, or help me on and off my camel. Fetch things for me and so on. In return, I'll share my food and water rations."

Oumar nodded. This was the offer he needed. "Thank you, Lucas."

"Good, because it's the only offer that will keep you alive."

A flurry of activity gripped the camp. One by one the Ansar Dine insurgents mounted their camels. Most slung wooden-stocked AK-47s across their shoulders and hid their faces behind black headscarves.

"Help me!" Lucas growled and stumbled before Oumar supported him. An insurgent nearby forced a camel to sit so a shaky Lucas could climb on. Oumar aided him, aware that Lucas was in agonising pain every time he moved. The camel grunted and complained as it clambered up on its spindly legs with Lucas unsteady on its hump.

"What about me?" Oumar asked.

"You walk."

Soon they headed west. The sun rose high above

AIDEN BAILEY

ragged outcrops defining the horizon. The temperature increased, and Oumar was soon sweating. Sweat meant lost water. It wouldn't be long before he needed to drink again.

Once the camel caravan found its stride, Saifullah rode up next to Lucas. "You don't look so good, Vautrin." His piercing blue eyes carried the intensity of cold precious stones, and his muscles resembled constricting pythons. Even the camel looked small under his giant body.

"My sister has the antibiotics I need, Shalgham."

"It is a day and a night's ride to reach her. Can you hold on until then?"

Lucas gritted his teeth. "Do you have any antibiotics?"

Saifullah shook his head and smirked.

"Then I must."

The Ansar Dine commander rode in silence for a moment. The long, curved scimitar strapped across his back and an AK-47 slung across the opposite shoulder reflected the bright sun off their metal. He resembled a Saracen, those warriors from the Middle Ages who fought the Crusaders invading the Holy Land a thousand years ago. Last night, Oumar had learned from overheard conversations that Shalgham was a battle-hardened soldier from Libya and Syria. The horrors he'd experienced in war had toughened his soul. Farid had been a weakling compared to this cold, brutal killer.

"There was five million U.S. dollars in the kidnappers' truck." Saifullah looked to both Lucas and Oumar. "You didn't mention it earlier. Where did this money come from?"

Lucas shrugged and winced. "I didn't know about it. I was too worried about my wound to focus on anything else."

"I don't believe you."

"Does it matter if I did or didn't? I didn't stop you taking it. As to where it came from, I honestly don't know."

"You feel some of it is yours by right?"

Lucas looked away. "Money's no good if you are dead. If I survive my wounds, then we can talk."

Shalgham's piercing blue stare locked onto Oumar's gaze. "And you? What do you know of this money?"

Oumar swallowed. "Farid said the money came from you, Sheikh Shalgham."

Lucas expressed genuine shock at this revelation.

Saifullah bared his clenched teeth, but his response was calmer. In his fear Oumar almost tripped and fell, which caused the giant to laugh. "Vautrin, your cripple calls me his leader. If only he knew the truth."

Lucas sneered. "Did you send them to kidnap me?"

Saifullah shook his head. "Of course not."

Lucas shrugged as he pointed to Oumar. "He wasn't the brains among them, Shalgham. And with his... lack of hands, the others never considered him a worthy confidant. Neither should you. He won't know who instructed them to kidnap me, or why."

Oumar shrank into himself, embarrassed and afraid. Did Lucas think so little of him, or was he protecting Oumar by talking down his capabilities in front of this vicious butcher; was it a ploy to keep Oumar alive?

Saifullah growled. "Where do you *think* the money came from, Vautrin?"

Lucas pondered the question for a moment, but Oumar suspected he had already prepared his response, rehearsed for when he was inevitably asked this question. "If I were to guess, I would say it was a reward offered by the Western invaders, for your capture or kill." A shaky hand gestured towards Oumar. "I'm guessing these bandits were lucky enough to stumble across it, and stupid enough to take it for themselves."

"I see." The giant paused in contemplation. "I'll ask again. You don't want a cut of the money? You stake no claim?"

Lucas laughed. "If you want to offer me half, Shalgham, I won't say no. But it was never my money to lose. So... keep it all."

Shalgham and Lucas rode for a time without speaking. Oumar trundled beside them. All the while Saifullah studied Lucas, searching for lies or trickery. Lucas only shivered, as if inflicted by chilling temperatures despite the radiating heat. He seemed to care for nothing more than his fever.

"If you are keeping the money, can I keep him?" Lucas nodded to Oumar.

"The Bambara cripple?" Saifullah asked, referring to Oumar by his ethnicity.

"I need help. He can be my assistant. At least until I am healed."

Saifullah nodded. "It amuses me to learn how he survives with no hands. That is the only reason he lives. If he aids you, Vautrin, keep him until you heal. If he slows us, leave him behind." He didn't wait for an answer as he rode ahead to join the front of the caravan.

A minute later, Lucas was laughing. "Don't worry, Oumar, I won't leave you behind."

Oumar nodded, not sure what to say and uncertain how long he could offer skills to prolong his value. He'd wanted to ask why Shalgham had butchered Jali, treated him as an infidel when his brother was more deserving to have lived and serve Ansar Dine than himself. He could have asked Lucas the same question, but he suspected the Frenchman didn't have answers and didn't care. Oumar also wished to understand why Saifullah had lied about the value of the money, claiming a discovery of five instead of the ten or more million he and Jali had counted, and why Lucas had let that lie pass without comment. Was it so that if Lucas had argued to split it, they would only be arguing over less than half the actual quantity, allowing Shalgham to deny the other six million existed, so he could pocket all that himself. As to Lucas's motives, did he, in actuality, have no idea how much money was involved? It seemed likely that Shalgham and Ansar Dine had not been the ones to orchestrate the kidnapping, so who had, and why?

But Oumar asked none of his questions. Instead, he asked, "Where are we headed?"

The Frenchman winced again as the roll of the camel's strides caused the flesh around his wound to twist and stretch. Sweat gushed off his face in torrents, and his body shook. Their water wouldn't last long.

"Towards destiny, Oumar."

"Destiny?"

"The French and the Americans think they have a war on their hands now, but it is nothing compared to what we will inflict upon them. Pray you live long enough to see our plans become a reality."

27

SAHARA, ALGERIA

After three hours of sleep snatched on a dune under starlit skies and in near-freezing conditions, Pierce felt rested enough to continue his journey.

In the morning light he ate an MRE, the infamous Meals Ready to Eat packs soldiers around the world "enjoyed" daily, and set off eastward. The Honda Africa Twin was the perfect desert bike, maintaining traction and speed on the sand. He made good time. The granite ranges of Adrar des Ifoghas appeared on the horizon, less than ten kilometres distant now.

His thoughts turned to the kidnappers and their hostages. His instincts warned that he was too late to rescue them, but he pushed on, knowing that he had to at least try.

As he passed one of many rocky outcrops breaking up the monotony of the dunes, the crack of a gunshot sounded, and in the same instant he lost control of his bike.

The Honda twisted underneath him. The jarring force hurled him towards a dune. He tucked in as his special forces training had taught him, and rolled when he hit the crest. The soft sand saved him from serious grazing as he disappeared over the lip of a dune.

A second rifle shot was fired. The Honda's gas tank burst into flames. Seconds later he heard a *whoosh* as the bike disintegrated. His M40A5 sniper rifle, flashbang and frag grenades vanished in the explosion.

Pierce didn't move as he watched and listened.

He hadn't seen the shooter. He had no sense of the enemy combatant's location. When no further shots followed, Pierce guessed he was beyond the sniper's line of sight. It seemed he'd chosen the correct side of the dune to roll into, away from the rocky outcrop.

Since no one was shooting for the moment, Pierce checked for wounds. His thigh hurt, and he saw why. The satellite phone strapped to his leg was now a shattered wreck of metal, plastic and circuits. While its destruction had saved him from a serious injury by deflecting the bullet, his only means of outside communication was now defunct. It hurt to move his leg, and bruising was spreading fast across his thigh, but the damage was superficial and had not broken the skin. He tested his weight on his leg, discovering no additional pain.

When he tried to unstrap the shattered phone from his belt, he fumbled with the catch.

He looked at his hands.

They shook.

In the past, adrenalin and action kept the shakes away, but not today...

He slowed his breathing and meditated, a strategy that sometimes dismissed or lessened his trembling.

After a minute he knew that strategy had failed.

What had changed?

Ignoring his physiological problem for the moment, he checked his possessions, but found he couldn't get a grip on any tool with his shaky fingers. He left his Glock 19 semi-automatic pistol and KAMPO tactical knife holstered to his belt. His backpack with food and water rations, the money, medical gear and night-vision goggles remained strapped to his back. Gone was his AK-47, flung into the desert when he'd crashed. He couldn't see it anywhere in his line of sight.

Pierce cursed. His shaking worsened, for he felt it in his legs now.

Clenching and unclenching his fists for several seconds to get the blood flowing, Pierce gained a level of control over his tremors. Before his muscles fought him again, he emptied his pack and wrapped the blue turban around it, then raised the fake "head" above the dune.

Another bullet penetrated the bag and knocked it from Pierce's hands.

With luck, the sniper now believed he had eliminated his target.

With shaky hands, Pierce repacked his backpack, slung it over his back, then sprinted down the dune, gaining distance from his attacker while remaining out of visual range. He stumbled several times when his legs gave out under him, but he pushed through his lack of neurological control. His muscles burned as he raced up the next dune and disappeared over the next crest. He looked back. Even from this crest, he remained out of sight from the now distant rocky outcrop.

At the rise Pierce examined the tracks he'd left behind that the sniper and his team could follow.

He jogged along the dune crest out of sight from the

trough he had just sprinted from, towards a position where the sun would be behind him if the attackers glanced in his direction. If he had his M40A5 sniper rifle *and* if he could get his shakes under control, the next step in his plan would have been simple, but with hundreds of metres between one dune crest and the other, a pistol didn't have the range to neutralise the enemy. Even with a rifle, his shakes wouldn't allow for a clean shot.

Pierce considered his predicament. Had the shot shattering the satellite phone also jolted his body, triggering the shakes? Was there another cause? In the past he'd always kept his tremors under control until the fighting ended. What was different about today?

He couldn't think about that now. First, he had to eliminate the enemy.

It was hard work exerting energy in the baking desert, so Pierce chugged water from his bottle. If dehydration was his problem, quenching his thirst might fix his shakes. He felt improved after guzzling more water than he would normally consume in a day, so drank more. Finally, his quivering lessened. Relieved, he rested on the dune and watched for the attackers to make their next move.

They didn't disappoint. Within twenty minutes two men, in khaki uniforms and with black scarves wrapped around their heads, stepped over the crest where Pierce had run from. Each wore an AK-47 ready for firing. Confusion replaced elation when Pierce's body was not visible.

As expected, the men followed the tracks.

Pierce snuck back along the crest, out of sight. He figured with the men's current rate of movement, he had about ten minutes to reach them before they crossed the next crest.

He sprinted through the soft sand and focused on not

slipping further down the dunes with every step. When he returned to where his tracks crossed over, he dropped and waited.

He willed his trembling hands to normalise, but they didn't.

If he had one advantage, it was that the insurgents had no proper training as soldiers. They were out of breath and discussing who the intruder on the bike might be, their loud voices giving away their position. When Pierce estimated they were almost at the crest, he took his Glock in his hands and slowed his breathing. Then he sprang from behind the dune and fired two bullets into each face as they stepped up onto the crest.

In that instant of sudden and violent action, Pierce operated by instincts alone. In that moment, shakes and tremors didn't exist. His aim was true. The insurgents had no time for surprise. As their entry and exit holes sprayed mists of blood and skull matter, they rolled fifty metres back the way they had come.

Pierce ducked down behind the dune and re-evaluated his situation. Two men dead, but neither carried a sniper rifle. At least one more insurgent waited, armed and dangerous and ready to kill him.

It took Pierce thirty seconds to plan. Shakes were best left unacknowledged if he were to survive this encounter, so acting on pure instinct, he was over the lip in seconds, racing to the fallen corpses.

He stripped one man of his clothes and turban and placed them over his own body. He took the man's AK-47 and marched back the way they had come. When he stood on the lip of the original dune, in the firing line of the sniper, he was gambling with his life. Standing on unsteady legs, he waved, pretended to be an insurgent. His motions aimed to be suggestive he was one of them, that the intruder was dead, and it was safe for the sniper to approach.

It took twenty minutes for the sniper to appear. Dressed like the others in khaki with a black turban wrapped around his head, he marched from the rocky outcrop, resting an old and battered Kalekalıp KNT-308 7.62mm sniper rifle over one shoulder. Every time he stopped to catch his breath and to beckon Pierce to come down to him, Pierce beckoned him to keep climbing. Pierce kept pointing over the horizon, as if a wonderful surprise awaited.

He would have shot the last man already, but his tremors made the long-distance shot impossible.

When the sniper was almost at the top of the dune and less than ten metres separated them, Pierce acted. He fired the old Russian assault rifle, peppering the insurgent's chest and guts with hot, fast-moving bullets.

The insurgent toppled and screamed.

Pierce readied his weapon for return fire in case more insurgents waited out of sight. When nothing threatened and no further bullets were fired, he marched to the fallen man and kicked the Kalekalıp far from his reach. With trembling hands, Pierce pressed the hot muzzle of the AK-47 into the insurgent's head. The barrel jumped around as if a strong wind buffeted it, but it was Pierce's tremors that caused the shaking.

"You're not...?" Blood gushed from the dying man's mouth.

Pierce shrugged. "No, I'm not, am I?"

The insurgent glanced at Pierce's shaking hands, and appeared confused by the affliction, despite the many other pressing matters he now faced, such as his impending mortality and uncertainty as to the fate of his friends.

"You're wondering what is wrong with me?" No one had seen Pierce like this before, but until today, he'd hidden his condition well. It didn't matter what this man learned, he would soon bleed out, so Pierce felt compelled to explain himself. "Concussion injury, perhaps... Stress. Lack of sleep. Nerve damage. Who the fuck knows...?"

The truth was Pierce didn't know.

The tremors had become more pronounced a year ago, after an operation inside Yemen where Pierce had been in close proximity to a grenade detonation. Before that, Pierce had been near plenty of other explosions and endured enough concussions during half a decade of secret missions before "officially" joining the CIA, so his condition could be neurological. He'd also operated in constant fear during that time, so stress was just as likely a cause. He had told no one about his symptoms, not even medical professionals. But there had been no need before. The tremors had never been this bad. "The devil has cursed you, for your lack of faith!"

"Sorry, bud. It's you he's cursed."

Pierce depressed the trigger mechanism one more time, delivering a silencing hole through the sniper's frontal lobe.

28

W ith his enemies eradicated, now was the time to rest and dismiss his shakes.
Pierce planted his ass in the sand, closed his eyes, slowed his breathing and otherwise remained motionless for many minutes, entering a state of mind where the sand didn't itch and the baking sun no longer bothered him.

When he felt centred, Pierce opened his eyes and stood. He didn't glance at his hands, but he didn't need to. Once again, he was in control.

He took the Kalekalıp sniper rifle from where it had fallen, then checked the dead insurgent for spare bullets, magazines and a sat phone. He found only bullets, which he pocketed.

Pierce checked the sniper rifle's serial number. It fell within a range Pierce knew, from earlier background research he'd undertaken on Victor Vautrin, was from a cache of Turkish Army weapons bound for the conflict in Northern Iraq, which had subsequently disappeared in transit. The weapon implied that Vautrin was Ansar Dine's and Kashif Shalgham's weapons supplier.

Utah and Arizona.

If only he could call in and share this intelligence with Mackenzie Summerfield. But that wasn't possible until he secured another satellite phone.

Focusing on his current situation, Pierce followed the dead men's footprints through the sand and up the side of the imposing rocky outcrop.

As he climbed, the view out across the desert grew vast, of occasional rocky peaks jutting from the dunes, dry mountain ranges in the west, a cloudless blue sky and hundreds of kilometres of uninterrupted sand disappearing towards all horizons.

The word desert had Latin origins, *desertus*, meaning "abandoned". Outside of Antarctica, the Sahara was the largest abandoned region on Earth. Almost devoid of life and covering nine million square kilometres, it was an area larger than the United States, and Pierce was in its centre.

He felt both welcomed and alien in this environment.

Then the stench hit him.

He couldn't guess the odour at first. Then he identified undulations in the sand. Arms, legs, heads and other partially buried body parts. Covering his mouth with his turban, Pierce walked among the desiccated husks. The fresher bodies he identified as Tuareg or Azawagh Arab men, women and children. People of the desert. The Imohagh, or noble ones as the Tuareg called themselves, but they weren't noble anymore. This was a slaughterhouse.

Pierce felt sick and not just from the stench. This was a genocide.

The footprints soon disappeared, replaced by a worn

path leading up the side and around the rocky outcrop. It led to a guelta waterhole where three mangy camels chewed on near dead clumps of grass or drank with long slurping mouthfuls. Each wore a saddle and a harness. Three camels. Three dead insurgents. Odds were that Pierce was alone now, and these domesticated pack animals were his transport out of here.

AK-47 raised and ready, Pierce took the path to the top of the outcrop. He discovered a tent and a sentry post from where the sniper had fired at Pierce. When he saw a dirty and beaten woman tied naked to a stake, he ran to her, only to discover she had no pulse. Pierce clenched his teeth and fists in anger. These men must be Ansar Dine, al-Qaeda or Islamic State, fundamentalists who believed in a single ideology of fanaticism and the genocide of all non-believers. They had used the woman for their brutal pleasure, then left her to die.

Further exploration revealed an Ansar Dine flag, rations of dates, couscous and cooked goat meat. Over a small fire brewed a pot of strong coffee. There were no radios and no phones. The weapons were primitive 1970s-era M2 carbines and AK-47 knock-offs. Pierce broke the weapons down to their component pieces and threw them from the rocky ledge. He ate the terrorists' food and drank their coffee while he searched through their packs, finding clothes, compasses, binoculars, more black flags with Islamic creeds of righteousness and copies of the Qur'an wrapped in cloth. He threw the flag on the fire and flipped through the Qur'ans, discovering in one a French-language contour map of the Adrar des Ifoghas ranges.

After identifying his current location, he memorised the pen marks that displayed routes taken by the Tuareg and other tribes as they fled the mountains towards international displaced person camps in neighbouring Niger and Burkina Faso.

This was not an Ansar Dine outpost to deter Western invaders from entering the mountains, but a watch post to ensure the local people didn't leave.

The Adrar des Ifoghas had witnessed some of the worst fighting during the 2013 French military liberation of Mali, code-named Operation Serval. The French had neutralised the insurgents during the war, but new opposing forces had occupied these lands since, with the largest of them being Ansar Dine, and thus had created a new flood of refugees fleeing the region.

CIA reports on Ansar Dine all stressed that the terrorist organisation wished to found a caliphate in the Adrar des Ifoghas, but for a caliphate to thrive, it required enslaved men, women and children. Incarcerated people forced to gather food, cook meals, tend to livestock and collect water for their captors. They married the unluckiest off to Ansar Dine fighters to satisfy their perverse pleasures and to provide them with children. With the number of refugees who had already fled, Ansar Dine could not afford to lose anyone else. Hence the need for these outposts.

Pierce had seen enough. He took food and spare magazines for the AK-47 strapped across his back, the binoculars and the Kalekalıp sniper rifle. He piled the remaining possessions together and set them on fire.

After drinking at the waterhole, he took the three grunting camels by their reins and connecting ropes and led them out onto the sand dunes. He forced one of the camels to sit, then mounted it. As it rose, Pierce leaned first backwards as it raised its hind legs, then forwards as its front legs rose. Once comfortable in the saddle, he tightened the reins and directed the animal west towards the distant mountains. Camels had an unusual gait, rocking him back and forth as they padded through the desert, and he soon felt his tailbone starting to ache.

At speeds of up to six kilometres per hour, the camels would reach the Adrar des Ifoghas mountains in two to three hours. Pierce settled in to enjoy the ride.

As the day progressed, the landscape transformed from dunes to ancient riverbeds. He passed mushroom-shaped rocks worn at their bases by sandstorms, and patches of white salt pans that from a distance resembled snow.

After a few hours Pierce entered the foothills of the mountains. Their rise was gradual as the landscape transformed from flat dry riverbeds into rocky plains and fields of jagged stone, plus wide sandy valleys surrounded by black granite peaks, ranging from a few dozen to a few hundred metres in height.

By mid-afternoon he spotted a caravan of camels and their Tuareg riders. Through his binoculars he identified that they dressed as he did, in blue turbans and long white cotton shirts that reached their ankles. The men carried assault and bolt-action rifles. Most men walked as the camels carried large blocks of salt, taken from mines deep in the desert for sale in Timbuktu, Gao, Mopti and other Malian settlements on the edge of the desert. These caravans were the last of their kind, for trucking companies now serviced many of the Saharan salt trade routes, surpassing the thousand-year-old transport method that Pierce now saw before him.

Pierce could avoid this caravan, and he would have done so if he had any suspicion these were terrorists or enemy fighters. The group was large, suggesting they travelled in numbers as a deterrent against the same insurgent forces Pierce wished to avoid.

He removed his turban so as not to offend, and rode towards the caravan.

The suspicious men raised their weapons.

Pierce kept his arms high and his hands free. "*As-salamu alaykum*," he shouted when close enough for the men to hear him. "I'm an American," he explained in Arabic as he climbed off his camel to appear less threatening. "Here with the United States Army. I wish to meet with your leader, Bachir Aghali?"

With their faces hidden behind their turbans, Pierce couldn't read the Tuareg's expressions. He listened while they discussed what they should do with him. They spoke in their own language, Tamashek, of which Pierce couldn't understand a word.

One man approached. He drew down his veil, revealing a young, dark-skinned face expressing a quizzical, uncertain smile. "I remember you." He spoke French.

"Tariq Aghali?"

"Yes, Pierce, it is good to see you again. May God bless you."

Pierce remembered the keen but somewhat whiny warrior he and Major Gabriel Travers had worked alongside during their many missions here. Tariq was the son of Bachir Aghali, and family bonds were strong among the Tuareg. An excellent marksman who could move unseen through any landscape, Tariq also complained constantly and questioned strategy often to the point of inaction. Working with Tariq was both educational and painful. "May God bless you, too. It's good to see you again, my friend."

Tariq nodded, expressing the worry Pierce expected from him. "While it is good to see you, you would not be here unless trouble is brewing in these lands."

"I think you already know what that trouble is. Ansar Dine. I'm here to help, and in return, I'm hoping your people can help me help you?"

Tariq gazed out across the unforgiving landscape. "Not for me to say. I will take you to my father, and he can decide."

Pierce grinned. The father, Bachir Aghali, was a man of far stronger character than his son. "That sounds perfect."

29

SAHARA, MALI

Baffled and overwhelmed, Mackenzie Summerfield stood among the carnage of Legionnaires and tried to understand.

Death and destruction were a job requirement. She accepted this whenever she watched the world's most depraved insurgents fight it out via live satellite or drone feeds, on video files uploaded on the Dark Net, or when absorbing their brutalities expressed through the words of after-action reports. She'd expected high levels of detached exposure to human carnage when she applied for and was accepted into a career with the CIA. Real-world operations, however, proved to be something else altogether.

Personal. Real. In her face.

Back when she was an analyst at Langley and then briefly working in the field, reality hadn't bothered her as much. Fieldwork had seemed easy, even exhilarating. Greece had changed all that.

Today the carnage felt too real. She could taste bile in the back of her throat...

Shaking her head to clear her anxiety, Summerfield focused again. She'd learned early in her career to compartmentalise feelings, as the CIA had trained her. She focused on the pieces, trying to build a picture of how this battle had unfolded.

Explosive detonations at two locations had vaporised the VAB armoured personnel carriers and their crews. Nine corpses lay scattered in the sand, peppered with fatal bullet wounds. No partially disintegrated corpses anywhere. The bodies included Major Gabriel Travers with his skull blown open and a shattered right hand. His dead facial muscles expressed both surprise and resignation.

Many Legionnaires presented similar sentiments, for most had had no time to retaliate against whatever forces had ambushed them. A lack of casings was proof enough.

"What do you see?" Idris Walsh asked. He had walked the crime scene twice already. As the CIA Head of Operations, North Africa, the lack of clues frustrated him as much as it frustrated her. "Summerfield?"

"Sorry, sir?"

Summerfield had difficulty hearing him over the spinning blades of the CH-47 Chinook heavy-lift helicopter that had brought her, Walsh and a contingent of U.S. Marines to investigate the aftermath of the battle and to collect bodies for their return home and a proper burial. The helo would never power down on the off chance they needed to leave in a hurry. A Reaper drone — invisible overhead — provided real-time intelligence on any suspected insurgent group movements that might present a threat. So far, they were in the clear.

Two French Foreign Legion investigators, a female lieutenant and a male sergeant, conducted their own analysis.

They had taken up the Americans' offer to fly with them to recover the bodies. The carnage baffled them as much as it baffled Walsh and her.

"Summerfield?" he said again in a harsher tone. "What do you see? Is the scene talking to you?"

Summerfield wiped sand and sweat from her brow. "It's too clean, sir. No insurgent corpses, and no tracks leading in or out."

Walsh growled. "Yes, that is odd." His cold tone suggested he had already thought of this.

Summerfield crouched next to a corporal with a ragged bullet hole in the back of his head. Hair around the entry wound was still sticky and wet despite the evaporating heat. Scorch marks suggested the killing weapon had been pressed against his scalp when fired. Dried vomit on his uniform completed the scene. Many corpses had expelled the contents of their guts before they died.

"Chemical weapons?" she asked.

Walsh shook his head and showed the portable gas detector array in his hand, programmed to detect airborne chemical and biological agents. "Everything came up clean."

"Why the vomiting?"

He shrugged. "Food poisoning? I've seen plenty of mundane explanations for horrible deaths in my time."

Summerfield stood. "All the Legionnaires get food poisoning at the same time? Then, while they're throwing up, insurgents just take them out?"

"Yeah, doesn't seem likely, does it?"

Summerfield sighed. Improvised explosive devices, land-mines and suicide bombers presented the biggest threats to armed convoys operating in Mali. Al-Qaeda, Islamic State and Ansar Dine had learned the hard way that direct engagement with Western forces was pointless and only resulted in mass casualties on their side. Why attack the convoy if the risks for failure were so high? Yet that was what they seemed to have done. And, if true, then why were they successful when no insurgent had been before?

Amelie, the female investigator, called Walsh over. The CIA man nodded to Summerfield, implying he would resume their conversation in a minute.

She hadn't shared with Walsh her knowledge of Juliet Paquet's and the DGSE's interest in the Victor Vautrin operation, or her suspicion that Paquet was an imposter. She considered if she should. The imposter seemed the perfect candidate to have orchestrated this bloody outcome.

Alone, Summerfield again studied the wreckage, taking her time to see everything in detail.

The scene resembled an impromptu battle, but the details suggested extensive planning and a coordination of many resources.

She noticed several of the dead soldiers had plastic water bottles lying nearby.

She grabbed one and smelled its contents and detected a metallic odour.

Following a hunch, she leaned in next to the mouth of a Legionnaire. Over the stench of his decomposing organs, she detected a garlic-like scent.

Could this be arsenic poisoning? Symptoms were vomiting, diarrhoea, cramping muscles *and* garlicky breath. If enemy operators had poisoned the crew using tainted water bottles, this suggested an inside job.

Summerfield closed the lid on the bottle and packed it in an evidence bag. They could test it for poisons later.

She scanned the scene again. The destruction of the

armoured personnel carriers and small protected vehicles had occurred in two tightly packed clusters. Convoys by convention operated at a distance from each other so if they came under attack, a single strike couldn't take out multiple targets. This suggested someone had moved the vehicles after the combat ended. But why go to the effort to group vehicles if the agenda was to destroy them, and if the soldiers were already dead from poisoning? What did the grouping of vehicles conceal? If the responsibility lay with the Paquet imposter, what was her motivation? What purpose did the attack serve?

Metal fragments were scattered far and wide, but there didn't look to be enough for eight vehicles.

Then the realisation hit her.

Was this a set-up?

Had the scene been engineered to look as if all the vehicles had been destroyed?

While in fact some of the UN vehicles had been stolen?

"That's the look of someone struck by inspiration, Summerfield?" Walsh had snuck up on her again.

Suppressing the urge to shudder, she said, "Look at the wreckage, sir. Not enough parts for eight vehicles." She explained her theory without mentioning Paquet. Mark had asked her to keep this information between them for now. With Walsh constantly watching her, she hoped this was the safest strategy.

"Could this be Vautrin?"

Summerfield paused. She hadn't considered this option but found no reason to dismiss it. "Maybe Vautrin wanted UN vehicles to move arms around without getting stopped at checkpoints?"

"That would make sense." Walsh massaged his chin. "Anyone else with a motive to steal a UN convoy?"

She paused, taking a moment to frame her answer. She didn't wish to give Walsh any sign she was holding back on him even though she was. "What do you mean, sir?"

"Exactly what I said."

She cleared her throat, even while knowing this was a visual clue that she was about to lie. "No, sir, I can't think of anyone else with motives for this."

He nodded, looked away and said nothing.

For twenty minutes they searched, finding nothing more, but together confirming the lack of parts for eight wrecked vehicles.

In the meantime, the Marines collected all the bodies and dog tags and loaded them onto the Chinook. "We're ready to leave, sir," said a sergeant, "unless you want to stick around?"

Walsh shook his head. "Right you are, Marine. We're done."

Within minutes the Air Force helicopter was airborne and racing south. The deafening noise of the engine and rotor blades inhibited conversation except through mics and headsets. The craft climbed and flew high to mitigate the risk of insurgent surface-to-air missile attacks. After twenty minutes Walsh spoke to the pilot via a comms channel off-limits to everyone else. A minute later they were descending into a vast sea of sand.

Why were they landing? There was nothing out here.

When the helicopter touched down, Summerfield realised that Walsh now pointed his Beretta Px4 Storm semi-automatic pistol at her gut. "Time to get out, Summerfield."

The Legionnaire investigators looked surprised, but not the Marines.

Walsh must have pre-planned this moment, prepped his men to his intentions. She couldn't imagine what prompted him to threaten her with a pistol, but his reason was sufficient for the Marines not to display any concern. This worried her more than the weapon lined up with her vital internal organs.

"I won't say it again, Summerfield. Get out, now!"

30

S ummerfield unbuckled her seatbelt and climbed from the helicopter. Walsh's grip on his pistol was steady, and the barrel never drifted off her centre mass. She hesitated before stepping out, but what choice did she have?

Walsh jumped down after her as the Chinook took to the skies and circled a mile above. Hot sand whipped around their clothes, and the noise of the distant aircraft was loud, requiring them to shout to be heard.

"What the hell is going on, *sir*?"

He waved his pistol towards her holstered Beretta M92 semi-automatic. "Take it out, carefully, then throw it to me."

Summerfield complied. She'd heard rumours Walsh loaded his Px4 Storm with hollow-point 9x19mm Parabellum rounds. When hollow points hit a target, the impact pressure causes the bullet to expand outwards in a process called mushrooming. A normal bullet often went right through a person, burrowing a bloody hole. Hollow points turned human organs and soft tissue into mush. If he shot her now, there was no coming back.

Walsh crouched, snatched her pistol from the yellow sand, pocketed it and then stood distant enough so she had no chance of rushing him. Close enough so he couldn't miss.

"You going to shoot me?"

He gave a smug grin. "That depends."

"On what?"

"How you answer my next questions."

Summerfield shuddered. What did Walsh know that she didn't?

"I'll make a deal with you. I'll only shoot you if you lie to me."

"Is this some kind of sadistic joke?"

"No joke, Summerfield. Just so we are clear, some of my questions I already know the answers to. Some I don't. If you answer with a lie, I shoot you in the gut and leave you to bleed out. In this heat and with all this sand, that will be an ending that is unpleasant beyond all measure. Are we clear?"

"You're insane."

"Maybe, but my methods work. Kept me alive for three decades when many colleagues are now long dead. First question: who else besides Victor Vautrin did you suspect might have attacked the convoy?"

Summerfield shuddered again. If it were she interrogating Walsh, she would have led with a question she knew the answer to. She had no choice but to answer with the truth. "Juliet Paquet. The DGSE operative."

Walsh grinned. "Good, Summerfield, now we're getting somewhere."

"How did you know about her?"

He shook his head, made a tutting sound. "Now, now, you're not playing by the rules. I'm asking the questions. But what the heck, I'll answer that one. I knew because I checked the paperwork. The French registered Paquet and seven of her protective duty officers as joining the convoy. None of their bodies are here. But you didn't check, did you?" When she didn't answer, he followed with, "That is question two, if you weren't paying attention."

She clenched and unclenched her fists. "You're right. I didn't know. I didn't check."

Her mind raced, tried to make sense of what was transpiring. She wasn't understanding the full picture. Walsh could be dirty as the office rumours suggested, a conspirator in league with Vautrin or the Paquet imposter, or both. He might also be clean, a patriot who suspected Summerfield to be just as dirty as she suspected him of being. With her limited information, there was no way of knowing which supposition was the truth.

"Question three. Was it really Paquet you suspected?"

She shook her head, surprised at how much Walsh already knew. "No. I suspect someone is impersonating her."

He frowned. This response seemed to interest him. "Question four. How did you come to that conclusion?"

She described the intel report on the dead woman discovered dissolving in acid in a bathtub. She recounted the strange condition Mark had reported on the imposter's disproportionate pupils not matching the descriptions of the real intelligence officer and concluded with how the switch could occur without the DGSE knowing.

"Pierce met with the Paquet imposter?"

"Yes." She relayed Mark's encounter in Gao and how the

imposter had failed to trick Mark into handing over the CIA files on Vautrin.

Walsh shook his head. "All these lies and deceit. I thought my sister was bad enough, lying to get more and more money out of me. What am I to do with you, Summerfield?"

"Is that a question?"

He laughed and raised his Px4 Storm so it pointed at her heart. "You and Pierce kept important information from me — don't answer that. It's not a question, because I know it is true."

Summerfield kept silent. She touched her lips, realising they were drying out, and she was thirsty. The hundred-plus-degree-Fahrenheit heat and the lack of shade caused her to sweat profusely. If Walsh's intentions were to leave her behind, she wouldn't last long this deep in the Sahara.

"Why are you lying to me, Summerfield? And remember, if I don't like your answer, you'll get a bullet in your gut."

The threat was clear. This was a life-or-death moment. Not knowing Walsh's true allegiances, even telling him the truth might get her killed. She considered if she was betraying Mark by telling the truth and if she could jeopardise his mission by doing so. But what choice did she have? Speaking the truth was her safest path right now.

"It's the money, sir," she said, using a title of respect to appease him.

"The money?" His frown seemed genuine, as if this revelation surprised him.

"Yes. It makes no sense to give insurgents eleven million dollars for a simple job. You could have swayed them into action with a far smaller sum."

"Oh, so that's it?" He laughed. "You think I'm corrupt?"

She nodded. "Pierce and I suspect you of misappropriating CIA funds. You seem overly eager to get the eleven million back, desperate even, as if your life depends on it."

Walsh stared at her. Then he smirked. Finally, he was laughing. "You think because my dumb sister is trying to screw every dime out of me, that I've lost control of my own finances? Fuck you, Summerfield!"

She wanted to ask what was so funny until she remembered the rules of the game.

"You're a fucking idiot, Summerfield. Pierce too." He shook his head, switching suddenly from laughing to fuming now. "Okay, I will tell you because I can't afford to have you two fucking things up any more than you already have." He took his canteen of water and guzzled. He didn't offer her any. "The money is part of a larger sting operation, to get the word out to al-Qaeda that their man Shalgham is running his own operations without their authorisation, and throwing around a lot of cash to do so. Cash he won't be able to account for, suggesting he sourced it from groups outside the Ansar Dine network likely not perfectly aligned with their fucked ideologies. The kidnapping was the first of many disinformation missions. Tactical arrangements make it necessary to get the money back for the next sting operation, because securing funds from Congress is a fucking pain in the ass."

Summerfield shuddered again. What Walsh said made perfect sense. His explanation might still be a fabrication, but his delivery and lack of any physical micro-signals that he was lying convinced her he spoke the truth. "Why didn't you tell us, sir?"

Walsh threatened with the pistol. "My rules. I ask the questions."

She kept quiet.

"I tell you what, why don't you guess why I kept you both in the dark? Or, specifically, why the Trigger Man can't know? Everyone keeps telling me how smart you both are, so work it out."

Summerfield thought through the logic. Then it hit her. The solution was simple tradecraft. "If al-Qaeda take Pierce in the field and torture him, he can't reveal information about the sting operation."

The CIA spymaster shook his head and lowered his weapon. "You are such a fucking disappointment, Summerfield." He spoke into his radio, calling down the Chinook. The helicopter pivoted and began its descent, and the noise of its engine and rotor blades grew noisier with every passing second. "From now on I'm keeping you on a short leash, but only because you are an excellent analyst. If you keep anything from me again, I'll see to it that the only way you return Stateside is in a body bag. People die in 'accidents' all the time here. Do I make myself clear?"

She nodded. What else could she say? If she had learned anything today, it was that Idris Walsh was a deceptively clever and dangerous man. Her next steps in this mission would need to be cautious.

"One more thing," Walsh yelled as the drone of the CH-47 drew closer, and he had to yell so loudly she could barely comprehend him. "I know what happened in Mykonos, three and a half years ago. Michael Abraham, the CIA paramilitary officer *I* trained along with the two dead CIA operators killed in the Sahel. Abraham abused you. He locked you in a cellar for days while Pierce was out in the field. Assaulted you repeatedly. Sometime later Pierce killed Abraham. Tell me if I'm missing anything?"

Without thought, she crossed her arms and looked away. Tears streamed down her face as the world receded from her. It had been more than a year since she had remembered the terror as vividly as she did now, triggered by Walsh accurately describing the harrowing events in too much detail.

She barely held her composure. It was almost too much to have her trauma thrown in her face mere moments after threatening her life. Was he trying to destroy her?

She nodded. "Yes. You're right." Strangely, her thoughts were not about whether Walsh would kill her, but rather whether she could bear the Marines' accusatory stares and judgements that she would receive when the transport helicopter landed. Did they all know about her past suffering? "How did you know?"

"I know people, Summerfield. I always know them. And most people never give me enough credit for just how astute I am."

Before the helicopter got too close and it whipped the sand around them, she heard his final words over the noise. "And for the record, Summerfield, I would have killed Abraham too, exactly as Pierce did. Even though he was my man, he was a fucking disappointment. He got what he deserved."

31

ADRAR DES IFOGHAS, MALI

The day dragged as the camel caravan traversed between peaks of dark Saharan mountains. Endless blue sky presented a sun that baked the vast plains of rock and sand and banished all clouds. Black craggy pinnacles floated on the horizon, distorted in the rippling atmosphere of mirages. Heat radiated off heat, letting no one forget this was an unforgiving landscape. There was nowhere to escape the burning rays.

The caravan comprised eighteen Tuareg cameleers, ranging from thin boys to leathery-skinned men who looked eighty but were more likely to be in their forties. On the rare occasions when the men spoke, it was in Tamashek, the local dialect of the Malian Tuareg. Pierce didn't understand a word.

The camels numbered sixty-eight, and each carried heavy blocks of carved salt with little complaint. When they reached an occasional acacia tree, the caravan stopped, and the camels chomped at the leaves, seeking nourishment despite the long thorny branches. The animals brayed and grunted until asked to march again at a leisured pace. An old man in the lead sang and chanted, providing a rhythm for the cameleers, reminding Pierce of drummers pounding out a beat for oarsmen on a Roman galley seen in movies he'd watched.

If it weren't for the assault rifles the Tuareg slung, this could have been a scene from the past, reminding Pierce that the desert people's lives had changed little in the last thousand years.

The men walked side by side with their camels, as the weight of salt already burdened the animals. Pierce found no appeal in the odd sway of the beasts, so he also walked. With the heat he'd lost his appetite for food but drank vast quantities of water. Out here in the desert, he could easily consume four litres in a single day.

If days were hot, nights were frigid. Pierce enjoyed the desert only in the mornings and evenings, when the landscape lit up in fascinating shades of reds, oranges, purples and blues and the temperature reached a sweet spot between the cold of night and the baking day. It was sunset now as they rode into the Tuareg camp.

Men, women and children ate bread, onions, couscous and tomato dishes baked in ovens dug into the sand. The men kept their faces covered; the women did not. Goats and sheep bleated as they searched for grass to eat and water to drink. Two young boys operated a rusty pump, drawing water from deep underground to satisfy themselves and the animals. Pierce guessed the pump was the legacy of a foreign aid programme from decades past, allowing the tribe to remain in this spot for an indefinite period.

Towards the centre of the camp, the cameleers marched around a parked older model Land Rover Defender, a British four-wheel drive manufactured in the 1990s. Rusted and beaten and covered in sand, it otherwise looked to be in perfect working order. He'd driven Defenders before, and they had impressed him with their versatility and simple maintenance regimes. It was an off-road vehicle that kept going long after other four-by-fours broke down and fell apart.

"You like?" Tariq asked.

Pierce nodded. Reliable and tough all-terrain vehicles, they were the perfect car for desert travel. "Where did you get it?"

"It was a gift, from a Swede who tried to drive solo across the Sahara — from Cairo to Dakar. I saved his life when he ran out of fuel and water. I got him home, so he gifted me his vehicle."

"That is some story, Tariq."

"That is why I am popular with the ladies, because I tell good stories."

Pierce laughed. He didn't believe Tariq. Bullet holes in the metal told a different story, that the Tuareg had commandeered the vehicle through force. These people were warriors, they protected their lands fiercely, and they took what they needed from anyone too weak to fight them.

"You can't have it, Pierce, if that is what you are thinking. You will drive it too fast and damage it."

Once the cameleers had tethered and watered the grunting pack animals, Tariq led Pierce to the largest tent. The fabric was dark goat hair, held high by poles and guy ropes. The inside was cooler, with carpets and cushions. The tent was separated into two areas, one for the men of the family and a smaller section to the back for the women.

"Father!" Tariq stepped forward and embraced the old

man seated on a cushion, drinking thick black coffee. He wore loose baggy pants and a blue turban. Although he covered all of his face except for his eyes, Pierce recognised him as Bachir Aghali. His distinctive grey irises locked onto Pierce and never blinked.

"*As-salamu alaykum.*"

"*Wa 'alaykum as-salam,*" responded Pierce.

The men embraced, kissed one another on the cheeks, as was custom.

"You have returned?" Bachir spoke Arabic, knowing Pierce understood the language better than he did French, the only other common tongue they shared.

"I have."

"Coffee?"

When Pierce nodded, Tariq poured cups for each of them. The three then sat together on cushions, ready to discuss matters.

Bachir spoke first. "I never know if I should expect to see you again, Mr. Pierce. Some days I think we will meet like today, you showing up from nowhere like a djinn." He gestured, as if to evoke an Arabic genie or a demon. "Other times I suspect you have been long dead, or that you have returned to America for good."

Pierce gave a short nod. "Ours is a strange world."

"It is. But what I know in my heart is, when you show your face, it is never a social call."

"True."

"You are here only because you believe my people can again aid your Western agendas of global domination."

Pierce said nothing. This caused Bachir to tense, a different man than he had worked with these last three months. The Tuareg leader wasn't speaking his mind, but Pierce needed to understand what motivated his ally.

"Am I wrong, Pierce?"

"No. I'm here for Kashif Shalgham."

"The so-called Sword of Allah? Saifullah?"

"The same. I'm here to kill him."

Bachir and Tariq laughed from their bellies.

The older man said, "*Insha'Allah*." *If God wills it.* "You are more of a fool than I thought, Pierce. You know who you are dealing with?"

"I know he is a man like anyone else. He bleeds like the rest of us."

"Maybe, but you have to find him to cut him. Do you know why he is so successful and has lived so long when many like him have not? Why he strikes terror into the hearts of everyone within a thousand kilometres of him?"

"Not me."

Tariq shuddered. His expression was the same as that of a man who had just escaped a violent death by luck alone.

Ignoring his son's moment of weakness, Bachir's intense grey eyes stared into Pierce. "He should scare you. If you really knew Shalgham, you would know what made him the inhuman monster he is today. Captain Shalgham was once an interrogator with the Libyan Army, which meant he was a torturer. He was very good at what he did. He got results fast. No surprise he soon came to Muammar Gaddafi's attention."

Pierce nodded. Gaddafi was as infamous as any dictator in modern history, ruling the North African country of Libya from the late 1960s to 2011, when he died after capture by rebels who shot him in the gut and impaled him through the anus with a bayonet. For forty years, Gaddafi had led a brutal regime that oppressed his people, murdered tens of thousands of dissidents, and exploited the country's natural resources. Gaddafi should have seen his demise coming, but megalomaniacs never did.

"By the late 2000s, Shalgham was Gaddafi's personal torturer. The position came with benefits, but also risks. When Shalgham refused to interrogate his own brother for plotting against the regime, Gaddafi executed Shalgham's oldest son. When Shalgham refused again, Gaddafi executed his second son and left the body for Shalgham to find, bound to a cross outside their home with his stomach cut open and his intestines spread across the dirt — his meat feeding mongrel dogs. Shalgham complied this time, brutally torturing his brother and killing him as ordered."

"That... explains a lot." Pierce now saw Shalgham differently than the mental image he had built up of his opponent these last months.

"Horror like that changes a man. When Gaddafi's regime collapsed and Libya descended into civil war, it was Shalgham who gave up Gaddafi's location to the rebels, shortly before Shalgham fled to Syria. If there was ever an aspect of Shalgham that was once human, it died in Libya. None of his family survived the civil war. He survived only by infecting the world with more brutality, threatening anyone who opposed him with the direst of bodily afflictions. That's why he joined Islamic State, changing his name to Saifullah, the Sword of Allah. Later he joined Ansar Dine, a group as barbaric as he is. He named himself after the ancient warrior Khalid ibn al-Walid, whom he admired."

"Wasn't al-Walid a general under Mohammad, during the seventh century?"

"Yes. It was under al-Walid's military leadership that Arabia was united under a single caliphate for the first time, and he is one of history's few generals who remained unde-feated in battle. Mohammad gave al-Walid the title the Sword of Allah, a title Shalgham now claims as his own."

"A high opinion of himself, then?"

"My problem, and your problem, is that he is very good at brutality. He terrifies everyone in the Adrar des Ifoghas. He should terrify you too."

"How do your people survive, then, if he is this ruthless?"

"*Insha'Allah*."

"*Insha'Allah*," Pierce responded, knowing this wasn't a real answer.

Again, Tariq shuddered.

Bachir nodded, acknowledging Pierce's sentiments, as his expression remained sombre. "Unfortunately, we rely on funds and weapons from the American and French govern-ments. Without your aid, Ansar Dine would overrun us. For survival, our tribes band together in larger, armed groups. We only travel as sizeable caravans, relying on safety in numbers of men and weapons."

"I encountered an Ansar Dine watch post on my way here," said Pierce. "Snipers murdering people fleeing these mountains hoping to reach the refugee camps."

"This is true," said Tariq, nodding. "Ansar Dine, like most fanatics, believe that they will one day achieve Islamic paradise on Earth. It starts with a caliphate, here, ruled under strict Sharia law. Caliphates require oppressed citi-zens if they are to prosper. People to enslave, rape, mutilate and murder. That is why they forbid anyone to leave the Adrar des Ifoghas. They can't afford to lose their slave class. And we can't afford to become their slaves."

"How do you deliver your salt to the southern markets, then?"

Tariq answered, "With great difficulty. We stockpile our salt, waiting for the opportune moment to risk the journey, but I fear that day will never come. I was not attempting to leave the mountains when you found me, rather we were transporting our stock to a new location where it will be more difficult for Ansar Dine to steal."

Pierce finished his coffee and nodded. "I can help. I can fix this."

"How?" Bachir asked, enraged. "I have one son left, Tariq. My other sons died fighting the self-proclaimed Sword of Allah. Ansar Dine's numbers are greater, their weapons more powerful, and their fighters more ruthless and fanatical. My people can't take any more losses. Pierce, we can't afford to help you anymore."

Pierce stared at the Tuareg leader. He saw what he had been missing. Bachir looked exhausted and defeated; old age was catching up with him. He had no fight left in him. "Then give me your intelligence. Information I can use to hunt Shalgham on my own."

"You are insane," blurted Bachir.

"Maybe. A few days ago, Ansar Dine insurgents brought several Western hostages into these mountains. They came in a truck. If I can find and rescue them, they should lead me to Saifullah. Your people must know where this truck is?"

Bachir's gaze lost its focus. "You are too late. The brutes would have killed the Westerners by now."

"Maybe... Maybe not... But you know of what I speak?"

"What exactly do *you* know, Pierce?" Tariq asked suspiciously. "We are a people on the brink of death. You can't ask any more of us!"

Pierce gritted his teeth, but saw no reason why he shouldn't share the intelligence he possessed. "One kidnapped man was not who the kidnappers thought he was. He was Victor Vautrin, an arms dealer. If you worry about the weapons Ansar Dine used against you in the past, they are nothing compared to the technological killing machines Vautrin is equipping your enemies with now. Weapons that will be used for the mass murder and enslavement of your people."

For the first time since their meeting, Bachir Aghali resembled his son Tariq, for he no longer masked his fear.

32

Tariq Aghali stared at Pierce in his confusion. He shuddered again. "You said Victor Vautrin?"

"You've heard of him?" Pierce asked, wondering how the young man knew of the arms trader.

Tariq shrugged. "During interrogation, captured Ansar Dine foot soldiers sometimes give up that name. My impression was that Vautrin supplies Ansar Dine with surplus small arms left over from the Libyan revolution — and Russian Kalashnikov knock-offs." He motioned to Pierce's AK-47 strapped to his back.

Pierce nodded. No less than seventy-five million AK-47s were in use across the world. They accounted for a significant proportion of the hundreds of thousands of human war-related deaths recorded each year. His weapon could have originated from anywhere, but it seemed likely his Russian assault rifle had entered Mali through Victor Vautrin's smuggling routes.

Firing a 7.62mm round, the AK used heavier bullets than British and American standard 5.56mm rounds, making the

AK a deadlier weapon than the MI6 and M4 carbine, which were more accurate weapons over longer distances. AKs sacrificed precision for stopping power.

Their simple design, minimal moving parts, reduced recoil, and their ability to function in the harshest environments made them popular weapons. Over twenty countries manufactured them, and fifty standing armies armed their soldiers with Kalashnikovs, making them common and accessible.

Pierce preferred the AK-47 for many reasons but mostly because he didn't stand out with one strapped across his back.

He poured himself another coffee. "Vautrin will arm your enemies with far more than Kalashnikovs."

The father shook his head. "I know this."

"Then help me."

"If I knew where the kidnappers' truck was, Pierce, I would take you there myself. But this is the Adrar des Ifoghas. A vast mountainous range that covers a quarter of a million square kilometres of inaccessible terrain. There is good reason Ansar Dine and al-Qaeda hide here. Even if you searched for a thousand years, you would not stumble upon the truck."

"I have to try."

"And I will not risk the lives of my people on this pointless quest."

Pierce didn't disagree. The mountains covered a larger area than the state of Colorado or the country of France. He would never find the truck on his own, but he needed to. It was his only lead.

"Then sell me your Land Rover Defender. I have ten thousand U.S. dollars. I'll pay you for it right now. I'll search for the kidnappers myself, and with the vehicle, I'll cover more ground faster." He studied Bachir and the son to sense their willingness to aid him. The younger man looked uncomfortable and agitated. "What is it you're not telling me, Tariq?"

The son hesitated. "I don't want to tell you, but I know where the truck is. Or at least where it was headed."

"You do? Where?"

He shook his head. "Our salt caravan spotted the truck from a distance."

"You didn't converse with them?"

"They stayed far from us, and they might have been insurgents. We left each other alone. Where it was headed, it's not an easy place to reach or find."

"But you can show me?"

He nodded and paused a long moment before he said, "I... can."

"Then show me."

"But the dangers!" Bachir spoke with a quiver in his tone.

Tariq's voice became raised. "I am not afraid. If you must go, Pierce, I will take you there, in *my* Land Rover so we can race across the desert together as you suggested. I do not wish to sell that beast."

"No!" Bachir interrupted. "I will not lose you, my last son."

Tariq gripped the old man's shoulders. "Father, trust me on this. Trust Pierce. I believe that Pierce is a fool as much as you do. But, unfortunately, he is correct. More weapons in the enemy's hands won't bring peace, just misery. For everyone."

Bachir trembled in his fury. "Send someone else."

Tariq shook his head. "It is not our way to ask our people

to take risks we are not willing to take ourselves. It has to be me."

Tariq's noble bravery surprised Pierce. The young man had never talked like this before. He always presented reasons why plans wouldn't work.

The old man seemed to shrink and lose his vibrancy. "You will go no matter what I say, Tariq, and ignore the wisdom of your father. This makes me sad." He turned to Pierce. "If I can't convince my last surviving son to remain by his father's side, you, Pierce, must promise no harm comes to him. When you find the truck, you send my son back to me!"

Pierce nodded. "If I can." His mission was to terminate both Vautrin and Shalgham with extreme prejudice. By joining Pierce, the young Tuareg was committing himself to fighting at Pierce's side until the mission concluded or Pierce was dead, for there was no easy means to return Tariq if Pierce were to retain the Defender as he planned. While Tariq was a natural fighter, he shied away from battles when the odds were against him. He could as easily become a liability as an ally, but Pierce now had no choice but to keep him by his side wherever his mission led him. "Do we have a deal?"

Bachir nodded. "I'm grateful for the help you provide my tribe, Pierce, but I fear my people bear the cost; they are paying with their lives."

"I don't disagree, but if good people don't fight when called up, the bad people keep winning."

Tariq spoke before his father could. "We will aid you in any way we can."

The old man frowned. Perhaps he too detected Tariq's unusual bravery.

Pierce said, "One more request, Bachir. I need to borrow a satellite phone. I need to report in."

Bachir shook his head. "No phones here. You Americans track them, then send drones to kill the users, thinking only terrorists in our country need to communicate with the outside world."

Pierce turned to Tariq. "What about you?"

The young man shook his head. "I'm sorry, Pierce. No phone either."

The two men shared a moment. Pierce suspected one, or both, had lied. For reasons not yet obvious, they must have a satellite phone but were keeping it secret. Pierce would search for it later. Mackenzie and Walsh would have to wait a little longer before he reported in.

"More coffee, Pierce?"

Pierce nodded, but then he heard men outside arguing in Arabic and Tamashek.

A woman screamed.

Pierce raced from the tent, not caring if Bachir or Tariq Aghali followed.

Several men dragged a young woman into the light cast by a campfire and threw her hard onto the dust. She fell supine before Bachir and Tariq, now standing next to Pierce. Her hair, thick with corkscrew curls, hung over her face. Her skin was a deep brown. Her dirt-stained cotton pants and purple and blue patterned shirt had many rips and tears. She looked up at Pierce, and he saw the bruises encircling her eyes and a split dividing her bleeding lip. His blood boiled witnessing the impact of the assaults these men had inflicted.

The group's leader stepped forward. He wore the same white robes and blue turban of his people, the Tuareg, and an AK-47 was slung over his right shoulder. His right hand held a large, jagged stone. "She is a witch!" he bellowed in Arabic, raising the rock high over the terrified woman.

"You're joking." Pierce locked onto the men's stares, sensing their fear and aggression. "Tell me you don't believe that... do you?" He knew superstitions were prevalent in the customs of these people, but even he felt surprised at how vehemently they seemed to believe this woman could be a witch. It resembled a surreal scenario dreamed up from the European Middle Ages.

The circle of men shrank.

Without conscious thought, Pierce's hand reached for his Glock, but he did not draw it. He sensed their anger, and he didn't wish to provoke a violent confrontation.

The woman sobbed but otherwise lay where she had fallen. Pierce turned to Bachir and Tariq, hoping they would defuse the situation, but both men remained stoic. Pierce turned again and eyeballed the man holding the stone. "Friend, put it down, now!" Pierce kept his voice level and even. This had the desired effect, for the man relaxed and stepped backward.

Then the woman spasmed like a high-voltage electrical shock was racing through her body. Her mouth foamed with spit, and her eyes rolled into the back of her head.

The man cried and raised the stone and readied himself to hit her with it.

The crowd behind him responded with cries and shouts in Arabic and Tamashek, encouraging him on, accusing the woman of witchcraft. She had cursed them all.

Pierce stepped forward, straddling the woman, protecting her while she thrashed in the sand in a seizure. He drew his Glock and fired a single shot into the sky.

The crowd drew back.

"She has epilepsy! Not witchcraft!"

Tariq and the men regained their senses and raised their weapons at Pierce.

"The first man who tries to harm her dies!" Pierce said without emotion despite the number of guns directed at him. His eyes locked on the stone-carrying man. The barrel of his 9mm pistol lined up on the soft spot of skin between his eyebrows. "That means you."

No one moved. No one lowered their weapon.

Pierce would shoot any man who threatened the suffering woman. He wouldn't be able to stop himself. He might incapacitate one, maybe two warriors, but that would be all. If he fought back, as he knew he must, they would spray him with heavy 7.62mm rounds, and he'd be dead before his body hit the ground.

33

SAHARA, MALI

The trek through the rugged Saharan mountains was a torturous ordeal. The daytime sun burned Oumar's bruised and battered skin. His mouth felt parched, and his head ached. He begged for water, which the insurgents rarely shared. Headaches progressed to exhaustion and dizzy spells, yet he forced himself to march with the camel caravan. If he fell behind, the insurgents would abandon him, and he would die alone of dehydration.

Lucas became less communicative as the day progressed. By afternoon his eyes lost their focus. By nightfall his fever had progressed to violent shaking, and Oumar couldn't get any sensible response from the man. A few hours after sunset when they had passed back into the flat desert, Lucas toppled from his camel onto the dry, compacted earth. He didn't move, just lay in the dust where he had fallen.

Desperate for water, Oumar fumbled for Lucas's water bottle. His teeth removed the plug; then he guzzled. In the starlight he hoped no one saw. By the time the first Ansar Dine insurgents rode close enough to shine a torch at

Oumar, he'd drained the bottle and positioned it over Lucas's mouth, pretending to hydrate the dying Frenchman.

"There was nothing left. He drank it all."

The insurgent stared at Oumar, then called for Shalgham.

The giant rode from the head of the caravan, pulled his camel to a stop and leaped off the beast. He pushed Oumar from his path, then bent to examine the prostrate Frenchman. "The fool finally died."

"He's not dead," Oumar said, overcome with guilt for not hydrating Lucas even though the Frenchman had no long-term interest in Oumar's well-being. "He is unconscious and very sick."

Shalgham pulled a semi-automatic pistol from his belt and fired a single shot into the man's face, which exploded in a shower of red gore. The noise was sudden and loud, hurting Oumar's ears. "No arguing now."

Oumar stood. He couldn't take his eyes off the shattered corpse. He forced himself to speak even though his facial muscles felt numb. "But he was your ally?"

Saifullah laughed. "I only need one Vautrin ally. His sister."

Trembling, Oumar feared for his own life. With Lucas gone, what reason did they have to keep him alive?

Shalgham searched through a saddlebag, using a flashlight to see.

Oumar noticed a first aid kit and antibiotics. "You had medicine that could have saved him?"

The giant froze. Then he turned and stared unblinking at Oumar, rage in his eyes.

"You didn't want Lucas to tell his sister about the

money?" Oumar realised. "Did you? You wanted him to die before we found her, so you wouldn't have to share?"

Shalgham laughed. "I thought you'd be more amusing, with no hands." He turned to the Ansar Dine fighters, all of them watching stone-faced from their camels. "I am no longer amused. Leave the cripple behind. The desert can claim him."

Shalgham climbed onto his camel, turned the head of the grunting beast with a pull of its reins, and kicked it until it marched again. He never looked back, condemning Oumar to his fate.

The Ansar Dine cameleers also ignored Oumar or stared with disgust, then disappeared into the night.

Oumar had briefly thought to argue or to beg for his life. But in an uncharacteristic shift in personality, he was too proud. These men were monsters. His brother and Farid were no better. Each in their own way had dominated him, abused him and taken advantage of his disability, and where had it gotten him?

Nowhere.

If he were to die, so be it. But if he survived, it would be through his own making. Hands or not, he *would* find his own path to salvation, or die trying. Only his own actions would determine the course of his life now.

34

AGADEZ, NIGER

Back at AB 201, Summerfield hid in an equipment store because she didn't want anyone to see her cry. Idris Walsh had rattled her, not with his interrogation and threats, but because he had revealed knowledge of the terrible details of her imprisonment in that remote Greek island villa. He'd forced her to relive the life-shattering seconds, minutes and days she'd spent years repressing.

Hiding was difficult in any military base because there were never opportunities to be alone. The operating intelligence centre, where she spent twelve hours each day, worked on a roster of around-the-clock shifts. Crammed bunkrooms with women sleeping, reading, exercising or cleaning their guns offered no personal space. Showers were communal, and the toilets didn't have doors that locked. And so, after struggling through the four and a half hours of her remaining shift in the OIC, still with no word from Pierce, she found an equipment store with spare uniforms, blankets and bedding, where she curled up in a corner and sobbed.

Her mind returned to where Walsh had taken her against her will: to her second mission with Mark Pierce and the first with the charming, handsome and utterly despicable Michael Abraham.

From their safe house on the party island of Mykonos, their mission was to observe a sleeper cell of al-Qaeda insurgents preparing to detonate a bomb at one of the many popular nightclubs.

Mark Pierce was the blunt instrument, the Ground Branch paramilitary operator responsible for direct action against the cell. Orders from CIA Headquarters in Langley, Virginia, dictated he act only when the insurgents received their explosives, which according to their information had not yet arrived on the island. Summerfield ran tactical operations and inventory and provided operational intelligence. Abraham was fresh from training and there to learn from two experienced operatives.

The mission turned sour the moment Abraham and Mark didn't get along.

At the time Summerfield believed Mark was the problem. She hadn't known Mark back then, and she didn't understand why he questioned Abraham's every action, berating him for sloppy tradecraft and challenging his skills as a field operative. Admittedly Abraham had only recently joined the agency and was prone to making rookie mistakes, but he didn't seem too bad in her eyes. She thought Mark had been too hard on him.

During a routine surveillance operation, al-Qaeda identified Abraham as shadowing them. A shoot-out followed, with two al-Qaeda dead and Summerfield with a bullet wound in her shoulder. A frantic escape in a stolen Mini Cooper saved their lives.

Back in the safe house, after Mark treated Summerfield's wound, he went hunting. With their covers blown, there was no chance al-Qaeda would receive their explosives. There would be no higher-ranking terrorists to identify and capture during the swap meet. Pierce sought to kill every insurgent still on the island before being ordered to return to Langley. He disappeared for three days.

That left Summerfield and Abraham alone together.

In time, Summerfield might have accepted the enemy sexually assaulting her, but not her own people...

Months of training should have prepared Abraham for the adrenalin come-down experienced after the shock of a violent confrontation. Instead, he lost his mind. First, he claimed it wasn't his fault the mission was botched. Later it was Summerfield's fault, then Mark's for being too controlling.

He sought Summerfield's reassurance, then her physical touch by always finding reasons to touch her himself. When that wasn't enough, she grew uncomfortable with his needy demands. She told him to stay away and get his emotions under control.

That had been the wrong approach.

Some men just couldn't take rejection.

Summerfield couldn't fight back with her arm bandaged and the painkillers numbing her senses. Abraham had beaten her, torn away her clothes and dragged her into the basement. He raped her and then locked her in the dark cell.

She'd clawed at the door for a splintered slither of wood, ready to stab the depraved operative when he next returned. But his next appearance surprised her. He didn't enter. Instead, he waited outside, talked for hours through the bolted door, apologising, telling her he was wrong, and acknowledging it was an awful mistake he would never make again. He promised that if she kept his "indiscretion" just between them, he would set her free.

Too scared to answer, she curled into a corner, hugging her arms around her trembling body, with the splintered wood tightly gripped, waiting for him to open the door.

For two days Abraham came and went but never tried to enter. Sometimes he would talk through the door like nothing depraved had happened. Other times he sobbed. More often he raged at her, blamed Summerfield for not comforting him when he needed it.

In her more lucid moments, she tried to understand how the CIA had missed Abraham's unstable tendencies. He would have completed many psychological assessments, but she knew no system was perfect. Abraham had seemed normal and stable enough... until the enemy had almost killed him.

Only Mark had seen Abraham for what he was from the beginning, a man unsuitable for field operations.

For two days she barely moved. She slept for only a few minutes at a time, couldn't eat and drank only from the water bottle Abraham had left her when her throat became parched.

When Mark returned, it was during one of Abraham's rages. She heard a fist fight and furniture breaking, which ended with one man collapsing on the ground and not getting up again. She had shuddered when Mark forced open her door, not knowing she was inside. He'd kept his distance while he explained that he would deal with every-thing. She would be okay now, and none of this was her fault. No one would hurt her again.

He returned to Abraham. She thought Mark must have

bound or otherwise restrained him because their spoken words seemed more civilised. She remembered Abraham arguing with Mark, insisting none of this was his fault. It was "her" fault, then Mark's fault. It was everyone else's fault except his.

That conversation ended with the "cough" of a suppressed pistol firing once.

Pierce returned with a blanket, took her upstairs and ran a bath. She didn't care that she was naked before him, but she couldn't bear his touch. She washed her dirty, soiled skin, then soaked in the warming waters while Mark disposed of the body.

Her own people had done this to her.

An American college graduate, educated and from a well-off family.

Summerfield soaked in the bath for hours, only climbing out when Mark helped her. In her mind she wanted him to dry her, but she couldn't bear the thought of anyone touching or looking at her ever again. She dried off alone and crawled under the covers of her bed, not rising until well into the next day.

Mark had to dress her, because of her near-catatonic state, despite how horrible it made her feel. He'd kept saying it was not her fault, never her fault. She was glad now, because while his words had been like chalk scraping on a blackboard at the time, the memory had stuck, and his words helped centre her later in moments of distress.

Pierce purchased a small fishing boat, which he used to get them to the next island. The lapping waves had a calming effect, and her mind cleared. They talked about the ordeal. Summerfield insisted that no one could know what had happened. She concocted a story that al-Qaeda had attacked her and Abraham in the safe house, killing the CIA man. She couldn't bear people knowing that an American intelligence officer had raped her.

Mark kept his promise.

For three and a half years, they kept their secret. She trusted Mark more than anyone, and he had proved again and again his loyalty to her...

So how did Walsh know?

The Head of Operations, North Africa had dragged those days from her repressed subconscious where she had locked them away. Buried memories had allowed her to maintain, at least on the surface, a normal life and career despite feeling scared all the time. The trauma forced her to give up field-work, but she could operate again as an analyst. Running the Trigger Man was the ideal compromise between both roles.

But not now. Walsh had sent her scampering to a store, neutralising her capabilities as an intelligence analyst and threatening her very career with the CIA. He must have known she would react this way. Walsh was too experienced an operative to believe he wouldn't tear open old scars.

She hadn't let slip to anyone what had really happened in Mykonos, and she didn't believe Mark had either.

So, who had?

The equipment store door burst open, breaking into her thoughts.

Two young soldiers, each out of breath, raced inside and slammed the door shut behind them. The male soldier forced his companion up against the wall, where she squealed in delight. Their mouths entwined in a wet kiss as he pulled at her uniform, opening it so he could seek delight in the curve of her breasts.

Summerfield stood and ran for the door. They displayed

no embarrassment and laughed as she exited. Embarrassment should have been theirs, not hers.

Outside, under the starlit skies, Summerfield hurried. She wiped tears from her hot eyes. She had to compose herself before someone asked if something was wrong.

Then, as she marched through the night, it hit her.

Which man had tried to claim her in Greece?

The culprit who had informed Walsh of those awful days had to be Abraham himself.

35

Pierce aimed his Glock 9mm at the accuser's chest. A dozen more Tuareg warriors behind the accuser glared at him with murderous eyes, all of them prepared to pepper his flesh with AK-47 rounds. What stopped them was Pierce's steady hand. They knew he would at best kill one of them before they shot him dead, but that was still one man less in their camp to protect them from Ansar Dine.

"What's your plan, Tariq?" Pierce called to the young man behind him. "Allow this to end in bloodshed?"

Tariq stepped past Pierce and the convulsing woman to speak with the men in Tamashek. The Tuareg argued and displayed no respect for the young man. Only when Bachir Aghali stepped forward and argued with his son did their combined words have a calming effect. The men lowered their weapons, spat on the woman, and walked away.

Only then did Pierce lower his weapon.

"They agreed not to kill you both." Bachir cast his eyes at Pierce and the woman. "But only if you leave now."

"Fine with me." Pierce holstered his weapon and crouched by the woman. He realised he was furious, but this moment was not about him. The woman's convulsions had ceased, and her erratic movements had slowed. Spit dribbled from her mouth. Her eyes were wide and once again aware of her surroundings. Pierce gently lifted her in his arms and carried her to the Land Rover Defender.

"Keys," he demanded when he laid the woman on the back seat.

Tariq shook his head.

Pierce stared down the young man until he glanced away. He gripped Tariq by the arm, startling him. "I'm going after Shalgham, with or without you."

"Give him the keys," Bachir interrupted. "And go with him."

Tariq's face contorted and made him ugly, as if he had no ability to express the many emotions overwhelming him.

"Don't look at me like that. The American is right. While Saifullah lives, none of us are safe."

Pierce held out his hand, palm open.

Tariq snarled as he placed the keys in Pierce's grip.

"Time to go."

After checking the vehicle had enough water and spare gas, Pierce climbed up behind the wheel and fired up the ignition. Tariq got in beside him, and Pierce drove off fast, churning gravel and dust, giving a final wave to Bachir before the night swallowed him.

After driving for an hour and convinced no one was following them, Pierce stopped, pocketed the keys and stepped out. He went to the back seat while opening his canteen of water. The young Malian woman was awake, her eyes wide with fear and her body rigid with tension.

"You speak French?" When she didn't understand, he switched languages. "You speak Arabic?"

She sat and nodded, then wrapped her arms about her. Bruises covered her bare arms and face. Cuts and scratches were many, while rope burns showed around her neck and wrists.

"Men kidnapped you four days ago. Right?"

She nodded again.

He offered her the water. "You're safe now. I promise I won't let any more harm come to you."

She drank quickly. "Who... who are you? American?"

"Yes. This is a rescue mission. Where are the others?"

The woman's head shook. She looked away.

Pierce's heart fluttered. "Only you survived?"

"The others..." She shuddered at the memory. "The others... didn't make it."

"Do you have a name?"

"Awa. Awa Sissoko."

Pierce nodded and smiled. "That's a cool name. I'm Mark. Mark Pierce. And my friend here is Tariq Aghali."

The Tuareg man nodded and slinked away.

Pierce grinned. "Don't worry about him. He's sulking, but he'll get over it. Let's talk about you. Are you hurt? Hungry? Thirsty—?"

"Tired. What happened to the men who...?"

"Thought you were a witch?"

She cringed.

"You have epilepsy?"

"That must disgust you?"

He shook his head. "I'm not bothered about it."

"Are you sure? Most people are."

Pierce held out his left hand. It trembled slightly and was

only noticeable when he paid attention to it. "It's not the same, but I empathise. No one understands my affliction either."

"What do you have?"

Pierce shrugged. "I'm afraid to find out."

She almost smiled. Pierce was getting through to her.

"I need your help, Awa. I must ask some difficult questions, many of which might dredge up memories you may not want to remember. But I need to know where the other prisoners can be found, so we can recover their bodies. Then I need to find the people responsible, stop them from doing this again."

"You will kill them?"

He hesitated before answering. Few civilians coped with that aspect of his work when he was forced to explain his particular method of solving the world's problems. "If I have to."

She shook her head. "You need not kill any of them. They are already dead. The only kidnapper who survived saved my life. He is a good man. He doesn't deserve to die."

"What makes you say that?"

Awa described Oumar's disability and how Jali and Farid had manipulated him, and Oumar's efforts to save Awa during their ordeal. "We must save him if we can."

"Sounds reasonable, but that means finding Oumar first." Pierce considered his next steps, whether the safest course of action was to drive through the night or rest here until morning. "Tariq?"

"What now?"

"Your men. Will they come after us, in a second attempt away from your father, to punish Awa as a witch?"

Tariq shook his head. "Not tonight."

"Good, then we'll make camp."

"Good, then I'll light a fire."

"No fire. We sleep in the car. Take it in turns while the other keeps guard—"

"But I just said my men won't come?"

"No, but Ansar Dine might. A fire will draw them straight to us."

"They wouldn't dare come this close to our camp."

"We don't know that." Pierce turned to Awa, concerned for her well-being. "You okay with the plan?"

She nodded. As he turned, her hand gripped his arm. "Don't leave me. Please." Her eyes glanced at Tariq.

Sensing her fear, Pierce nodded. "I'll keep you in sight at all times."

"Thank you. You'll keep your promise, Mr. Pierce?"

He grinned and nodded. "Even if it kills me."

"Don't say it like that, but thank you."

Keeping his distance, Tariq unslung his AK-47 and began cleaning it. "I don't like this plan. I don't like that you've brought her along."

"You don't have to like it, my friend, you just have to abide by it." Pierce took Tariq's assault rifle before he could disassemble it and pulled back on the slide, chambering a round ready for action. "I'll take the first shift. And in the morning, you'll take me to the truck."

Tariq stared into the still blackness of the night.

Pierce still sensed the young man withheld critical information regarding their current situation, but what that might be or why he kept his silence, Pierce did not understand. His instincts mirrored Awa's, for he didn't completely trust Tariq to be alone with the nurse.

"You understood what I said?"

"Fine."

Pierce looked to Awa. She had curled up on the back seat of the Defender and was already asleep. "Tariq, you sleep in the front."

"Why?"

Pierce could give a dozen reasons, but he was in no mood to explain any of them. "Get some sleep, Tariq. Everything will look better in the morning."

36

Tariq snored like a rutting pig.

Frequently Pierce wanted to wake him, to stop the snoring and change watch, but he never acted on these impulses. He didn't trust Tariq would be diligent enough to protect them. Better no sleep than to never wake again.

Years of operating in special forces teams had trained Pierce to forgo sleep for days at a time, so one night without rest was manageable. He kept his eyes on the horizon, watching for any group that might approach. Anyone encountered this deep in the Sahara he would treat as a hostile. Any movement, therefore, was a threat.

Later, when the moon rose, visibility improved. Pierce drank cold coffee from a flask found in the Defender. He considered sitting, but chose not to. If he did, he might fall asleep. His eyes were sore and his head foggy. That was one of the side effects of his tremors, a reduced ability to operate for long periods without rest. He could still operate for days without sleep, but not as well as he had a year ago. Perhaps he would catch a few moments of sleep tomorrow while Tariq drove.

Around 03:00 hours he heard movement within the cabin. A minute later Awa Sissoko stepped outside. She wrapped a blanket around her against the cool air and approached.

"How are you feeling?" Pierce asked.

"Better." Her hands touched her corkscrew curls. She was an attractive woman, with sensual lips and a tall slim body that moved with a graceful fluency. Her eyes were the same rich brown as her skin. They blinked less often than Pierce expected and seemed to notice the detail in everything around her. "I can't remember if I thanked you before."

"For what?"

She laughed. "For saving my life."

"Oh, that. I think you did most of your 'life saving' yourself."

Awa looked ready to say more, but also lost as where to begin.

"Let me tell you what I know," said Pierce. "Two insurgents snatched you and four Westerners off the streets of Timbuktu and drove you north into the desert against your will. Somewhere along the way they came across eleven million dollars."

"How do you know all this?"

"I'm with the American military. Our people have been working on a rescue plan."

She looked away. "You're too late..."

"You said that. What happened to the others?"

Awa hugged her arms tighter. "Jacqui died a few nights ago, choked to death. Isoline, the priest and Jali..." She shuddered, reliving the memory as tears flowed from her eyes. "They crucified and disembowelled them. It was horrific."

"I'm sure it was. Can I ask, how did you escape?"

Awa retold her story, adding further detail on how Farid had tried to rape her and how another kidnapper, Oumar — the man without hands — had saved her life. She had watched from a hidden vantage point in the mountains as Ansar Dine fanatics murdered the Westerners and Oumar's brother, the killing blows delivered by a giant with a curved sword. They spared one man, a young Frenchman called Lucas, who seemed in allegiance with the killers. They took Oumar as their prisoner. Awa had fled after the killers, Lucas and Oumar rode off on their camels.

"Afterwards I returned to the waterhole and waited. I didn't know what to do. I couldn't bear being around the dead, but if I left the waterhole, I knew I would die of thirst. I waited until the Tuareg found me. I asked them to take me to Timbuktu, but they only laughed. It was then I discovered that I had lost my epilepsy medication. I had a seizure, so they beat me, accused me of being a witch. I begged for mercy, but they said only their leader could grant me that wish. They took me to their camp, where I had another seizure. That was when you found me. You know more about what happened after that than I do."

Pierce digested her story as he rubbed his eyes and tried not to yawn. Not because her tale bored him, but because exhaustion was catching up with him.

"You're tired?"

"I've hardly slept these last couple of days, but I'm okay."

She nodded and cast her eyes towards her feet.

Recalling the description of the journalist in the MINUS-

MA's super-base, Pierce asked, "Was this Lucas guy in his late twenties, handsome with a wiry but fit frame?"

"Yes, that's him."

Lucas was the name of Victor Vautrin's son, supposedly killed in the U.S. air strike in Afghanistan. Could it be the same man? Pierce wished he could contact Mackenzie Summerfield so she could compile the sketchy clues he kept discovering and piece them together into a plausible scenario.

"Awa, I'm sorry about what happened to you."

"Thank you, but it is not your fault."

"Regardless, you have my sympathies."

They both remained motionless, neither speaking. Pierce felt awkward, not sure what he could say that was comforting. Despite the support and space he had provided Mackenzie over the years since her assault, he knew from experience there was only so much he could do. Some wounds never healed, and with Awa it might be the same.

"What now?" she asked.

Pierce motioned to the Defender. "Tariq will take us to the bodies. I'll mark the location so my people can recover them..."

"And then what?"

"A helicopter will come, U.S. Air Force. They'll take you home to Timbuktu, or to Gao, at least, where we have a base. You'll receive medical attention and counselling if you want it."

He noticed she examined his hands. When he looked with her, they were shaking. He rubbed his palms together in an effort to hide his tremors.

"When do they occur?" she asked.

"What?"

She crunched her eyebrows. "I'm a theatre nurse, so I know a thing or two about medical conditions. I might be able to help you."

Pierce re-examined his shaking hands. The condition had worsened these last twelve months, and he had done nothing about it, avoiding medical professionals because he suspected they could do nothing for him. He also feared that if his official records noted this condition, someone might use it as a reason to dismiss him from active service.

"You've seen no one about it? Why not start with me?"

Pierce hesitated.

"Do you know the cause?"

"No... I've been too close to a few detonations in my time."

She took his hand in hers. Her skin was soft, and her touch reinvigorated him. "Can you control it when you focus?"

"Actually, it's more when I don't focus that I get it under control."

Awa looked up and grinned. "It's probably stress-related, Mr. Pierce. You can cure that."

"Mark."

"Sorry? What?"

"Call me Mark. That's my first name."

She tucked a loose curl behind an ear. "Very well, Mark. Have you been under much stress lately?"

He laughed.

"What is so funny?"

"It's kind of my job description."

"What exactly is your job?"

"Solving problems. Eliminating others."

"When was the last time you slept—"

"Yesterday—"

"I was about to say, when did you last sleep for seven hours or more straight?"

Pierce laughed again. "Never."

She rubbed the back of her slender neck. "Why don't you sleep now?"

He shook his head and stared out across the silent and still desert mountains. "I can't. I need to keep watch."

"For the terrorists?"

"Yes."

"What about your friend? Tariq?"

Pierce shrugged, not sure how he should articulate his concerns to a woman he didn't know.

"Let me keep watch?"

He adjusted the strap of the AK-47 over his shoulder, his only effective weapon against any threats they might encounter out in the still darkness. "That is not a good idea."

"Mark, I told you I'm a theatre nurse. I've stood for hours paying close attention to patients with their organs exposed and anaesthetics pumping through their bloodstreams. I'm always ready to respond to the doctor's needs. I'm trained to keep my attention focused. Besides, with epilepsy, it's not safe for me to drive, and I don't want you exhausted when you are behind the wheel tomorrow."

Pierce felt tired, more than he should, given his training. He'd turned thirty towards the end of the year, not old by any measure, but his body had taken a beating and endured all kinds of stress and trauma for the last fourteen years. He needed a break, even if that was a single good night's rest. His body needed time to heal, physically and mentally, and Awa's offer was tempting...

"You don't believe I can do it?"

"I do, Awa. I..."

"Don't trust easily?"

Pierce nodded.

Awa laughed. "Would it help if I said I don't trust easily either?"

He rubbed his eyes again. He felt weak, that he was giving in. "Yes..."

"Rest against the car's tyre. Hold on to your gun. If anything worries me, I'll wake you straight away."

After a moment of deliberation, he nodded, figuring he was no good to anyone fatigued. "Okay. Thank you." He gave her his binoculars and sat as she suggested against the front wheel of the Defender. He wasn't concerned that Tariq would drive off without them. Pierce had the keys and had removed critical elements of the ignition, which he kept in his pocket. He still didn't understand why he didn't trust Tariq, but he was too exhausted to think upon it now, so it was a problem for the morning.

"Mark, get some rest."

He closed his eyes, his arms gripping the assault rifle in his lap, and within seconds he was asleep.

37

AGADEZ, NIGER

When Summerfield had a hunch, very little stopped her from finding the answers she sought.

The next morning, she was back in the operations intelligence centre, working alongside her co-workers, who had always ignored her. She logged in and commenced her investigation into the Mykonos mission from three and a half years ago. Summerfield didn't care that Idris Walsh might check her logs. She wanted him to know.

First Summerfield accessed the NSA Communications Database, a vast metadata repository of trillions of phone conversations, searchable by phone number, location, device model, carrier, calls and known user identifiers.

She pinpointed the exact longitudinal and latitudinal coordinates of the Mykonos safe house, narrowed her date ranges to commence when Pierce had left and ending with his return from hunting al-Qaeda, and searched within those parameters. The exact time and location when and where Michael Abraham had destroyed her.

The metadata of a single call blinked back at her. Duration: twenty-seven minutes, fourteen seconds.

The receiver had answered from an unregistered phone in Boston, Massachusetts. The location was the Carlyle Lodge, an antiquated gentleman's club where old men enjoyed whiskey, cigars, gambling and spending time with other old men. Summerfield sensed she was onto a promising lead. Boston was Idris Walsh's hometown, or so it said in the parts of his personnel file she had access to.

She next checked Walsh's known cell numbers. One of those numbers exactly matched the cell phone that had taken the call from Abraham inside the Carlyle Lodge, and that cell phone had been in the exact location of a phone registered to Idris Walsh. Walsh had carried two phones that day, one registered with CIA and one that was a burner phone, used for clandestine, off-the-books contacts.

Abraham must have confessed his crime to his mentor.

As soon as the call had ended, the burner phone had been shut down and deactivated.

Her suspicions had been correct. This must be how Walsh knew.

Summerfield checked the logs on Walsh's CIA-registered cell phone across the following weeks. Walsh made no further calls on his registered phone until the following day, and that was only to his sister in Italy.

Had Walsh, disgusted by Abraham's crime, refused to help him? It seemed likely, but it also seemed he had done nothing to help Summerfield either, just left her to her fate.

Her hands tightened. Her teeth clenched. She had trouble processing his callousness, that Walsh had kept silent for all this time. Conversely, he must have known

Mark or Summerfield had killed Abraham, and had never sought retribution.

The spymaster was playing a complex game with a long-term agenda that Summerfield could not understand, but she knew it must also involve the missing money. None of his actions made any sense. No agenda was obvious.

Why unsettle her now, when he could have so many times in the past?

Her skin prickled.

She twisted, expecting Walsh to have been standing behind her, watching her every keystroke.

No one stood behind her.

Summerfield shut down her workstation and fled the operations centre.

She felt many eyes watching her, but they could have been figments of her imagination.

What felt much more real was the notion that Walsh was herding Mark and her into a trap.

38

SAHARA, MALI

Sergeant Jean Denault stood alone in the desert as he watched the distant caravan of camels materialise amid the hazy horizon. Spied through Steiner 210 10x50 tactical binoculars, he counted a dozen camels, most with Ansar Dine riders in black turbans and slung AK-47s. Kashif Shalgham, the infamous Sword of Allah, was recognisable because of his huge height and the curved scimitar strapped across his back. The megalomaniac considered himself a Saracen warrior, defender of holy Islamic lands whose purpose it was to fight against the evil Christian, Jew-loving invaders. Denault also knew that Shalgham's reputation was a front, for he enjoyed his wine, women and modern Western luxuries. He was a fanatic of convenience only.

Denault considered if he himself better fit the profile of a modern-day Crusader.

He was certainly a warrior; he was trained in combat and had fought many bloody battles. He had journeyed far across the world to fight Islamic Jihadists, who believed the dogma of their ancient religion could remain relevant in a world dominated by capitalism, science and technology.

The contra-argument was that Denault didn't believe in any god, as Crusaders once had. He didn't believe he was an honourable man either and had never followed a chivalrous code. If he was honest with himself, he was a real "badass motherfucker". He'd killed his fair share of men and women and, dare he even admit it, children too. If hell existed, then it was his ticket in the afterlife, he had no doubts about that. He wondered how many deluded Crusaders waited for him in damnation.

Lowering his binoculars, Denault adjusted the FAMAS assault rifle slung under his right arm and checked again that the magazine was full and that he carried plenty of spares clipped to his combat vest. Not that he planned on a battle; Ansar Dine and Hanna Vautrin were in partnership, but insurgents were crazy fucks, and sometimes it required a long cold stare into the business end of a high-tech assault rifle to keep them civilised. Denault laughed. He supposed the FAMAS was his equivalent of a broadsword.

Ten minutes passed.

The caravan didn't seem to get any closer.

Denault observed them again through his tactical binoculars. The dumb camels plodded slowly through the flat sand, one ugly foot after another. The group didn't seem much larger than last time he looked.

Earlier, when Shalgham had not shown up at the agreed meeting time, Hanna had sent Denault into the desert to search for the crazy giant and his volunteers. She'd concluded they might not find the hidden UN vehicles unassisted, even though she had provided Saifullah with their GPS location. Tardiness had forced Denault to wait in the baking forty-five-degree-Celsius heat, guzzling litres of water and wondering why he hadn't pissed all day.

He looked for Hanna's pretty-boy brother, Lucas, in the crowd, but didn't see him. Denault supposed the rich kid wore a turban and robes like the rest. Once the group came closer, he'd confirm if Ansar Dine had rescued the idiot as promised.

Denault reflected on how he had ended up wet-nursing a bunch of uneducated fanatics in the middle of the world's ugliest desert. He supposed it had started long ago, before he even knew there was a hellhole called the Sahara. When he himself was an uneducated fanatic, whose ideology was drug dealing and its promise of wealth and power if he ever hit the big time.

Orphaned when his drunk father stepped in front of a truck, there had never been a mother he remembered, so he was alone from age ten. Years in foster homes and shelters across Nice had taught Denault that nobody gave a fuck about him. Low test results at school would not bode well for future job prospects, and selling drugs to other kids was his only means of making money to survive. He proved to be a cunning fighter, scaring other kids with his vicious retaliations against anyone who challenged him. Several boys ended up in the hospital because of his punches, kicks, bites and breaking of limbs. Prowess positioned him well, as a prominent drug pusher in his badass neighbourhood.

This strategy worked for a time, until most of his friends ended up overdosing or in prison. He figured he'd face the same fate soon enough if he didn't take action and change his fortunes.

At seventeen, he completed school despite his best intentions not to, and realised he was at a crossroads. Without a plan, he knew he'd be dead in a few years, shot by the police or stabbed by an inmate when the authorities finally locked him away. He'd never taken hard drugs himself. His highs came from beating people to near death or until their bones broke and blood gushed from their orifices. His was a high he would never overdose on. Denault figured his best solution was a career that paid him to pursue his drug; therefore, his future prospects lay with the military.

On his eighteenth birthday he applied for basic training with the French Foreign Legion, who quickly recruited him.

The next eleven years of his life were better than anything he'd ever experienced. Denault excelled at fitness, weapon training and ordering lesser ranks into action. He travelled the world, killing dumb-ass insurgents, enemy combatants and rebels across North Africa, Latin America and the Middle East. He enjoyed living in the world's shit-holes, where he was anonymous and could pay prostitutes to pleasure him in every imagined coupling, then disappear never to see them again.

His downfall occurred when he returned to the Legion's Quartier Captaine Danjou in the south of France, where he was to deliver basic training to new recruits. He enjoyed pushing the men and women, seeing whom he could break physically and mentally, but he had forgotten that proximity to the powers in charge meant that he was under close observation. After he'd killed his third recruit in three months, the Legion dishonourably discharged him.

Denault disappeared into Asia, settling into Ho Chi Minh City, Vietnam. After blowing his savings on gambling and prostitutes, he took up contract work with Russian, Chinese and local criminal groups smuggling guns. In his personal time, he took part in cage fights, never losing against an opponent. He soon came to the attention of one foxy yet ice-cold Hanna Vautrin. Denault proved his worth, opening up supply routes to various Asian buyers, including questionable but cashed-up insurgents and criminals. He also proved himself as a capable and ruthless bodyguard. In time, Denault gained Hanna's trust, and he ensured he would never betray her. His pay had never been this good. The kills had never been this satisfying. Jean Denault was riding a new high that he didn't want to come down from.

But now he had a problem, and it was infuriating his every waking moment.

Not since his father died had anyone beaten him.

Every fight, every confrontation, Jean fought viciously until he was the victor. He'd killed men while bleeding from knife wounds and had once strangled an insurgent to death while ignoring his own broken arm. Over one hundred men, women and children had died at his hands. He survived because he fought harder, pushed through pain that no one else could, and he never allowed himself to lose.

That was until Mark Pierce had bested him.

The wound in Denault's leg hurt like hell. Thankfully, the bullet had passed through his flesh with no serious damage. No broken bones and no major nerves or arteries severed. He could stand okay, even run with the painkillers he popped daily. It wasn't the nature of his wound that bothered him; it was that he had allowed Pierce to shoot him through a wall, then render him unconscious with a blow to the head. An embarrassing and unforgivable insult.

Revenge consumed Denault. Once Hanna Vautrin's mission was complete, he would hunt down Pierce, beat him in battle, and make him suffer until he expired from a slow, painful death. The record needed resetting. He would not allow Pierce to tarnish his reputation.

Bored with standing in a baking landscape of nothingness, he looked again through his binoculars. Ansar Dine were closing in, but they weren't in any rush. He considered firing a warning shot over their heads to get them to hurry along.

Then the earth exploded.

Men and camels were torn apart and flung as meaty chunks across the arid flatness.

A dust cloud of brown smoke propelled in every direction.

Ducking and covering his head with his hands, Denault wasn't certain what had happened. No flare of a missile, no sign of other combatants for kilometres in any direction. Somehow, Saifullah and his men had blown themselves to pieces.

He watched for a moment. It took several minutes for six men and three camels to get back on their feet and stagger like drunk teenagers at a rave. A few maimed insurgents rolled in the sand, clearly in agony.

Denault chuckled when he realised what had happened. Like all insurgents, they were stupid. They had clustered together, so when one stepped on an IED, it took out most of their group. And that improvised explosive device had likely been placed there by Ansar Dine themselves.

He supposed he should get into his PVP armoured vehicle and see if he could help these idiots.

It took Denault two minutes to drive the distance Ansar Dine would cover in twenty. He parked a hundred metres from the carnage in case of further buried IEDs. Bloodied human and camel limbs and organs and shattered rifles littered the flat, baked earth. The giant Shalgham wandered among the dead and dying. Trails of blood on his face and hands had dried in the heat, presenting him as a Christ-on-the-crucifix figure. Sunlight glinted off his curved scimitar blade, which he swung, decapitating the men who wouldn't survive their injuries. He left the camels to expire on their own.

Saifullah was well over two metres tall, with muscles like thick mooring ropes berthing a ship to port. He was an imposing warrior who loomed large over everyone. Yet, despite his physique, the man moved with controlled, precise motions. The blue eyes were the most unsettling; they seemed to burrow into the minds of anyone he stared at, as if understanding their deepest fears in an instant. Few people caused Denault to shudder and recoil, but Shalgham did.

"What happened?" Denault asked, trying to sound casual. He watched where he stepped to avoid any more buried surprises.

Kashif Shalgham grunted. He wiped the blood off his sword using a dead man's headscarf.

"IED?"

"It'd better not be a trap you laid, Denault."

The French mercenary shrugged. "Fucking not likely. IEDs are stupid. Kill and maim your own side as often as they debilitate the enemy." He scanned the survivors. "Where's Lucas Vautrin?"

Saifullah laughed. "He's dead."

Denault's jaw dropped. "What? Did he get blown up with the others?" It would be his misfortune to come close to reuniting Hanna with her brother, only to lose Lucas in a stupid, avoidable accident.

Shalgham took a moment to consider his answer. "Yes. Probably it was his camel that stepped on the mine."

Denault nodded. He didn't care about the brother. Hanna was the smarter of the two, so the Vautrin arms smuggling empire wouldn't take much of a hit with the brother gone. "You can break the news when we meet up."

Shalgham ignored the comment. He looked to each of the five surviving, superficially wounded warriors. Six fanatics in total were the number required to complete their mission, so enough had survived. He watched as they removed five heavy saddlebags from one dead camel in particular, then carried them carefully as instructed by Shalgham. Perhaps they contained copies of the Qur'an and other holy scriptures Denault cared nothing for.

The giant sheathed his scimitar in the scabbard across his back and stood tall. "Where is this outcrop where you are hiding my UN vehicles?"

Denault pointed to a rocky peak three kilometres south and shimmering in the heat. "Not far. We'll get there quicker now that I'm driving." He gestured to the PVP. "If you want to keep your camels, assign two men to ride them in. I've had enough of standing in this fucking heat."

Shalgham's piercing blue stare locked onto Denault, murderous intent in his dark irises.

The former Legionnaire took a step back. Had he offended Shalgham? Why was he suddenly afraid?

Instead of threatening the former Legionnaire, the Sword of Allah gave a slight grin and said, "Very well. We'll do it your way."

39

ADRAR DES IFOGHAS, MALI

After an uneventful night and morning prayers to Mecca, they drove again. Pierce behind the wheel, Tariq in the passenger seat and Awa asleep in the back.

The Defender's air-conditioning had failed long ago, so the heat was soon oppressive. Open windows allowed air to blow through the cabin, mildly improving their condition. Navigation was difficult, as Tariq had only traversed the landscape on foot or camelback and was unable to distinguish between ground conditions a camel could traverse that a car couldn't. Many false starts led to impassable cliffs or rugged terrain, requiring them to double back multiple times.

"No satellite phone?" Pierce asked.

Tariq turned away and touched his ear. "No. I said that before."

Pierce almost slammed on the brake to forcibly search Tariq, but he needed the young warrior's cooperation more than he needed to report in. If an outside means of communications existed, hidden in the man's robes, it could wait.

"There!" Tariq pointed to the battered, abandoned truck ahead. "I knew it would be around here somewhere."

Pierce drove to within a hundred metres of their target. He climbed from the Defender, took his AK-47 and pressed it against his shoulder, with his fingers on the stock and trigger grip, and approached. He watched for insurgents lying in ambush and for signs of buried improvised explosive devices. Pierce covered the distance in three minutes, discovering the truck was devoid of water, luggage, cash or bodies. He did, however, smell the scent of death. The pungent odours of rotting flesh were noticeable every time the wind picked up.

He heard the frantic buzz of flies.

Pierce waved his hand high, motioning them to approach. Tariq drove the last hundred metres.

"Is this what you expected to find?" Tariq said.

He saw the dead then, not in the truck but at a distance. Four crucifixes, three with disembowelled bodies: the priest, one aid worker and a young African man. Nearby lay a sprawled insurgent, his skull crushed. Maggots had hatched in the corpses' wounds and transformed into the flies he heard.

Pierce's stomach turned in knots. Despite the unlikeliness of him succeeding in his mission, he felt disappointment that he hadn't saved these people. They were probably all decent individuals and didn't deserve to die as they had. Could he have reached them earlier? Would an infil on a U.S. Air Force Chinook helicopter have brought him here in time?

He remembered his flight from Gao to Agadez and the

advice he had given the airman gunner. He gave himself the same advice now: accept that he had done the best he could, and move on; otherwise self-doubt would destroy him.

Pierce examined the crucifix without a body. Tied ropes but no man.

Of the young Frenchman, who seemed likely to be Lucas Vautrin come back from the dead, there was no sign. This suggested the Vautrin family were in league with Shalgham and Ansar Dine. Arizona and Utah were the same as the Sahara. New Mexico, the original kidnappers, were not.

He turned when he heard a noise. Without thought he raised his assault rifle, ready to shoot hostiles.

Instead, Pierce discovered Awa lined up in his sights. She gasped at his sudden reaction. He lowered his weapon so as not to scare her further. "Sorry!"

"I shouldn't have snuck up on you."

"It's okay. You're almost silent when you move. I'm not used to stealthy civilians." He motioned to the corpses. "You sure you want to see?"

She shrugged. "I saw when it happened, but from a distance. I've seen worse in the hospital. Many of our patients have third-degree burns, missing limbs, infected wounds..."

Pierce nodded, remembering that she was a nurse in a country at war and hardened to all kinds of horrors. "As you said, Lucas Vautrin is missing, and so is Oumar."

"I don't know why the insurgents took them. I watched them both ride off on their camels, in that direction." She pointed southwest. "Although they made Oumar walk."

Pierce calculated, if they travelled in the indicated direction, they would eventually reach Gao. He looked for Tariq, who waited inside the Land Rover Defender. Pierce checked to see he still had the ignition key in his pocket, then wondered how the Tuareg man was coping. "Awa, you seem to take this all rather well?"

She sneered and crossed her arms. "You expect me to be a weak woman, needing saving?"

"No. It impresses me, that's all. I've seen plenty of men, and women, who've coped far worse after enduring far less."

She laughed. "Perhaps I hide my feelings too well. Reality is, I'm terrified, Mark."

"I would never have guessed from your calm exterior."

She shuddered. "They kidnapped and tortured me; I was almost raped and murdered. I've probably lost my job at the hospital in Timbuktu because of my absence. My mother can't look after herself, and I'm worried about her. Pierce, I hope you take me home soon, so my life can become normal again."

"I will. I promise."

"But first, you will find those responsible?"

"Yes."

"And then, what...? You will kill them?"

"Yes. I doubt they'll surrender to me."

After a moment of contemplation, Awa said, "Good. They deserve to die."

Her opinion relieved Pierce. She at least saw the realities of the situation as he did.

"But you are only one man."

"I won't do the actual killing. First, I need to find a satellite phone so I can call in support. Once I report Shalgham's location, an air strike should bring us resolution."

"What about Oumar?"

Pierce frowned. "The insurgent who saved you, the man without hands?"

"Yes."

Pierce thought about his answer before he spoke. "If I can save Oumar, I will."

He examined the ropes that had bound Oumar, guessing how he had slipped from the knots. The crucified bodies, with their hands and wrists bound tight and with purpled fingers, had expired from more immediate injuries.

He turned, for he had seen enough. The dead were dead. Nothing he could do for them now. All he could do was protect Awa and prevent Kashif Shalgham and his men from causing more death and destruction. If he could save Oumar, he would, but he wouldn't put himself at risk to do so. "We should move out. Another team will collect the bodies."

She pointed to his hands. "How are they?"

He held them out. The tremors were there, but they were slight, almost unnoticeable. "The shakes have gone."

"No, Mark, they have not."

He chuckled. "I can't hide anything from you, can I?"

"No, you can't. I still say it is stress." Awa held his gaze. "If you discover what makes you a better man, and act on it, I'm certain you'll solve your problem."

40

SAHARA, MALI

Hanna Vautrin clenched her teeth and tightened her fists. She was furious. Denault had one job this morning, to bring Shalgham, Lucas and the Ansar Dine martyrs to their hideout. A simple exercise without risk or danger, or so she thought. Instead, her brother, Lucas, was dead, and the volunteers were half the numbers Shalgham had promised. She wished to cry her pain and scream her fury, but Hanna did neither. No one would ever witness her vulnerable side. Retribution would instead be unleashed through her orders and actions.

"My brother is dead!"

Denault scratched his head and looked away. Shalgham acted like she hadn't spoken. Hanna realised neither man cared that her last surviving family member had just died.

"Explain what happened."

Denault looked to the imposing Shalgham, the self-appointed Sword of Allah. Under differing circumstances, Hanna would have been fearful of a giant sadist like Shalgham, but not with grief consuming her. Plus, she knew

Shalgham needed her more than she needed him. The plan was hers, the will to make it happen was hers, and the negotiations and deal-making, they were all hers too. Everyone else in this scheme were just participants, not instigators, happy to come along for the ride and the wealth and power she promised. Without fear for herself, she would accuse this brute of all kinds of ineptitude, and he'd just have to take it.

"Talk to me!"

Shalgham waved his hand in a dismissive gesture. "Lucas rode his camel onto a buried mine. He killed himself and half my martyrs."

"What?" Hanna kept eye contact, straining to look up at the deep aqua blue encircling the man's black pupils, like pools of inky oil. Physically, Shalgham represented a nightmarish monster, and her understanding of his past atrocities didn't lessen this perception, but she would show no fear. "*You* let him ride in front?"

"Lucas disobeyed me. The infection in his shoulder, it drove him mad. I realised too late what he was doing."

"This gets worse and worse. How was he wounded? How did his shoulder become infected?"

"A kidnapper shot him, several days back."

"How did *you* let that happen?"

Shalgham smirked. "It happened before I reached him."

Hanna growled. "Who are these kidnappers anyway? Why did they have my brother? Who paid them?"

The giant shrugged. He didn't care. "We don't know, but they are no longer a problem."

"Explain?"

"They were merely three young jihadist hopefuls, with

crazy ideas in their heads, and I executed them. They claimed to be working for me, but I gave no such order."

Hanna growled again, concerned that another party had involved themselves in her affairs. Someone who knew something of her intentions and had paid the kidnappers to hold her brother ransom, but why, and who was behind it? For a moment, she dreaded it might be her former intelligence officer, Brad Tegmark of the CIA, wishing to get back at her for not allowing him access into her inner circles and a cut of her business empire fortunes. But Tegmark had been out of the picture for close to three years now, and she had long suspected he was dead, killed in some war zone somewhere while trying desperately to make a name for himself. He was that kind of guy, conniving and reckless and destined for an early grave.

She turned to Shalgham, who appeared bored. She guessed he needed only a single Vautrin to ensure his side of the plan succeeded. In this moment, she would have put a bullet in his head, but she still required him for the final stage of their mission.

Hanna turned to the Ansar Dine martyrs, assessing their quality. All were bloody and bruised, with tattered and soot-stained clothes. One had lost two fingers on his right hand. Another was missing an ear. Each man looked ready to fall over and die rather than to commit one last act of retribution, guaranteeing them — in their minds, if nowhere else — a place in heaven. The virgins who waited to please these poor examples of warriors would certainly feel they could have done better. "What happened to you all? And why only six warriors?"

She looked first to Denault, figuring he was more likely

to be straight with her, the only man not blackened and scarred by the explosion.

"Like Shalgham said, ma'am, one of the Ansar Dine camels, perhaps Lucas's, for I didn't see, stepped on one of their own IEDs." He laughed, but no one joined him. "Come on. Who is idiot enough to die from their own traps?"

Shalgham whispered, "It was a French mine."

"Bullshit! Neither the Europeans nor the Americans use mines."

A hand shot forward so fast that, as Hanna blinked, she didn't see it move. Shalgham's thick fingers encircled Denault's throat, choking him. In his shock, Denault dropped his FAMAS, so it hung loose at his side while he tried to pry the vice-like fingers from his neck. His face turned red. His eyes bulged. Despite his impressive physique, Denault didn't possess the strength to beat this brute.

"Enough!" Hanna said.

Shalgham held the grip a few seconds longer before dropping Denault to the gravelly floor. It took Denault a moment to recover his breath. Then, in an instant, he was on his feet, a knife in his hand.

Hanna had expected the former Legionnaire's action, so she held out an arm, blocking him. For all his skills, it frustrated her that Denault could never keep his emotions in check when someone bested him. "Stop it! You are like children." She stared at both men until they each nodded their capitulation.

She gazed at their makeshift hideout. A rocky outcrop in the sandy desert, close to a sea of dunes. Wind had weathered the base of one cliff wall, providing a natural alcove to hide the four UN-marked VAB and two PVP vehicles. One hundred kilograms of C-4 explosives in each VAB, and fifty kilograms of the same explosives in each of the PVPs. Bags packed around the explosives were filled with metal shrapnel, and each vehicle was wired for detonation, using a deadman switch placed under the driver's dashboard.

Six suicide bombs.

Six fanatics.

"The vehicles are ready. The six of you can leave when—"

"Five." Shalgham corrected her.

"I can count. Six vehicles. Six men."

The giant shook his head as he glanced to the saddlebags on his camel. "I never agreed that I would be a martyr."

"Then who's driving the sixth vehicle?"

Shalgham shrugged and looked to his walking wounded. "You have five of my best, most loyal men. Your brother killed the rest. They will have to be enough."

"We agreed on six targets."

"Abandon one of them. Use two vehicles in one location, detonate them side by side. You agreed, six of your mercenaries would take my men to the locations, so you have enough drivers for the six vehicles. And don't worry, my martyrs will give your men time to get away before the detonations."

Hanna maintained eye contact with the giant, searching for an explanation for his obstinate behaviour. Something had changed. When they formed their alliance, Shalgham's passion had been pronounced, he had been motivated to bring retribution and fear to the West, bitter and angry against all the pain the world had brought him. Now Hanna detected something else. Was it hope? Did he have a purpose in his life again? She had liked him so much more when she thought he was angry and miserable.

"We have five men. No more. No less. They are martyrs chosen by Allah to bring glory to Islam in these forsaken lands. Do not cheapen their sacrifice by questioning their commitment."

"Five targets it is, then." Hanna nodded. "In the scheme of things, one less target makes no difference."

41

Hanna and Denault kept a respectful distance as Shalgham led his martyrs in prayer. Afterwards, he thanked them for their sacrifice. The men didn't hide their fear, but Hanna could not question their resolve. Five men willing to give their lives without regret or question, she had to respect that.

Denault spat into the dry earth. "What makes men throw their lives away?"

"You think you and I are any different?"

Denault looked to his employer, his brow furrowed. "What do you mean?"

"In our profession, Denault, we take risks every day. Risks that might cost us our lives. You are a soldier. I am an arms trader. Our daily decisions, if we get them wrong, will kill us."

"Yes, but our intention is to live, to achieve a payoff when we succeed. We don't choose death as the *only* option, like these fucks do."

Hanna laughed. "And yet Mark Pierce obsesses you, even if your pursuit of revenge will be your undoing."

The former Legionnaire growled. "That's different. No one defeats me. Besides, ma'am, you won't lose sleep if I remove him from this world."

"I will if your obsession costs me your service. Focus on our objective. Think upon the money we will make when we pull this off."

A snarl fixed upon Denault's face. He couldn't look at her.

"Will you go after Shalgham too? Earlier he almost killed you and would have done if I hadn't intervened." He didn't answer, and she saw she'd guessed correctly. "Of course you will. You can't win every battle, Sergeant."

"Yes. I. Can!"

Denault, despite his anger issues and obsession with always being the most powerful man in the room, was a competent soldier, a formidable assassin, and an efficient and loyal bodyguard. She needed people she could rely upon, and he was one of the few men she did trust. If she didn't allow Denault his retribution, she would lose him. "I tell you what, when this is over, I'll give you time off to hunt and kill Pierce, and Shalgham too, if it will make you feel better. But only after we've seen this mission through to completion."

It took Denault a moment to realise this was the best deal he would get. He nodded his capitulation. "Thank you," he said with a grin as the disfigurement on his face twisted in a malicious mockery of a second grin.

"Was it really the Cambodian who gave you that scar?"

Denault looked surprised that she questioned his earlier

story. His body tensed before he answered. "I have my father to thank for this."

"Didn't your father die when you were young?"

Denault nodded.

"Did you kill him?"

He shook his head.

So, one man *had* beaten him, and Denault had spent the rest of his life making up for that single failure. Hanna had gained an appreciation of how Sergeant Denault had become the man he was today.

Interrupting her thoughts, Shalgham nodded to each martyr, embraced and kissed each man on the cheeks. He said his goodbyes, then approached Hanna and Denault. "We have a problem," he said in his calm, monotone voice. "An American soldier named Mark Pierce is approaching. He'll be upon us before midday."

"Pierce?" Denault shuddered with what Hanna presumed was excitement. "He's here? How do you know?"

"I have my sources too." Shalgham gave the slightest nod. "You know him?"

Hanna stepped forward. "He's not just a soldier. He's a CIA paramilitary operator. A government-sanctioned assassin, if the label fits, and he's been hot on my trail for some time. Is he alone?"

The giant shook his head. "Two others. They approach in a civilian four-wheel drive." Shalgham described the identities, capabilities and motives of the companions. "They should be no problem for you to deal with."

"Us?" Denault sneered. "You're leaving?"

"Yes. My part in this operation is at an end." He glanced again at the five saddlebags on his camel, far more than was usual. "Call me when it's done. Then I'll commence the next stage, as agreed. The Malian politicians will tremble in their boots when I do."

Hanna itched to know what was inside the saddlebags, but suspected she would unleash Shalgham's wrath if she dared to ask. She told herself the contents were likely inconsequential to their mission, so she put the thought from her mind.

"What about Pierce and his team?"

"I'll tell you exactly where to find them, and when. I've arranged for their incapacitation, so they won't resist when you arrive."

"How?"

The giant grinned. "You'll find out."

Hanna nodded, accepting his offer. "Good luck, Saifullah. We'll be in contact soon."

He nodded while his face returned to its expressionless mask. She knew his lack of emotion was a defence mechanism against the world, much like her own.

After Saifullah provided Pierce's location, she watched him ride alone into the desert, astride the first camel in his caravan of three; then he disappeared into the haze and shimmer of the flat desert that stretched beyond their rocky outcrop.

"He's still in range," Denault whispered behind her. "A sniper bullet he'd never know was coming. Then I'll see what he has in his saddlebags."

Her trusted right-hand man had also noticed the anomaly.

As tempting as his offer was, Hanna shook her head. "No. If we kill Shalgham, we lose the loyalty of his martyrs, and we'll need others like them to escalate the war. Better to let

Shalgham live so he can spread the word of the martyrs' deeds... for now."

Hanna felt the heat in her eyes and resisted the urge to cry. When she looked up, a baffled Denault stared at her and asked, "What's wrong? We're all about to become fucking rich."

Hanna simmered. "I lost my brother today. We might have hated each other, but we were family. It was love — twisted love, for sure — but that is what it was."

"You'll miss him?"

"Of course I'll miss him, you fool."

Denault nodded in a masquerade of sympathy. "And Pierce? What about him?"

"For God's sake! Is he all you can think about? Bring him here alive... also for now."

42

W ith the Adrar des Ifoghas far behind them, the Sahara transformed again into flat and featureless stretches of sand. The surface felt as hot as the sun, and the hazy horizon stretched out as though it continued forever.

When Tariq identified camel tracks, Mark Pierce increased their speed. The Defender churned a dust trail as they raced towards the insurgents. Pierce kept his eyes focused. Any signs of metal and he would slow and take an alternative route. An improvised explosive device or mine would end their lives and their mission, and he hadn't journeyed this far just to die now.

The heat became more unbearable as the day progressed. With no air conditioning, they kept the windows wound down to circulate a breeze through the cabin, but all surfaces felt hot and dry. Still, Pierce felt he was nearing his target and achieving his objectives.

"What's that?" Awa pointed to a shape on the track ahead, her skin wet with sweat.

"It looks like a man," Tariq answered.

"Or a corpse," Pierce mused. "Two corpses."

Pierce slowed. The shapes were two men, both lying prone and unmoving. Pierce exited the Defender and approached with his AK-47 raised and his eyes tracking down the sights of the weapon. The first man was dark-skinned with soiled clothes and dry flesh. Pierce detected the rise and fall of his chest. The man wasn't dead, but he wasn't far off.

Then he noticed the arms without hands. Not a recent injury, but old, healed wounds.

"Oumar!" Awa raced to the fallen figure and cradled his head in her lap. She used her water bottle to wet a cloth and squeezed it into his mouth, hydrating the near-unconscious man.

"This is the insurgent who saved you?" Pierce kept his weapon raised, not trusting that the situation was as benign as it presented itself to Awa.

"He's not an insurgent! Oumar's as much a victim as I am."

Pierce checked on Tariq, who crouched low to examine the second Caucasian man. A single bullet fired into the skull had shattered the face, creating a mess of bone, meat and blood. A second older, infected wound showed on his shoulder. His clothes were a tailored European cut, tattered and torn from rough living in the harsh Sahara.

Tariq stood and scanned the horizon. "We're on the right path."

"This is Lucas Vautrin?" Pierce asked.

Awa nodded.

Oumar's eyes fluttered open. He stared up at Awa as she cradled him. "Am I in heaven?" He expressed his elation in

French, then he looked at his absent hands, and his eyes lost their hope. "I guess not."

Awa offered more water straight from the bottle. "What happened to you?"

It took thirty minutes for Oumar to tell his tale while he rehydrated. While he spoke, Awa treated his sunburn and fed him small portions of food.

Despite himself, as Pierce listened, he felt sorry for the insurgent. All he had wanted in his life was to study and qualify and then practise as an engineer. He never wanted to be a fanatic. And it was true; Oumar didn't have that stare of death many terrorists did. He looked like a normal person, someone who believed life was worth living regardless of the challenges it threw at you. The absence of hands would have made his life near impossible in a country as poor and unstable as Mali. Pierce was impressed he had survived as long as he had.

"That's an interesting story," said Tariq as he drank from a water bottle, then passed it to Pierce.

When Oumar finished his tale, Pierce drank himself, then summarised. "So, Shalgham murders Lucas Vautrin, steals the eleven million dollars your brother and Farid took from the dead CIA operators, and is now on his way to Lucas's sister to escalate the war in Mali?"

Oumar nodded, then bowed his head. "I am afraid so."

Pierce asked, "Who hired you to kidnap Lucas Vautrin and the others?"

The man shrugged. "I don't know, that was my brother and Farid's doing. They told me Ansar Dine."

Pierce nodded. "That makes no sense, if Shalgham is Ansar Dine himself, and Lucas Vautrin was working with him already?"

Oumar's eyes grew wide with fear. "I don't know, sir. I'm sorry."

Pierce sensed he was telling the truth. He considered again if the kidnapping had indeed been a false-flag operation, with another party pretending to be Ansar Dine to stir up trouble. American deserts being and not being like the Sahara... but Pierce still did not understand who really was in league with who.

"What now?" Tariq retied the knots around his long white shirt and blue outer robes, and his face again became hidden behind his turban, after so much time having been exposed. "Do we keep advancing until we run into Ansar Dine? If so, I say that is madness! How can you expect the four of us to take on an army of bloodthirsty butcherers?"

Pierce recalled again the reason Tuareg men hid their faces, so they would never betray their emotions. He couldn't help but sense Tariq was not being honest with them. "Not take them on, Tariq, but to gather intelligence. We observe from afar." He looked back at Awa Sissoko helping Oumar into the Defender. She searched for a first aid kit to patch Oumar's many bruises and lacerations. "Then I call it in, and the U.S. Army or Air Force deals with them."

Tariq expressed hope in his eyes. "A drone strike?"

Pierce raised an eyebrow. "As simple as that, yes. I'm not crazy. I'm not a one-man army." His head felt foggy, like exhaustion was catching up with him.

"Two," Tariq corrected him. "I'm with you on this one regardless of whether I like it or not. But I agree, it is suicide to fight."

"The problem is, Tariq, I don't have a satellite phone. This can all end now... if you give me the phone... the one you've kept hidden in your robes."

Tariq shook his head. "I wish... I could help you... Mark Pierce."

Pierce stiffened. Tariq's use of his full name felt forced and wooden. He knew Tariq was lying. "Where... is the satellite phone?" he demanded as he stumbled on his feet.

Tariq stood his ground, then tripped as his legs shuddered. He didn't say a word.

Pierce rushed the young warrior, grabbed his arm to spin him around, the other hand knocking the AK-47 from his grip. He patted Tariq down, searching for the phone hidden in the folds of his robes, when Tariq's hand went up to protect himself.

Pierce felt woozy.

He looked to Awa and Oumar, also struggling to remain upright. It seemed as if none of them had control over their legs. Pierce watched in horror as Awa and Oumar fell unconscious to the earth.

"What... have you... done?"

"I... drugged us all... You would have... noticed... if I drugged only one water bottle..." Tariq snarled, then dropped to his knees. "You should have... stayed away, Pierce. I can't let you bring... the Americans... here..."

Pierce's brain struggled to understand as it desperately fought the drug, but within seconds the world receded, and nothingness consumed him.

43

Pierce's first semi-lucid memories were of his body being dragged through the sand. Tight rope bound his hands. Men talked in hushed tones, using French and Arabic. A woman struggled next to him. He tried to remember who she was.

Laughter. Cursing. His vision and hearing faded in and out until men in desert camouflage uniforms and assault rifles came into focus.

He felt heat.

He sensed a shadow pass over him.

Pierce tried to move, then speak. He felt his skin tingle, but none of his muscles responded.

The woman sobbed.

He heard a knife cutting at cloth.

A second rope looped around the knot binding his wrists. The men yanked him upward until his feet flirted with the sand. They removed his boots and belt, then cut away his clothes until he was naked.

He heard the woman sob again. He gained enough

control of his muscles to swing in a circle. Awa swayed naked next to him, from metal hooks hammered into cracks in a large rock above them. Her hands were also bound. Bruises and lacerations covered her, but none were recent. They were inside a semi-cave, or a large overhang of rock in the desert. His head hurt, and his vision blurred as he tried to concentrate on details.

The woman sobbed again.

Pierce spun awkwardly, suspended in the air, so he could see her, three metres from him. He tried to speak, but he couldn't get his mouth to work.

Awa's wide eyes, full of terror, stared at him. She talked, but her voice sounded muffled, like she was speaking underwater.

Pierce focused and tried to remember what had happened to bring him to this predicament.

Tariq... had drugged them all.

Had Awa woken earlier because Pierce had ingested more of the drug and therefore remained unconscious for longer?

The shapes of men in uniforms moved around them. Pierce blinked several times, then screwed his eyes shut for a moment. When he opened them again, the men came into focus. White Caucasians, muscular in desert-pattern military fatigues. Each carried FAMAS assault rifles. These were the French mercenaries who had accosted him in the Gao bar where he had met Juliet Paquet, the DGSE operative.

He returned his attention to Awa. "Have... they hurt you?"

She struggled, twisted her slender body back and forth, trying to loosen her binds.

The mercenaries laughed.

"She is untouched," came a voice in a soft French accent. "My men won't touch her. Not like that. No woman deserves that."

The woman's pale skin and slim muscular physique was as Pierce remembered, as was her distinctive dilated left pupil. She was dressed like the mercenaries, in desert fatigues with combat rigs and body armour. What had changed was her hair. Black roots showed through her fake blond colouring.

Pierce chuckled, but there was no humour in the sound. "Back from the dead, Hanna Vautrin." His mouth was dry, and he was thirsty. How long had he been unconscious?

She raised an eyebrow and smirked. "So you finally worked it out. I was glad I covered my tracks earlier. I was worried you might have seen through my ruse when you invaded my Gao safe house, the one time when you could have actually done something to stop me. Seems you didn't."

"I see it now. The discovery of your dead brother, shot in the head by Shalgham, clinched it." The comment seemed to take her by surprise, so he said, "Oh, you didn't know?"

She clenched her teeth as her facial muscles tensed. "You lie!"

"Drive to where Tariq drugged us. See for yourself."

"An IED killed him, Pierce. Not Shalgham."

"Your so-called ally lied. Lucas's corpse has two bullet wounds. It was the second one from Shalgham that killed him."

Hanna's skin reddened.

Pierce grinned, but it was all show. They would torture and murder him soon enough, so to keep the pain and finality of death at bay, he would taunt her, keep her talking until he came up with a plan to escape. "How did you dispose of the real Juliet Paquet?"

"I might as well tell you." Hanna laughed. "Denault excels at that kind of work. Thanks to corruptible contacts within the DGSE, we were led right to her. Parquet and I look very similar. Denault killed her the moment I needed to make the switch, then used acid to destroy all forensic evidence. Apparently, he did similar work for criminal gangs operating in Asia, before he joined my organisation—"

Awa called out, "Mark?"

He turned to the nurse, a feat he could perform with more grace now that the drug was wearing off, and he was in control of his muscles again. Her eyes were wide. Fear gripped her.

Fear gripped him too. Torture was the worst fate an operator like him could face, and with it an ending that would involve mutilations, pain and suffering beyond what any human could endure. He'd rather die quickly than die at the mercy of butchers.

"Please don't let them…"

"Awa, I'll get us out of here, unharmed. I promise."

Hanna laughed again.

Mark kept his focus on Awa. She was shaking. Her eyes rolled back towards her skull, and froth erupted from her mouth. The full length of her body shook with convulsions.

"Cut her down!" Pierce demanded. "She'll die if you don't."

No one answered. Hanna and her men watched with dispassion. Awa convulsed for many minutes, and he could do nothing to support her. He kept waiting for her mouth to explode with blood, a sign that she had bitten into her own tongue. He couldn't even raise his legs to support her, the distance between them was too great.

Then he thought, if she died now, she wouldn't face the tortures and humiliations that awaited them, and that might be a good thing.

After several minutes, when Awa's convulsions ceased, she slipped into unconsciousness and hung limp from her ropes. Her breathing at least remained consistent. Pierce noticed that he secretly felt relief, because if she lived, he might still find a means to save them both despite how unlikely that seemed in this moment.

Pierce swung towards his captors. "Why are we still alive?"

While he waited for their answer, he examined his surroundings in further detail. The hideout was the base of a rocky outcrop overhanging the desert sand. The natural structure created a semi-cave perhaps five metres high and forty across. Sand and rock made up the floor. Eons of wind action eroding the base must have created the cave.

The uniformed men numbered seven, including the leader of the group, the scar-faced Denault. Joining them were five dark-skinned, Middle Eastern men, looking like they had nearly died during an arduous and prolonged battle. Each carried the stares of men who had given up on life, or who were preparing to enter the next one. They dressed in dark robes and headscarves, like the Ansar Dine insurgents he had encountered in the Sahel. These were Kashif Shalgham's men.

Pierce counted four French-made VAB armoured vanguard vehicles and two PVP small protected vehicles, each painted white with UN markings. These were vehicles from the convoy Major Gabriel Travers had planned to drive to Tessalit in northern Mali. He glanced inside the closest vehicle, saw the C-4 explosives inside, packed against many bags filled with metal shrapnel.

It all came together in Pierce's mind; he saw now who aligned with whom and the nature of the ultimate scheme they aimed to achieve.

"You're right." Hanna stepped close to Pierce. "There is no reason to keep you alive, or her."

"Then why are we still talking?" He hoped when the end came, it would be quick for both of them. But he also hoped that they would leave them alive and intact for a little longer, so Pierce could put his single strategy for escape into action. But he couldn't act now, not with some many hostiles poised to shoot him down quickly and easily. "Hanna, Hanna Vautrin?"

She grinned at his use of her real name, as if him speaking those words made this identity real, then glanced behind to the smarting Denault. He grinned, and his scar twisted. "My boy is not happy you shot him in the leg. He has a long and painful death planned for you both."

Pierce snorted. "What a surprise, he's motivated by revenge alone."

She nodded. "Unfortunately for you, Denault's loyalty is more important to me than your well-being."

Pierce swallowed against his dry throat. His nostrils and mouth felt crusty. The heat was stifling. Now he knew he had to keep Hanna talking and unsettle her further, or he would find himself in Denault's clutches. "What was the Gao farce about?"

Her smile was conspiratorial. "My father died in Afghanistan. Not Lucas or I. I knew you were hunting the Vautrin family, but I needed to know which Vautrin. You confirmed the CIA thought all this was my father's doing, which suits me."

"Why is that important?"

She grinned. "You want me to give a speech, lay out my plan? That is so cliché."

"I've got nothing better to do."

"If you must know... The French president will soon pardon Lucas and myself of all our crimes. He is one of our most profitable clients, but he insists on discreet face-to-face meetings when he needs to negotiate and lay out terms, so there is no paper or electronic trail. But that required Lucas and me to meet with him personally, so he realised we still lived. We convinced him our father lived too, but was in hiding, and that we had faked our deaths to protect ourselves from our father's enemies. The president accepted our story, which he found easier to believe if he thought we held no real power in our arms empire. But we knew that if he knew of the agreements Lucas and I, and not our father, made with Ansar Dine, he would rescind the pardon. So I decided that this operation — as far as it concerns Western powers — was to be orchestrated by my father even though he is dead. He will officially 'die' during the attacks we have planned. Then I can step forth with my pardon, as the legitimate business owner of the Vautrin empire, and be free to trade with whomever I want, without fear of French retribution. An eloquent enough scheme for you?"

"What about Oumar?" Pierce called out. "Did you kill the poor man after everything he's been through?"

She took the bait and kept talking. "He's joining us on our mission, masquerading as one of our team and linking the attacks to the kidnappers responsible for snatching my brother. It will add authenticity when he dies with Shalgham's martyrs. Also, it serves as a fitting revenge for Lucas's passing. Did your CIA masters orchestrate that? Pretended to be Ansar Dine to hire Oumar and his friends to kidnap my brother. Was it a feeble attempt to turn the Ansar Dine inner circle against each other?"

Pierce twisted. His arms ached from being elevated for so long. His hands were numb from the lack of blood pumping through his fingers. The longer he remained hanging like a piece of meat, the weaker he would become, decreasing his chances of escape. But until he had a plan, he would keep her talking.

"I can't confirm nor deny that."

She sneered. "Fuck you, Pierce."

Pierce cleared his throat and focused on what was important, his escape and survival. "So, Hanna, what's the scheme? Drive six UN-marked vehicles into the MINUSMA's super-base in Gao, detonate the vehicles and, what, take out as many foreign soldiers and aid workers as you can?"

"Not quite. The UN protect MINUSMA too thoroughly. The target, or targets I should say, are six refugee camps in neighbouring Niger and Burkina Faso. Their security is far less sophisticated, so much easier to get into. The results will be the same. The travesty will bring in more foreign soldiers, and just like Iraq, Syria and Afghanistan, the war here will escalate."

"This is all about driving market demand for arms, which you'll cash in on? But at the cost of thousands of innocent refugee lives? Even for an arms dealer, that's low."

"The targets are deliberate for more complicated reasons than that, Pierce. Ansar Dine, like Islamic State, want their own caliphate they can lord over, but if people keep fleeing these deserts, they have no subjects."

"What? So, if you destroy the refugee camps, that will make them think twice about fleeing Shalgham's tyranny?" He remembered the snipers he had encountered entering the Adrar des Ifoghas, and the many corpses of Tuareg and other tribal people who'd hoped to flee the violence gripping Mali. "I don't think that plan will work."

Hanna circled Pierce, her gaze seemingly admiring his muscular physique. "It's a shame you aren't more corruptible. I could use a man like you in my organisation. I'm sure your unique skills and expertise are hard to find."

It was Pierce's turn to sneer. "You're getting off subject."

"I didn't think we had anything to talk about? Well, nothing more that interests me."

"Are you sure?"

She raised an eyebrow. "Okay, I'll humour you, Pierce. What else will you tell me?"

"Where is Shalgham?" He gestured towards the desert. "Gone already?"

Hanna shrugged. Pierce saw signs in her unusual eyes that she was concerned and trying to hide it. "What if he has?"

"I've only just worked it out, the one part of this equation you aren't aware of..."

"Which is?"

"The eleven million dollars." He gauged her response. He realised through her flicker of surprise that she knew nothing about the money. "The CIA didn't false flag the kidnapping of your brother and the other hostages. The CIA actually tried to pay off the kidnappers with eleven million dollars to return the hostages, only Seigel, Wong and Rowlands blew themselves up by driving over a land mine. The kidnappers took the easy money. Then, when Shalgham killed the kidnappers, he took the money from them — for himself."

Hanna's intense eyes grew wide as her jaw dropped despite herself.

"You didn't know?" Pierce laughed. "Shalgham won't build his caliphate now. He hates the desert as much as you or me. He killed your brother so Lucas wouldn't tell you about the money, Hanna. Shalgham didn't want to be in a situation where he might have to share it with you. Tell me if you see it differently, but that's about as deceitful as any human being can get."

Hanna fumed.

Pierce smiled. He had unravelled her again. "He's taken the money, Hanna, silencing your brother in the process, and will soon disappear forever to live a decadent life somewhere else. You are all alone in your scheme now."

44

Ten metres from Pierce, Hanna argued with Denault. Harsh words soon turned to shouting. Pierce had bought Awa and himself some time. Now he had to use it.

"Awa?" he hissed. "Awa? Wake up!"

Her eyelids fluttered as she regained consciousness. Recognising her predicament, she struggled against her binding ropes with rising panic.

"Awa!" he said again. "Look at me."

"What's happening? Why are they torturing us?" She struggled further. Then, accepting the futility of their situation, she surrendered and hung limp like Pierce. "You promised me you'd take me home. You promised we wouldn't get so close to these people."

"I'm sorry. I didn't know Tariq was a traitor."

His words had a calming effect, for she slowed her breathing and focused on Pierce. "How did we get here?"

"Tariq drugged us all, himself included. Clever really, and I didn't see it."

"But why am I involved? I'm just a nurse. I save people. I'm a good person." She glanced around, taking in her surroundings as Pierce had. "I hear it is the same everywhere there is war. Men fight each other, kill each other, and brutalise women and children. Men are always the problem."

She looked exhausted as she faced Pierce. Her breathing slowed. Her hope was fading.

"I promise you I'll get us out of here."

"How, Mark?"

Pierce had figured that they would be moved from this location before they were killed, and he was about to tell her how, then remembered a past operation in Eastern Europe. He'd been in a similar situation, imprisoned with several civilian hostages. He had told them his plan, but one hostage had thought it a better strategy to tell the terrorists what Pierce hoped to do, bargaining for his life by betraying Pierce. That operation had not ended well.

"Trust me on this." He remembered that Denault had a slow, painful death planned for them, so they had time. "I have to wait until the mercenaries aren't watching, but I'll get us free."

"Look at our situation. Look at these men, and us, bound like carcasses in a butcher's shop. Stripped and humiliated. Our chances are not good. How can you be so sure?"

"Because I've gotten out of more difficult situations in the past, that's why."

It was a lie — this was the most challenging imprisonment he had faced in his paramilitary career — but he had faith he could escape, nevertheless. That was what special forces training did, conditioned you to solve one problem at a time, then move on to the next problem, and the next

— rather than worry about the futility of the bigger picture.

"You have?"

"Yes, Awa. Trust me on this," he repeated. "By today's end these men will be dead, and you and I will walk away unharmed."

He spotted Tariq Aghali entering the cave. The young man looked tired and worried even though only his eyes showed behind his blue turban. So much for Tuareg men masking their emotions. While he wasn't a bound prisoner, he carried no weapons, which suggested Tariq's own situation was less positive than he had hoped for.

When he spotted Awa and Pierce, he approached. He said nothing as he removed his water bottle and held it out for Awa to drink. "This time it's not drugged."

She looked to Pierce, and he nodded that she should accept Tariq's generosity. Awa drank fast. Not all the water entered her mouth, and streams ran down her chest and legs, evaporating in the heat.

Tariq approached Pierce and offered him water, too. Pierce drank. Soon his throat lost its dryness, and the headache he hadn't consciously known of until then subsided.

"Thank you," Pierce said. "That was clever, drugging yourself the same time you drugged me, knowing that these mercenaries were already on the way to collect us. You would wake a free man while the rest of us woke as prisoners. Did Shalgham teach you how to apply the drugs?"

Tariq frowned. "It's not my fault you are in this predicament."

"You think they'll let you live, Tariq? You're as dead as we are. Hanna Vautrin wants zero witnesses."

The Tuareg warrior shook his head. "Did you ever wonder why my father and our people survived since the fanatics overran Mali? Not because of the American weapons or our fierce fighting reputation, as my father believes. Or even your efforts, Pierce. It's because I made a deal with Saifullah. I paid him money. I sold out foreign soldiers whenever they entered the Adrar des Ifoghas. I sold you out in the past too, but each time you slipped away before they could snatch you... until today. In return for my loyalty, Ansar Dine protect my people. You would have done the same in my situation."

"No, Tariq, I wouldn't have. You might have bargained with Shalgham for short-term gains, but he will kill you and enslave your people when neutrality no longer serves his purpose."

"You are naïve, Pierce, seeing the world through privileged Western eyes. Men like you don't understand the reality my people live with every day."

"Does your father really not own a satellite phone, or did you purposely lose it for him?"

Tariq nodded. "You got me there. I convinced him it was dangerous to own one."

"So it was you alone who betrayed us?"

"Yes, I texted Shalgham our location each time I prayed to Mecca."

"You got it all worked out, haven't you, Tariq?"

"I have to work it out. My people are at risk if I don't. People of the desert, myself included, make daily decisions that if wrong, cost us our lives."

Pierce spoke slowly. "They will kill you too, Tariq—"

He was about to say more when Sergeant Denault came up behind Tariq and squeezed him hard on the shoulder. Tariq winced. "No more taunting the prisoners, Tuareg."

The young man turned and looked up at the muscular ex-Legionnaire, then slinked away as instructed.

Denault took a long minute to stare at Awa's naked form, licking his lips. "You are beautiful. Such a waste that we have to kill you."

Awa gazed into the distance, her face resolute.

"I wanted to keep you close at the end, to watch you both expire before my very eyes, but Ms. Vautrin thinks I will be too distracted for my mission if I do. No matter, you will still both die in the manner of my choosing." Denault chuckled and turned with a leer to Pierce. "Nobody beats me, Pierce. Nobody ever has, and nobody ever will."

"I beat you, Denault," he said with a smirk. "Nothing will ever change that."

Denault stepped close to Pierce, sniffed the air. The man's hot breath felt like sandpaper on his face. He had a plan, and Pierce knew it would soon cost him. "Let me see... How did you beat me, exactly? Oh, that's right. You shot me in the leg."

He lunged, and Pierce felt an intense pain explode in his left leg. He could hear Awa's screams. Blood gushed from a hole in his calf where a screwdriver impaled his muscle. Pierce grunted against the agony. He had taken bullet wounds in the past. This was similar.

Denault yanked the screwdriver clear, and the pain doubled. For a second Pierce thought he would pass out, but he didn't.

"Are we even now, Pierce?" Denault asked with an ugly sneer, his scar twisting on his face.

Pierce didn't answer. He looked at his wound again,

knowing that if Denault had punctured a major artery, he'd bleed out in minutes, and then there would be nothing he could do to save himself, Awa and Oumar. Testing his leg cautiously, he found he could still move it, even though it hurt to do so, so no major nerve damage or broken bones.

"Have I forgotten something?"

"You seem the forgetful type," Pierce jested through clenched teeth, with the perspiration pouring off his face. "So probably."

"Oh yes, I don't think we are even yet, because..." Denault curled his hand into a fist, swung it hard, clobbering Pierce in his temple.

His skull shuddered like a bell struck by a hammer. He tried to fight unconsciousness... and failed.

45

"Mark!"

Pain. Wind. Heat.

"Mark!"

Pierce sluggishly emerged from a dream. As he regained consciousness, the sting of his leg wound and the throb in his head took over. He lay on his back while being jostled up and down. The heat was worse than before. His arms remained bound, and his naked skin was uncomfortably hot. Opening his eyes revealed the sun bearing directly down on him.

So he hadn't bled out.

"Mark! You're alive."

"Where... where are we?"

He turned his head. A still naked and equally bound Awa lay next to him. They were both tied to the roof of a VAB as it sped through the flat sandy deserts. Their skins were turning red from the scorch of the sun. Wind rushed past, fluttering Awa's corkscrew curls around her face. So this was Denault's plan, leaving them on the roof of the suicide vehicle to bake to death under the heat of the Saharan sun. A slow and painful passing.

She yelled over the noise of the wind, "You said you'd get us free?"

"I will."

He felt for the skin kit on his wrist, pulled the bandage-like escape tool from his real skin and gripped the tiny flexible metal saw in his hands. Pierce cut at the rope that bound him, and within a minute he was free. A trick he could have used in the cave, but with that many people watching, he wouldn't have gotten far.

He sat up. The hot metal of the armoured personnel carrier had blistered his back. The vehicle raced at over sixty kilometres per hour through the flat desert. He spotted the remaining convoy, three more VABs and two PVPs, on the road ahead.

"How did you do that?"

He showed her the blade. "Hold still."

She spread her hands apart so Pierce could cut her bindings. In less than a minute, she was also free. Sitting and, like him, covered in burns and blisters, she asked, "What now?"

"We take command of this vehicle."

He stood, and the pain from the screwdriver wound fired through his leg. He grunted against the agony while maintaining his balance. When he had his pain under control, he tested his weight on the leg. It could support him, so no lasting damage, even if the wound still seeped blood.

He raced to the roof hatch and banged his fists against the metal once, hoping to mimic something falling on the roof.

His actions had the desired effect. The hatch opened, and a French mercenary stuck his head out.

Pierce was ready. He yanked the man's head upwards and twisted his neck at the same time. The vertebrae snapped, and the body became limp as his FAMAS assault rifle dropped into the cabin. Pierce pulled his body up and snatched the PAMAS G1 9mm semi-automatic pistol from the dead man's holster in a swift action.

The VAB lurched upwards. The occupants inside knew something was wrong.

Pierce dropped the body back into the hatch. He pulled back the slide on the PAMAS, ensuring a chambered round, then reached down and fired several shots towards where the driver and passenger would be.

The vehicle wobbled.

After a few seconds, when no gunshots were returned, Pierce glanced down. The insurgent behind the wheel was dead.

"Follow me," he yelled to Awa over the noise of the engine and wind rushing around them.

Pierce climbed inside. The deceased driver had his foot on the accelerator. His body slumped on the wheel. They were driving in a straight line across the flat desert.

After helping Awa clamber down, he stripped the mercenary whose neck he had broken, and dressed in his clothes and desert boots. The camouflage shirt was wet with blood, but Pierce ignored its stickiness. His leg agonised from the wound in his muscle, but there was nothing he could do about it right now. He pushed the dead driver from the wheel and took command of the vehicle. So far, it seemed that no one else in the convoy had realised Pierce and Awa had taken over the last vehicle.

"You killed them, just like that?" Awa asked, standing behind him.

He looked her up and down. She was still naked and red from sunburn. "Grab some clothes."

"From where?"

He motioned to the dead insurgent.

"He's covered in blood."

"Or stay naked, I don't mind. But we've got some action ahead of us." He glanced behind. The back of the VAB contained over one hundred kilograms of C-4 explosives wrapped in metal shrapnel. He'd been lucky that a bullet hadn't hit them when he fired into the cabin; otherwise Awa and he would be dead already. "Did you see where they put Oumar?"

"Yes, he was in one of the smaller vehicles."

"A PVP? That makes things easier. And what about Tariq?"

She shook her head.

"Doesn't matter."

She pulled off the dead insurgent's long shirt. "What is your plan?"

Pierce picked up speed. "Originally, it was to call it in. Now, I'm going to end this myself."

46

Pierce increased the speed of his vehicle, closing the distance between his VAB and the next armoured personnel carrier in the convoy. The UN-marked vehicles had maintained a distance between each vehicle as they sped across the flat desert. If one had an accident or came under fire and the C-4 detonated, the resulting blast wouldn't consume the others. Pierce planned on using this strategy to his advantage.

He glanced at Awa. The insurgent's shirt hung on her like a dress, and the baggy pants looked too big on her, but at least she had clothes again.

"You're trembling," she said, slipping on the insurgent's sandals.

Pierce held out a hand. It shook like he had Parkinson's disease. He returned his grip to the steering wheel. "I'm fine," he said, knowing that if he didn't think about the tremors, they couldn't affect him, or so he told himself.

"Why are we going after them? There are so many. Shouldn't we run?"

Pierce paused. He had promised Awa he would protect her from harm, and now he was about to throw her into a bloody battle where they could both die. It was the lives of thousands of refugees that propelled him forward. His chance to stop the strikes was now, and he'd never forgive himself if he didn't try.

"Convoy Six?" chirped the radio. "Why are you increasing speed?"

Awa and Pierce stared at the radio.

"Convoy Six? Answer me!"

It was Denault. The mercenary sounded aggravated.

"You're right," Awa answered her own question. "We have to save Oumar and stop these terrorists detonating the bombs. What do you want me to do?"

"Can you drive?" Pierce asked with a grin.

"Yes — I mean no! I mean I know how to drive, but it's dangerous for me to drive with epilepsy."

"I'll take that risk. Get behind the wheel." He positioned himself away from the driver's seat while Awa slotted in and took control of the VAB. "You need to put a lot more strength into turning the steering wheel than you do in a normal car or truck."

"I'm getting the hang of it."

"Good."

"What are you doing?"

"There's an M2 machine gun back here."

"You will shoot the truck in front? Isn't it loaded with explosives as well?"

Pierce laughed. "Exactly. So get close, but not too close."

Pierce grabbed an ammunition belt and the machine gun, then opened the hatch and attached the weapon to the vehicle hard point. Years of practice on firing ranges had taught Pierce how to load and ready most weapons within seconds, so the M2 was no challenge.

When Awa had them within a few hundred metres of their first target, he opened fire.

In normal operations, the VAB's armour was protection enough from M2 fire, but Pierce was counting on the bullets finding a gap in the metal. He saw one. He maintained trigger pressure, concentrating his aim on the windows at the back of the VAB. The mercenaries had left the armoured window shield up, exposing the glass. An oversight they would soon regret.

The M2 burned through hundreds of 12.7mm x 9mm NATO rounds. Soon the target VAB started swerving, responding to the attack with evasive manoeuvres.

But they were too late.

A round hit.

Pierce expected a sizeable explosion, but what he witnessed surprised even him. One minute there was a VAB racing ahead on the flat-packed sand. The next a huge cloud of dust and dirt erupted into the sky like a meteorite had hit the earth. Shrapnel flew in every direction and pounded their armoured shell. Pierce clambered back inside only just fast enough, before a large metal chunk impacted their roof, tearing away the M2, while the ensuing sand cloud enveloped them.

Awa was jittery behind the wheel. She made tiny cries of surprise as metal fragments bounced off their armour and windshield, frosting the bulletproof glass with spiderweb fractures.

The dust cleared in time to see the destroyed VAB shell fall from the sky.

It bounced and rolled towards them.

Awa yanked at the wheel, but she wasn't strong enough. Pierce helped her, and they turned with seconds to spare before several tons of chassis tumbled past, close enough to touch. He felt gravity shift, so he fought to correct the wheel alignment before their vehicle flipped.

Then the blast crater loomed, thirty metres across. Now Awa corrected just fast enough to avoid barrelling into its deep edges.

Within seconds they passed the destruction and were back on the flat desert, picking up speed again.

"Did we just do that?"

He caught his breath, surprised they were still alive. "Yes, we did!"

The radio chirped. Denault's voice boomed across the frequencies. "What the fuck! Pierce?"

"Do we answer him?"

Pierce shook his head. "Not yet. Keep them guessing."

Two down. Four to go. Superior odds compared to where they were an hour ago.

47

Denault fumed. One compromised VAB disintegrated in an instant, close enough to feel the blast reverberations through his VAB's chassis as he gripped the wheel to keep it under control.

The African insurgent seated next to him, watching and learning how to drive these beasts of machines, glanced at Denault with an idiotic expression, which he had maintained effortlessly since their pairing. The man shrugged, to say he did not understand what was transpiring either. Of course he didn't. In Denault's view, the man was an idiot. At least he had mastered the basics of road operations, so could drive them in a straight line well enough. Denault might need him to do so soon.

Denault grunted and checked his side mirrors again. The VAB designated Convoy Six now sped through the dust cloud that marked Convoy Five's destruction, with Six now closing the distance on Denault's VAB. The situation was very wrong.

"What's going on, Sergeant?" chirped the radio. Hanna

Vautrin in the PVP just ahead expressed the same annoyance and frustration he felt about the unfolding situation.

"Assessing, ma'am. Looks like Convoy Five's lost. Convoy Six is…"

"Is what, Sergeant?"

He cleared his throat. He detested losing control of situations, and suspected Pierce had somehow escaped his bonds and taken control of the VAB that was supposed to be his death sentence. But to admit that was to admit he had underestimated the American again, and Vautrin would see it as entirely his fault. "Compromised, ma'am."

Denault expected a berating from Hanna, not the silence that followed.

"You there, ma'am?"

"Of course I'm here, Sergeant, you fool! Convoy Six is Pierce, and now he's got the better of you. You fucking should have just shot him when I told you to!"

Denault swallowed, feeling the itch in his throat. Hanna rarely swore, and he had never witnessed her this angry before. "I'll engage."

"Don't be an idiot. If you shoot him, we'll lose another VAB."

The former Legionnaire frowned. "What shall I do?"

"Ram him! Make him crash."

"Into what? It's flat desert."

"Look ahead, Sergeant. Think with your intellect rather than your misplaced pride for a change."

Denault stared along the horizon where the sands transformed into the familiar crests and troughs of low dunes. Spread among the dunes were hundreds of sand-worn pinnacles of rock, three to ten metres in height, resembling a petrified forest. He caught Hanna's meaning and grinned with both his mouth and scar.

He turned to the dumb insurgent. "Still can't figure out how a real man handles the road? Watch and learn."

Denault slowed his armoured personnel carrier. When he felt he was in position, he turned to the insurgent and said, "You take control, and stay close to that VAB." He pointed into the rear-view mirror as the distance between his and Pierce's VAB shortened.

He wanted Pierce to get close. He would kill his enemy on his own terms.

With the African behind the wheel, Denault opened the central overhead hatch, where his M2 machine gun waited, ready to be used for maximum effect.

48

Pierce knew their deception had ended when the radio chatter turned silent.

Back in the driver's seat, he floored the accelerator pedal and pushed up the gears, closing the distance between his vehicle and the next.

"What are you doing?" Every muscle in Awa's lithe body tensed.

"Closing the gap. They're packing C-4 explosives, but so are we. If we're close, they won't shoot. It would kill both us and them."

"That's insane."

"I know."

The compacted desert racing under their large wheels lost its flatness. Low dunes less than half a metre in height rose out of the desert, which the VAB burst through, creating explosions of sand clouds behind them. Pierce never let off on the accelerator. Only speed would save them now.

He spied a gunner on the closest VAB prepping an M2 machine gun. Pivoting to aim, the man fired high-velocity rounds that traced their vehicle even though it was dangerous for them all to do so.

Pierce squared off. The C-4 was in the back. Bullets were less likely to hit the plastic explosives from shots at their front, where there was an engine to block them and more metal to travel through.

Awa ducked her head as bullets bounced off their armour plating and bulletproof windshield. She pressed her hand against the dashboard and tensed.

The gunner kept firing. Their windshield frosted each time a bullet hit, and Pierce could barely see the path ahead. What he noticed between the frosted bullet grazes on the windshield was fields of rocky pinnacles, a maze of weathered sentinels that would slow them all down.

Pierce almost had to lean into the accelerator to achieve further speed, and soon they were doing over seventy kilometres per hour. His distance to the VAB ahead was closing... Three hundred metres.

Two hundred.

One hundred.

The gunner stopped firing, knowing the risks of hitting the C-4 at this range.

"What do we do now?"

He wouldn't tell Awa what he planned, knowing he'd scare her.

"Look!" she cried.

Pierce followed her pointing finger. The trailing VABs were closing ranks, one slowing so it could drop behind Pierce while the other kept in front, to constrain Pierce from the front and rear.

The VAB he'd been catching ahead also slowed.

They expected Pierce to slow with them.

But he didn't.

Pierce enacted his plan and sped up.

The rear of the VAB with the gunner came up in front of them fast.

They collided.

The impact was jarring. The VAB wobbled on its wheels and almost rolled over. Then the driver corrected at the last moment.

Pierce raced to its side. Rammed it again.

Both vehicles shuddered, but kept moving.

"Mark!" Awa cried.

He looked up.

A large rock came hurtling at them from nowhere.

Pierce yanked on the wheel, and the VAB pivoted.

So did the armoured personnel carrier at his rear, and they both avoided ploughing headfirst into the ancient rock formations looming around them.

The vehicles broke away, then closed in again.

Pierce looked to the closest VAB, the one he had rammed several times already. He recognised Denault, who was surely cursing his name.

Another rocky pinnacle loomed.

Pierce took a gamble and rammed Denault's VAB again.

The vehicles locked onto each other.

Pierce pulled on the wheel, pressing their bulk together, committing them both to a head-on collision with the next rock formation.

Awa screamed.

There was a *thunk* on the roof as Pierce disengaged.

Denault's VAB couldn't turn fast enough and rammed head-on into the ancient rock just as Pierce braked suddenly in case the *thunk* was someone jumping onto his vehicle. No body propelled forward over the windscreen, so he sped up again, knowing that if a foe remained on the roof, he'd have to deal with them later.

For many seconds nothing happened while the convoy sped past the carnage. Then there was an explosion from the crashed VAB, which was deafening, even from a distance. The fireball was brilliant in the already hot sands.

The shock wave spread rapidly. Pierce's VAB shook, but it kept moving, so he knew they couldn't have sustained serious damage. Again, no one was thrown from the roof, so it seemed likely if anyone had been up there, they had fallen off the back and were far behind them now. He looked through the intact rear-view mirror. No bodies but one VAB and two of the smaller vehicles, the PVPs, still in the game.

And as he glanced behind him, he also spotted his backpack in a corner. The French mercenaries must have concluded his equipment was worth salvaging.

Suddenly Awa screamed, "Mark, pay attention!"

He looked back through the windscreen to see a rocky pinnacle, already precariously balanced, now tipping forward, likely dislodged by the compression waves propagated through the sand by the earlier detonation.

He turned as sharply as the VAB would allow, missing by a few metres the hundreds of tons of rock about to squash them like pancakes.

It wasn't just one rock falling. Millennia of winds could only carry sand particles so far off the ground, thus eroding bases faster than the height of the rock. Mushroom-shaped protrusions had weak foundations and left the rock topheavy. The second explosion that had destroyed Denault's VAB had sent a shock wave through the pinnacle field, as he had suspected, and now rocks were falling everywhere.

Pierce turned fast and often, altering his direction every few seconds and pushing their speed higher.

Massive rocks crashed into the sand, creating what felt like mini earthquakes. Gravel and sand detonated into the air, forming localised dust clouds. Visibility dropped, but Pierce didn't slow. He saw two pinnacles fall onto each other, creating an arch, which he only just drove through in time before the columns collapsed behind them.

And then they were out of the rock formation, onto flat open sands and racing onwards.

Pierce pushed their speed to over a hundred kilometres per hour.

One VAB still chased them.

"What are you doing?" cried Awa.

He grinned. "Making this up as I go along."

Then the turret hatch in the centre of the cramped VAB interior flung open, and Denault leaped down. Miraculously, the French mercenary must have jumped on the roof before his own VAB crashed, and had managed to hold on through the detonation of his vehicle and the carnage of the pinnacles. That must have been the thumping Pierce had heard earlier: Denault fighting to stay alive on top of his vehicle. Now he was inside, with Pierce and Awa.

Pierce looked up only fast enough to see the scarred Frenchman lunge at him with two meaty fists. Trapped behind the wheel, Pierce barely blocked the blows.

Soon Denault had his muscular arm around Pierce's neck, and then he was pulling him back into the cramped cabin of the VAB while screaming, "No one fucking beats me, Pierce!"

Pierce couldn't breathe. His face grew hot. He couldn't

turn his arm far enough to reach the PAMAS pistol holstered at his belt.

The VAB's cabin shuddered, then started to slow now that no one was driving.

"The... wheel... Awa!" he managed between strangled breaths.

She'd been searching for a gun but hadn't found one. But, aware that no one controlled the vehicle, she jumped in behind the wheel and wrestled with the shuddering steering wheel.

One problem solved, but the grip around his neck was a more pressing problem.

As Denault throttled him, the CIA paramilitary officer knew he had one chance to save his life.

With Denault's firm grip around his throat, he stretched for his backpack, but it was just out of reach...

49

The flash and reverberation of a second explosion startled Oumar. He wasn't certain what had just happened, but he knew that once again, his situation had hope.

Tied by his neck and feet in the back of the armoured PVP, Oumar appreciated he was being driven to his death. The Tuareg nomad, Tariq, sat hunched over by his side. Although unbound, the French mercenaries had stripped Tariq of his weapons and the satellite phone that he'd had hidden on his person.

As Oumar heard further gunfire, Hanna yelled to Denault over the radio, instructing him again and again to kill Pierce. Then she ordered the French mercenary seated next to her to get up through the hatch in the centre of the vehicle and prep his assault rifle ready to protect them. Soon only the soldier's legs showed, with the rest of his body outside the vehicle.

Hanna ordered the other drivers to close in on Pierce. Oumar concluded the American must have escaped his bonds, destroyed two VABs and was now turning the fortunes of this battle in his favour. He hoped Pierce had saved Awa too.

Oumar glanced through the tiny window at the back of the vehicle. The towering rocks, weakened from the explosions, had fallen all around the two remaining VABs. Yet, somehow, the two had driven from the chaos intact.

It was time to act. This was likely his only chance to save himself. He'd survived a multitude of impossible situations these last few days and could survive a few more. He turned to Tariq and spoke in Bambara, a language he was certain the French would not understand, and said, "Cut my bonds!"

The nomad's eyes were red. His expression equal parts anger and sadness. He shook his head, betraying that he spoke Oumar's native tongue.

"Tariq, they will kill you as quickly as they will kill me."

"No! I made a deal with Saifullah. These people work for him. If I betray the mercenaries, I betray the Sword of Allah, and in retribution Ansar Dine will slaughter my family and my people. I'll die before I let that happen."

Oumar tensed. Without hands, he couldn't untie the knots. But that was the only help he required from Tariq, freedom from his bonds. "Loosen them, please. That's all I'm asking. No one will know it was you. I'll fight her myself."

Tariq snorted. "You are a cripple."

"I am. But I will not let my deformities define everything about me anymore. Please loosen my bonds."

Tariq hesitated, doubt in his eyes. Oumar sensed the man recognised his own misplaced loyalties and appreciated that soon the mercenaries would kill him too.

"No one will know."

Tariq looked to Hanna and the soldier, the latter with

half his body outside the central hatch of the PVP, tracking the movements of the other vehicles and unable to see what transpired inside. When Tariq could see no one was looking, he loosened the rope around Oumar's feet and neck. "You're on your own now."

Oumar nodded his appreciation as Tariq looked away. He freed himself of the remaining rope, then took several long breaths, preparing himself.

Hanna still yelled into the radio, furious with her men; she remained distracted.

If he pondered too long on what he was about to do, Oumar knew he would lose his courage. So he leaped up and propelled himself at Hanna and tightened his limbs around her throat, pressing into her neck as hard as he could, strangling her.

Caught by surprise, her hands slipped from the wheel.

50

P ierce struggled to breathe. Denault's grip across his throat imposed a strength greater than he could resist. The only reason Pierce hadn't suffocated was the pull of his own fingers against Denault's forearm, holding back the pressure that would otherwise crush his windpipe. But he still couldn't reach his holstered pistol, trapped just out of reach for both of them.

"Just fucking die, Pierce!"

With his left hand, Pierce reached out again for his backpack. This time he found purchase on a strap and managed to pull the bag towards him. His Swiss Army knife slipped out, slid across the floor and was soon beyond his grasp.

The VAB raced through the desert with Awa behind the wheel. She cried out when the other VAB nudged them, causing their vehicle to rattle. But she kept her cool and focused on keeping them in a straight line. Still, if she suffered an epileptic fit now, it was all over.

Pierce pulled again on the strap of his backpack, and it inched towards him. He was close to blacking out and fought the urge to succumb to the darkness. He reached into a pouch at the side of the bag and found the aerosol can where he had packed it. Grasping it, he managed to bring it up and spray it in Denault's face.

The former Legionnaire merely laughed. "It's just deodorant, Pierce. Thought you'd scare me again with fake drone-tracking nanoparticles?"

Then Pierce flung the can at Denault's head. The mercenary grunted from the impact and, in the same moment, lost the grip he had around Pierce's throat.

Pierce moved fast. He dropped, using the momentum of his own body weight to unbalance Denault, and the two men lost their balance in the bouncing vehicle and were soon somersaulting across the cabin. Pierce twisted in time for Denault to impact with the C-4 explosives packed against the armoured cabin. In the same motion Pierce's body crashed into the Frenchman.

This time it was Denault who wheezed for breath.

Pierce staggered to his feet. He went for the pistol, but Denault was faster, kicking it away as Pierce reached it.

Pierce retaliated, going in with punches and kicks, but Denault was a proficient fighter, blocking Pierce's every move. With his greater size and muscle mass, he soon turned defensive blocks into offensive strikes and came at Pierce's eyes and throat. Soft, vulnerable body parts.

Pierce ducked and blocked, then landed a punch in the kidney.

Denault winced but didn't slow. His right fist powered forward. Pierce ducked but not fast enough to avoid a glancing blow to his head. Disoriented, he lost his balance.

Then Denault grabbed at and unravelled a long length of rope, looped it on a hook on the rear cabin wall, and tried to wrap it around Pierce's neck. Pierce intercepted the rope with his left hand, only for Denault to loop it around his hand rather than his neck. Using this to his advantage, Denault yanked Pierce forward with a tug on the rope, while just at the same moment Pierce caught the other end of the line and wrapped it round his opponent's leg.

Pierce tried to pull the rope to unbalance Denault, but the mercenary simply came at Pierce again, his beefy fists pounding against the CIA man's forearms.

Pierce dropped low, landing a fist on Denault's jaw.

Now, with the mercenary dazed at last, Pierce kicked Denault's legs, and the man staggered backwards, colliding with the rear door. Pierce leaned forward, pulled on the latch, and the door flung open.

Denault fell out of the back of the VAB, but not before he pulled at Pierce's shirt. Pierce barely had time to snatch the fallen Swiss Army knife from the vehicle floor before he was dragged out into the desert.

They hit the sand together, its softness cushioning them from breaks and skin abrasions, but not from the force of being slammed hard into the ground. Sand exploded around them. The grains of sand had heated up through the day and burned Pierce's already sunburned skin.

Pierce coughed and spluttered as he rolled onto his back. He thought the VAB would race away and the sand clouds would dissipate, until he realised he was moving too. The rope, still wrapped around his left arm, was attached to the vehicle in its middle, looped around the handle of the now open back door, and he was being dragged behind it.

Denault too was tangled in the rope, caught on the opposite end to the length that had Pierce. The VAB pulled him by his leg, a few metres behind Pierce. Their eyes locked, both men surprised at their predicament. Despite the air that was surely rushing into the vehicle, it seemed Awa hadn't noticed their disappearance from the vehicle and kept up her speed. From his briefest glances her way during the fist fight in the cabin, she had seemed nervously focused on the road ahead.

Through the sand clouds bursting around him, Pierce saw the pursuing VAB only a few dozen metres behind them. The driver had noticed Pierce and Denault sand-skiing behind their VAB, and was now responding by closing in to run them over. Perhaps the driver thought he was skilled enough to avoid Denault and take out Pierce, but Pierce doubted it, and from Pierce's perspective, it didn't matter what the driver believed because he was attempting this stunt anyway.

Being closer to Awa's VAB than Denault was, Pierce managed to grab both their ropes, then used his pocketknife to cut the length dragging Denault.

Pierce watched as Denault cursed and came to a halt as Pierce's own VAB pulled him onwards. He hoped the Frenchman would disappear under the tyres of the approaching VAB, but the vehicle swerved in time, and Denault rolled away to safety.

Now the VAB continued on, aiming for Pierce alone.

Pierce had expected this. It was a long shot, but the length of rope only looped around the door handle, and him having hold of both ends gave him an opportunity. Not much of an opportunity, but a slim chance of survival.

As the VAB gained on him, he released the rope so only the end looped around his wrist stayed with him. He slowed as the rope unravelled from the door handle, then rolled, and managed to get underneath the approaching vehicle, ducking to avoid the four huge black tyres as they sped over him. The knife disappeared from his grip and was lost in the sand.

He hoped to vanish out the other side unharmed. And he did, but to his surprise the long length of rope trailing behind him caught in something on the underneath of the enemy VAB. A wheel axle perhaps. Whatever it had caught on, it now meant this second VAB was dragging him through the sand again like a jet ski surfer.

In a moment of confusion, Pierce glanced back at the now distant Denault and saw the former Legionnaire getting up onto his feet.

He also saw the two PVP vehicles still in the chase.

The rope wouldn't hold for much longer, and if it was caught in a wheel axle, it might tangle further and pull Pierce into the large spinning tyres, crushing him, so Pierce dragged himself through the near-suffocating sand. He heard gunfire and guessed it was from insurgents in the pursuing PVPs trying to take him out.

Pierce scrambled faster, pulling himself up along the remaining length of rope and grabbing a purchase at the back of the VAB.

A PVP closed in as he did so. They had given up shooting him and were now about to crush him.

He pulled himself up just in time, as the PVP rammed the VAB, attempting to squash him between the two vehicles.

Pierce climbed onto the roof of the VAB, found the central hatch and swung it open.

The mercenary inside was ready and fired his FAMAS assault rifle in Pierce's direction.

Pierce ducked as he felt bullets rush past his face.

The soldier emerged from the hatch, assault rifle ready.

Pierce knew he had a single chance, and he took it, kicking the weapon aside as the man fired.

But with the vehicle bouncing, Pierce lost his balance and came crashing down on top of the man's head. His foe momentarily stunned, Pierce used the precious few seconds awarded to him to twist the man's head and snap his neck, killing him. He pulled up the mercenary's FAMAS assault rifle and used it to put a bullet into the interior cabin and into the head of the Ansar Dine insurgent driving the VAB. The man fell forward, his weight collapsing on the steering wheel and his foot jammed on the accelerator.

Meanwhile, he spotted that Awa was racing away; he judged that she was far enough to avoid any potential ensuing blast radius if any of the C-4 in the vehicle he was firing into were to detonate.

Maintaining his balance on the bouncing and rattling PVP roof, Pierce reached in and pulled a flashbang grenade from the dead mercenary's combat harness. The flashbang had a magnetic grip, so he attached it to the FAMAS, waited until they passed over the crest of a low dune, pulled the pin and dropped both inside the VAB.

He launched himself off the back of the VAB, tumbled down the opposite side of the dune crest as a super-explosion ripped across the bright blue sky above him.

Covering his head, he waited for debris to cease falling out of the sky.

He was unharmed.

He was also unarmed.

The enemy VAB was little more than an empty shell of blackened metal.

But there were still two PVPs to deal with.

The Trigger Man 321

This scenario was the main reason why he had never wanted to be a lone man in an open desert in the first place.

Pierce glanced back. The PVPs had dropped back during the explosions, but the dunes were not sufficiently high enough for him to hide behind. They now knew where he was, and they came for him.

He had nowhere to run. Nowhere to find cover.

He was a dead man.

At least he thought so until one PVP flipped, then smashed into the other, which sent both vehicles to a grinding halt.

What had happened?

51

Pierce looked to his hands. They shook. Badly.

So did his legs.

But it wasn't over yet. Oumar or Tariq in one of the pursuing PVPs must have fought back. He needed to help them and eliminate any further mercenary or insurgent threats. He raced to the wreckage of the first PVP. As with the previous vehicles, its occupants were comprised of one French mercenary and one Ansar Dine insurgent. The insurgent was on his back, convulsing and coughing up blood. Pierce's hands felt around his seat, the driving controls and steering wheel, searching for the dead man's trigger to detonate the explosives, but it was nowhere to be seen or found. The Frenchman was dead, his back snapped at an unnatural angle.

Pierce drew a PAMAS G1 9mm semi-automatic pistol from the dead mercenary's holster and shot the insurgent in the head. Twice. He ensured that the angle of the bullets travelled through the skull and down the spine. He didn't wish to risk hitting the wired-up C-4 explosives packed inside this vehicle.

Pierce then grabbed the soldier's FAMAS assault rifle and approached the second crashed PVP as Oumar and Tariq clambered from the hatch. Both men staggered and were bleeding from multiple wounds, but none of their injuries looked life threatening. It seemed they had fought back after all, but Pierce remained suspicious. He aimed the rifle at Tariq. "You, hands up high where I can see them."

"I helped," the Tuareg cried out. "I freed Oumar—"

"Is that true?" Pierce asked.

Oumar nodded. "Tariq realised he was as dead as the rest of us. What happened? Where is Awa?"

"She's fine. The rest I'll explain later. Who else is in your PVP?"

Oumar gestured with his right limb. "The French soldier is dead, crushed when we rolled. Hanna Vautrin is unconscious at the wheel... Maybe she's dead."

"You!" Pierce kept his weapon pointed at Tariq. "Turn around and face the desert. If you turn towards us, even glance back, I'll shoot you. Understand?"

The Tuareg nodded. Pierce sensed the man's fear and shame.

After patting down Tariq to ensure he was without a weapon, he checked the PVP. Hanna, slumped on the wheel, with a large bruise across her forehead, was regaining consciousness. He checked her for weapons, found a fighting knife, a PAMAS automatic pistol and a satellite phone, all of which he pocketed; then he dragged her from the vehicle.

Once on the sand, Hanna proved too groggy and disoriented to stand, so he left her on a patch of empty sand and transmitted on the radio. "Awa? You copy? This is Mark."

Only static returned.

"Hold down to speak. Only one of us can talk at a time."

He heard her let out a squeal of excitement. "Praise Allah! You're alive!"

"Yes. So are Tariq and Oumar. Everyone else is dead or our prisoner. You can stop now. We'll come to you in a minute."

"Oh, that's a relief," she said through laboured breaths.

He heard her disengage the accelerator and the engine revs drop. Looking south towards the horizon, her VAB was easy enough to spot. Perhaps two kilometres away. "Turn around and come back to us."

She hesitated for the briefest moment, then: "Sure, I can do that, Mark. The closest smoke plumes?"

"That would be us."

Hanna was on her haunches now and trying to stand.

Pierce approached, PAMAS ready.

"What's your plan now?" Her dyed blond hair with black roots showing was in disarray, and her face was covered in soot and bruises. She remained a stunning woman, but she had lost her polish and poise. "You going to gloat before you kill me?"

Pierce waited a moment before he answered, "No."

"Then what?"

"I don't kill women or children. Only professionals."

She laughed. "I'm a professional."

He shrugged. "You've got to have standards; otherwise it's easy to slip into being the bad guy."

"How noble of you." She stood, and Pierce didn't move to stop her. He checked the pockets of his commandeered clothes, finding zip ties as he had hoped. He threw one to her. "Put it on. Use your teeth to tighten it."

Her eyes grew dark and her stare piercing as she obeyed. "If you take me alive, I'll end up in French custody. It won't be long before I'm released, and then I'll be back running my operations."

Pierce cocked an eyebrow. "Is that an invitation to kill you? Go against my personal standards?"

"No. But you must have concluded this yourself already."

He nodded, understanding her hidden question. "I don't know what will happen to you, but I know the CIA runs many black prisons across the globe. I will hand you over to them, and they'll report that you died today, so no one will come looking for you. Not even the French."

She bit her lip and looked out across the baking sand dunes. Pierce saw her fear. Perhaps her gaze was her way of memorising this moment, knowing that she wouldn't be staring at many horizons in her future.

Pierce looked to Tariq. He stood where Pierce had left him, away from the group, with his back still turned and his body trembling.

"Tariq?"

"Y-yes?"

"You can turn around now."

The man did so. Fear in his eyes suggested that he too believed Pierce was about to execute him. Instead, Pierce threw Tariq another pair of zip ties. "You know the drill."

With Tariq and Hanna constrained, he checked their cuffs and tightened them. He went to Oumar, who had been watching the events with equal trepidation. The two men didn't really know each other, yet Pierce felt he knew him well enough already to know there was more to this man than a mind confused by fanatical doctrine.

"You going to cuff me?" he asked, holding up his stumps.

Pierce shook his head. He didn't trust easily, and this man could still surprise him. But he was also handless and had acted to save Pierce during the earlier combat. "Awa speaks highly of you. I trust her judgement." Pierce wouldn't treat him like a prisoner, but he'd keep one eye on him at all times until reinforcements arrived.

Oumar nodded and said nothing.

Taking Hanna's satellite phone from his pocket, Pierce recognised it as a model the NSA had hacked and inserted a backdoor into its operating system. By entering a simple code, an overlay and temporary "shadow account" was activated, allowing the phone to make secure calls to the CIA that would never show up on the phone owner's account or IP address. Pierce activated the device and called Mackenzie Summerfield.

It wasn't Mackenzie who took Pierce's call, but Idris Walsh.

"Code in?"

"Three, one, Delta, one, Echo, nine, Bravo."

"Breakfast preference?"

"Muesli." Pierce gave the correct coded response.

"All right, Trigger Man. Tell me everything."

Pierce relayed the events of the last few days and the details of Ansar Dine's and Hanna Vautrin's now foiled plan. He provided their current location and details of the people with him, allies and enemies alike. Walsh responded that he had a U.S. Air Force CH-47 Chinook on its way. Then he asked about the missing money.

"I don't know where it is," Pierce said, as Awa pulled up

in the only surviving VAB and climbed out of the cabin. "But I know how I can recover it," he said, looking to Tariq.

"What is your plan?"

"I'll tell you when you get here, sir. Too many listening ears."

Walsh paused, then said, "Very well. ETA at your position will be ninety-four minutes. You have everything under control until then?"

"Yes, sir. Just one more thing."

"What's that, Trigger Man?"

"I need a drone. Preferably a Reaper."

52

I t was hard work, running in forty-five-degree-Celsius heat across soft sand in the world's largest, driest desert, with a slow-healing leg wound. But Sergeant Jean Denault wasn't like other men. He was better. He was a former French Foreign Legionnaire, trained and honed to perfection by one of the toughest and most effective fighting forces in the world. The sustained run, even in this heat and with his injury, was no problem for him.

His target was the rocky pinnacles they had chased Pierce through earlier. He needed cover from drones and U.S. and French aircraft. The radio silence left him with no doubt that Hanna, the other mercenaries and the insurgents were all dead. Pierce might be among the deceased, but Denault couldn't take that risk. He had to presume that Pierce had survived and now compromised Denault's position.

However, the former Legionnaire now had a plan that extended past mere survival. Hanna Vautrin's scheme might have turned to shit, but that didn't mean he would have nothing. Shalgham was still out there, with eleven million U.S. dollars stuffed into the saddlebags of his camels. Denault would catch the Libyan, gut him and use the money to escape Africa once and for all. Then he would disappear, change his identity and live the life of a playboy, but not before he hunted down and killed Pierce. He had to complete that last phase, keep his record straight, ensuring no one ever defeated him.

Eleven million dollars would go far. He'd make this work.

Denault kept running despite the ache in his calf. He stopped only to guzzle the water he carried on him. He had enough liquids to sustain him for days. With the sun dipping towards the horizon, the temperature would drop, and he wouldn't need to drink so much. He only had to get to the rocky overhang and take the Land Rover Defender that they had found with Pierce and Tariq. Then he would catch Saifullah soon enough.

Despite everything that had gone wrong today, Denault felt he had maintained a solid position.

His satellite phone rang.

Not expecting a call, Denault checked the number.

It was Hanna's number.

He thought it prudent to answer. If Hanna had survived and had enough resources to continue with her plan, he might as well rejoin her after he recovered the money from Shalgham. Hanna had promised Denault sufficient rewards, and besides, he enjoyed the spoiled bitch's company — most of the time. Watching her finely shaped ass was also a pleasant daily distraction.

He hit accept. "You survived?"

"I did."

Denault tensed. It wasn't Hanna who answered but Mark Pierce. He should have expected this. "You should have killed me, Pierce. I'll find you again, one day. That day will be your last."

There was a pause.

Denault said, "I know you're afraid of me. I saw how you fought. I'm the better warrior. Faster. Stronger. More ruthless."

Pierce didn't answer at first, then said, "Is Shalgham with you?"

"What?"

"Also known as Saifullah? Did you run to him for protection?"

Denault recognised Pierce's taunting, but he wouldn't let the American get to him. Denault was the victor; he was the one in control here. "I'm alone, Pierce. I'll take you on, man to man, if that's the purpose of your call. To save you from all that fear, worrying about when I will find and gut you."

"Thanks, Denault, that's all I needed to know."

"What are you talking about?"

Pierce laughed. "You were right about it being deodorant... the first time."

It took Denault a moment to understand Pierce's meaning. He lowered the satellite phone, realising that infrared markers covered his face. He couldn't rub them off. It didn't matter where he tried to hide, he would be lit up like a lighthouse in the night. There was no cover in the kilometres of sand dunes that stretched in every direction.

His fists tightened. His teeth ground against each other.

Every muscle in his body tensed with the urge to break the CIA assassin in two.

"See you in hell, Pierce."

Denault looked up. He knew he wouldn't see the drone, but instead the tail flame of the Hellfire missile racing towards him, and then...

Nothing.

53

Pierce, Awa and Oumar watched the explosion rise on the horizon. A few seconds later, they heard the rumbling blast. Pierce stared into the inferno, concluding that another threat was eliminated. The CIA had equipped him with infrared aerosol markers for some time. He had never used them until now, but they were an effective tool.

He turned his attention to Awa.

She had been busy cleaning sand and dried blood from his leg wound where Denault had stabbed him in the cave, a painful experience for Pierce but a necessary one. Satisfied with her work, she applied disinfectant swabs, taken from the trauma kits she had found in the wrecked PVPs. Then she bandaged it. "You were lucky, Mark. The wound doesn't look like you'll need stitches."

He grinned. "And no major arteries hit."

She smiled with him. "We wouldn't be having this conversation now if that were the case. But I need you to take these pills for the next week." She passed him a packet of broad-spectrum antibiotics. Pierce buckled up his pants and swallowed one pill. "Clean the wound at least twice a day and apply fresh bandages."

"Yes, ma'am."

Awa laughed. She took his hand in hers and held it. "Look at that."

"Look at what?"

"You're no longer trembling."

Pierce glanced at his fingers and palms. She was right. In the past, he'd become a mess after a brutal battle, but not today. "What's different?"

"At a guess, I'd say you achieved much good today. Your mind is at peace with what you accomplished."

Pierce reflected on her words, not sure what to say, and sensing that she might have unlocked one mystery about how his subconscious operated.

"Western medicine has forgotten that the body mirrors your state of mind. The shakes, the tremors, they are your body's way of saying all is not right."

"So if I keep doing what is right, help people and make the world a better place, I should be okay? This isn't a degenerative disease?"

She shrugged. "I could be wrong. I'm not a doctor, but it makes sense to me. Does it feel right?"

Pierce nodded.

"Our subconscious is a powerful force we give little credit to. If you understand what your subconscious wants, and act on it, your life will improve."

"I don't doubt that. Thank you." He glanced over to Tariq and Hanna, both bound to the VAB. While they waited for Walsh and the Marines, he didn't want any of them trying to escape — not that there was anywhere to run to, this deep inside the Sahara. Both prisoners looked worried. They should be, as both their futures were about to experience unexpected transformations.

Pierce caught Oumar staring at him. Pierce had earlier instructed him to keep his distance from him if they wished to remain friends. "What's up?"

"What about me?"

Awa pushed her curls from her eyes and stood between Pierce and Oumar. "Mark, I know Oumar was with the kidnappers, but he didn't have a choice. And remember, he saved both our lives back there. He just wants a normal life, to become an engineer."

Oumar looked surprised that Awa had remembered his hopes and aspirations.

Pierce stood and gave a salute to Oumar. "Very well, Oumar. I have a lot to thank you for, and I'll get you out of this."

The man nodded. "Thank you, Mr. Pierce."

They heard the approaching Chinook long before they saw it. It flew high to avoid surface-to-air missiles, dropping only when it was above them. Sand whipped up into the air as it settled into a soft landing on the flat desert. U.S. Marines with M4 assault carbines secured a perimeter.

A sergeant approached and saluted, and Pierce returned the salute. She shouted over the noise of the helicopter, "Sir, I understand you have two prisoners ready for transfer of custody?"

"Only one for custody." Pierce nodded to Hanna. "The other stays with me."

"Understood, sir." She took a black hood from a pouch.

"She won't need that, Marine."

"I'm afraid she does, sir. Orders from up high."

The Marines bound Hanna with metal handcuffs around her wrists, waist and ankles. Her stare expressed neither despair nor anger but focused on Pierce as the hood was pulled over her head. She complied as they led her to the Chinook. Pierce felt he would never hear about her ever again; she would disappear like she had never existed. Pierce felt sorry for her in that moment, but remembered that she had tried to murder thousands of innocent refugees for revenge and profit. Maybe she deserved her fate.

Walsh and Mackenzie stepped from the Chinook; they were both wearing civilian clothes coloured to blend with the desert. Walsh threw Pierce a bundle of similar clothes, which Pierce changed into. He wasn't shy, but for modesty he turned his back on them so they would only have to glimpse him naked momentarily from behind.

"Congratulations, Pierce." Walsh spoke without looking at Pierce, and his lips barely moved.

"Yes, well done." Mackenzie beamed from behind their boss.

"Summerfield, I was being sarcastic." Walsh turned to Pierce. "You saved only one hostage, and you didn't recover the missing money." He spoke in English so Awa, Oumar and Tariq wouldn't understand. "You're about as useful as the idiots I was dealing with on my last operation in Turkey."

The new pants felt clean and comfortable to Pierce. Now he buttoned his shirt, glad to be out of the clothes tainted with other men's sweat, spit and blood. "You shouldn't be so down, sir. We prevented a major terrorist attack occurring against several refugee camps, saving the lives of thousands and preventing an escalation of this conflict. We're close to neutralising a major Ansar Dine fighting force and killing or capturing a high-value target. And I can still recover the money."

"Yes, about that. You said you had a plan?" Walsh turned to the Marine at his side, motioning with his eyes that he wanted to speak with Pierce and Mackenzie alone. The Marine obeyed and motioned that Awa should come with him, as she was the only other person within hearing distance.

"What about me?" Awa protested in French. "And what are you saying?"

Pierce answered in Arabic. "It's all good, Awa. They won't take you anywhere until I say so."

With a scowl, Awa let the Marine lead her away.

Walsh spoke when they were alone. "That was presumptuous of you."

"You know," Mackenzie interrupted as she gazed out across the expanse of dunes and the sun on the western horizon, ready to set in about an hour, "I keep thinking of the deserts I've visited in California, but they are nothing like this."

"Stay on topic, Summerfield. Plan your vacations in your own time."

"Sorry, sir." She straightened her back and grasped her hands behind her waist.

Pierce stood tall, now that he had finished dressing, and smirked. Mackenzie had just told him that she believed Walsh was operating alone and unaligned with any of the groups Pierce had battled in the last few days. That would make the next steps in his plan easier to accomplish.

Pierce pointed to Tariq. "He's Bachir Aghali's son. He thought he could protect his father and his tribe by paying off Shalgham. However, Shalgham planned on killing him during the suicide attacks to make the Tuareg people complicit with the fanatics. But I believe his real value now is his knowledge of Ansar Dine's operations and details on their local headquarters, the rock formation they call the Hand of the Prophet. Shalgham will take the money there to hide it. Once Tariq tells us its location, you can send in a SEAL team, Army Rangers or CIA Special Operations Group forces to take them out and recover the money."

"Will Tariq Aghali willingly give up Ansar Dine's location?"

"He will if you offer him his freedom and buy yourself some leverage."

Walsh frowned. "I sense you already have a plan how to do that?"

Pierce nodded as he pointed to the mercenary and Ansar Dine bodies. "We have many dead insurgents at our feet. Photograph Tariq with the Marines, basking in the glory of their kills. Put out the word it was Tariq's heroic actions that led to their downfall. He'll become a hero to his people and a sworn enemy of Ansar Dine, al-Qaeda and Islamic State for siding with the Americans. We secure the Tuareg's loyalty, because he won't dare go back to an enemy he has betrayed."

Walsh smirked through thin lips. "You are a cunning and scheming individual, Trigger Man. I'd hate to find myself on your bad side."

"Let's ensure that never happens."

"You want to join the raid? Destroy this so-called Hand of the Prophet?"

Pierce shook his head. "I'm sure you can handle the situation without me, sir. We came here in a Land Rover Defender." He pointed north where they had raced across the desert. "I'll return Tariq to Bachir, talk him up. Cement the story about his heroic actions. I also want that man with me." He pointed to Oumar.

Mackenzie asked, "Isn't he a kidnapper?"

Pierce had used the last hour to reflect on the man's fate, watching him as he talked and laughed with Awa, and he'd concluded the nurse was right about him. He was no threat to anyone, and he had saved Pierce's life. "Technically he is, but look at him. The man has no hands. Oumar's lived as a beggar these last few years. He's got nothing, and he put himself at great risk to aid me in my mission. He's not fanatical. If he gets on that Chinook, we both know he'll end up in chains with a bag over his head and a bleak future in a black prison. He doesn't deserve that."

Walsh considered Pierce's request. "What will you do with him? I'm not sure he could survive out here on his own."

"Awa, the kidnapped nurse, says he has family in Timbuktu," Pierce lied, knowing from earlier conversations with Awa and Oumar that the man's sister was in Tangiers. "I'll reunite them when I've dealt with Bachir and Tariq."

Walsh spent another moment in deliberation. Pierce suspected the spymaster did so only for show, for Walsh didn't strike Pierce as a man who ever had a problem with making quick decisions. Walsh said, "Very well. You sure you don't want to join us on this raid, see it concluded?"

"No, sir."

Walsh shook his head. "Your plan sounds sensible."

Mackenzie spoke up from behind the CIA spymaster. "I need to go with him, sir."

"You, Summerfield? For what purpose?"

"I speak Tamashek, the Tuareg local language, and

Pierce doesn't. I bet Bachir won't fear voicing his real plans in the open, knowing that we won't understand. We might learn a thing or two."

Pierce watched Walsh calculate many future scenarios on how the next few days would pan out. The Head of Operations, North Africa knew Pierce and Mackenzie were scheming something, but it appeared he hadn't yet figured out what that was. Pierce was counting on Walsh being more interested in his primary objective of recovering the money than that of controlling them in the short term.

"Do you want her along, Pierce?"

"No, sir," he said, keeping his face impassive. Pierce wanted Mackenzie with him, but he didn't want Walsh to know that.

Walsh studied them both. "Very well, Summerfield. You go with Pierce. Once you've delivered Tariq to his people, I'll send in a helo for your ex-fil; then I'll debrief you both. From there, we'll decide both your futures."

54

The Chinook flew Pierce and the others to the rocky outcrop where Tariq had left the Land Rover Defender. Pierce had minutes at most to say goodbye to Awa Sissoko, a shouted conversation over headphones because of the competing engine noise, spinning rotor blades and the fast wind blowing through the open helicopter.

"Awa, you'll receive medical attention and a debriefing in Agadez. Afterwards we'll return you to Timbuktu and reunite you with your mother. We'll also sort out any misunderstandings with the hospital where you work. Everything will be back the way it was. Unless..."

Awa pushed the fluttering corkscrew curls out of her eyes. "Unless... what? Mark?"

Pierce shrugged and shouted again, "My country owes you. I owe you. If you and your mother want U.S. citizenship, I have contacts in the Immigration Department who owe me favours. We could make that happen."

She looked away, and Pierce sensed her conflicted state of mind.

"It's your choice," he assured her.

Awa turned to him as her eyebrows furrowed. "I could take your offer, Mark, and it sounds generous. But if I left Mali, I'd be abandoning my people. I know my country has a long path to follow before it becomes anything like your beloved America, and I know I face discrimination here every day because of my gender and my epilepsy, but I'm still a Malian. This is my culture. These are my people."

Pierce nodded. He had already guessed her response, but it would have been remiss of him not to offer.

"What I remember most these last days are men being violent to men, women and children. Not women being violent to men, women and children — except for Hanna Vautrin, but even she restrained herself compared to the others. I know countries only stop warring, become stable and advance politically when women receive education. I'm an educated woman, which makes me lucky. If I leave my people, I'm abandoning everything I believe in. I'm like you, Mark, I believe in something bigger than myself."

He smiled and shouted his answer. "Then it's solved. You'll still receive compensation from the U.S. Treasury. You won't say no to that?"

She smiled. "If one good thing resulted from this, it was that I met you."

"I feel the same."

"Will I ever see you again?"

He shrugged. "I hate to be honest, Awa, but no. We'll probably never see each other again."

She smiled. "Then good luck. I hope your life is far longer than you might expect it to be."

The helicopter landed. Pierce, Mackenzie, Oumar and Tariq departed with their gear and enough provisions and water to last them several weeks in the desert — not that they planned on being there that long. They watched the Chinook disappear south as the sun set. Then they found the Land Rover Defender parked on the flat sand between rugged peaks. It was night by the time Tariq and Pierce performed a maintenance check and ensured it was operational.

Tariq said, "We should camp for the night, Pierce. It's too dangerous to drive in the dark."

Pierce scratched the back of his neck. "Will Shalgham travel at night?"

"Have you changed your plan? I thought you were returning me to my tribe now that you've manipulated my loyalty with those staged photos?"

"That is where we're ultimately headed, but first we kill Shalgham."

"I told your people where the Hand of the Prophet is. Won't your Marines now kill him?"

Pierce wiped his greasy hands on an old cloth he'd found in the Defender. "They can't, because he won't be there."

"What?"

"He's running."

Tariq frowned. "Why?"

"Because Shalgham has the eleven million dollars, that's why. He was a fanatic only because he had no choice. His skills were useful to Ansar Dine when he needed financing, but with money like that in his possession, he can now disappear."

"How will he disappear? How will you find him?"

Pierce gazed to the heavens. The stars were out, and the

Milky Way was a clear line of stars and gas reaching from one horizon to the next. He saw a single shooting star live for less than a second, and he spotted his favourite star, Aldebaran, twinkling in the zodiac constellation of Taurus. "By airplane. I'm betting you know where the closest abandoned Adrar des Ifoghas airfield is. You know what I mean, Tariq — a strip once used to fly in tourists and petroleum geologists before insurgents took control. The nearest runway will be where Shalgham is headed."

"You lied to your own people?"

Pierce laughed. "So did you, Tariq."

"Of course I lied, to protect my people. You wouldn't understand."

"I understand. It's why you're here and not in a CIA black prison. I wanted to ensure you'd forever fight on the right side."

"I thought you would kill me?"

"No, Tariq. Despite our differences and disagreements, you and I are friends. We'll be working together for some time yet. Now, do you or don't you know where this airfield is?"

For the next thirty minutes, Pierce interrogated Tariq on the location and details of the abandoned runway. Once satisfied that he had everything Tariq could provide, he went to Mackenzie and explained his plan. Oumar was nearby and already fast asleep inside the Land Rover, but not before he had hurriedly consumed three meals, the "ready-to-eat" variety.

"Why didn't you tell Walsh any of this?" She spoke English so the others couldn't understand.

"Because of the money. Hanna and Lucas Vautrin didn't know about the cash, and neither did Shalgham and Ansar

Dine. We can also exclude Bachir, Tariq and the Tuareg. So that leaves only—"

"Idris Walsh."

"Exactly. You confirmed as much with your earlier California desert comment."

Mackenzie wrapped her arms around her chest now that the temperature was dropping. She explained to Pierce how Walsh had played mind games with her, made her question her worth and threatened to murder her in the desert, and she told him about the half-truths she'd spun so Walsh wouldn't fire her or have her reprimanded for insubordination. "I don't know what he's up to, but I don't like any of it."

"Neither do I, but if we recover the eleven million dollars, he might have to tell us to get it back."

Mackenzie looked to the horizon, as if she suspected someone watched them. Another shooting star burned for less than a second. "One more unexpected discovery just before I flew out. Walsh reported the eleven million lost four days ago, destroyed in the car explosion that killed the three CIA operatives. I checked the time and date. He made the report straight after your first call to him."

"So Walsh must be running his own personal black op, which this money funds and is unwittingly paid for by the CIA. Nothing to do with Vautrin, Shalgham and the others."

"Mark, that was my conclusion too. But what operation? And why did he let us loose when he knows we suspect him?"

"You said it earlier, Mackenzie, the Sahara is a huge place to disappear in, forever."

"You think he'll come after us? Silence us permanently?" She shuddered at the thought.

"When he discovers the money isn't at the Hand of the Prophet, yes."

Neither spoke for a moment. Mackenzie's face became glum.

Pierce said, "Or the money pays for a legitimate sanctioned op we don't have the clearance to know about, and we're committing treason by standing in Walsh's way."

She made a face. "Put a positive spin on it, why don't you?"

"Mackenzie, why are you here?"

"What do you mean?"

"This is the Sahara's heart and ground zero on the War on Terror. You didn't have to join this mission. Fieldwork is not your role if you don't want it to be."

She touched the back of her neck. "I know. I've been thinking about that, Mark, and what happened... to me... in Greece. Some men, they do that to control women... Have power over them. Abraham wanted to control me, and Walsh used my trauma to control me too. I realised I'd given over my control, externalised it. While you were in the field these last few days, I had an epiphany; I don't want to be afraid anymore. You're right, I don't have to be here. But I choose the field, and I choose being brave; otherwise I'll forever remain a shell of the person I really am. I'll let others keep putting me in a box that constrains me."

Pierce nodded, not sure how to respond. She didn't need his approval, so he said nothing to suggest this. "Thank you for telling me."

"We're friends, right?"

He smiled. Nobody had called him a friend for a long time. He realised that was what they were, friends. He didn't trust anyone else in the world the way he trusted Mackenzie Summerfield. "Always!"

She wiped tears from her eyes, pretending they weren't there. "Enough of all this sentimental time wasting. What's the plan?"

Pierce grinned. "We go hunting."

55

ADRAR DES IFOGHAS, MALI

With the morning sun rising behind them, Pierce and Mackenzie watched the abandoned airstrip from their hideout on a desolate hill, three hundred metres distant. Summerfield used their new M40A5 sniper rifle's scope, while Pierce used binoculars. The Saharan landscape was mostly flat gravelly sand with a few patches of low dunes. To the north were the outlying peaks of the Adrar des Ifoghas, shimmering in the haze. Pierce often thought the Sahara resembled an alien planet, for there was nothing in their line of sight to suggest life could have ever existed here, even though he knew this wasn't true.

A sand-coloured tarp, included in the equipment Walsh had provided them, covered Makenzie and Pierce, offering concealment from aerial observation. The similarly covered Land Rover Defender remained out of sight behind the rise, with Oumar and Tariq inside. So far, it seemed no one had spotted them.

"Shalgham must be nearby." Mackenzie spoke softly so

her voice wouldn't carry in the winds. She held the sniper rifle steady. "His camels, we spotted them on the drive here, at that nearby guelta. So, where is he?"

"It's a good question, Mackenzie." Pierce watched the empty, cracked runway. No signs of movement anywhere, yet Pierce sensed Kashif Shalgham had to be somewhere in their field of view. They had arrived in the early hours, well before dawn, and established an over-watch position. Since then, it had been a waiting game to see who showed. "The other question is... who'll come for him?"

Summerfield answered without hesitation. "Moroccans."

"Really? What do you know that I don't?"

"Lots of things."

He chuckled. "I've never doubted that." When she didn't answer, he asked, "What, specifically, about Shalgham don't I know?"

Trained in a variety of firearms by the CIA, during an advanced field operative course, Mackenzie kept her eye planted on the scope, as her instructors had drilled into her. "His cell phone history. The few times the NSA positively identified Shalgham, he made calls on burner phones to Casablanca. And before you ask, we never identified his contacts; otherwise we would have moved on them long ago. Some group who knows how to mask their identities well."

Pierce thought of Oumar and Tariq in the Land Rover. With the vehicle's battery cables in Pierce's pack, Tariq couldn't drive off and escape, and would instead sweat in the heat, guzzling water to stay hydrated. Pierce knew Ansar Dine and his own people terrified Tariq now, so the idea of running wouldn't be at the front of his mind. Pierce didn't care for Tariq's troubles; he had plans for them both, assuming their encounter with Shalgham went as planned. Plans that benefited them all.

"Morocco is ideal."

"Because of Oumar?"

"Exactly."

"Eleven o'clock," she said, giving directions.

Pierce dropped his binoculars and looked until he found the approaching low-flying aircraft. He switched to the binoculars again until he had a bead on the plane. "A C-212 Aviocar. Medium-range cargo plane. No country markers I can make from this distance."

Mackenzie licked her lips against the dryness of the air. "With extra fuel tanks, that's range enough for Morocco."

"You sure they're Moroccan?"

"Are you sure Shalgham is down there?"

Conceding her point, Pierce scanned the runway. The twin-prop airplane would land in minutes. If Shalgham was in the vicinity, he had buried himself somewhere nearby or had covered himself with a tarpaulin like they had.

"Mackenzie, here's my plan. You keep over-watch. I'll disguise myself again as a Tuareg and drive with Tariq to the plane. If the occupants don't immediately start shooting, I'll try to convince them I'm Shalgham and see what they say."

Mackenzie kept her eyes at the scope, tracking the plane as it came in for a landing. "It's rough, but I can't think of a better plan."

"Neither can I." He touched the voice activation pod on his chest rig. "Comms check?"

"Copy that."

"Okay. Mission on."

Pierce shimmied back to the Defender. To their credit, Tariq and Oumar had remained inside and out of sight.

Pierce tore off the desert-camouflaged tarpaulin cover and opened the door. Both men sweated and drank from their water bottles. Oumar's ability to perform simple tasks with only stumps impressed Pierce, and he imagined what the young man could achieve with proper prosthetics.

"New plan. Oumar, get up to Mackenzie. Can you use binoculars?"

He nodded.

"Good. You act as her spotter. You must identify targets for her if a gunfight erupts."

"Sure, I can do that. Is that plane here to collect Saifullah?"

"We have to presume so, which is where the next part of the plan comes into play. Tariq, you're coming with me." Pierce found white robes and the blue turban worn by Tuareg men that Tariq had left in the Defender. "I'll disguise myself as Shalgham. You are my bodyguard. We drive down now."

"Are you crazy? They'll shoot us."

Pierce shrugged. "Probably. Just make sure when you shoot back, you don't hit the plane. We'll need it to fly out of here."

The young nomad pressed his hands against his forehead and gritted his teeth. "Is that your plan? It's suicide."

"It won't be. They'll think we're friendlies." Pierce didn't necessarily believe this was likely, but he needed to heighten Tariq's confidence that this deception could work.

"Come up with a different plan."

"No. It's time to move."

Oumar disappeared up the rise towards Mackenzie.

Pierce got behind the wheel, then ensured his M4 carbine was by his side and ready. He passed Tariq magazines for an AK-47 they had brought with them. This was the first time since the man's betrayal that Pierce had trusted the Tuareg with a weapon. It wouldn't take much for Tariq to turn traitor again and shoot Pierce, but he didn't see that the Tuareg man had much choice in the matter now but to help him. Pierce hoped Tariq would be sensible enough to fight at his side. Ideally, he would have had Tariq drive, freeing Pierce to engage targets, but he didn't trust Tariq that far.

Pierce started the engine. He heard the C-212 on approach for landing. From their hidden position behind the rise, the Land Rover would seemingly come from nowhere, but so might Shalgham. He sensed the terrorist was nearby, but where?

"You saved my life, just to kill me now?"

Pierce sped up, churning a cloud of sand behind them. "What happened to the brave warrior all the young women are interested in? That was all show?"

Tariq snarled and looked away. "I am brave. I need not prove it to you."

Pierce shook his head. "No, you don't, but you might have to prove it to yourself in a minute."

The plane had touched down and pulled to a stop by the time Pierce reached it. He was in easy firing range now, and the pilots weren't trying to take off again because of his sudden appearance, which he took as a positive sign.

He was about to apply the brakes when a low dune exploded outwards. A man, previously hidden by a tarpaulin covered in sand, now rose out of a foxhole in the earth, with a weapon pressed into his shoulder.

Pierce didn't have time to see the make and model, but he recognised a rocket-propelled grenade launcher when he saw one.

The missile fired, streaking through the blue skies.

Pierce pulled on the wheel, willing himself to turn from its path fast enough.

He might not have identified the weapon's model, but he knew the man operating it was Kashif Shalgham.

56

P ierce pressed all his weight into the steering wheel. The rocket shot past, hit the gravelly sand behind him, and detonated with a thunderous explosion.

It was then that Pierce realised he had overcorrected.

The Land Rover flipped.

They rolled, over and over.

He saw Tariq disappear out the window. The fool hadn't worn his seatbelt.

Sand sprayed everywhere, got in Pierce's eyes and mouth. His arms and head bounced off the cabin's interior as he lost control. After it had rolled over twice, the vehicle skidded to a sudden stop.

In a daze, Pierce realised the Land Rover had landed the right way up.

The engine was still running.

Blood dribbled from the back of his head where shattered windscreen glass had cut him. He ignored the pain and glanced through the rear-view mirror lined with spiderweb fractures.

Three men in jeans and shirts approached with Steyr assault rifles at the ready. One fired a burst into the back of the Land Rover.

Pierce flinched. Then kept his body still.

He felt for pain, glanced without moving his head for signs of blood. He feared for a moment that he had taken a bullet, or three, but he remained unharmed.

The soldiers drew closer.

When they were within a few metres, Pierce engaged reverse and raced backwards, hitting all three men, driving over them. Bones crunched, cracked and shattered. Muscles and organs made popping noises.

He spun the wheel, turned in an arc, grateful that the Defender responded to his demands despite its battering. Two more identically armed men ran at him and raised their Steyr rifles.

Pierce lifted his M4 carbine and fired one-handed through the open window. His shots went wild, and the men had time to duck for cover. Pierce slammed down on the brakes, skidded to a stop, then took proper aim with his weapon. He was about to shoot when a series of bullets burrowed through their skulls, killing them instantly.

He spoke into his radio. "Thanks, Mackenzie. Nice shooting. I owe you."

"Oumar spotted them. You okay?"

"I am. Cover me while I ground the plane."

"Roger that."

He drove again, parked the Land Rover across the runway so the C-212 couldn't take off.

He kept his body low and behind the four-wheel drive as

he climbed out. The aircraft's main door was open but with no signs of movement.

Pierce spoke into his mic. "I'm approaching. If you see trouble, fire over the top of the plane."

"Roger that."

Pierce jogged forward. When he was next to the cabin door but out of sight to anyone inside, he called out in Arabic, "I'm counting to five; then I throw a grenade inside. One... Two..."

Two men in pilot uniforms scrambled out, their arms raised.

"Down on the ground. Hands behind your heads."

The pilot and co-pilot complied.

"Anyone else on board?"

"No."

"If I discover you are lying, I'll shoot you."

"*NO!*"

Pierce believed them.

Mackenzie yelled over the mic, "Mark!"

Pierce heard two shots fly high over the aircraft as he spotted Shalgham near the tail of the plane. The blue-eyed giant held Tariq as a human shield, the long curved blade of his scimitar pressed against the young warrior's throat. The battered and bruised man had survived the car roll, only to face death at the hands of a sadist.

Pierce lined up Shalgham's head with the sights of his M4. He might kill his enemy with a single shot, but with Tariq thrashing and struggling, Pierce could hit the wrong man. "Drop the weapon, Shalgham. I say the word, and my sniper drops you."

Shalgham snarled and edged forward. "I don't think so.

Shoot me and the bullet goes through my body, damaging the plane you have fought so hard to win."

"We can patch bullet holes."

"Not when the fuel tank is right behind me."

Pierce tensed and gritted his teeth, knowing that Shalgham was correct. "Mackenzie?"

"Yes, Mark?"

"Is he in your sights?"

"Affirmative. I'll take him out when you give the word. But be careful, he's correct, the fuel tank *is* right behind him."

"Copy that." He returned his attention to the self-professed, reincarnated Sword of Allah and his sweating prisoner. "It seems we are at a stalemate."

"Drop your weapon."

"No."

Shalgham pressed the blade against Tariq's neck, drawing blood.

"Okay, Shalgham, I'm complying." Pierce slowly lowered his M4, ejected the magazine and threw both far from him.

"And your sidearm."

Pierce complied, withdrew the Glock 19 and dropped it at his feet. This weapon he kept armed and close enough so he could go for it should circumstances change in his favour. "Now your turn. Release Tariq or the sniper will kill you. You can have the plane. We'll take our chances with the Land Rover."

"That is acceptable. First, the pilots return to the plane."

"Kill him!" Tariq yelled as he struggled, frustrated that he was in a vulnerable position once again.

Ignoring Tariq, Pierce nodded and gestured to the pilots

that they should return inside as instructed. They hurried on board.

"You get on that plane, Tariq, you're a dead man."

Tariq panicked and struggled further, which was what Pierce wanted him to do. Shalgham kept Tariq's body positioned so a sniper bullet would go through his prisoner first before it went through him, but the struggle kept Shalgham preoccupied from noticing what Pierce was collecting in his left hand.

"*Rattaek!*" Summerfield shouted in Pierce's ear. "Tell him to *Rattaek!*"

Pierce presumed that was a Tamashek word. "Tariq? *Rattaek!*"

The words calmed the warrior, and he stopped using his legs to hold his body upright, despite the risk that the action might cause the blade to still cut him, and let his body fall to the earth.

Shalgham, not expecting this, lost his balance, then stumbled forward as Tariq's weight pulled him down.

Pierce whispered into the mic, "I've got this." He didn't need bullet holes in the plane, or for the auxiliary fuel tank to ignite and incinerate them all.

"Copy that!"

Shalgham growled, dropped Tariq, then came at Pierce, swishing his scimitar through the dry air in wide arcs.

Pierce heard Summerfield cry out, but he kept his cool, only sidestepping at the last second as the sharp steel blade slashed down towards his forehead. Shalgham overbalanced and stumbled forwards. Pierce turned to face his foe, who was now staggering on his feet.

Shalgham tried to raise his weapon but found he had no

strength. He looked down at his side. It was covered in blood. A wound gushed with his life fluids.

"You missed." Pierce smirked and held his bloodied KAMPO tactical knife in his left hand for Shalgham to see. "I didn't."

Shalgham tried to speak. Instead, blood gushed from his mouth. He fell to his knees, then his eyes rolled up towards his skull, and he fell forward, face down on the old tarmac.

Pierce gathered up his Glock semi-automatic and put two bullets into his skull, just to make sure.

fter securing the aircraft and binding the pilots with zip ties, Pierce led the two men back outside again.

Tariq was up on his feet, dusting himself off. "You..." he blustered. "You... saved my life."

Pierce nodded.

"Why?"

Pierce patted Tariq on the back. "You're not a bad man, my friend. Just misguided. But look, you've just killed Kashif Shalgham, the infamous Saifullah. You'll be a hero among your people."

"But I didn't kill him. You did!"

"Did I?" Pierce grinned. "That's not how I remember it."

Tariq gritted his teeth. "I suppose... I should thank you. If you'd betrayed me to my enemy, I wouldn't be so forgiving."

Pierce shrugged. "Just don't do it again, Tariq. Besides, the U.S. will have decimated Ansar Dine operations in the Adrar des Ifoghas by now. Any future resistance you and your people face will be minimal." He looked south. Now they'd received the all-clear, Mackenzie and Oumar were jogging across the flat gravelly plains to join them.

While they waited to regroup, Pierce checked the dead paramilitary soldiers and the living pilots, took their photos with a smart phone and searched for passports and other identifying papers, all of which identified them as Moroccan but were probably forgeries. He photographed them anyway.

"Who was the leader?" Pierce asked the pilots.

The older of the two men gave a dismissive nod to one corpse who looked ten years older than the others. "Him."

"Who are they? Al-Qaeda? Islamic State?"

The pilot shook his head. "We don't know. We do this only for the money."

"Of course you do." Pierce crouched low. There was nothing remarkable about any of the men, yet Pierce sensed there was nothing about their dress style, postures or their state of health to suggest these were typical terrorists. They instead resembled a sophisticated American or European hit team.

The dead leader's shirt clung to his skin with sweat. His right arm had fallen up over his head when he died, allowing Pierce to see the imprint of a tattoo under the wetness of his shirt.

He ripped off the fabric. Inside the right bicep was a tattoo of two circles, one inside and at the base of the first and half the diameter of the larger one. A straight line bisected both circles. It was not a symbol he had seen before, although it reminded him of diagrams found in mathematics textbooks. It could have been a random tattoo, like the many decorations people across the globe sought out every day, with personal meaning but nothing more.

But Pierce suspected it meant something else...

Pierce examined the other dead soldiers and the reluctant pilots for similar tattoos, but no one else carried the same or similar markings.

Mackenzie and Oumar joined them, both out of breath from the heat. He waited until they drank from their water bottles. Another day where the temperature had surpassed forty degrees Celsius.

"Nice shooting, Mackenzie."

Her face lit up. "Thank you!"

"Enjoy being back in the field?"

She kept breathing hard. "It's scary, but exhilarating at the same time."

"And how are you?" he asked Oumar in Arabic.

The man clasped his stumps together in prayer. "I don't know how to thank you both. You saved my life. You gave me my freedom. At least I think this is what you are doing?"

Pierce laughed. "You saved yourself, Oumar, from what I hear. And as for freedom, these pilots will fly us to Morocco. You want to reunite with your sister?"

Oumar beamed with joy. "Oh, thank you, sir. Thank you so much!"

"Mark, please. Call me Mark."

"Why do you do it?" Tariq asked then. "Risk your life to help people you barely know? Fight battles that aren't yours?"

Pierce considered the question for a moment and remembered Awa's parting words. He checked his hands. They weren't trembling, and he had just saved the lives of many, so maybe there was a connection. "If I didn't, I think I'd be an alcoholic by now. This is a messy profession where many innocent people die all the time. Doing good where I can — it keeps me going." He caught Mackenzie staring at him, looking close to tears. He needed to redirect the conversation before it got too emotional for them all. "Mackenzie, you, Oumar and I need to get to Morocco. I checked the fuel tanks. I'm certain there is enough to get us to Tangiers, or at least Marrakesh."

"What about me?" Tariq asked.

"The Land Rover is operational and fully kitted with weapons, water, food and fuel. If not, there are the camels Shalgham left at that guelta."

Tariq nodded. "I might take both."

Pierce walked to the spot where Shalgham had materialised from nowhere with the rocket-propelled grenade launcher. As Pierce suspected, there was a foxhole dug into the hard earth and covered with a hide made of goatskin the same colour as the sand. Inside were provisions, weapons and five saddlebags stuffed with money. He sifted through the cash and estimated its value. All one-hundred-U.S.-dollar notes; the sum was somewhere between ten and eleven million dollars.

"Was it worth it?" Mackenzie asked while watching him count the money.

Pierce closed the last saddlebag and stood. His stomach twisted in knots, as realisation struck him that the situation was not as he had expected. "We'll find out when we get to Tangiers. Can you pilot a twin-prop?"

She laughed. "No. And neither can you."

"You sure about that?"

She shrugged and smirked. "You let the pilots live. Doesn't that answer the question?"

58

RABAT, MOROCCO

Pierce and Mackenzie had remained busy since their arrival in Morocco. They had flown through the night, to land at a private airfield outside Tangiers. After securing the pilots, they commandeered a car and drove into the city. A phone call to Oumar's sister reunited the siblings, and she proved ecstatic to have her brother back in her life, whom she had long thought to be dead. By the time Mackenzie and Pierce left them, they were already talking about getting Oumar prosthetic hands and how he could complete his engineering degree.

Pierce and Summerfield then drove south in a rental car under false identities, arriving in the capital of Morocco late at night. The ocean breeze was refreshing, after spending so much time in the desert. Navigating both the modern and antiquated streets of Rabat, they soon reached the U.S. Embassy and parked outside.

Neither of them moved.

Mackenzie's eyes narrowed as she clenched her teeth. She was angry, and he didn't blame her.

"We agreed, Mark, we hand the money over to the CIA together. If it's officially received, Walsh has to account for it."

Pierce said nothing. He knew he had been cold towards her since departing Mali, but he had his reasons. He had to protect her, and to do so, she had to remain ignorant of his motives and why he had to disappear.

"Don't do this, Mark."

"Do what?"

"You've gone cold again. Shut down, like when I first met you. When you came back from whatever horrible work you did before you 'officially' joined the CIA."

Summerfield knew nothing of Pierce's life before they had teamed up three and a half years ago, but she had understood his personality without having to understand his past. She recognised his mental scars that were not visible to others.

"Whoever they were and whatever they did to you... I know it can't have been pleasant."

"I can't talk about it."

She gripped the dashboard until her knuckles turned white. "I'm not asking you to."

He didn't respond even though he knew this infuriated her.

"I thought we were friends?"

"We are friends," he blurted, meaning it.

"This is a difficult profession we chose, I know, but friends have to have a level of trust between them."

"I didn't choose this profession. Not really."

She turned to him, stared until he looked back. "You will disappear tonight and go underground. I know it. Don't lie. Just tell me why, Mark?"

He reached over and opened her door. The message was clear. It was time for her to leave.

"Why?"

"Trust me."

"That's all you've got to say?"

He nodded, pushed the five sport bags they had transferred the money into onto the pavement, and waited for her to get out. She was emotional again. He was hurting her, and he felt awful. But if he didn't push her away, he'd drag her into the mess he had blindly walked into.

"Look after yourself, Mark," she said, without looking at him, then marched off, not once looking back and ignoring the money.

He watched her reach the embassy gates, where she showed her passport to the Marine guards. She gave the corporal the standard code, identifying her as an American intelligence officer. She pointed to the road where she had left the money bags, then disappeared inside.

Two Marine guards approached, so Pierce drove off fast.

He exhaled, not realising he had been holding his breath. Mackenzie Summerfield was physically safe, for now. Career-wise and mentally, that might be another story.

The next twenty-four hours would determine whether he could save them both in the long term.

59

Shrouded in lines of shadow and the reflections beamed off display monitors, Idris Walsh sat motionless at his foldout desk, studying real-time head-cam feeds from six assets in the field, all confident ex-soldiers proficient at tradecraft and surveillance. So far, Walsh liked what he saw.

The assets had monitored their target, Mark Pierce, since his arrival in the capital, Rabat. Mackenzie Summerfield, who had been with him yesterday, had disappeared into the American Embassy and was beyond Walsh's reach now. Walsh didn't care about her; his target was the Trigger Man. He'd known Pierce would run rather than seek refuge with his own people. The Trigger Man was predictable like that.

It was early morning in the Medina. Sunrise was not far off, so a few citizens wandered the streets, heading off to work. The smell of freshly cooked bread and sweet pastry wafted from the bakery below. In an hour, crowds would flock into the narrow streets, providing more opportunities for Pierce to slip away, but for now the man was in the open and easy enough to track. Walsh assumed that Pierce knew he was being followed, for the Trigger Man was running a surveillance detection route, doubling back, stopping at random spots, changing his pace and switching between walking and running. But he wasn't good enough to fool Idris Walsh.

The assets trailing Pierce were the best money could buy. Two Australian former Special Air Service Regiment soldiers who'd operated for years behind enemy lines in Afghanistan. An ex-Mossad operative who'd foiled Lebanese and Saudi attempts to incite Palestinian uprisings in the Occupied Territories. A Turkish army intelligence officer with a sociopathic streak that made him perfect for eliminating innocents who got in his way. A self-trained assassin from Algeria who boasted over twenty professional kills on his resumé. And the last man, the best of all of them, was Walsh's team leader, a former German intelligence officer who'd switched to the private sector for the money and had excelled as a specialist in wet work staged to implicate other organisations and governments as required. The team had cost a small fortune to secure, but not enough to seriously dent Walsh's funds. They would be worth the money if they could close off the loose end that was Mark Pierce.

While the Trigger Man might be skilled and cunning enough to outsmart the six assets, he was unaware that Walsh also tracked him with three mini-surveillance drones. When his men had to drop back so they would not give away their position, the football-sized drones would fly close to the whitewashed buildings of the Medina as cover and keep their target in sight. Trigger Man would be prepared for surveillance, trained and experienced in identifying, so the drones working with a human team lessened the likelihood he would spot his tail. One drone now watched Pierce force entry into a residential block, then climb the stairs.

"Swordfish One, this is Swordfish Actual." Walsh radioed the former German intelligence officer. "Target just entered this building." He gave the address. "Sending you drone feed now."

"Copy that, Swordfish Actual." The German sounded pleased, as if finding Pierce here had been because of his skills, and not Walsh's subterfuge.

"You'll have him cornered now. Get it done."

"He's just made his first mistake, sir. We'll have the building surrounded shortly."

"Remember, I want him alive."

"Yes, sir."

The drones had saved the day, proving again that robotic assets were becoming more reliable than human assets. These drones featured the latest in artificial intelligence software, providing them with limited self-determination. Programmed with the Trigger Man's facial and kinematic data, the drones would autonomously search for Pierce under these parameters, making them effective hunter-seekers. Their only downfall was battery life, as Drone Two's battery light was already flashing red. Time to return it to base and recharge. There was a slight, unexpected wobble in the drone as it hit something — maybe a bird — then it continued on its way unperturbed, as instructed.

Drones One and Three had at least two hours of charge remaining. Enough time to trap and apprehend Pierce.

The German spoke over their secure comms. "Swordfish Actual, this is Swordfish One. All operatives in place, and the building is surrounded. He's not getting out."

"Good work, Swordfish One. Get ready to move on my command."

Walsh switched the drones to tracking mode, limiting their range to the building Pierce had entered. Zipping from window to window, their cameras would peer inside, seeking their target. Once pinpointed, Swordfish One and the rest of the team would move in, ready to incapacitate the Trigger Man.

Walsh grinned; his plan had worked too perfectly: Mark Pierce was exactly where he wanted him. Within minutes they would subdue the rogue CIA soldier, and within hours they would have the Trigger Man bound, hooded and drugged, and on a plane flying out of Morocco.

Walsh savoured the drone feeds as they appeared on his monitors, glimpses into the private lives of ordinary citizens who lived here. At this hour most people were asleep, but not all. A pregnant woman seated at a kitchen table seemed enraptured by a modern romance novel. An old man studied a backgammon board as if trying to understand how he had lost a game. A blank-faced, thin teenager played *Ghost Recon* on his Xbox like he was half asleep.

"Any sign of the target?" chirped the radio.

"Patience, Swordfish One. He's in there."

The first signs of daylight crept along the horizon and into Walsh's window. The Muslim morning call to prayer started, broadcasted through tinny speakers across the city. The wrought-iron gates of the bakery creaked open, allowing access for the day's first customers. A pigeon landed on his window.

The depleted drone flew through the open window of Walsh's operations centre and set itself down. Walsh drew his attention from the monitors and plugged a power cord into Drone Two. Once satisfied that it was charging, Walsh returned to his seat. Then stopped. The camera feeds on Drones One and Three showed only static.

"What the—"

"Swordfish Actual, this is Swordfish Three. We have a problem."

It was the Turkish asset. He sounded panicked.

"Sit rep, Swordfish Three?"

"The drones, sir. They're smashed — no, someone shot them up."

Walsh felt his gut tighten and his skin prickle. He recognised the sensation as fear. "Escalate. I repeat escalate. Work from the bottom up. The target is in there somewhere."

His assets were propelled into action. They abandoned stealth and switched to assault mode. Walsh heard them kick down doors, terrify occupants as they searched each room by knocking over furniture to seek places where Pierce might hide.

"Ground level clear," reported Swordfish Six after several minutes of door-breaking, glass-shattering and resident-whimpering.

"Level one clear," echoed Swordfish Two, one of the Aussie SAS soldiers.

"Level two clear."

"Same here, level three clear."

It had taken the assets five minutes to sweep the apartment block. Walsh didn't doubt their efficiency, but they should have subdued the Trigger Man by now. They were the best European and Oceanic assets available at short notice for this kind of work, yet they had failed him.

"Have you checked the roof?"

"Yes, sir," reported Swordfish One.

"Check again."

"Copy that."

Walsh clenched his fists. Thirty years in the business of spying and covert operations, and Walsh had always been a careful and meticulous planner, but it seemed all his contingencies and double-guessing counted for nothing when applied to a man with Trigger Man's many and honed skills. Walsh thought he had not underestimated Pierce, that was why he chose only hardened professionals for this operation, yet he couldn't help but feel that Pierce had led them all into a trap.

"Swordfish Actual, this is Swordfish One. We have another problem."

"What problem?"

"It's only myself, Swordfish Three and Swordfish Four on the roof. We've lost radio contact with—"

The next sounds over the mic were three loud noises, like sneezes, then three weights falling hard. Then... nothing.

"All units, report in."

The comms channel returned only hissing static.

Walsh switched to the emergency channel with the same result.

He felt his insides tighten, knowing that Pierce had bested them.

There was no time to reflect on what had gone wrong. There was only time to disappear. Walsh executed shutdown codes on all the laptops, a programme that copied random data over the hard drives again and again, clogging the memory and wiping anything that could compromise their operation while also ensuring any computer forensics couldn't later reassemble their data. As an added precaution, tiny bombs would detonate once the programme had copied over the drives at least a dozen times, melting the hardware.

Trash bins doused with accelerants were strategically placed within the room, including one under the drone receiving and recharging station. Walsh lit the bins just before he walked out. Flames danced higher and higher, and within minutes, fire would consume the apartment.

Walsh slung his prepared field kit over his shoulder. Once through the door and onto the interior balcony, he checked that his SIG Sauer had a full magazine and a bullet in the chamber, then headed downstairs. The stairwell caused his skin to crawl, but there was no point letting his past traumas cripple him in this critical moment.

Like the building Pierce had entered, this was a residential block, with a courtyard in the middle featuring potted plants and a fountain bubbling at its centre. No one was up and about except for scrawny cats rubbing their backs against mosaic-tiled pillars.

Walsh unlocked the front door and locked it again behind him, then hurried in the direction away from where Pierce had taken out his six assets. The Medina streets were narrow and arranged like a labyrinth, but Walsh had studied the various paths and already had his exfiltration route planned. Despite the morning prayer, and the fact that the bakery was open for business, few people were out at this early hour, and those who were barely glanced his way.

After he'd navigated several alleyways, Walsh felt he was in the clear — not that he was happy about the outcome. He needed to be out of Morocco soon so that he could salvage this catastrophe; plus his whole operation hinged on bringing in the Trigger Man alive. Still, he had backup plans supported by additional professionals, so everything still might proceed as planned.

He kept walking.

Walsh sensed he was being followed. Then he knew he was.

He halted.

The barrel of a weapon was pushed up against the back of his head, without Walsh hearing or sensing the assailant approach.

The Trigger Man had him.

60

"Careful now." Pierce spoke to the back of the spymaster's head, his suppressed Glock 19 semi-automatic pushed up against his skull. "Your team is dead. I killed them all. Ending your life will be my simplest kill today."

"I don't doubt it." Walsh spoke slowly and kept his raised hands still. "I holster my pistol under my jacket, left side. And a knife in a sheath on my left arm."

"Well then, you know the drill."

Walsh opened his jacket. Pierce reached in and removed the weapons, pocketing them both. His leg ached from tonight's exertion. The screwdriver wound had reopened, and he felt the stickiness of blood on his cargo pants, but he still patted Walsh down in case he concealed further weapons. He found nothing else.

Walsh said, "Surprised I found you so quickly?"

"No." Pierce snorted a laugh. "I found the tracking device you sewed into Mackenzie's shirt yesterday, but not soon enough, it seems."

Behind them, Pierce heard screams, then the sounds of emergency sirens. The faint scent of smoke hung in the air. Walsh had torched his operations centre. Pierce had expected this but knew it was at the cost of innocent citizens' lives and their homes. The spymaster was both ruthless and efficient.

With quick glances Pierce checked the narrow alley where they hid. For the moment they were alone. "Turn around."

Walsh complied.

Limping on his injured leg, Pierce handed over zip ties, which Walsh bound around his wrists without complaint.

"Not too tight, Walsh. I know if given the opportunity, you'll try to shear them off with a forceful strike against your chest."

The spymaster grinned. "You think you are in control here, Trigger Man?"

"I have the gun."

He led Walsh further into the empty alley until they found a narrow, angular corner hidden in shadows. He told Walsh to face the wall and to keep his arms raised above his head.

"How did you find me?"

"Easy; a tracker dart fired into your drone."

"Ah... How did you defeat my assets?" Walsh's tone remained confident, like he still believed he would walk away from this encounter unharmed.

"Easily."

"Indulge me."

"I raced up that apartment block, then jumped three metres to the next building." Pierce felt the pain in his leg, knowing that it was the jump that had reopened the wound.

"I raced down the second building, then came back up the first again, taking your assets out from behind, one by one."

"I never thought about it before, Pierce, but you always talk in metric units. That says something about you, I think."

"Good point, it will be a nine-millimetre bullet shattering your brain, if that's important to you."

"How did you know you'd be able to jump?"

"I know Rabat." Pierce laughed. "I've operated in Morocco many times, which you'd know if you *really* had access to my redacted files."

They heard police and fire engine sirens. Crowds were gathering of local citizens curious as to the cause of a fire and authorities trying to restore control. Pierce didn't have much time to question Walsh before someone discovered them; therefore his questions needed to be pertinent. "I know about the forged eleven million dollars."

Walsh nodded. "Ah. How did you work that out?"

"Just by looking at the notes. You should have hired better people, for I've seen better forgeries than those. It wasn't difficult to draw the connection to Mackenzie's intel on the Istanbul counterfeiters. That's where you operated before showing up in Agadez. Until I saw the money, I kept thinking you might be legit. Not anymore, so where is the real money? The eleven million you would have sanctioned from the CIA, to swap out for the fake money?"

"You were smart, sending Summerfield into the embassy alone while you ran," Walsh said. "Made it look like you'd duped her, and you alone were behind the forgery. She'll still lose her job, for incompetence. The CIA flew her back to Langley last night, for 'intensive questioning'."

Pierce gritted his teeth. Walsh had guessed at his motives to protect Mackenzie Summerfield, but at least — if Walsh wasn't lying — she was no longer in immediate danger. "You didn't answer my question."

Walsh turned to face Pierce, but kept his arms raised. It was a defiant move, but not threatening, so Pierce allowed him his tiny victory. "In an offshore account, Pierce. Been there since before we first spoke. You would never have found it. Never will."

His body tensing, Pierce resisted his instincts to shoot Idris Walsh now, as he needed answers. He needed to know just how deeply Walsh had compromised him, and why. "You sent three CIA operatives into the Sahel with the fake money, hoping that they'd be killed by Ansar Dine terrorists, drive over a mine or perish in some other tragic circumstances. You also false flagged an Ansar Dine operation, convincing the three kidnappers to snatch Lucas Vautrin off the streets and bring him to Shalgham, even though Shalgham never authorised it, causing more confusion and distrust. You also worked out who Juliet Paquet really was, that she was Hanna Vautrin, and you leaked intelligence to her through back doors that I was hunting her father. I don't know how you did that, but we'll come to that in a minute.

"Then after feeding Mackenzie and me a bullshit story about your sister costing you a fortune, suggesting you were broke, you had me search for the money while you acted all suspicious about it. You knew I'd go after the money and keep it from you when I found it, as leverage to discover what you were up to. But I see it now. The whole scheme was all about bringing several distrusting groups together, to cause carnage and to squabble over the money, so that eventually it disappeared or was destroyed during all the fighting you knew would erupt because of it. Confabulating the whole situation so no one would ever begin to suspect you had disappeared with the real eleven million dollars you took in the first place." Pierce's gut twisted, thinking through how thoroughly Walsh had framed him.

The spymaster chuckled. "You were perfect, Trigger Man. You're an outsider, operating to your own agenda. Paranoid to the point you don't trust anyone. I needed a fall guy for when the money went missing, any fall guy, and you were perfect."

In a sudden, brash movement, Pierce cracked the butt of his Glock over Walsh's head. The spymaster dropped to one knee and cried out his pain. "Hanna Vautrin and Kashif Shalgham and their mad scheme to wipe out refugee camps to cause a war had nothing to do with your plans? They were just convenient pawns, like me and Mackenzie?"

Walsh laughed through his pain and staggered to his feet.

Pierce clubbed him again, this time in the shoulder. "Stay down until I tell you otherwise."

The older man shook his head, recovering from the pain. "Yeah, I had no idea that Hanna Vautrin and her brother were up to anything that elaborate."

"How did you know Juliet Paquet, the DGSE officer, was actually Hanna Vautrin?"

Walsh shrugged. "Deep cover operation from years back, a time when I was Brad Tegmark. Which was a legend, of course. The CIA wanted me embedded well inside the Vautrin organisation to confirm that dad, son and daughter all died in the missile strike they had planned for them. I reported back what my masters wanted to hear, but I figured, by first saving them manipulating a vulnerable Hanna and Lucas who had just lost their father, I might gain control of their inherited empire's substantial cash funds. Make me rich like I've always wanted to be. Didn't work out then, unfortunately. So, when Hanna shows up unexpectedly in Gao, pretending to be French Intelligence, her file crosses my desk. I put two and two together and decide it's time to get her messed up in this whole confused operation, just to get back at her. Just like I'll get my revenge on you, for taking the forged money back to the CIA. The one place on the earth I never wanted it to be."

"You asshole. At least I'll have the satisfaction of knowing you'll never get a chance to spend any of it."

"You think you will kill me." It didn't sound like a question, but a statement.

Pierce licked his lips. "Maybe. Maybe not. It depends on..."

Walsh looked up, blood trickling from a gash in his forehead, and cackled. "Depends on what, Pierce? You fool, you know the truth now. You know you can't kill me. I'm the only one alive who can clear your name."

Pierce gritted his teeth and tried not to let his hands shake, as they were about to.

"Eleven million dollars is a lot of money, Pierce. Enough to retire comfortably on, even with a million as contingency for tying up loose ends. But it's nowhere near enough if the CIA will hunt you down for the rest of your life."

"This was just about money, about lining your own pockets?"

Walsh nodded. "Most people's motives are basic when it comes down to it, mine included."

Sirens grew louder. Pierce heard someone yell out the Arabic word for blood. His leg wound might have dripped a trail to their location.

"You wanted us to take the fall for your theft? Why me and Mackenzie? Why frame us specifically?"

"I just told you, Pierce. You are an outsider, and so is Mackenzie. Easy targets. You might have saved Summerfield, but the CIA thinks you've run, disappeared with the money. Even Summerfield will think so now." He laughed manically. "Don't tell me, you didn't tell her you worked out the money was fake, so you sent her into the embassy with her believing it was real? So after the CIA interrogate her to learn the truth, she'll come out the other side smelling of roses, an innocent victim of your dastardly forgery scheme. You are too noble, Trigger Man. You've just convinced both her and the CIA that you set them both up. I couldn't have done it better myself."

Pierce knew Walsh was correct, but he had to protect Mackenzie, even if he couldn't protect himself until he'd had the opportunity to bring Walsh in. "So this has nothing to do with Michael Abraham? He wasn't 'one of your prodigies'?"

"No. He deserved what he got. I didn't care about him."

Pierce paused and thought. Walsh had framed him from the start. But there was one advantage the Trigger Man had that the spymaster did not. "Your team is dead. You're operating alone now, with no backup."

"Maybe, but the difference is, the CIA believe I'm on their side."

Pierce grinned. "No. The difference is I have a gun. You're coming with me, a hostage until you tell the CIA what you did. I can hide you for a very long time if I have to, and I won't make our time together pleasant. Don't think I haven't treated other traitors the same way in the past."

Walsh held Pierce's stare. His eyes were cold and his face as impassive as stone.

"Get up, Walsh."

The spymaster did as he was told.

Pierce heard a crowd of early shoppers approaching from a nearby alley.

He heard shouts that someone had spotted a man with a gun.

A knife suddenly materialised in Walsh's hand, with which he struck at Pierce's shoulder. A weapon he had successfully concealed despite Pierce's early search.

Pierce was ready for this. He fired his Glock, and a single bullet bored through Walsh's guts.

The spymaster stopped rigid, surprise on his face, then pain. He fell backwards, hit a stone wall and slipped onto the cobbled street. A trail of blood smeared the wall behind him.

"Over there!" someone yelled.

Pierce was about to put two further bullets into Walsh, both in the head to be sure of a permanent death, when bullet fire from someone else's weapons erupted around him.

He heard police calling in Arabic to drop his weapon.

With the distraction, Walsh managed to drag himself into an alcove, out of sight.

Another shot fired close to Pierce.

He had no time to finish the job, or he'd end up dead too.

He ran, and as he did, he noticed that Walsh had dropped his satchel. Scooping it up, Pierce fled into the early morning. Walsh might bleed out, or he might survive, but either option left Pierce facing many problems and in serious danger from his own people and who knew else.

He fled through the Medina, then after he had sprinted three blocks, hid in an alcove and changed into a loose grey thawb, or thobe, he had brought with him, disguising himself as a Muslim man. A fake moustache and beard adhered to his face completed the picture, and Pierce quickly blended with the gathering early morning shoppers out for a bargain. He walked without rushing, and when two police officers ran past him in a hurry towards where Pierce had shot Walsh, they never glanced his way once.

Out of the Medina and into the more modern districts of the city, Pierce hailed the first bus he spotted and climbed on board, paid for his ticket and took a seat.

He sat for a while as they journeyed, listening to the other commuters, men and women mostly speaking in Arabic or sitting by themselves, lost in their own thoughts. He didn't think any of them were working for Walsh and had trailed him, but he wanted to be sure.

He changed buses twice, then walked into a café and sat away from the entrance, with his back to the wall and his eyes watching everything.

When he felt convinced, again, that he had made his escape, he decided to look inside Walsh's bag.

Carefully opening it, angled so only he could see, Pierce was shocked by what he first saw.

A military-grade Geiger counter waited inside. A device commonly used to detect the presence of radioactive nuclear materials.

Pierce shuddered. What the hell did this mean?

But he couldn't think about this. He didn't have answers.

Not yet.

It was time to run again.

It was time to go dark and hide in the shadows, for however long it took to clear his name. When at last he could re-emerge, he would only have one mission. Find Walsh.

EPILOGUE

CADIZ, SPAIN

With controlled effort, Sergeant Alex Trager pushed the forger's face into the water-filled basin. Immersed, his captive soon struggled to breathe, but with his wrists bound behind his back, and Trager's more powerful muscles holding him down, his life was completely in the hands of the former Special Air Services Regiment soldier.

Trager counted to twenty before he yanked the forger's head out of the bathroom basin. The terrified man sucked mouthfuls of air and panted like he had run a marathon. He burst into tears and wailed before mouthing words without speaking them, begging for mercy.

Trager gritted his teeth. In his time, he'd hunted down and slaughtered dozens of the most vicious Taliban warlords in the wildlands of Afghanistan, so the forger was no problem for him to bend to his will. "I'll say it again. Mark Pierce was here, in this apartment, yesterday evening while you prepared fake identity documents for him. Afterwards, he boarded a train headed for Seville. What I don't know is the name and nationality you listed on the passport that he is now travelling under."

When the forger didn't answer, too exhausted to speak, this infuriated Trager even more. The Australian saw that the Spaniard was still trying to grasp how close to death he had come, so Trager pushed his head back into the basin and left him to thrash and panic again.

When the forger started losing his will to struggle, Trager pulled him back by his saturated hair and said again, "You know what I want. So tell me!"

The forger gasped. His bloodshot eyes were unblinking as they stared up at Trager. "Please, let me tell you. I *did* prepare a fake passport for him!"

"The name? What was the name on the passport, and the nationality?"

"Dimitri... Dimitri Levendis. Ukrainian passport. They are easy to come by, with the war and refugees fleeing that country. And Ukrainian passports are also easy to forge."

Trager smirked. "See, mate, that wasn't so difficult, was it?"

He allowed the forger a moment's rest so he could imagine that the worst was behind him. He watched as the Spaniard nodded, as if agreeing with Trager, that cooperation wasn't so difficult and would only serve to prolong his life. Then, when Trager had regained his strength from their earlier torture session, he pushed the forger's face back into the basin and held him thrashing for a count of well over a minute while he struggled to live.

Eventually, the forger gagged and involuntarily opened his throat and filled his lungs with a flood of fatal water rather than the oxygen his panicked mind would have hoped for. Seconds later, he ceased struggling altogether, and his body went limp.

Trager waited another twenty seconds, still holding the head under, then dropped the lifeless body onto the bathroom floor with a loud, wet thud.

The name and identity were all Trager needed to recommence his hunt.

He dialled a number on his burner phone, using an encrypted line, and waited for the connection.

"Yes?"

Trager recognised Idris Walsh's voice immediately, but there was a croak to it. Not surprising, it had been three weeks since Pierce had shot the CIA spymaster in Rabat, and Walsh was still in post-surgery recovery. Trager felt comfort in the fact that Walsh had survived, but only because it ensured their bold covert scheme remained in play, and Trager might still get rich from it.

"Pierce was here, sir, as I said he would be."

"Good. What else?"

"Three days ago, he crossed the Strait of Gibraltar from Tangiers into Spain, and I tracked him from there to Cadiz. He'd left just before I arrived, so I secured the identity and nationality of the passport he will next travel under, which will make him easier to track."

"And the identity is?"

"Dimitri Levendis. Ukrainian."

"Makes sense as a cover. Pierce speaks fluent Russian, as thirty percent of Ukrainians do. I'll run it through the system, and if I get a ping, I'll keep you informed."

Trager didn't answer.

"Sergeant?"

Trager's lack of response was because his thoughts had

drifted to his buddies Adam and Liam, the two ex-SASR soldiers Pierce had cowardly butchered in Rabat. Now they were dead, and he wanted Pierce to pay for their unjust passing. The thought of firing a bullet through Pierce's skull had occupied nearly every waking minute of his days ever since.

"Sergeant!"

"Yes, sir?"

"You know we need Pierce alive. If this scheme we have cooking has any chance of success, it will only be if Pierce takes the fall for it. But he can't do that if he's dead!"

Trager sneered, then nodded, not that Walsh would see this, speaking over an encrypted line as they were. "Okay, you're right, sir. I'll take him alive and bring him to you. But while I understand why... When this is all over...?"

The CIA spymaster snorted. "Don't worry, Sergeant. Long before all this is over, Pierce's life will be the worst hell he could never have imagined. He'll wish many times that you had killed him straight off."

"Good."

"So take him alive. You hear me?"

"Yes. It's understood."

Before Walsh could lecture him further, Trager ended the call, dismantled the burner phone, and crushed the SIM card under his foot. Placing the cell phone and SIM card pieces into his pockets, Trager was soon outside, in the streets and moving fast while looking out for garbage bins to dispose of the burner's many components. He didn't like what Walsh had asked of him, but knew the American was correct. There was a bigger picture here to consider.

But on the plus side, he was on the hunt again, just like in Afghanistan.

And this time, Mark Pierce was his prey.

ACKNOWLEDGMENTS

Special thanks to all those from across the globe who read the early drafts of this novel and provided invaluable feedback, helping me to shape the book it has become. They include Bodo Pfündl, Deep Ranjan, Brian Drake, Ross Sidor, Roxy Long, Dori Barrett, Don Shetterly, Terrill Carpenter, Andrew Warren, Kronos Ananth, Samuel Carver, Travis Spencer, Kenneth Karcher, Steve Lepper, Sarah Tilby, Freidrich Reher, Kashif Hussain who also provided cultural background, Rob Doran for his first-hand experience in the operations and maintenance of Land Rover Defenders, and Robert Adamcik and Timothy Burrows for technical help with military aspects of this story. I thank you all.

Thanks also to my editor, Alice Latchford, for working with me and her insightful editing processing that really enhanced the final book.

My thanks also go to Peter Gratwick, Sarah Townsend, Brigid O'Neil, Emma O'Neil, Haoran Huong and especially Bec Short, for your belief in me, support and encouragement.

This book was one hundred percent written and edited by humans. No artificial intelligences were involved.

ABOUT THE AUTHOR

Aiden Bailey is an international bestselling thriller author from Australia. Formerly an engineer, he built a career marketing multi-national technology, engineering, and construction companies. His various roles have included corporate communications with the Australian Submarine Corporation, technical writing for several defence contractors, engineering on an outback petroleum pipeline, a magazine editor and art director, and engineering proposal writer for the Royal Australian Air Force's surveillance and intelligence gathering aircraft and drone enabling works. Aiden has travelled widely in six continents and his experiences are the basis of many of his stories.

Did you enjoy *The Trigger Man*? Please consider leaving a review to help other readers discover the book.

www.aidenlbailey.com

Printed in Great Britain
by Amazon

40205209R00229